MYTHBORN II

BANE OF THE WARFORGED

Mythborn II: Bane of the Warforged

MYTHBORN II
Bane of the Warforged

Cover art by Raymond Lei Jin and Na Sun
Map by Ralf Schemmann, Raymond Lei Jin

Certificate of Copyright Registration:
TXu 1-887-058

ISBN: 978-1-64058-079-4
ASIN: B07B8CYWHB (Kindle)

Dawn's Light Media
Noble Sun Press
SillanPaceBrown Publishing, LLC

www.mythbornmedia.com
www.dawnslightmedia.com
www.sillanpacebrown.com

Mythborn II: Bane of the Warforged

Hail, good fellows and well met! I hope each of you gains a small measure of excitement, happiness, and comfort, losing yourself in the world of Edyn.

CONTENTS

WHAT HAS GONE BEFORE

I n *Mythborn I: Rise of the Adepts*, we meet Silbane
Petracles and his apprentice, Arek Winterthorn. They are
leaving their secluded Meridian Isle on a mission to
ascertain whether a Gate has opened between their world, Edyn,
and Arcadia, the realm of the demonkind. This Gate is in the
besieged fortress called Bara'cor.

Silbane has been ordered to use Arek's ability to negate
magic to seal the Gate shut. This will likely result in Arek's
death, a fact that has been kept from him and leaves his master
conflicted.

On the eve of their departure Arek gets into a fight with a
fellow apprentice, Piter, and kills the boy by accident. When he
awakens he learns of the fight and death, and that the lore father,
Themun Dreys, has ordered him and Silbane to leave the Isle on
their mission immediately.

An enigmatic group known as the Conclave orders
Rai'stahn, an elder dragon-knight, to kill Silbane's apprentice
before he reaches the Gate, but their reasons are unclear.

Rai'stahn carries Silbane and Arek to the Altan Wastes on
his back before he confronts Silbane with his orders to kill Arek.
During this exchange, Piter appears as a shade to Arek, hateful
because Arek killed him. Despite his malevolence, however,
Piter seems to be trying to keep Arek alive. He shows Arek how

to use something called a Far'anthi Stone to escape the dragon. What he does not tell Arek is that the Stone will only take him to Bara'cor, the ancient dwarven fortress now occupied by King Bernal Galadine and his besieged forces, and potentially the location of the Gate between worlds.

When Rai'stahn attacks, as ordered by his Conclave, Silbane comes to his apprentice's rescue, allowing the boy to escape using the Far'anthi Stone. Before a victor can emerge, both the dragon and Silbane are captured by a red mage known only as Scythe, who is allied with the nomad tribes besieging Bara'cor. Meanwhile, Arek appears in the bowels of Bara'cor.

After Silbane and Arek's departure from the Isle, there is an assault on the adepts and students by dwarven assassins, sent by an unknown master called Sovereign. This attack results in the deaths of several students, Adept Thera Dawnlight, and Lore Father Themun Dreys.

Kisan Talaris, another master of the Way and mentor of the dead apprentice Piter, casts an illusion transforming herself to look like one of the assassins, whom she killed before concealing his body. She infiltrates the dwarven team, joining them on a boat heading to an unknown destination. Soon the team gets new orders: to infiltrate Bara'cor and kill Arek and King Galadine.

After Arek escapes the dragon, Silbane and Rai'stahn find themselves at the mercy of the archmage Scythe, who has used his considerable powers to delve into Silbane's mind, where he learns of Arek's ability to negate magic. Scythe worries that the Gate he has worked so hard to open to the demon realm will be closed by Arek's presence. He forces Rai'stahn to utter a Binding Oath, allying him with Scythe to protect the Gate from any threats.

Meanwhile, Arek finds himself in Bara'cor and comes face

to face with the Princess Yetteje Tir, her cousin, Prince Niall Galadine, and his personal guard. We've heard Arek is good with a blade, but watching him fight shows just how much better his training is than the two heirs and guards of Bara'cor. Though an alarm is given, Arek incapacitates everyone, but refrains from killing them. Only the arrival of Ash Rillaran, the second-in-command of Bara'cor, stops Arek from getting cleanly away. Instead, they face each other, and Ash's greater combat experience tips the balance in his favor. Arek is apprehended as a spy, and without a logical explanation for his sudden appearance, he endures torture that ends with his foot being severely injured.

The besieged King Bernal Galadine has sent his queen Yevaine to Edyn's capital city, Haven, on a likely fruitless quest for reinforcements. He is desperate to save Bara'cor, and his son and heir, Niall. Eventually persuaded that Arek is not a spy for the nomads, the king requests that Arek use his finder, a magical amulet that will transport Arek to Silbane, so that the king's men may follow Arek into the enemy camp and assassinate the nomad leader to end the siege. Arek agrees, but brazenly asks for his torturer's life in return.

The king refuses, but Arek's enchanted blade, Tempest, comes alive and carries out Arek's wish by using the torturer's own life energy to heal Arek's foot. Arek falls unconscious.

When he awakens, Arek is befriended by Princess Yetteje Tir and Prince Niall Galadine. Yetteje's family has been murdered by the barbarians now besieging this stronghold and she wants revenge; Niall wants to prove he will be the warrior his father wants him to be. Arek sees the shade of Piter again, this time cajoling him to search under the fortress for his destiny. Yetteje and Niall mistake Arek's desire as a quest for a weapon to use against the barbarian nomads and decide to accompany him on an adventure into the dark heart of Bara'cor. Here, the shade of Piter leads Arek through a secret passage to Lilyth's Gate, a portal like a blue sun sitting atop a pyramid within an underground cathedral, named for the demon queen who created it.

Meanwhile, the dwarven assassins of Sovereign have found their way into the fortress. Kisan, still disguised as a dwarf, has managed to contact the new lore father, Giridian Alacar, who orders her to kill Arek as an enemy of the Way. Giridian has been approached by the leader of the Conclave, a being known as Thoth, and told about the creation of "nulls," children like Arek who consume the Way. Sovereign, who attacked the Isle and seeks to remake the world, cannot succeed unless more of the Way is freed. With all the people of Edyn draining its potency, the world remains safe. In fact, Arek's power doesn't destroy magic—it frees it, making him a danger to all life in the realm.

Kisan, who still resents the death of her apprentice, finds herself hunting Arek with the assassins who killed mages and children on the Isle. The assassins split into two teams, with the leader, Prime, going after Arek, while the rest go after the king and his men. Kisan can only follow one path, and decides to save the king's men, since Prime will kill Arek for her, leaving her hands clean of the actual deed. She kills the dwarven team of assassins and sifts through their memories in an effort to find Prime and Arek.

Arek, Yetteje, and Niall are about to inspect the pyramid and Gate when they are attacked by Prime. Piter helps Arek understand how to summon and use his flameskin, a defensive tactic used by masters of the Way. Arek and Yetteje team up and take down Prime, while Niall freezes with fear. In an attempt to be a hero and close the Gate, Arek touches the portal to the demon realm. Instead of closing it as the lore father had hoped, his power breaks the remaining barriers between Edyn and Arcadia, and the demon queen Lilyth emerges, the leader of the Aeris and repeated attacker of Edyn. She claims that Arek is her son and she welcomes him and Niall into Arcadia.

Meanwhile, Kisan finds King Galadine and his men, and uses the Finder to help the king infiltrate the nomad camp so that she can rescue Silbane and Bernal's Firstmark Jebida can kill Hemendra, the leader of the besieging nomads. Silbane, Kisan, and Firstmark Jebida Naserith battle Scythe and the oathbound Rai'stahn. Silbane cleverly captures Scythe, and most of them escape back to Bara'cor. Jebida stays behind to challenge Hemendra, and dies killing him.

When the companions reappear in Bara'cor, the portal leading to the nomad camp stays open. Silbane dives into Scythe's mind to unravel the spell, where he learns the true identity of Scythe. He is Lore Father Duncan Illrys, ancient archmage and wielder of the Old Lore, now driven insane in the quest to find and rescue his wife and son from Lilyth's realm.

The group, with Duncan as prisoner, journeys downward beneath Bara'cor looking for Arek, Niall, and Yetteje. They run into Yetteje, who has managed to escape. She tells the king that Niall and Arek have gone through the portal to Lilyth's kingdom, Arcadia.

The Aeris cannot exist in Edyn without bodies, necessitating possession, and the Lord of Storms, Baalor, has taken over Prime's body, which seems to have more power and connection to the Way than those of beings from Edyn. Baalor demands they turn over King Galadine. Baalor uses his power over the Way to free Duncan, but despite being able to run, Duncan takes a Binding Oath and stands with the others.

King Bernal Galadine offers himself to Baalor if the rest

may pass. Since Lilyth's orders only concern the king, Baalor agrees. Duncan, in a moment of lucidity, charms the king's weapons with an enchantment, but before he can tell the king what it does, his moment of clarity passes. The party leaves the king to face Baalor alone as they go through the portal to rescue Niall and Arek. Yetteje carries the king's bow, Valor, to give to Niall. Silbane releases Duncan from his oath so he can continue his search for his wife and son.

Bara'cor is surrounded by a blue shield of energy that lets the Aeris temporarily survive in Edyn without bodies. Thousands now infest the fortress, possessing any who remain within its walls.

We begin *Mythborn II: Bane of the Warforged*, with King Galadine facing Baalor, while the king's newly promoted Firstmark Ash Rillaran, his niece Yetteje Tir, and the master adepts Silbane and Kisan journey to the demon realm of Arcadia to rescue Arek and Niall.

KINGS

"I do not relish facing the man who,
when knocked down a sixth time,
grasps his bloody blade,
grits his teeth, and grimly rises a seventh."

- Toorval Singh, Memoirs of a Mercenary

King Bernal Galadine shifted his shield to his arm, his gray eyes never leaving the hulking mass of the stormlord Baalor towering over him. The Lord of Storms had been worshipped as a god by the people of Edyn, his power plain for all to see in the dance of lightning and the boom of thunder that swept across the land whenever anvil heads formed. It was his hammer's beat that shaped the world upon which they lived. Bernal nodded to himself. No matter, for today either he or a supposed god would die. He stepped forward, ready.

"Hold, King," Baalor's voice boomed into the open space in where they stood.

Bernal's eyes narrowed, but he remained silent. Only moments ago the adepts, his niece Yetteje, and Firstmark Ash Rillaran had disappeared into the bowels of the fortress, pushing onward in an attempt to save his son and that apprentice. His stand must buy them time.

"Be not so quick to throw away your life," said the Lord of Storms. "There are many chances to save your people. I offer you one."

Bernal waited, knowing every moment helped his friends, then said carefully, "Speak."

Baalor gestured, and from the smoky mist rose Sergeant Alyx Stemmer, struck down by Yetteje during the last skirmish, after the sergeant was possessed.

Bernal stared at her, stunned. He had seen Stemmer fall, possessed by demons, as Yetteje's blade sliced her from shoulder to waist, cutting the young sergeant almost in half. Yet here she stood, whole and mostly uninjured. The only evidence of the strike lay in the sliced jerkin and the visible scar beneath, which even now was healing and fading.

"King Galadine," said the dead sergeant, spreading her arms in supplication. "We do not wish war, only life. You can save our people and yours."

"How?" He refused to say her name, for this could not be the same Alyx Stemmer who had served him so faithfully. This was something else, a parasite, an imitation used to lull him into a false sense of familiarity and trust. Bernal could only pretend to listen, buying precious time and with it hope for his son's rescue.

"Join us willingly, and you will be given everlasting life and power beyond your ken. The Aeris call it *Ascension*. You will need its power to face the true enemy." Alyx bowed, fist to chest, a perfect execution of the salute he had seen a thousand times before. It unnerved him, but Bernal had also heard what the wraith of his former sergeant had said.

"How?" he asked again. Here was information he could use, perhaps something to help fight these creatures. Was "ascension" responsible for Stemmer's resurrection? Hearing the demon speak could shed light on possession and what now inhabited his former sergeant's body. It was also a chance to delay them further.

Baalor stepped forward. "I offer myself, King Galadine. I offer myself to save our people. Join me through Ascension and together we will become one, a being of true unity as our forefathers intended."

Bernal stepped back. "Join..." He gasped as the implication of what Baalor said hit him. "Become possessed? Like you have done with my sergeant and others? I will not—"

Baalor interrupted, "No, you will be as you are now, but stronger." The stormlord drew closer.

"You face an enemy you cannot comprehend. Sovereign comes, and none can withstand where his hand falls. He will remake the world in his image and we *all* will be less than a memory, lost forever. Be not so hasty to refuse, for in the end true death awaits. Yet through Ascension we can become more powerful. I will join with you brother, not as the possessor, but as the Way that obeys your will."

A moment passed. Bernal listened to his own breathing. His heartbeat was strong and steady in his ears. He could feel the soft leather of the grip of his blade. His shoulder flexed, his shield a comfortable reassuring weight upon his arm.

He let go of his breath slowly. It washed out of him and took with it any remaining doubt. Though he did not hold the same abhorrence to magic as his forbears, he knew no demon ever spoke the truth. He always knew he would die in battle and this moment felt like an old friend come to visit him again. He would not listen to this demon. For him, death held no fear.

"You will never possess me," he said.

Baalor's armored head tilted, and though only the glow of

his eyes could be seen, Bernal felt a wave of sadness wash out of this god of storms. "You are wrong, King of Bara'cor. You will serve our needs, just as have all those who have died under your command."

In response, the mist surrounding the area congealed into dozens of armored forms, then hundreds. They were the fallen of Bara'cor, possessed and now raised again from the dead by the power of the Aeris lords. They pulled back as Baalor steppd forward, creating a circle around the two from which there was no escape.

"Only power sufficient to match that which you already carry will be brought to bear upon thee, mortal." The armored god paused and said, "We shall take measure of one another as required by the First Laws."

What I carry with me? Bernal assumed Baalor meant the enchantment he'd seen Duncan perform prior to his departure with Ash and the rescuers. The man was unhinged, seldom making sense during Bernal's brief encounter with him. Then again, perhaps this was Duncan's way of ensuring Baalor brought his full might to bear, for the Galadine family was no friend of the insane archmage.

He turned to Baalor and stated, "I did not ask for Duncan's aid."

Baalor shook his head. "The Old Lord did nothing to change this outcome. Your blade and shield speak for themselves, baned to destroy our kind. Your feigned ignorance is unbecoming. Your family's name has caused our people much harm and woe."

The statement about his weapons came as a shock, but did not exactly surprise Bernal. Rumors abounded of the weapons and armor of the Galadine line had been enchanted against demons. After all, they had been forged at the outbreak of the

Demon Wars. Still, to hear confirmation fall from this demon's mouth called to question his earlier belief that everything they said was a lie. The point about his name bringing woe to Baalor's people... that *did* surprise him, but he was careful not to let anything show on his face. If what Baalor said was correct, a small part of him dared to hope he might yet prevail.

"Very well," he answered, "let us have at it. This endless chatter is useless." Bernal's shield snapped up and his blade Anzani sang as Bernal slid it against the edge of his shield.

The ebonite-armored giant did the same, the flex in his legs and arms promising carnage. The mace came up, blue threads of lightning arcing down its length, tainting the air with a metallic tang. Bernal watched grimly as Baalor circled without another sound.

Then the stormlord attacked, bounding forward with steps that shook the granite ground. His mace, dancing with lightning, rose and fell like a blacksmith's hammer as Baalor went to the labor of shaping what he desired most from the world. It was bloody work, for the thing he sought to shape was the body of Bernal Galadine.

Bernal dodged to his right, keeping his shield between the mace and himself. The downward strike shattered the stone where he had stood, causing a tremor to run through Bara'cor's walls. The smash was followed by a swipe that narrowly missed Bernal's head. As Bernal had seen before, for all his size and bulk, Baalor was as fast as a sky serpent with his strikes.

Bernal crouched and deflected the mace upward, his arm and shoulder taking the brunt of the massive blow that would have knocked his head completely off his shoulders. The strike sounded like thunder, blasting him backward and shaking his very bones. Yet his shield held, showing no sign of damage from the storm god's blow. Even more surprising, the force of the blow wasn't nearly as harsh as he'd expected.

Bernal spun, using his shield to pivot around Baalor's strike before riposting with his own blade. It cut through the air, the razor-keen point thirsting for the stormlord's blood. Bernal was sure had he connected, the strike would have gone through Baalor's chest. But the blade sparked and skittered, deflecting off the giant warrior's interposing armored forearm. Then Baalor swung his off-hand in a tight arc.

An ebonite fist caught Bernal and flung him away to land in a heap. At first it looked as if he had been knocked unconscious and the ghosts of Bara'cor crowded inward, thirsting for any drop of Galadine life. Then the wraith-like soldiers pulled back as Bernal stirred, not so incapacitated as they thought. None would challenge the sanctity, it seemed, of Baalor's duel.

He levered himself up and shook off the blow that could have felled a dozen men. His shield lay more than an arm's reach away. It had been torn from his grasp by the leviathan blow it had absorbed, yet its surface still looked unmarred. Likely, mused Bernal through pain-filled eyes, his shield and blade would be the only witnesses to his final stand.

Bernal wiped the back of his hand across his mouth, noting it came away wet with blood. Either the strike or the fall had broken something inside him. Regardless, this fight would not last much longer if he yielded. He gritted his teeth against the pain and rose, his stance unsteady. But when his blade came up, its point never wavered from Baalor's eyes.

Something flitted across the storm god's face, and the giant tilted his head forward and said, "You will beg to join us when your life hangs by a thread." Then the armored god attacked again, swinging his mace in an arc trailing lightning at a speed that made the earlier attack seem like sparring practice. Clearly the stakes had been raised.

Despite his injuries, Bernal couldn't hesitate. Hesitation meant certain death. He moved forward under the swing and could feel a broken rib grinding in his side. The coppery taste of blood filled his mouth. He ignored it, his blade thrusting out.

Baalor dodged the strike then brought his knee up, catching Bernal under his jaw. A second strike from the pommel of Baalor's mace smashed Bernal's face, breaking his nose and flinging him spread-eagled onto his back. A cough of blood punctuated his impact, spurting into the air above him like a red cloud. His sword fell from nerveless fingers, ringing as it bounced off the fine stonework of Bara'cor.

"I have fought battles for endless lifetimes, king. Power is not enough. *Puissance* is required, and you are outmatched. Accept my gift and be healed. Do not seek to become legend."

At first, nothing happened. Then Bernal stirred, rolling onto his stomach with a groan and pushing himself to all fours. His vision swam. Noise came to him from inside what sounded like a deep tunnel. Yet his right hand crawled across the stone with a mind of its own, finding and slowly curling around the hilt of his blade.

He sighed, and the sound came out like a wet gurgle, ending in a spit, spattering the ground with his blood. He rose slowly. There was nothing to say, but every beat of his heart drew time. Every moment bettered his son's chance to be rescued. It was a worthy sacrifice. Staying alive meant everything. He drew another shuddering breath and levered to his feet. He wavered there for a heartbeat, then leapt again at the Lord of Storms.

His blade danced out: right, then left, then right, aiming alternately at the juncture of the storm god's neck and hips. The blows came true and exact, a testament to his lifetime of training. Even exhausted, his body would not let him deliver anything less than perfection. Talin would have been proud, had the armsmaster lived. He'd always said we fall to the level of our training. Bernal was proving that now. His eyes watered from the pain as he ducked under a counter and struck again.

Baalor's mace swung back and forth in short arcs, catching Bernal's blade on its haft. Each impact created a starburst of blue, a flash that left afterimages of yellow in Bernal's eyes. At the last strike Baalor turned his mace over Bernal's arm, forcing it down. The demonlord's elbow came flying over the top and smashed into Bernal's skull.

Pain and blackness exploded in Bernal's vision. He felt rather than saw himself hit the ground. A part of him winced with detachment as he absorbed the thundering impact, even as another cried at the damage being done to his frail mortal body.

"Your sacrifice achieves nothing," Baalor's deep voice whispered. "Accept your fate. Accept us."

Weariness far deeper than anything physical came over Bernal. It would be easy to lie down, to give in and let the pain end. Another wet cough racked his chest, a spasm of pain that brought bloody splatter to his lips.

Though he felt this deep within his bones, his body still would not listen. He rolled over again, feeling the gritty ground under one cheek, his betraying hands pushing him up to a knee. He paused there, head hanging, as his vision slowly returned. He could feel something like small rocks in his mouth and spat them out, only to watch as his broken teeth scattered like bones tossed for prophecy. He didn't even look at them. He knew his future.

His head tilted back and he gazed up at the stormlord, a goliath wreathed in lightning. *He is wrong*, he thought. *This is worth it.* What he imagined was a grotesque smile made up of split skin, jagged teeth, and broken bone greeted his opponent. When Niall was rescued, it would be worth every drop of blood spilled here.

Baalor stepped forward and growled, "King Bernal Galadine, since you will not allow Ascension, I claim you and will add your strength to my own." The Lord of Storms raised his mace, the white lightning increasing to a buzzing crescendo as it gathered at the tip of his weapon like a star. A feeling like thousands of ants crawled across Bernal's skin. *At least*, he thought, *the end will be quick.*

Then a red flash erupted behind Baalor. An arch opened in the middle of the hall, a new portal showing a dark room made out of branches woven together on the other side. A scream sounded and from the opening streamed dark figures, dangerous and fast. They slammed into Baalor's ghost army, using long wicked spears and shields in interlocking groups of three, pushing the demons back.

Their discipline was obvious. Each set of three would form a triangle, two in the front and one in the rear. While the two forward shields slammed into the line of opponents, the third man stabbed into the fray with lethal effect. These small units would then band together with others to form larger interlocking phalanxes where needed, pushing back the enemy and then stabbing through them with deadly efficiency before contracting back into a defensible shield wall.

Bernal had never seen synchronized close-quarters combat so well executed. These were clearly highly trained and battle hardened men. But on closer inspection they were not men. They were blue skinned, with ram's horns curling from their foreheads. Yet the question remained—who did these horned creatures fight for?

The red gate snapped shut as fifty or so of the blue-skinned warriors continued their sweep into the forces of the Lord of Storms like a scythe through wheat. They stabbed and sliced with weapons that glowed an unearthly blue, much like their skin. They left nothing in their wake, for each Aeris they killed disappeared in a cloud of smoke and ether.

Baalor moved back from the new troops he seemed genuinely worried about and shouted, "Fall back!"

The strident orders had the desired effect. Baalor's forces melted away, seeping into the cracks of the fortress like a living mist.

The Lord of Storms looked at the leader of the blue-skinned attackers and said, "Malak, your high lord revels in ruin, and does not see the true enemy."

The blue-skinned leader replied, "You are the only ruin this world will face if it trusts your Lady's word."

Baalor looked back at Bernal and said, "Do not trust elves. They are the children of lies and hubris." A moment passed with a single tortured breath from Bernal. Then Baalor said, "Even in death, know you have traded worse for worst." With that, he sank into the stone floor, disappearing near the entrance where Ash and his team had descended in search of Niall, a moment separated from now by what seemed an eternity.

The blue-skinned creatures Baalor had called elves moved into formation around the shattered king, who could not raise himself past his one knee. One of them, no different looking than the rest and yet clearly their leader, crouched down and came eye to eye with Bernal. He laid a gentle hand on his shoulder and said, "I am Firstmark Malak. My men stand with you."

Bernal looked at the blue warrior dumbly, a part of him registering the glowing circular sigils tattooing his skin. Yet the pain and damage made it all but impossible to react. His mind worked slowly, coming to the most obvious question like a man fumbling in a dark room for a lantern. Finally, a single word croaked out.

"Who?"

Firstmark Malak looked at Bernal with sympathy. "My healer will see to you, King Galadine. Rest easy. We are succor and hope." Even as the firstmark spoke, another warrior detached herself and came forward, crouching behind Bernal.

She assessed him expertly and then met Malak's gaze and whispered something to him that Bernal could not hear. At Malak's nod, her hands came up and touched Bernal's back and shoulder. At a signal from her commander, a soft glow grew from under each palm, a blue light that seemed to soak into Bernal's skin. A moment passed, then he felt his breathing become easier and his mind begin to clear. She moved her hands to his face and mouth, still glowing, her light permeating his skin.

Malak turned his attention back to Bernal and said, "Sparrow says you came close, perhaps within a few heartbeats of making your son the new king."

The offhand comment caught Bernal's attention, for it seemed out of place. Something in the back of his mind tickled a warning, but it was too faint and his body too damaged and battle-weary for him to take more notice.

Instead, he looked about with the sight of a man given new life at these blue-skinned warriors who had saved him, arrayed now in a tight defensive formation. Except for the two who continued the ministrations, the soldiers kept their attention outward, holding vigil against any threats.

Many thoughts ran through Bernal's head, but with his growing clarity he asked the one question most important to him at that moment: "Who sent you?"

Firstmark Malak took a moment before replying, "My men and I are at your disposal. We serve House Galadine."

"You didn't answer me, Malak," Bernal rasped. Whatever the woman was doing eased his pain, but he wasn't fully healed yet. His jaw felt better, and a warmth was clearing his lungs. He coughed up a bit more blood and spat to one side, noting that even his teeth seemed to be restored. What sort of magic was this? He then rose unsteadily to his feet, but his voice came out firm. "Who sent you?"

Malak rose as well, and the look on his face was one Bernal knew intimately from years of campaigning, that of an officer giving a superior unpleasant news. No matter the army, the look was always the same.

Bernal pursed his lips and ordered, "Out with it."

The firstmark looked at Bernal, then produced something and handed it over, saying, "Your forefather, Highlord Valarius Galadine, sir."

Bernal stared at the blue-skinned commander. Valarius? The man was a legend, and dead for over two hundred years! What mockery of his family was this?

Then the object in the firstmark's hand caught his attention. It was a signet ring with the Galadine symbol and a House crest engraved upon it. Only those of the royal family had such a ring, but that was not the detail that shocked him most.

As if completing his thought, Firstmark Malak said, "I have been instructed to help you secure Bara'cor." He hesitated again before adding, "Your cooperation is greatly appreciated." With that, Malak handed Bernal the ring, then he and the woman he called Sparrow took a knee. The fifty or so remaining elven warriors banged their spears against their shields and shouted in unison and fealty, but did not break their vigil.

Despite their show of loyalty and service, the message was clear. His cooperation was expected, and their objective was to take Bara'cor. Whoever or whatever had sent Malak and his men made sure Bernal understood his place. While the ring showed the symbol of the Galadines, the crest was not of House Valarius.

Bernal knew the crest on this ring—it was identical to his own. The golden lion of Bara'cor stood rampant on its face, a sure sign it could have come from only one place. He held Niall's ring in his hand. These blue-skinned elves had his son.

Kings

ARCHMAGE

It is said a man is only as smart
As a woman half his age plus seven years.
A simple thing to remember in conversation.
Harder when your life is at stake...

- Alain the Farflung, A Guide to Westbay

The pain of transition was welcome, a sharp reminder that he was still alive. Duncan appeared where he'd expected, the invitation from Lilyth depositing him almost at her doorstep. He stood some thousand paces from her castle, a white structure that rose out of the ground like daggers pointing at the sky.

He took stock of his surroundings. The smell of pine and a cool crispness permeating the air marked the season as spring. The sky was lit orange by a sun that looked larger than the one he was used to. The analytical part of his mind immediately wondered if he was still in Edyn, or some other world connected by Lilyth's Gate. It likely did not matter, as getting home was not a matter of distance but of his own perseverance.

Almost done, he thought with a clarity he found refreshing. It was as if his centuries in Edyn had been a fugue, a mental lassitude Lilyth's realm cleared away with a fresh breeze. He was seeing things now with a crystal acuteness that extended as much to his thinking as it did to his vision. The world before him was unambiguous in its reality, defined by sharp edges and clear outcomes. Suddenly choice had relevance, consequences had meaning.

Before he could spend much more time appreciating this simple fact, two figures detached themselves from the castle's wall, like gargoyles come to life. They flew toward him, angling downward to land lightly. Then one stepped forward and said, "Greetings, Lord Scythe. Welcome to Olympious. The Lady will see you now."

Duncan nodded, his pale eyes drinking in their details. They looked like twins, bearing bronze-colored breastplates, greaves, and blades. Their features were essentially like his, except for the fact that their skin seemed to be made of a white stone, like marble. They waited patiently, evidently for his approval.

"Lead on," he said, gesturing.

The two bowed, and began walking to what could only be the main gates. Neither looked back, assured that he would follow. Duncan's first task in finding Sonya would be to face the Lady. He knew she would not have brought him here if she had all she wanted. He would have to play his hand carefully.

It was not long before he was crossing a bridge that led to the main pyramid-shaped spire, the sunlight shining through the parapets to paint alternating stripes of orange and shadow on the white bridge's deck. Normally a bridge without anchor points below would need to be suspended, yet he noted no cables or lines. Curious, for it bespoke a level of magic or materials used that exceeded those found in Edyn. Regardless, the bridge and castle were beautiful to behold.

Something blue caught his eye, and when Duncan moved to

look, he was surprised to see this castle's 'moat' was actually a chasm that fell past dark walls to blue sky below. They were floating!

He looked back up and saw what he'd missed before, mainly because he'd not expected to see it. The sky was dotted with small shapes—dozens, then hundreds came into view. Were these islands like Lilyth's, each floating in the serene firmament? None looked nearly as large, but that might have been a matter of perspective and distance.

As Duncan neared the main entrance, guards snapped to attention and he was smoothly handed off to two others who led him inside. These fell in ahead and behind, silent and implacable, like living statues leading him inward and up.

Lilyth's castle was more than a simple stronghold. It consisted of multiple spires surrounding a small city that rose up the pyramid sides in steps. Each level was framed by four spires of white, one at each corner, needles pointing to the sky. Everywhere he looked, he saw people milling about and children running around under the watchful eyes of their parents and the city guards.

The soldier in the lead motioned and they turned to enter an open courtyard, following a paved road that led in an orderly fashion around Lilyth's city. What he'd taken for the main spire had, in fact, been merely an entrance in the outermost wall. Concentric rings circled the castle grounds, each "ring" a living space filled with markets, houses, and more children accompanied by their parents. Life here did not seem so different from a city in his own world, yet something bothered him, like a book that did not close because a page had folded upon itself. It was just enough to keep him cautious and alert.

In moments, they had entered a thoroughfare that was wider and more ostentatiously decorated. It sloped upward, bisecting the rings and cutting a line directly to the center of the palatial grounds. His escorts picked up their pace as the speed of those around them became faster.

Soon, they stood in front of massive doors flanked by winged guards, the wings a sign Duncan had begun to associate with the Aeris. No doubt a preferred method of travel in a world of floating islands. At some unheard signal, the guards opened the doors and backed away with a bow.

"Be welcome and enter," Lilyth's voice echoed out clearly. The room was filled with courtesans and other folk, and even more children. They ran in between the legs of adults, scurrying about like mice at play. Clearly whatever laws the demon queen enforced, she did not impose any limits on where children were allowed to play.

He took a step in and looked around, unable to identify Lilyth, for the throne seat was empty. Looking to his right he caught his first glimpse of the Lady through her royal retinue, standing near an open arch by herself. Her aura of power was unmistakable, bringing a certain coldness to her beauty. While that did not surprise him, her blue skin did. Wherever bare skin showed from beneath her simple silver gown, he saw a soft blue that seemed to shimmer with its own light.

Her form was lithe and tall, though not quite as tall as he. The curve of her back ended in a long, delicate neck, with dark hair gathered into a small mountain of curls. Her large eyes shone from a heart-shaped face, deceptively young for a demonlord reputed to be many centuries old. When she turned those eyes upon him they glowed blue, but he wasn't sure if it was magic or just the light from the setting sun.

She leaned casually on the stonework, gazing at the world spread out before her. On the other side was a vast stretch of land, so vast that Duncan could not see its end. He realized with a surprise that they were in the spire, so high that looking down gave him vertigo, though he had no fear of heights. Her lands fell away from the city and downward, continuing the pyramidal slope until it merged with a vast plain that continued for as far as the eye could see. He had not recalled climbing stairs of any type, yet the vista spread outside the arch was a silent testament to the height of his vantage.

He bowed and said, "My lady." A calmness had descended over him, so unlike his near frenzied state inside Bara'cor. *Another byproduct of Lilyth's power?* he wondered. *Perhaps.* Yet his purpose had not wavered, and in a voice laced with deadly intensity he asked, "Where is she?"

Lilyth looked at him, her gaze casually straying from the red gold sky to appraise him through half-lidded eyes. "Welcome to Arcadia, Lore Father: home of my people. We meet at the moment when small actions have great meaning."

Her voice was filled with a kind of melancholy, as if the simple words of welcome had drained from her any interest she might have had for discourse. He found himself moved to sadness, though he did not know why.

She traced a single finger on the rough stone of the sill upon which she sat, then rose slowly, moving away from the arched window. Her blue skin caught the light in such a way that it seemed almost iridescent, changing from its deep blue to a color tinged with an almost aqua green. She smiled softly, revealing perfect white teeth, and said, "We are both blacksmiths, you and I."

Duncan moved closer to the window and the spot she'd just vacated, his eyes searching the verdant landscape. Her unwillingness to be straightforward irked him, but not so much that he wasn't willing to be pleasant. "How so?"

"We shape that which needs shaping." She paused as some

children ran across her path, her face still set with that same soft smile that hinted of sadness, though the sight of the children brought a glimmer of something happier. "We forge flesh, readying it for battle."

Duncan scoffed, not taking his eyes from the world of Arcadia stretched out before him. "I don't care. Do what you will with Edyn, but return me my wife. It is only for her that I bargained. I have no interest in your war."

"Really?"

The shock of the voice coming from so close behind his ear caused him to spin in surprise. Lilyth stood there, silently regarding him with eyes so deep blue they called to mind the sky at sunset. He found himself unable to speak, his mind able to focus only on her proximity. Her sensuality was a physical thing, pulling at him, though his heart belonged entirely to another. She was madness in the making, and Duncan took a step back. It took more than a moment for him to gather his wits. Her closeness felt like a violation.

Lilyth smiled and said, "Even now my world infuses you with health, sharpens your thoughts, lends you fortitude. You see my beneficence, and yet what will happen when this is all gone?"

When Duncan didn't respond she continued, "Sovereign intends on remaking the world. When our worlds die, where will you and your family hide?" She said this casually, her eyes moving over his tall form in a way that made his skin crawl.

He gathered his composure and replied, "And your answer is better? Possess them all?"

Lilyth shrugged. "Ascension, possession, is there a difference? It is only a matter of who looks out from behind your eyes. That you are Ascended means one of Thoth's feeble Watchers has been possessed. From Lord Scythe's point of view, are you not the possessor?"

Duncan suddenly felt himself at a loss for words, her question forcing him to reassess things. Then he shook his head, refusing to let a demon's lie open a small crack in a door that would lead him to question his own deeds.

"I don't care," he repeated. "Where is she?"

Lilyth closed her eyes and took a breath, then said, "Lore Father, I have stayed Sovereign's hand or his first course of action would have been to execute all the people of Edyn. Kill the dreamers and the dreams die, too. Then the world will be remade."

"Stayed his hand? What do you mean?" he said, looking around at the room, drinking in details like a dry sponge thrown in water. Perhaps she spoke the truth, that her world was healing him. He didn't know enough to believe her, but with his mind now strangely sharp, many questions crowded to be given voice. He thought for a moment, then ignored what he'd asked earlier and raised the most important one first. "Why does Sovereign seek to remake the world?"

Lilyth bent her head, and it seemed she was really considering how to answer.

"Sovereign believes the world is broken, imperfect, a bad dream, perhaps nothing more than a nightfright," she replied. "When the sleeper wakes, the nightfright is gone." She paused then said, "Sovereign will survive the remaking of the world but we—your people and mine—will be gone."

Duncan blinked, his thinking still clear, and asked, "How can you stop something you claim is so powerful?"

Lilyth gestured, and Duncan's eyes were drawn to the children running around the throne room under the watchful eyes of their parents. Wait—children? He'd seen children upon entering the palace grounds, in the marketplace, even here in the royal chamber. His mind was whirling. He'd seen children *everywhere*.

He stumbled back and sat down on a ledge near the sill, a hand to his head. Were these people really parents? He took another look and realized that while each watched with loving care and earnest, they did not interact as birthers would, but more like... guardians.

Then the history of Edyn hit him like a hammer and he found it hard to breathe. "You took them," he said, the accusation coming out as a gasp. "The children who disappear from the land, taken by demons." He looked up at her as if daring her to deny it.

She did not. Instead, she sat down next to him and took his hands in her own, "Lore Father, these children are the only reason Sovereign has not wiped out your people."

Too much... it was too much to take. His mind rebelled against the sheer number of children he'd seen in just his short walk, a walk he now knew had been engineered for his own benefit. If she could whisk him to her castle through a gate, why hadn't she? No, she'd paraded him through a city built by her actions, trying to justify her choice to kidnap, capture, or worse.

He looked at her, his pale eyes meeting her own deep blue ones, and asked, "How many?"

Lilyth looked at the many children gathered around them, then back at the archmage and said, "How many is not as important as who. They carry the blood of the first families to walk upon Edyn, blood like yours or the Galadines. Sovereign cannot remake the world if he harms these children."

"So you're holding them hostage?"

"There is a chain of hostages, for no small purpose. Sovereign cannot remake Edyn without using the Way, and he cannot draw upon enough of the Way to do so unless he also destroys Arcadia. Yet he dares not destroy Arcadia when it holds this precious blood. Hostages, yes, but for the good of both our worlds."

"If what you say is true, why hasn't he come after them here?"

"He needs to use the Way to do that as well, and there are enough of my people drawing upon it with their very lives that he cannot muster the force to break into Arcadia. It's a stalemate."

She grabbed his hands and her voice became insistent, her eyes wide and searching his. "We have a chance now that the Gate has reopened. My people can flee Arcadia and take bodies in Edyn. We have a chance to free ourselves! Join me in this fight. Our people, yours and mine, deserve better."

Duncan closed his eyes, his newfound grip on clarity finding its first challenge in this world, slowly cracking like the top of cooled magma when the hot caldera below bubbled. He began to shake, the quest for his wife and child threatening to overcome any semblance of fortitude this place had carefully propped up.

He moved slightly away from the sill's edge, and in a voice echoing his grief he said simply, "Release my wife. My debt is paid in full."

The Lady watched him, her eyes seemingly measuring the tenuous hold he had on his own control. She let out a breath and said, "Sonya is the captive of Highlord Valarius on the isle of Avalyon."

"*What?*" he screamed, unable to control himself any longer.

Her guards reacted, as did the children, scattering behind the protective legs of their guardians. Everything in the throne room came to an awkward halt.

"Careful, archmage," she admonished, her eyes flashing like

living sapphires. "You are not the only one here with power." Slowly, the room regained its balance and things returned to normal. When he'd calmed himself enough, she continued, "I told you, 'all may not be as you wish.'"

"You expect me to believe Valarius Galadine survived? That he still lives, here?"

"Yet you exist and believe the same of your wife? How is your quest any less foolhardy?" she asked in a tone that managed to be both genuine and condescending.

Duncan stayed silent, the idea Valarius had survived not entirely surprising him. Oh, the man was irritatingly full of himself, and if anyone could have cheated death it would have been Val. That thread of logic led him to his next realization. That would mean Valarius and Sonya had spent the last two hundred years together... alone.

"You look ill, Lore Father," said the blue-skinned demon queen. "May I get you something?"

Duncan ignored her, trying to catch his breath. Was Sonya truly Valarius's captive? They had stood against Lilyth together, and fought for the safety of Edyn. The three of them had been friends once, but that had been so long ago. "Where is Avalyon?" he asked carefully. Then he forced himself to smile, for he knew he was very much at Lilyth's mercy.

Lilyth paused, searching his face, then said, "It stays between realms, appearing only when necessary, else my Furies would have found it by now and destroyed Valarius. He and his elves distract me from the more important battle with Sovereign. But you," she looked at him calculatingly, "can accomplish a critical need in my efforts."

"What?" he barked, the idea of yet another task laid at his feet irritating him beyond reason. Had he not been her agent in good faith these many years? The measure of their bargain had been the return of his wife, and Duncan was quickly coming to the conclusion that he would have to visit Val and secure Sonya's release on his own.

She blinked once, then said something that seemed unrelated, startling him out of his reverie. "Did you know you have a son?"

Duncan felt the world tilt beneath him. He knew Sonya had been with child, but to know the truth... the baby had survived! Then the reason for her comment became clear. "You have him."

"Born of Sonya, raised by me. He's a fine boy, one that may yet make his father proud."

Duncan moved forward with a snarl, but Lilyth raised her hand and he felt himself clenched in a hold so tight it was just short of crushing his ribs. He gasped, feeling his feet lift off the ground as the demon queen held him in her grasp.

"Do not tempt me, Lore Father," she said. For the first time in their conversation true malevolence bled through her regal demeanor. "You're nothing to me, a means to an end. If you become unmanageable, I will discard you like a useless tool and raise your son as my own. Having been born here in my lands, am I not also in some way his mother?"

He knew he could call upon the Way, but to what end? What was the chance of one man prevailing against a demonlord who'd withstood the combined might of the council and the armies of Edyn? Here, she was all-powerful and the threat to his son was real, measured by the conviction he saw in her eyes. Her sudden display of power had the same effect as a bucket full of cold water splashed in his face, returning a modicum of control over what he could objectively see now as his own madness.

"Release me," he said calmly.

She watched him, her gaze so direct it seemed to strip away any deceit he might harbor to peer at the control of the man underneath. Then, apparently satisfied, she dropped her hand and the crushing grip was gone. Duncan fell the short distance, stumbling to all fours.

"You do not doubt his existence?" she asked with a tone of curiosity, as if nothing untoward had just occurred.

Duncan shook his head briefly, "She was pregnant when she fell through. If she survived... let me see him." He looked up at her from bent knee, but his voice did not plead. It demanded.

Lilyth had turned away and put a gentle hand on one of the many children that, having remembered play was foremost, ran in and around her again. "And why would I do that, Lore Father? Shall I show him to you, giving you a face to suborn all reason? You will dedicate yourself to saving him, and then what of my needs? Anonymity seems a better hand for me to play right now. I will reveal him when it suits my purposes."

His head hung wearily when he asked again, "Is there no end to your demands?"

She laughed, then turned to face him, her tone growing serious, "I have a mission for you, simple in comparison to your work in Edyn. Accomplish it, and I will release your son, unharmed. You and your family may go in peace and live out your days for as long as I'm able to hold out against Sovereign."

She stopped, then said, "Though if I fail, you may regret not joining me when you could have made a difference." Lilyth spun and made her way up the dais that led to her throne, the act of seating herself as much a command for him to come forth as if she'd ordered it.

Duncan watched her, and could hear his escort leave their stations to flank him. He could feel his will crumble, and knew he'd do anything for his wife and son, even though he'd never met the boy. In a tired but determined voice he asked, "What do you want?"

Lilyth's gaze did not waver from Duncan's own when her demand fell from her lips. "Kill Valarius."

Archmage

KINSLAYER

I find a penurious reflection of myself in life.
Perhaps in death, I shall find peace.

- Jebida Naserith, Should I Fall

S ilbane's party appeared amongst trees, the shock of transition fading slowly with a tingle, like ants crawling across skin. Silbane was the first to quickly take in their surroundings. They had appeared in a clearing, with canopy above and enormous trunks twisting out of the earth around them like massive vines made of white wood. It was like being surrounded by a forest of entwining bones, bare and stripped of flesh as they reached upward greedily for the sunlight, only to spread their fingers at the top in bursts of luxuriant green.

"Seems calm enough," commented Kisan, looking around, "though that's often the last thing people say before chaos breaks loose."

"We didn't appear where the image showed," added

Silbane. He looked around again then said, "And the Gate is gone."

"Of course," Kisan offered, her voice flat. "Surprised?"

Silbane ignored her question, knowing how she thought, then asked, "Did you feel—?"

"Sideways," Kisan answered the unfinished question, "like we shifted as we moved."

"If that's true, we could be anywhere," said Yetteje, her eyes wide, drinking in the details. Her fear was plain on her face, now that the actual transition had happened. Saying you're going to walk through a gate to a demon's world is different once done. Silbane could sympathize with the sudden dash of cold reality.

"You stand in Arcadia, Lilyth's realm." The female voice came from the direction of Ash, who looked down in surprise at his belt.

Silbane stepped around the others and came face to face with Ash. "Tempest?"

"Yes," she replied, with just a hint of laughter behind the voice.

The elder master's eyes narrowed and he drew a breath. "And are there other overlords besides Lilyth?"

There was silence to that. Silbane turned to Ash, who in turn shrugged and said to the blade, "Please answer."

There seemed to be almost a sigh before Tempest replied, "It has been centuries since I lived amongst my kind. I am called 'Kinslayer' for a reason."

She seemed ashamed at that, but then she said, "When I was here last, this world was much like your own, with fiefdoms and lands belonging to one lord or another. But things change as your beliefs wax and wane."

Yetteje was the first to speak, asking, "Our beliefs?"

Tempest laughed, her hesitation and anger disappearing when addressing the princess. "Of course, little sister, the Aeris are your beliefs brought to life. In the last war, those who stood with Lilyth were called Furies. This land we stand upon is theirs, a place where they hope and dream for life again."

"Then they're not alive, not real?"

Yetteje looked at Silbane when she asked this, but it was Tempest who replied, "The Furies are real and very dangerous. They have bodies here, for they are a manifestation of pure faith. They are the vanguard of Lilyth's forces and are fearsome to behold. If they gain a body from Edyn, they can move between worlds. You stood witness to this with Baalor. Should that body be living, they will be far more powerful." Tempest was quiet for a moment then added, "But even now our presence attracts the weaker ones, those who hunger for living flesh. You have seen the mistfrights, but there are worse. When they possess you, you become a living extension of their will. The presence of Ascended will give them pause, but we must still make haste."

Silbane held up a hand to stop Yetteje from asking another question, his eyes narrowing. "Ascended?"

The blade seemed reluctant to answer, if that was even possible, then simply replied, "Those who are one with the Way... you can hurt the Aeris."

And then Duncan's words came flooding back into mind, that only those gifted with the Way could combat these ghostly wraiths. Yetteje whispered, "Like Alyx, her blade passed right through them and they took her." She was speaking to herself, but Silbane didn't miss the importance of what she'd just said.

He looked back at Ash and Tempest and said, "We have Furies and mistfrights to deal with. Anything else?" He looked at Ash meaningfully. "Anything that might not want to kill us?"

There was silence to that, which Ash finally broke by saying, "You'll answer him because I wish it." His words seemed in response to something Tempest had said but they could not hear. Clearly the firstmark was dealing with the sword's acerbic personality in the best way he could, but his patience, it seemed, was wearing thin. Finally he exclaimed, "Now!"

There was silence at that, then the bitter voice of Tempest said, "Watchers. At one time they stood opposed to Lilyth, but are few in number, if they have survived at all."

Despite Tempest's information, the blade quite likely had an agenda of its own. Something, some undercurrent of danger pricked Silbane's senses whenever Tempest spoke. Regardless of her affection for Ash, this latest contest of wills did not reassure him the blade would always agree with the firstmark, and that thought became a point of concern when it came to their safety. Still, they needed to make some decisions.

He turned to Kisan and asked, "How would you do this?"

"Recovering Arek is our highest priority—"

Both Yetteje and Ash stepped forward at that, but Kisan stopped them with a glare and continued, "We did not separate during transition. For that reason I think Niall will be with Arek."

Silbane nodded, not surprised at Kisan's conclusion. He dropped his head, deep in thought. How would they know the right direction? He'd been so sure before they arrived, though perhaps blinded by the need to do something to recover Arek. He knew they had few choices, but wandering a land infested with demons held little appeal. Then an idea jumped into his head and he looked out across the rolling hills surrounding them, opening his dragon-given gift of Sight.

The whole world became suddenly more vivid, sharpening

into focus. Details became clearer, lines more distinct. It was as if his vision had magnified in both clarity and scope, yet also remained the same. At first he did not see the yellow particles that made everything up, as before at the Far'anthi Tower. Everything here looked the same, but if he concentrated he could see those particles lining the edge of everything, like a tiny aura.

So much! His mind found it hard to conceive that the Way could be so concentrated that it took on real solidity, the same way that substance did in his world. It was humbling.

When Silbane turned back to the group, he got his second shock. His eyes fell upon Kisan, who stood closest. His eyes slowly drifted up, taking in the sight. "You..."

She tilted her head to one side, and the massive being superimposed on her, in black armor edged with crimson, did the same, as if it was her.

"You what? What do you see?" The image of the winged angel over Kisan followed her every movement, like the massive ghost of her true self.

Tempest laughed. "He sees the truth."

Silbane looked, only to find the blade made out of the shape of a diminutive woman. Her head and eyes made up the pommel, her arms the cross guard, and her legs the blade. It was not an actual woman, but the distinct ghost of a woman superimposed on the blade. Her alabaster skin and silver hair gave the impression of fine argentium, almost as hard to forge as ebonite. His eyes were drawn to the emerald eyes, shining with life and light, like the gem on the pommel of the blade. Those eyes grew hard as Tempest returned his inspection with a glare and said, "Do not let your gaze linger too long, miscreant."

Silbane shook his head, unsure why Tempest seemed to hate

him so much. Still, he looked away, trying to respect the blade's wishes. He saw nothing else superimposed over Ash, but when he turned his attention to Yetteje, a ghostly form, deadly in its own way, shimmered around her. It did not look as massive or as solid as Kisan's angel, but the figure was definitely there. And there was something else.

"Remove your bow, Tej," Silbane said softly.

The girl moved to obey. As she did so, the creature moved with her, like a second skin. When the bow was removed and held, a quiver appeared on Yetteje's back. It and the bow had a yellow aura of small particles, surrounding them like a halo. Silbane could see arrows would manifest themselves as long as the bow had the Way to draw upon.

That was not all. He saw a second aura and asked Tempest, "What is it?"

"Who placed a second enchantment?" she replied simply. Though she did not qualify her question in any way, she implied "dullard" by her tone.

Silbane ignored the jibe, concentrating on the bow, his eyes widening. Duncan! He was seeing the enchantment placed by the insane archmage. He moved a bit closer and asked, "Will you hold the bow up?"

Yetteje complied, holding the bow lightly in an archer's stance, without drawing the string. As she did so, Valor hummed with power, but the aura did not change.

"Valor is a simple tool," Tempest added derisively. "Its only redeeming trait is its yearning to kill."

For most, Tempest's attitude would have meant very little. Yet Silbane had been a strategist for his entire life and the blade did not seem to mince words. His thoughts narrowed along with his vision and the intent of the archmage became clear. "A finder?"

"Perhaps," dismissed Tempest. "It's difficult to fathom the motives of the insane."

Having a blade echo his fears about Duncan did not put Silbane at ease, but he replied, "So the king could find his son?"

"Or a son could find his father." The blade said this plainly, then added with a tone of boredom, "It's useless here. Do you truly care?"

"Yes," Silbane said, looking at the group. "Why useless?"

When Tempest didn't answer right away, Silbane carefully pressed, "Why would it be useless here?"

Kisan's voice piped in from behind. "Because Niall doesn't have the bow. Whatever Duncan did linked the king's weapons together. At best if the king survived, he could find the bow, which is with us." The younger master paused for a moment then added, "Perhaps Duncan thought better of Bernal's chances than we gave him credit for."

Silbane chewed his lip. It had been an oversight on his part not to see the connection between the weapons created by the enchantment of the archmage. Duncan had almost said as much when he remarked he'd wished someone had done the same for him. Knowing his obsession with recovering his wife, Silbane had overlooked the obvious, but Kisan hadn't. His protégé was not one to be underestimated.

As if echoing his thoughts, Tempest added, "Dull is forever."

"Indeed?" offered Kisan with a small laugh, her eyes filled with mirth. She seemed to understand the blade was insulting Silbane, and covered her smile. Then looking out over the landscape she said, "I didn't particularly like that comment"—she looked at Silbane with a teasing eye, drawing out the moment—"about, 'hunger for living flesh.'"

Silbane searched his memory, piecing it together. He knew

there was no point in wandering about, but if the bow was as useless as Tempest said, how to find Arek? He'd told the group that he would find his apprentice, and now they relied on him. The master began to doubt his own words, until something caught his eye.

A motion, a ripple just below his vision. The world shimmered, if that was even the right term. Although the Way permeated everything, there was a flow to it, like the effect of wind on snowfall. Something acted like a distant lodestone, drawing the Way toward it. What could cause that? It was familiar somehow, then Silbane remembered where he'd seen this before.

Arek. The thought snapped into his mind, including all that had been said with Rai'stahn at the tower. He had Seen this before, hadn't he? Rai'stahn had claimed his apprentice absorbed these particles of the Way, and now these same particles flowed toward some distant place. Could Arek be the cause? Silbane breathed in, quickly realizing it didn't matter. They had no other options or clues.

He turned to the group and motioned them to gather. When they had formed a loose circle, he took a breath and said softly, "Rai'stahn gave me a gift, a type of vision. With it, I may be able to track Arek and the king's son." He left out the dragon's claim that his apprentice devoured the Way.

Kisan started to say something but paused. Her eyes flicked back and forth as if mentally weighing her words, then she asked, "If you fall, how will we continue?"

Pragmatism, the most enduringly annoying of Kisan's many tiresome traits, now came to bear.

"I'll try and spare you the inconvenience of my death."

Kisan, oblivious to his sarcasm, replied, "Good, but we still need a contingency plan."

Silbane conceded she had a point. "I can see a flow in the Way... it goes there." Silbane pointed at a V made by the peaks of two hills. "I believe the Way flows toward Arek."

Kisan cocked her head at that, but said nothing. Something in her eyes, however, made Silbane feel she knew more than she was saying. What would cause Kisan to keep information to herself? The thought made him a little nervous, and he quickly looked away under the pretense of surveying their path.

"Olympious," supplied Tempest, speaking to no one in particular. "Lilyth's abode."

"We're that close?" replied Ash.

"Distances can be deceiving, my love," replied the blade. "Olympious lies in that direction, but it is many days travel from here."

"You can lead us?" Kisan asked, but the question came out like a statement, and wasn't directed to Silbane. Annoyingly, it was clear the younger master had dismissed him from her strategic planning.

Silbane took a deep breath and blew out. He reminded himself that Kisan's behavior was no surprise. She had the ability to cut through the chaff and create clear goals... a reason she was picked so often when it came to missions. Instead, Silbane continued to look out over the land with his enhanced Sight. There was beauty here, and life. It emanated from everything like a halo of health and potency.

"And what do you see when you look upon yourself, Lord of War?" Tempest's voice came floating from behind.

Silbane looked down at his hands, his body, and legs. White armor, overlapping scales of protection, covered his torso. Gauntlets, vambraces, greaves, all ghostly white and edged with a deep blue. He looked up over his shoulder and saw white wings edged in the same blue, like the sky just before sunset.

Each wing was made of keen blades instead of feathers, conveying the promise of death despite their ethereality.

Tempest said again, "Know your own worth." Tempest met the master's eyes but there was no kindness or friendship there. It was clear no one saw what he did. Only Silbane saw the true form of Tempest, who continued, "You give dread, purpose."

Silbane watched the creature a moment longer, then nodded. "Is that why you hate me?"

"Hate you?" The others paused as Tempest answered, "To hate means one must care first."

Silbane pursed his lips, then looked at the blade and said, "If I have given offense, it was unintentional. Please forgive me."

There seemed to be no reply, but the firstmark looked up at Silbane and said, "Let's give it some time." Then he looked a little sheepish, probably realizing he was talking as if Tempest was an unruly child.

Silbane nodded slowly. "Okay, but we need to move."

"Agreed," replied the firstmark, "we'll follow you and—" he paused for a moment, listening to Tempest, then addressed the group "—we need to guard our thoughts. According to Tempest what we think has effect on us here, understood?"

Silbane stood, brushing himself off. "I do."

"I don't!" replied Yetteje, her voice edged with fear. "We're not supposed to worry?"

Kisan came over and gently took the young princess by the arms. "You were the first to say we'll find Arek and Niall and bravely join us through the portal. Now we're here. Do not despair."

Their eyes met and through his gift Silbane saw some of Kisan's strength flow into the girl, imbuing her with fortitude that led to calmness. Her breathing relaxed, and she hefted the bow a few times, reassuring herself. Then her amber eyes met Kisan's own and she smiled. "It's just so much has happened."

"I know, but this is a long run, not a sprint. You must gird yourself. We have to keep going." She directed the last of her statement to Silbane, who caught her meaning.

He focused his Sight, and could again see the Way flowing toward twin peaks in the distance, like a dust storm made up of pinpoints of light. It did not obscure his vision, yet the particles were everywhere. "Let's move."

Tempest chose then to say, "Mistfrights and worse will appear, drawn to my beloved as moths to flame."

"And we'll deal with them as needed," replied Silbane.

Tempest grumbled something in reply, only to be silenced by Ash's hand over her pommel.

Making their way through the forest was an exercise in ease for some, effort for others. For Silbane and Kisan, the path was clear and the terrain did not seem to hinder them. Silbane noted that Yetteje's steps seemed buoyed, as if the very ground gave her a bounce of helpful aid.

Ash, it seemed to him, had the worst of it. Though the forest floor seemed flat and unobstructed, hidden roots, small dips, and irregular terrain threatened to twist his legs out from under him. It was as if the land itself tried to slow him down, but for what reason remained unclear.

At the trip of the fourth hole that seemed to appear from nowhere, Ash stopped and cursed.

"I'll break an ankle like this." They stood in a clearing of trees, a path through the forest still showing the way to the V-shaped peaks Silbane had identified earlier.

"It is my fault, beloved, for the land has no love for me. Yet we must keep moving," came Tempest's soft reply.

"Did you notice that?" It was Yetteje that asked the

question.

Silbane responded, "What?"

The princess looked around, then back at the elder master before saying, "Everything gets clearer when we stop. Like the world comes more into focus." She stomped and the ground and remarked, "The ground feels flexible under my feet when I move, but now feels steady and hard. Why?"

The voice of the blade said, "Your thoughts, little one, for you are favored here. But we must not tarry."

"We create solidity around us?" Silbane replied. "Fascinating."

"Logical... how much do you pay attention to your surroundings when you move, rather than where your foot will be placed next?" Kisan turned to Ash and said, "And how often do we believe the land hates us, that we are troublesome? Here, it becomes what you fear."

"Is this what you meant?" Ash asked Tempest. His question was clearly born of frustration, and he took to looking at the ground and muttering under his breath.

Silbane looked at the group, thinking. He made eye contact with Kisan, using their familiarity rather than mindspeak or voice, asking her to be silent. Then he came before Ash and said, "I can make your way easier."

"How?" asked the firstmark, still looking at the ground with disgust. It seemed his boots had already sunk a bit more than anyone else's, as if he stood in his own personal quicksand.

"A spell," Silbane said, his statement causing the firstmark to look up. "I can enchant your boots, if you and Tempest will trust me."

"We should make haste," Tempest urged, an edge of fear now in her voice.

Her concern began to infect the group, but most of all,

Silbane, who wondered at her sudden desire to move. What did she know?

Then the firstmark spread his arms and said, "Fine. I've never been against magic, and this is intolerable." His feet were buried to his ankles. He looked at his blade, and Silbane imagined he had told Tempest to allow him to cast his spell.

At the firstmark's nod, Silbane knelt. He placed his hands over the boots and called on the Way. A small flash occurred and then disappeared just as quickly. "Done."

Ash looked down, then took a tentative step forward, and his foot came resting on hard ground. He took another step or two and found the ground unyielding and supportive. He looked up, astonishment spreading his face in a smile. "Thank you."

"Of course, firstmark." Silbane turned and walked back to the lead, a private smile on his face.

What spell was that? Kisan mindspoke to him privately with a laugh.

It wasn't. But if he believes... It seems that's all that matters here.

They started to move when another voice piped into both their heads, *I heard you!*

Silbane and Kisan spun, looking at the wide-eyed princess, who was clearly in shock. "I heard you... the spell is fake?" Yetteje looked at both of them, not realizing she had spoken this last aloud.

"What?" Ash's eyes searched everyone as the realization that what Silbane had done had been nothing more than a false palliative, a way to convince him and his blade that his boots had been ensorcelled. His feet sank back into the ground. He looked down in misery.

Silbane rolled his eyes but Kisan let out a small laugh. Then she turned to Yetteje and remarked, "How is it that you heard us?"

"Better question," Silbane said, looking directly at Yetteje, "how do you feel?" He knew something of the Way flowed through the girl, especially since her ghostly otherform had been revealed. Given her Galadine heritage, the fact that she could command the unseen forces of the world to some extent without training did not surprise him.

However, the act of mindspeaking would normally drain someone unused to it. A simple statement between he and Kisan was bearable by the masters, but Yetteje should be feeling something more noticeable. The girl shook her head no, which caused his interest to rise. In fact, once he thought about it, even he didn't feel the normal drain of using mindspeech. *Curious.*

"They've found us." The statement came from Tempest, followed by a sudden silence that blanketed the area. They had grown so accustomed to the small sounds of the forest that this stillness filled them with a nameless fear, leaving no time for Silbane to follow up his question to the princess.

The two masters moved to either side of the party, which closed ranks despite having no idea what direction the threat came from.

"Who?" asked Silbane, searching their clearing for any sign of pursuers.

"Draw me, beloved. At least we shall see our end together."

Her tone was mournful, so much so that it seemed to give life to Ash's hand. Despite what Silbane knew was a real fear on the firstmark's part about using the blade, Ash drew Tempest from her sheath. "You're not very confident."

Her gem lit in a flash of emerald, casting its pure light around them. In that light her meaning became clear. Dark shapes surrounded them, hundreds, all with glowing yellow eyes. They rose from the ground like mist, featureless and yet real in a dark and terrible way. Silbane knew them from his childhood, as Yetteje did from Bara'cor. Mistfrights. Each watched silently, unmoving, as if waiting for something, or someone.

"We are well met, my lord."

Silbane turned to the voice and beheld a giant stepping from the thin air, his form wavering into solid reality. He was dressed in bronze armor, with blue eyes glowing from beneath white brows under a bronze barbute topped with four black feathers. His arms were massive, encircled with a bronze-colored metal, the same at his wrists and waist. A simple bronze cuirass and faulds, and bronze boots completed his defensive garb. In his hands he held a long spear, ending in a razor-sharp leaf head. Appearing behind him were a dozen more men, slightly smaller, but similarly attired.

"And you are?" Silbane asked.

"I am Anhur." The being bowed, hand first to forehead, then sweeping out as he rose. "And I ask you to step aside from the Kinslayer."

The greeting reminded Silbane of Baalor, the stormlord. This giant must be one of the Furies Tempest had mentioned.

"I'll drink your blood before you take him," Tempest warned.

Anhur seemed to take this in, but did not respond. Instead he looked back at Silbane and said, "We wish neither you nor Lady Artymis harm, but Lady Lilyth has ordered your companions be brought to her." He then turned his attention back to Tempest and said with obvious relish, "The Kinslayer, of course, is ours."

Silbane heard Kisan's sharp intake of breath, but did not let it distract him. "I'm afraid I can't step aside. They're under my protection." Then an idea occurred and he asked, "If you're going to Lady Lilyth, why not let us accompany you?"

The blue giant tilted his helmed head, considering. Then said, "I have no orders concerning you, my lord, but would agree if the Kinslayer is turned over to us."

"No!" Tempest roared in fury. Her green gem flashed even brighter, pushing the entire crowd of dark shapes back and causing the giant and his men to raise their arms to shield their eyes. But it was short-lived. The weapon seemed to grow tired and lose luster, as if exhausted. "I won't let you take either of us."

As her light dimmed, Anhur said, "Do you still yearn to feed on your own kind, sister?"

Silbane intervened, worried what Tempest might do if cornered. "If we separate them, she could kill him. Why not let them travel together?"

The giant seemed to consider this too, and replied, "As I said, I have no orders concerning you, but all may accompany us. However, the Kinslayer must be surrendered. She will face judgment for her actions. By refusing, you cast your lot in with her."

At that, Silbane realized what the giant meant. They would kill everyone and then do whatever they wished with Tempest. It was intolerable, and he felt his own anger rise again. In an instant, he called on the Way to ignite his flameskin and could feel Kisan do the same.

There was a sudden detonation of white—an explosion of power that left Silbane dazed. When his vision cleared, it seemed the giant had shrunk. Anhur and he were now eye to eye, until he looked around and saw the truth. The ghost-like mistfrights were no taller than his leg, and the clearing seemed small by comparison.

White armor edged in deep blue encompassed him. He'd taken on the tangible aspect of the ghostly being he'd seen earlier. Kisan stood next to him, encased in black armor edged in red. The two war angels faced Anhur and his men, who had fallen back and brought their weapons up to the ready.

"My lord!" Anhur said in surprise mixed with awe. "We thought you dead."

Silbane moved forward and the giant retreated a step. "Dead?"

Anhur nodded, though his weapon did not move to a less offensive posture. "We knew of the Ascension of Lady Artymis," he said with a nod to Kisan, "and that you, too, were clearly Ascended, but we thought you lost."

Silbane rose to his full height, feeling every minute detail of the armor encasing him as if it was alive. He could feel air against its skin, on each blade of his wings, could even flex them individually as if he had been born knowing how. His gaze met Anhur's own, who stood ready with his company of giants, and took a calculated guess. "You would face Azrael in combat?"

The Fury hefted his spear, which began to glow. "I would never have believed today would be our day, and we do not wish to take your lives. Yet you must also know that Lady Lilyth will do far worse to us if we fail to bring the Kinslayer to justice. Like you, we are bound by duty."

Kisan stepped forward. "Then you'll die today, Lord Anhur."

"Perhaps," Anhur said with a shrug, "but everything dies." He stepped into line with his men and bowed with his helm. "Fate will decide."

There was a short horn blast, a signal from the line of Furies. They locked shields and advanced with a shout. Then, from behind and on all sides, the crowd of mistfrights gushed forth in a deluge of black fur and yellow eyes. They smashed into the four at the same time, like a tidal wave made of blades, teeth, and claws.

For a moment the bright light of Tempest flared in a burst of pure emerald before it was buried by the onrush of creatures screaming with hunger. Silbane had only a moment to see Ash and Yetteje standing alone and small near their legs before the wash of enemies swallowed and buried them all under a black sea of bodies.

PRINCES

Never trust those who give you something for free.
Assume what they receive
far exceeds what they gave in value.

- Argus Rillaran, The Power of Deceit

A rek felt the cold shock of transition to the demon plane. Then just as suddenly, the cold was gone. The two youths stepped into a warm breeze, heavy with the smell of spring grass and brightness of sunshine. The sound of birds could be heard coming from some distance away, but nothing stirred that spoke of habitation or people.

Squinting, the new adept looked over a verdant expanse flowing down the hill upon which he stood. The horizon was a clean, distinct line, an intense slash separating the vivid green from the wholesome blue of the sky above. Shapes in that sky appeared almost like floating islands. The surreal nature of landscape was jarring, and Arek surmised this was only the first of many things likely different between this realm and his.

Arek closed his eyes, feeling the world suffuse him with energy. He took a deep breath, then another, and then looked around. With each breath the colors grew brighter and more

distinct. The very air seemed to hum with something, a vibrancy he could not quite put his finger on. Then he knew what it was.
Power.

It fell upon him like the sunlight itself, permeating his skin, soaking into his very bones and warming them from the inside. It was a feeling of "rightness," of sustenance he could not gain from food or drink, and the energy it brought with it gave him boundless excitement. He looked back at Niall, a smile already lighting his face.

"What happened?" Niall asked, groggy. He seemed to be coming out of whatever fugue state Lilyth had imposed. He rubbed his face as if clearing away cobwebs, then his features went from confusion to wary alertness and he looked around quickly. "Where are we?"

Arek smiled and said, "We're in Lilyth's world." It was hard to hide the exuberance in his voice.

"What?" Niall exclaimed, clearly aghast at the thought. "Why?"

"You don't remember?" Arek looked at him in confusion. "You said you trusted me."

Niall shook his head, uncertainly. "The last thing I remember was standing with Tej, looking up at you climbing the pyramid. How did we get here?"

Before Arek could answer, a deep voice came from behind them. "Stand easy. We greet you in peace."

They spun at the voice and were shocked to see a company of blue-skinned beings silently regarding them. How long they'd been standing there was uncertain, but their stance mimicked the very earth and trees around them, natural and steady.

They seemed as much a part of the world as the grass or

sky.They had horns curling up from their foreheads like rams, and a circular sigil burned into their shoulders, chests, and brows. They were armed, but held their weapons in relaxed hands.

At their head was a taller blue-skinned figure in armor. A winged helm sat atop his head like a crown, and caught the sunlight in a flash of yellow fire. His silver armor was magnificent, shining like a knight from a tale, yet this was overshadowed by the most remarkable thing about him—he had the wings of an angel.

They grew out of his back, spreading and enveloping him like a mantle of power. Each shining feather ended in a knife-edge. It was glorious and beautiful, and at the same time dangerous and deadly. Arek could not believe he'd not noticed this man and the blue-skinned creatures with him before this. It was as if they'd appeared out of thin air.

The figure removed his helm, revealing a hornless head of black hair framing a square-jawed face. Flawless blue skin stretched over high cheekbones and a sharp nose, marred only by circular sigils burned into the center of his brow and down each cheek. For some reason he looked familiar, a face Arek had seen before but couldn't place.

The figure took the helm and handed it to a waiting yeoman, then stepped forward, smiling. "I greet you, Lord Arek. Your arrival has been a cause for eager anticipation and celebration." He stepped back and bowed, looking up at Arek from amber eyes.

Arek looked back with confusion. "You're with Lilyth?"

The man smiled, a flash of white teeth. "We serve what is best for our people, and you are most important to that end." The man paused and turned back to his yeoman to whisper something. The blue-skinned warrior bowed and ran off, his sprint barely leaving a trace or sound.

Arek could feel the harmony between these creatures and their environment. Then Niall grabbed his arm, pulling him closer.

"Don't trust him."

"Why?" Arek whispered back.

"Don't tell him who—"

The man turned back, interrupting whatever Niall would have said, and explained, "Forgive me, but we must make haste. We are your escort."

He then seemed to notice Niall and turned to address him with a formal bow. "It is a great honor to meet one of the old blood, Prince Galadine."

Before Arek could say anything Niall answered, "You know me, too?"

The man paused, his eyes flitting to Niall's hands before answering, "Of course, Your Highness. We have been instructed to escort both of you to Lord Arek's father."

Shock brought silence to both of them, but Arek spoke first. "My father?"

The man in armor nodded. "He has been most eager to meet you, but until now circumstances have made your reunion all but impossible."

"Circumstances?" asked Niall.

The man looked rueful when he answered, "The war has exacted much from our forces. Guaranteeing your safety was paramount and required immense forbearance. Your father is most patient to have let his desire to be reunited with you wait this long."

Arek felt confused and asked, "War? Lilyth said there's no war in her realm."

An uncomfortable silence grew as the man seemed to be

searching for an answer. He finally said simply, "You did not appear within her lands. There is danger, and we must make haste." He looked to his men and issued commands in a language neither of the boys understood. The blue-skinned warriors moved quickly into formation.

When they had assembled, the man turned back and said to Niall, "Your Highness, may I beg your favor?"

Confusion ran across Niall's features, but he nodded for the man to continue.

"Many envoys were dispatched at the news of your arrival. Whoever greeted you first was to send back proof of your identity, something specific to you. Upon confirmation, soldiers will be sent to protect our passage."

"Proof?" replied Niall. "What kind of proof?"

The man in silver flexed his wings, a smooth motion that started and ended with the casualness one would use to move an offending lock out of one's eyes. It was this very offhandedness that made the gesture seem inhuman, causing both Arek and Niall to take a step back. He tilted his head and gestured to Niall's hands, still smiling.

The prince looked down, at first not understanding. Then he noticed the glint of his signet ring, and asked, "My ring?"

"I can appreciate your confusion, Your Highness, but in a realm where thoughts are reality—" he raised his hand and a sparkle of air coalesced into a crystal flute filled with an amber-colored drink—"the highlord must be certain he's sending his forces to the right place."

He took a long swallow then tossed the glass into the air where it disappeared into a scintillating cloud of particles. "Your signet is something unique to you, and difficult to conjure because of its exactness. It is more than a simple aperitif."

Arek could feel Niall look at him again, clearly hoping he

had an answer to this strange angel's demands, but this time he said nothing. The cloud of particles still held his attention. They dispersed quickly, but for a moment swooped and spun like a flock of birds or a swarm of insects. Why would these particles have intelligence? The young adept thought for a moment, then looked at the man and asked, "What is your name, sir?"

The man bowed. "I am Gabreyl, and I promise Prince Galadine's ring will be returned safely to him. It is the highlord's greatest wish that you come to no harm whilst under his aegis." He bowed again, his wings curving around his shoulders to drape him in a regal argent cloak.

Though there was nothing about this man that made Arek trust him, he also understood they were alone and at the mercy of whatever dangers stalked this world. Better to be aligned with his mother's forces than not, he thought, rationalizing it as simple expediency. He turned to Niall and said, "If this land is dangerous, it might be prudent to have soldiers with us."

"Do I know you, sir?" Niall asked the angel.

Gabreyl smiled and said, "Perhaps. Do I remind you of someone?"

Niall seemed to consider that for a moment, then shook his head. "I can't place it but you seem familiar in some way."

Arek looked at his friend in surprise, having thought the very same thing only a moment before. Something about blue skin, warm to the touch, brought a faint feeling of comfort with it, like a smell or taste from childhood. Perhaps the prince was more astute than he'd given him credit for.

"Here." Niall slipped the ring off his finger and handed it to Gabreyl.

The messenger took it gingerly, then made a strange sound, almost a whistle. The sound echoed out, becoming louder. In answer, a deeper whistle echoed back. Whatever made that sound was bigger.

Gabreyl turned back to the two young men and said, "A wingblade has been summoned. They are fearsome to behold, but mean you no harm."

The approaching sound grew louder, a *whump whump* of stomping feet running at a fast clip. Even as the two young men watched, the crowd of soldiers parted and a rider on what could only be described as a giant running bird appeared. The rider was horned and tattooed the same as the rest of the blue-skinned warriors.

It was the bird however that caused both Arek and Niall to hold their breath in shock. The wingblade stood almost nine feet tall from the ground to its majestic crest. It was resplendent in iridescent colors that shifted from a deep cerulean blue to a bright turquoise, depending on the angle from which it was seen. Even in this vivid landscape, it stood out.

Gabreyl said, "In addition to their speed, they are armed." He gestured to the bird's feet, which revealed wicked crescent-shaped talons, each adorning a toe. It was clear the bird could disembowel a man with one slash.

It turned its black eyes on the pair, blinking as its rider reached down. Gabreyl handed over the ring and said something else in that strange, almost musical tongue. The rider nodded then turned and kicked the bird into motion. It shot off in a blur, almost faster than the eye could see. Another rider joined her. Soon they were out of sight.

"Sparrow will ensure your ring is properly delivered." He smiled and motioned to his men again, who promptly fell back into formation.

"Is that the bird's name, or the rider's?" Niall asked.

Gabreyl didn't look back but he laughed and said, "The rider's. She has been riding since she could climb onto a saddle.

Nothing will stop her."

"How far does she have to go?" Niall asked.

Gabreyl smiled and said, "No farther than we do, Your Highness. She makes her way to a henge not too distant, along with her sacrifice. From there to Avalyon is only a step." He looked at his men and then back at the two young lords. "As I said before, we must make haste. May I give the order?"

Arek nodded slowly, not understanding the context of the word "sacrifice." But it sounded ominous. He also wondered if they truly had any choice. He did not know where Lilyth's realm started or ended and wandering the countryside, beautiful or not, seemed counterproductive. Better they let these "men" escort them, especially if they meant to take him to his father.

At that, he turned to Gabreyl and asked, "What do you call yourselves?"

"We are the seed of your father's work, born from his blood and indomitable will, bound to protect and serve his House," Gabreyl said with a smile. He motioned to the warriors surrounding them and added, "They name themselves 'elves,' and serve your father faithfully as defenders of his realm."

Arek didn't miss the distinction and asked, "You said, 'they name themselves'... you don't count yourself amongst them?"

Gabreyl tilted his head as if acknowledging Arek's insight and offered, "Though I share kinship with these elves, I am bound by more than flesh to my House, my lord."

"Who is my father?" Arek asked directly.

"Ah, I regret I cannot answer that yet, my lord. Your father has asked that he be the one to properly introduce himself."

"That doesn't seem right," Niall said.

The winged man in armor bowed and replied, "Nevertheless, I am under very specific orders. May we continue this discussion as we make our way to the highlord's abode? I promise all your questions will be answered, but we are in danger if we linger here too long."

Arek turned to Niall. "What do you think?"

"What choice do we have?" replied the prince of Bara'cor, as if completing Arek's earlier thought. "We can't just wander around."

Arek pursed his lips, his eyes running over the elves assembled as their escort. Despite the claim that this area was not safe, Gabreyl seemed unwilling to rush them along without their consent. That made him cautious. Arek was aware the man in armor had skillfully avoided answering any question too directly.

He thought about it a moment longer, then nodded and said, "Very well, you may escort us, but please provide us your station, sir, so that we may address you properly."

Gabreyl bowed once and said, "Armsmark Gabreyl, Your Highness. I am the highlord's messenger."

Princes

FLASHBACK:

SACRIFICE

"The only measurable mark of true love, is sacrifice."

- Duncan Illrys, Remembrances

Highlord Valarius Galadine stepped around the bend, his arm wrapped protectively around his wife. They had been together for close to two centuries now, and in that time he'd found his love for her had become deeper than he could imagine. Together they had survived in a world that was intent on killing them, and that shared triumph had become their common bond.

"Are your preparations going well, my lord?" she inquired.

Valarius smiled and nodded. "Soon we will walk again under the cool sun of Edyn, beloved."

They walked down the wooden halls of Avalyon, the forest city that served as home to his elves. It floated by itself, a vast ball formed from a network of living trees and home to over ten thousand of his elven children. Life had not been easy in Arcadia. The Way flowed strongly here, so much so that thoughts had to be guarded lest nightmares give rise to real demons.

Valarius did not worry, for his disciplined mind had persevered and overcome his banishment since the Demon Wars. He'd created a new race, utterly loyal to him. His blood had been the key, the power to shape his very flesh into these beings he'd named elves. They were his defense against the Aeris demons that called Arcadia home.

The key to blood magic was the sacrifice of something the spell weaver cared for deeply. This sacrifice, combined with the use of his flesh and blood, had been the means for creating an island like Avalyon. Faith could be brought to life here, using blood and the power of the Way, and give the stronghold of the elves a place in the clouds.

Of course, blood magic was forbidden by the council, but what could they do to him here? They'd sealed their fate the day they'd pushed him through the rift. Now he and his wife were close to his final goal: to return to Edyn at the head of an army of elves and restore order to the land. No sacrifice, he reminded himself, was beyond him now.

He looked back at her as they entered a large chamber, her radiant gaze smiling back at him. This chamber was where they birthed their elves; entering it filled him with an undercurrent of hope every time. On one end was a raised dais that led to a podium with a single piece of wood grown into the shape of a bowl. No cuts or carpenter's marks marred its simple beauty, just like the rest of Avalyon, for it had grown in answer to his will. Valarius stepped up and gazed at the thing hung on the wall behind it.

A man—or the mummified remains of a man—was

crucified there, his tattered robes now musty as centuries had slowly eaten away at the cloth and leather. The highlord's head tilted to the side, his contemplation of the figure wistful. So much had been sacrificed to give his people life. He quickly blinked away any emotion and turned, a smile once again on his narrow, angular face.

"Are we creating another archangel?" asked his wife.

Valarius shook his head. "No beloved, I'm waiting for Malak and his men." He gestured with an open hand and she walked up the dais to join him. "Stand here with me," he said, kissing her gently on the forehead. "We'll address the men together as highlord and queen."

A few moments passed in silence, then Firstmark Malak entered along with a platoon of men, all clad in light armor and armed with spear, sword, and shield. The firstmark bowed to them both.

"We have it." Malak reached into his belt pouch and withdrew something. He tossed the highlord a ring, which glinted gold in the soft light of the chamber.

"When?" Valarius asked, inspecting the rampant lion embossed on the ring's face.

"Sparrow—" Malak gestured and one of elven warriors, a slim woman with fierce eyes—"recovered it hours ago."

"Then he's here?" asked the queen in a whisper, as hope, love, fear, or perhaps all three stole her voice.

Valarius watched Malak risk a quick glance at his queen, knowing she did not mean the ring's owner. She spoke of their son, Adem, who had been sent to Edyn for the safety of all Arcadia. Now he had returned and with him came the need for desperate measures.

Malak gave a brusque nod saying, "He's here. Gabreyl brings him along with the other boy. Sparrow came ahead so that we could act in time."

Valarius nodded, saying, "Gabreyl has done well." Then his eyes hardened as he met Malak's own and said, "This portal comes at great cost. Remember, I cannot bring you back, and we cannot follow unless Lilyth's Gate is aligned with Avalyon. Succeed or we are lost."

Malak nodded and replied, "We'll not fail you, Highlord." He caught the ring Valarius tossed back to him deftly, putting it back into his pouch.

Valarius gave a curt nod, then turned to his wife. "You know we will save them, right?"

She nodded. "I cannot believe Lilyth would risk everything by bringing him back."

"She's desperate, and her foolhardiness will cause the death of us all." He held her at arm's length. "If not for you, I would have been lost forever." He pulled her in, squeezing her in his warm embrace. "I love you so."

She closed her eyes, "Beloved, you do not have to—" Her eyes opened wide and her mouth made a small O. A strange sound, a keening like escaping air, hissed out of her.

Valarius slowly bent his left hand down, forcing his wife's head toward the wooden bowl using the slim dagger he'd pushed through the base of her skull. When her neck was over the bowl, he took another blade with his right hand and slit her throat.

Blood painted black in the lurid light gushed out into the bowl and despite his preparedness, a sob escaped his lips. At that sound, the platoon of elves went to a knee as one, paying homage to the sacrifice their highlord paid to open this one-way gate back to Edyn.

Highlord Valarius Galadine turned to the assembled men and said, "Sonya's death must mean something. Defend

Bara'cor and find Lilyth's Gate. Give me a path back to you. You are Avalyon's last hope."

A flash of blood red fire flashed from the bowl then, lighting the entire room in a crimson glow. That glow flooded the chamber and a vortex opened below the platoon, painting their blue-skinned faces purple in the blood light. Malak looked at his highlord and Valarius saw the love shining in his firstmark's eyes. The elven commander saluted, fist to chest. "We stand eternal."

Valarius didn't answer. Instead, he looked back down at his wife, her form now still in death. His heart was near breaking, but he finished the spell.

Sacrifices had to be made, and his love for her powered this single escape from Arcadia. Though he could not take it yet, he knew what he did offered life for all his people. In a red-white flash, the entire platoon, fifty of his best warriors, disappeared.

The Lens of

Arcadia

*The easiest way to deceive someone
is to tell them small truths instead of lies.*

- Argus Rillaran, The Power of Deceit

What?" Duncan was at a loss for words. He wasn't sure he'd heard Lilyth right.

"Valarius is a thorn. You would be doing the land a favor in dealing with him," she replied.

Duncan looked at her as if she'd lost her mind, then asked the question most obvious to him: "You've failed to kill him for almost two centuries and expect I'll succeed?"

Lilyth leaned back, her eyes becoming half slits, like a viper assessing her prey. A moment passed, then two.

"You and Valarius were once friends."

Duncan felt a clinical detachment, a strange ability to ascertain his own mental state. He tilted his head, "Not—"

"And now he has your wife."

He stopped short, her comment nudging his deepest fear— what had actually happened over the last two hundred years between them? Was Sonya truly an unwilling captive? Yet was killing Valarius even right?

Lilyth, in a strange echo of his own thoughts, said, "Killing him ensures your family's reunion. The man has brought more misery to our worlds than can be believed. Would this be such an injustice?"

As if she thought his surrender was inevitable, she beckoned a hand servant who approached with a small box on a silver platter. Lilyth took it and met Duncan's eyes, opening the box casually. With two fingers she gingerly extracted a crystal, thin and circular in shape, and held it up to the light.

"Do you know what this is, Lore Father?"

Duncan shook his head. He did not recall ever seeing one before. The crystal was clear, smooth, and maybe a bit smaller than the size of his palm.

"This is a lens," she said, turning it over slowly.

He noted that the edges were beveled, catching and refracting the light into sudden small flashes of rainbow colors.

"While lenses can still be found in Arcadia and Edyn, they're rare, and this one is exceedingly so."

"Why?" he asked, more than a little intrigued.

He'd heard of some ancient tomes entitled lenses, but had always imagined they had been books made from parchment. Now it was clear lenses were crystals, but how did they convey information? He supposed he could search the stored memories of the ancient lore fathers, now that he knew what to look for. Clearly his interest showed.

"This particular lens deals with locations," Lilyth explained. Her eyes left the crystal, wandering back to meet his own. She leaned forward, extending her hand, offering it to him.

Duncan rose and took a step closer, still cautious, and asked, "How does it work?"

The demon queen smiled and said, "It is simpler if I show you."

Her hand remained extended. She wanted him to take it. At first he rebelled at the idea, but slowly curiosity won over fear. If she'd wanted to kill him, she could have done so with less trickery. No, she wanted something else.

At her nod, he took the crystal and held it warily. It felt smooth and warm to the touch. It described a circle and a convex surface that fitted perfectly into the cup of his palm. He placed it flat on his hand and looked at Lilyth.

"Turn it like this," she said using her forefinger and thumb.

Duncan did so, rotating the lens in his palm. At the half-turn mark, his palm felt a tingle and the lens adhered to his skin, bursting with a sparkling light. All around him floated islands—hundreds, perhaps thousands! They filled a sphere in which he was the center.

Islands orbited his position, each irregular and misshapen. One gargantuan island had a bright star on it, which he quickly surmised was their location.

"We are here," he said.

Lilyth looked at him, her features calm and measured. Then she smiled and said, "You are intuitive, Duncan Illrys. Yes, this is us." She made a pinching motion with her fingers. "Trace this motion on the surface of the lens and you will see more around you. Reverse it—" she pulled her fingers apart—"and the view will move closer to the object you are looking at."

Duncan tried it, and could immediately see how to zoom his view in or out on the map. He looked back at her.

Lilyth smiled and said, "There are other ways to manipulate the map. I leave discovering them to you." She directed his attention to a small island not far from their bright star and said, "Now, touch this island."

Duncan reached out and touched the island she had indicated. The world shrank and then expanded in his vision, and he no longer stood inside Lilyth's castle. Instead, he had been deposited on a plateau overlooking open air. Below him spread the sky, with islands floating serenely beside him. The transportation had felt instantaneous, not cold like the transition from Edyn to here. He looked up over his shoulder and saw Lilyth's domain, an immense island floating majestically in the distance.

He could leave now, a part of him realized, just continue his search for Sonya and abandon a son he'd never met. The thought flitted by but could find no purchase on the smooth wall of his now level-headed detachment. Oh, he'd not given up, by any means, but a cold logical reasoning had taken over. He needed more information in order to formulate any strategy, and that required he return to the demon queen's spire. She must've known this or she would never have let him leave. His brows knitted as he looked back down at the crystal disk, then he traced the half circle again.

Once again the map showed itself, springing into being around him. He could easily see Lilyth's castle and touched it. The world collapsed and expanded, and he stood again in her throne room.

"You are a quick learner."

Her comment was delivered as if she acting the part of his proud mother. She smiled at him, but her eyes never softened.

Duncan held up the crystal, "Why give me something so powerful? Why not use it yourself to jump to Valarius or this Sovereign you speak of?"

She laughed. "I do not need a lens to travel, mortal." Her gaze grew thoughtful and she added, "We Aeris do not manipulate the Way as you, using blood and other unseemly things. And even if we did, you saw how the lens behaves. The travel is instantaneous, but only for those you are in physical contact with. It is not a gate I can run an army through."

"You would ease my travel just so I can kill a friend?"

She looked down from her station. "We spoke of Sovereign and his desire to remake the world. I and my Furies oppose him and believe, despite what has evolved on Edyn, all is as it was meant to be. You've seen our worlds are different. Each island bespeaks the faith your people have in us. Your people believe in me and have so for millennia, and because of this my lands range farther than any other."

Duncan shrugged, unsure where Lilyth was going with this but content to let her speak. Every word uttered gave him more information.

"My fight's not with Valarius and his elves. They are a nuisance, true, but Sovereign is the real enemy." She looked at Duncan carefully before continuing, "Somewhere deep inside the mountain of Dawnlight lies Sovereign's stronghold. I mean to destroy it and him, and set our people free, but I cannot do this while Valarius distracts my forces."

Duncan's eyes narrowed. "Dawnlight disappeared after the last war. So did the dwarves and their kin throughout Edyn."

"Dawnlight has always been a nexus between realms. Something about the mountain itself makes the path between worlds thin."

She smiled at his raised eyebrows and said, "When it became clear Sovereign sought their end, the dwarven king did something unexpected. He found a way to escape Sovereign and my Aeris, moving his people into a version of Dawnlight that exists in-between Arcadia and Edyn. We call it, 'phase.' Do you understand this term?"

"You said Sovereign is holed up in Dawnlight," Duncan

reminded her, not answering her question. He wanted her focus on Dawnlight.

"The mountain in Edyn is now Sovereign's demesne, a clear declaration to the dwarves saying, 'Your land is now mine.'"

She leaned forward and said, "Dawnlight coexists in all realms. Each has its own unique denizens. In Edyn it's Sovereign, in Arcadia it's unexplored. The dwarves who survived my attempt to free Edyn escaped the realm into phase. None may enter Dawnlight unless they also exist in the same realm with it."

Duncan ignored the characterization of her invasion as "freeing Edyn" and instead said, "You know I faced Baalor. He had a new body, one that could change form, move through rock. Perhaps he can be trained to enter the dwarven mountain, like a pet with a new trick." He let the barb stick. Let's see how she reacts when someone didn't bow their forehead to her feet.

Lilyth's eyes narrowed and she said, "Despite your insult, Baalor is an honorable warrior and friend. Do not belittle him with your penurious understanding of his actions." Her eyes did not waver when she finished, "He did what I asked."

"Attack us? Kill the king?" When Lilyth seemed about to respond Duncan held up a hand and said, "You'll not get tears from me at the death of any Galadine. My war with them started the day one put an arrow through my wife."

"Then killing Valarius Galadine will not be such umbrage to your soul."

"You forget that Valarius too was the first victim of his brother's vengeance. He shares that honor with me and my wife."

"And your child?" There was silence at that as Lilyth drew a soft breath. When she spoke again, it was as if she wished to start an entirely new conversation, an attempt to set them on the right path forward.

"I asked you to end Valarius. His elves travel throughout the realm, attacking my Furies with impunity. They're ensorcelled to destroy my Aeris, something I cannot abide."

She paused, then added, "Worse, Avalyon can appear whenever he wishes. He cannot leave Arcadia, but has mastered staying hidden from me. It is only a matter of time before he learns how to shift Avalyon back to Edyn, and then your world will face a Galadine who is insane. His thirst for war will end only when he has subjugated every soul in Edyn and brought Galadine rule down upon their heads."

"And with Avalyon hidden, you cannot send in your forces. You want me to unravel how Valarius hides himself," he said.

Lilyth nodded and said, "Yes, Lore Father. You and he know the Old Lore, a kind of magic we do not need. Remember, even as we speak, the black-clad assassins of Sovereign scurry between our realms like vermin, attacking and killing those of the Way. Very few can stand against them, and for every Fury and Master they kill, for every dwarven builder they capture, Sovereign is able to draw upon more power. Killing Valarius allows me to engage the full might of my forces against Sovereign."

Duncan considered that, finding it hard to believe an enemy eons old, the maker of these worlds, would do such a thing without reason. It was more likely a trap, for rarely did someone's mistake give you exactly what you want. Still, he said nothing. They were speaking only because Lilyth still held his son.

So instead of debating the intelligence of Sovereign's tactics, Duncan said, "Killing Valarius may free you to act, but how do I know it's for the good of Edyn?"

"Since when have you cared? Your only request was for the

safe return of your wife and family," the demon queen retorted. "Deal with Valarius and you will be rewarded."

It amused him how her use of the word 'reward' sounded more like a threat. He did not answer right away, his thoughts turning the conversation over. Not everything she'd said fit, so he said, "You've obviously tried before."

Lilyth sighed. "Of course, Lore Father... but Valarius is more than cunning."

"Your men failed?" he asked, a part of him liking the idea she'd also contended with failure.

She smiled at the challenge, a hint of malice edging through when she said, "My men died."

"Nothing dies," he said softly.

Lilyth's gaze did not waver when she leaned forward and answered, "Here, everything does. If you are killed, Lord Scythe is freed from your possession." She kept her eyes on him, her gaze turning icy. "His enslavement will be over and no one will remember you. You will fade from existence, permanently."

Duncan looked down, taking a deep breath. It was interesting that she thought of his bonding with Scythe as an act of possession by him. It was also unclear whether his newfound clarity or the fact he was so close to achieving his goal filled him with this fear and doubt. In the past, with beings like Rai'stahn, he'd had none. He would not have thought twice about killing anyone to achieve his ends, a fact many had come to know firsthand. Now, for some reason he could not fathom, the idea of killing filled him with revulsion.

Something in his thoughts must have shown on his face, for Lilyth said, "You feel uncomfortable playing the role of assassin. If it will make things easier, I withdraw that request. I cannot enter Avalyon. As you know, it means death for me or my Aeris. However, if the lens is there, I can fix Avalyon's position, anchor it within phase. If you manage to get it into the city, I can bring the full might of my legions to bear. I will eradicate Valarius and your hands do not have to be dirtied."

Ah, he thought, *and now the reason for the lens was revealed.* He took note of that, and of Lilyth's ability to divulge information only when necessary. Some facts were beginning to fall into place, but there were still two glaring holes in her logic, ones he did not yet give voice.

First, it was on her word alone that Sovereign even existed *and* was malevolent to Edyn. The only attacks he'd witnessed over the last two hundred years had been Lilyth's own.

Second, how would he unravel the spell Valarius used to hide Avalyon? According to Lilyth, the island had no physical location, but instead existed within this "phase" between worlds. The problem was deeper than just finding something on a map.

Then she said something that sounded completely unconnected, a sure sign she was using her entire arsenal of diplomacy to bring about his support. Clearly his actions were important to her, though he could not discern why.

"We found something floating amongst our isles."

"What?" he asked.

Lilyth gestured with her chin at the open window but that movement seemed to take in the entire world of Arcadia. "A metal tomb etched with unfamiliar runes. The metal itself is hard, like ebonite, but gray and covered with minerals. Quite ancient. When we opened it, we found a woman." She paused, making sure Duncan was listening, then said, "A dwarven builder dressed in strange garb."

Duncan now looked at the demonlord with renewed interest. "She's alive?"

Lilyth nodded. "She was in a deep slumber, but awakened

shortly after the tomb was opened. I was going to use her to bargain with Dazra." When Duncan looked confused she added, "The leader of the dwarves."

"Bargain, how?"

"While Dazra and his dwarven people are not aligned with me, they're not yet my enemies. Perhaps the gesture of returning one of his own people to him might help reduce his fears enough for him to meet."

"To join in your efforts against Sovereign?" Duncan inquired.

Lilyth smiled and said, "With his guard down, my forces will attack and subjugate the dwarves, bringing them in line against Sovereign." She paused, then added, "So, yes... in a manner of speaking."

This was said so matter-of-factly that Duncan was nodding before he caught himself. Then the simple truth that thousands would be possessed by this act of subterfuge hit him with a sickening finality. His morality, the strange new feeling emerging as a result of this place's beneficial healing, forced him to ask, "You'd betray and possess those who meet you in peace?"

"I grow tired of explaining this." Lilyth slammed her palm down with a thunder crack and stood. "My Furies need bodies, archmage! They cannot survive Sovereign nor can they do battle with his forces on Edyn without real flesh, without substance. Somewhere deep in Dawnlight Mountain the coward Sovereign sits, plotting the end of your world and mine and you speak as if possession is a choice! Do you understand what's at stake?"

Duncan had fallen back a step at the demon queen's vehemence. As her anger cooled, he knew he'd have to be careful what he said next.

"Then why give up the prisoner?" he asked. "Why give

away this opportunity you've so eloquently outlined?"

"Do not feign ignorance now, it is beneath you. My world rebuilds you beyond such shallow façades. Did you believe I could not ken your strategy to entice me to chatter away? Were I so feeble-minded, you and yours would already be victims to Sovereign's dreams."

She turned to him and asked directly, "Do I need the dwarven woman now?"

Duncan thought about that, his mind quickly turning over all the facts. Lilyth had managed to capture one dwarf—wait, this was the second builder she'd captured! The first was... when the answer revealed itself, he looked at her and acknowledged, "Baalor."

Lilyth nodded, saying, "My general now has a builder's body and can enter the dwarven city freely – his new trick, as you so churlishly offered earlier. This leaves you with the chance to do the same at Avalyon."

"You think this woman can breach Avalyon's phase?"

Lilyth shook her head, a hint of exasperation showing itself before being quickly hidden behind her sapphire eyes. Then she sighed and began to talk more slowly, as if he were a dimwitted child.

"Like me, Valarius has long sought a true builder. This prisoner may be a good reason for the elven highlord to allow you into Avalyon. You meet an old friend, and come with gifts. He may even give you your wife in trade."

At that, Duncan felt the barb. Give him his wife? His disgust at Lilyth rose to new heights but he kept it carefully hidden. He laughed instead, a short bark that brought raised eyebrows from the demon queen. Lilyth could not gain entrance to Avalyon with a thousand dwarves to trade. Valarius would never trust her enough to open his isle. But Duncan...

They had never been friends, and his haughtiness had put Duncan and many others off, but maybe he could convince Val to let him in. Having the dwarven prisoner might be just enough to convince the conceited archmage to treat with him. Still, he kept his emotions carefully neutral and said, "It will not be easy."

Lilyth cocked her head at that and asked, "Why?"

Duncan's smile was derisive when he replied, "Because we hate each other. Always did. He's pompous, entitled, arrogant and overbearing. Mix the worst of a Galadine with an archmage of incredible power and you get an ass with a crown. He's thick-headed and stubborn. It's no wonder he's a thorn in your side. He's been far worse to others."

Lilyth seemed unprepared for that, and she fell back in her seat. Yet his statement did not seem to change her mind and her fortitude was plain for even Duncan to see. He steeled himself as she rose and said, "You have your task. Accomplish it if you wish to see your family."

And that, he realized, was it. He had no other argument. In the end she only cared about results. He was careful when he looked up at her, smiling in a way he hoped was agreeable, and said, "You'll inform your men I come to take the prisoner?"

Lilyth leaned forward, her mouth slightly parted as if she were about to question him, the tip of a pink tongue delicately touching her white teeth. Then she leaned back again and said, "If I did that, how would you convince Valarius you are not in league with me? Do what you must to secure the builder. Any Aeris I lose will be a small sacrifice for a greater cause."

She continued to look at him, blinking once like a reptile clearing its eyes, and said, "Do you know why we've never recovered a dwarven body until Bara'cor?"

Duncan had grown accustomed to the manner in which

Lilyth approached things. It was seldom direct unless she was angry. Instead, she came at it from many angles, like a warrior fighting. This made him both interested to hear what she had to say, and wary. In his experience, those who spoke well seldom had good intentions.

"They come for their own, Duncan." Lilyth leaned back, "Their ability to phase gives them unfettered access to almost anywhere in the realm, and they retrieve the body from wherever it lies. Always."

Duncan's eyes narrowed as he thought this through. "They can enter here, yet they don't attack? Why?"

Lilyth shrugged. "I don't know. Until the dark assassins of Sovereign began their assaults on your people and mine, we never saw a dwarf. Even during the last war, not a single dwarf killed an Aeris."

It was Duncan's turn to scoff. "You forget I was there. The dwarven axers did their bloody work, just like the rest of us."

"And killed the bodies of those possessed, but no Aeris died." Lilyth closed her eyes, looking it seemed, back in time. "Only Valarius and your mages caused us any real harm." There was silence as the demonlord reminisced, but when she opened her eyes they bore into him like lances. "Killing an Aeris is harder than you think, but you and your kind have nonetheless proven yourselves up to the task. I remember your part well, and your stand at the Fall."

"Valarius was out of control," he replied simply.

"Perhaps, but your actions caused all of this." She gestured around her. "Were it not for you, the Aeris would have achieved Unity already."

"And Edyn would be lost."

"Lost?" Lilyth laughed. "How does one blind from birth know what vision is?"

Duncan paused, careful how he answered next. "I'd do so again, but this time I'd not walk so blindly back to the Galadine line." He looked around the chamber, his mind coming back to the prisoner. He looked at Lilyth and surmised, "This tomb you found... they didn't come for her?"

"Not yet," she answered, "but she has awakened. It is unclear if they will try to effect a rescue."

"That's a huge chance you're taking."

"Coming from a man who has gambled on the idea of 'chance' for almost two hundred years, it's hard to take you seriously."

Lilyth's blue eyes danced with amusement, but to Duncan it was a thin disguise beneath which true danger lurked. Then her expression changed to one of real earnest.

"But I am not the one taking chances, Duncan. You are. I hope for your sake that you're wrong about you and Valarius being enemies, or I fear you walk to your death."

To Duncan, she didn't seem the least bit concerned for him, but rather resigned that one way or another, she was getting him out of her way. A sudden thought occurred so he turned to her and asked, "If the dwarven woman can shift as they can, how has she not escaped already?"

"Their ability is blocked by this." She reached down and lifted a copper, ring-shaped torc Duncan knew all too well. "I see you recognize it."

"A gift from the Galadines to the world." Duncan spat, unable to hide his distaste or the fact that he'd felt powerless when Silbane had used the same thing on him.

Lilyth shook her head, correcting him, "A gift from Valarius to the Galadines." She laid it back to rest and said, "Do you know what happens if this is put on an Aeris?"

When Duncan didn't respond, she said simply, "I said we

are hard to kill, but this insidious ring, this basest of metals, brings true death to my people. You worry about losing your connection to the Way when wearing this," she said, looking at the collar like it was a stinging insect, "but my children *are* the Way. They die when this collar closes upon them. One reason amongst many you should kill Valarius and feel nothing but pride."

"Valarius created these?" Duncan asked softly, almost to himself.

Lilyth nodded. "Oh, I doubt anyone knew where they came from, but the Galadine magehunters put them to effective use."

"And nearly wiped us out," finished Duncan. "Why would he help to wipe out his own people?"

"What better way to get rid those who betrayed and left you here for dead? Throw in the fear of Aeris 'demons' and blame at my feet, and you have a world willing to kill those saving them from eradication. Give them a weapon to destroy us, and you foment war. In this I believe you when you say the archmage is a pompous tyrant."

For a very brief moment sorrow etched her features, but she finished in a hard-edged voice, "Do whatever you need to do to get into Avalyon. That is the only outcome that will be rewarded."

"I want to hear you say you're offering me my wife and son, unharmed."

"Get inside Avalyon and you will be reunited with your family."

Duncan cocked his head at that, dread forming a pit in his stomach. He asked the question then, the one that a part of him did not want answered. "Do you know... is my wife truly captive?"

Lilyth waved a hand dismissively and said, "I told you all

may not be as you wished."

Duncan did not know how to respond to that, for she'd not answered him definitively. "Captive" could mean more than one thing, but he did not want his mind to start dwelling on an idea that Sonya had stayed with Valarius willingly. The thought was too much to bear and threatened to spiral him out of control. The expression on Lilyth's face said that she was not going to say any more, so he forced himself to focus on his present situation.

He looked around. The children continued their play, running in and out of the obstacles made by adult legs or anything else, as kids were wont to do. This could not be her endgame, a nursery of thousands upon thousands of hostages. Then a thought occurred to him, and he pointed at the children and asked, "Why have you not possessed them already?"

Lilyth smiled, her eyes sparkling with something akin to hunger as she explained, "Purebloods may not be harmed, not even by Sovereign, as the First Laws decree. Possession would alter them. They would be mixed with my Furies and Sovereign would no longer stay his hand from the people of Edyn. So long as they stay purebloods we are at an impasse, a stalemate, as I said before."

So they served her purpose now, unpossessed, but what about after? Then he remembered her words. *We need bodies, archmage.*

His eyes narrowed as he asked, "And what happens when you win, Lady? When Sovereign is no more?"

Lilyth smiled, and for the first time her face took on a feral, almost predatory look. "My people still need to live. As I asked you before, what difference does it make whether it is you or Lord Scythe that looks out from behind your eyes?"

At that moment Duncan finally understood that Lilyth, for

all her claims of being misunderstood and of having a virtuous cause, would remake the world too, only to suit her own needs. Her Furies would be the new race of Edyn, possessing these children and able to leave her realm with new bodies of their own. Families would welcome back their missing children and grandchildren, only to be possessed in turn. It was an insidious, different kind of war, designed this time to win without drawing a single blade.

He breathed in, knowing his life now hung in the balance. If she did not feel he was truly aligned with her, he would not leave this castle alive. Lilyth would not chance his interference, so he played the only hand he'd been dealt. She was right, when survival was at stake, he could be exceedingly clever. He nodded slowly and said, "I'll find a way to get to Valarius."

Lilyth smiled and nodded back, "I have every confidence in you. And what will you do when you see him again?"

His pale eyes met her own deep blue ones, and a sardonic smile lifted the corner of his mouth as he answered, "We'll both get what we want."

TRAINING

Traitorous doubt, ever victorious over us
'ere we give our task true attempt.

- Rai'kesh, *The Lens of Leadership*

L ower!" Giridian shouted, his eyes never leaving Tomas's stance. "When you're comfortable, you're vulnerable." The boy took that moment to shake out his legs and reposition himself, which only caused the master to roll his eyes in frustration. What part of "comfortable" and "vulnerable" did he not understand?

Grabbing a thin rod the lore father moved in closer, striking the back of Tomas's thigh with a painful *thwack*. "Get down!"

"Oww!" cried the boy, grabbing his hamstring and hopping out of reach of the rod.

The lore father moved in quickly, striking two more times to the other leg and arm, then upending his student onto his back. Tomas's breath burst out with a *whoosh* as he slammed into the ground.

"What's the matter with you?" Giridian demanded, poking him in the chest. He knew the boy was unharmed, except for a bruised ego. "You're acting like a White, mewling at pain and looking for excuses to rest."

Tomas looked away, and Giridian could sense fear and shame in the boy's thoughts. Using that as a clue, he offered him a hand up, then pushed him back onto a waiting stool.

"What's going on?"

Tomas looked up, but not directly at the lore father, and one could see he did not have the confidence to meet his teacher's gaze.

"Nothing, Master."

"Nothing?"

Giridian looked away and then back, crouching so he was eye to eye with his student. "You're distracted and fearful. You weren't like this before, so I ask again. What's going on? Answer me truthfully."

The boy struggled with something, finally blurting, "They killed them right here and even the lore father couldn't stop them!"

The assassins who had infiltrated and killed Thera and her students had left a lasting mark on the Isle. None had escaped unscathed from their attack, least of all Tomas.

Giridian took a deep breath, then said, "You must remain focused. While this world allows for distractions, your upcoming Test doesn't. You must redouble your efforts; we need another Adept to join our ranks."

"What if I'm not ready?"

Giridian clapped the initiate on one burly shoulder. "You're ready."

"How do you know? Initiates fail all the time!" said the student, looking down at the ground.

"Tomas, you know everything you need to know. If there were an easier way than practice, I would be the first to show you, but there are no secrets or shortcuts. Training is the only way to pass the Test, and I cannot say more. Now, focus." He raised the boy's head up and met his gaze with a reassuring smile. "Believe in yourself."

Tomas's face was screwed up, his brows knitting over eyes squeezed shut. It was as if the boy was trying to forget a memory. Then the initiate rubbed a hand over this face and released a held breath.

Tomas turned to Giridian and nodded, saying, "Let me try again, Master."

Giridian gave the boy a reassuring shake and stepped back, grabbing his stool and retreating to one side of the training area. There was so much work to do, yet it was in these moments that he felt he was accomplishing the most. He put the stool down and then sat heavily, signaling Tomas to begin.

The boy began with the ceremonial bow, but quickly leapt into his kata, his strikes precise and his stance strong. As he wheeled and struck, fighting imaginary opponents as he practiced how to execute perfection, Giridian listened to his rhythm and breathing. Any mistake the boy made would first manifest itself there. As Giridian watched with one eye, his mind wandered, thinking through the many things they'd faced already.

It had been a few days since Dragor's departure with Jesyn. The two Adepts would have made the coast by now, yet Giridian had not yet heard from them. While that wasn't worrisome in itself, the idea of them facing the assassins who had attacked the Isle. Despite their prowess, Jesyn was untested as an Adept, and Dragor was still young. Neither had the power or experience of Silbane or Kisan.

"Impressive."

Giridian started at the voice to his right, and was more surprised when Thoth appeared, materializing in midmotion, like smoke brought to life. He began to get up but the Keeper motioned for him to stay seated.

"Only you can see or hear me, Lore Father. How goes the training?" The Keeper's eyes assessed Tomas quickly, before looking back to Giridian again.

Giridian paused halfway up, then reseated himself and shrugged. "One cannot rush the day."

"Poetic, but we both know this one must pass. Our ranks grow thin."

Tomas whirled, striking out at unseen opponents. He executed a perfect flip over one and then jumped, spin-kicking another. His foot contacted the palm of his own hand with a sound like a whip cracking before he landed without a bounce, his stance rock solid.

When Giridian didn't answer, Thoth raised a hand and the scene slowed. Tomas had begun his jump, and now hung frozen in the air, pirouetting around imaginary foes as he reversed himself to strike something behind him. The entire world, it seemed, waited on Thoth's next breath.

Giridian hung his head and asked, "Why? Answer me plainly or I won't help. I can't take more ambiguity."

Thoth seemed to consider this for a moment, then said, "I have been excruciatingly honest with you, Lore Father. Why do our ranks grow thin? Because fewer and fewer of you prove worthy of Ascension, leaving more unbonded Aeris trapped in Lilyth's realm. They are of little use there when the fight against Sovereign will be here, on Edyn. Some even lose hope and join the Lady's ranks."

Giridian sighed. This was not the only time he and Thoth had spoken since their first encounter in the Vaults. The Keeper had kept true to his word and whenever new information had been discovered, he had shared it openly, though Giridian questioned the Keeper's timing when revealing important facts.

Oh, he'd been correct that Arek needed to die, but what had not been clear at that time was that Arek needed to die *here*, in Edyn. The fact that the boy had escaped to Lilyth's realm meant dire consequences for everyone involved. If the boy was killed there, it would destroy the Aeris and leave Sovereign unchecked. When he'd first heard this he'd reached out to Kisan in an almost blind panic. It was only hours later, when he'd awakened to the taste of coppery blood in his mouth and the concerned voice of a student calling for help, that he realized he'd pushed himself to the very brink of death. Frustratingly, informing Kisan would have to wait until she was on this side of the Gate. Giridian could only hope she was unable to complete her task before they finally spoke.

Did that make the demon queen and her armies allies of Edyn? Perhaps for a time, but Lilyth had no intention of rescuing his world. She meant to rule through possession and would see herself as monarch of everything under the sun. So a delicate balance had to be maintained, one where Lilyth could keep Sovereign in check, and Giridian's Council and Thoth could keep Lilyth in check. Key to this, according to Thoth, were more Adepts able to take the fight to either realm.

The Lore Father's head swam whenever he sat back to think about it. His mind was clearly not made for the complicated web being drawn between worlds. He preferred the straight fight, not these behind-the-scenes maneuverings. He had not appreciated Themun's machinations, and appreciated it even less with Thoth. What he did know was training students, and when he cast a critical eye at Tomas, he could not lie to the Keeper.

"The boy is not ready. He doubts every step, which comes as no surprise. He saw his friend killed, then the Isle attacked, and the greatest of us felled by assassins." He meant Themun, and even now he could not bring himself to fully believe the lore father was gone.

"He will gain confidence," said the Keeper. He took a moment to look at the boy before saying, "It will take effort but you are up to the task."

"He doubts. Do you understand that will kill him?

"We have no other option."

"We can delay—"

"We have no other option!" shouted the Keeper, turning on Giridian. He caught himself, his chagrined expression mixed with shame and worry.

Then his voice dropped to a whisper and he confided, "We have no other option, Lore Father. Only these Adepts, each fully trained and bonded, can stem the tide unleashed in Lilyth's realm and match Sovereign's forces here on Edyn."

He placed a hand on Giridian's shoulder and squeezed. "Forgive me, but you cannot allow doubt to cloud your mind either. You must persevere, be the rock upon which these initiates can rest their faith, so they can earn their place amongst the Ascended."

Giridian placed a hand upon his brow, rubbing it as he watched dust motes freeze in the air. The boy's hand was sloppily chambered, his foot wasn't correctly canted, his knee was locked... three mistakes he could see without even trying. Worse, he knew Tomas could do better, so these simple mistakes spoke to problems rooted deeper in his mind.

As if he knew what Giridian was thinking and wanted to distract him, Thoth said, "I want to introduce you to someone."

Thoth motioned and from the air stepped another figure, a girl not much older than Tomas by the look of her. She stepped forward and bowed, one fist to her chest. It was then that he noticed her golden eyes and the wings that sat folded neatly on her back. This was no girl.

"Greetings, Lore Father. Fate falls unfairly upon thee," said the girl, "yet I greet thee with open arms. I am Sai'ken."

Giridian blinked, then the memories he'd shared of Themun's youth flooded back and he said, "Your father is Rai'stahn."

"Verily," said the girl, smiling. That smile revealed row upon row of fanged teeth. Sai'ken looked up at him from under arched eyebrows, her golden gaze almost piercing his soul. "I hath been charged by the Conclave to lend aid to thine Adepts. Wouldst thou share with me their path?"

Giridian looked from her to Thoth, not entirely sure what to say.

The Keeper then filled the silence, saying, "Finding Armun Dreys is the key, and Sai'ken knows him. Your adepts could use the help."

"I've... ," he began, then paused to clear his throat. "I'm not sure what to say." At least here he was being honest.

"Ken my only service is protecting the land and all her people. We dragons serve the Way, just as thee and thine doth. However," she paused, looking at him in that discerning way he'd come to believe only dragons could do, "Sais serve for the sake of vitality and potency. Do not believe thou art being misled in my ability to aid and succor thine adepts. Though we are not Rais, we bring much havoc with our name." This last was said with an arching eyebrow, as if daring Giridian to gainsay her point.

"And you want to find Dragor and Jesyn and do what, exactly?" His mistrust had not diminished despite her openness.

Sai'ken looked to Thoth, who nodded once. The dragon looked back at him and said, "Armun may be held by the

Sovereign. Thine adepts art ill-equipped to suborn his release. I will aid thee, and thereby assure success."

Giridian absorbed this, still thinking. Before Kisan had disappeared she'd related that Rai'stahn had bonded with the red mage and fought against her and Silbane. They'd barely escaped with their lives. Now Rai'stahn's daughter asked for the location of two more of his people. Telling this dragon the whereabouts of his adepts did not sit well with him, so he did the next best thing. He told the truth.

"I only know they strove toward the Dawnlight Mountain. Part of their effectiveness stems from being given a certain amount of latitude to carry out their orders. Their exact location is unknown to me now."

Sai'ken's golden eyes narrowed as she seemed to ponder his answer. Then she sighed and said, "I shall hearken unto Dawnlight and search for their scent. Mayhap Fate's fortune shall smile upon us yet."

Rather than say anything else, Giridian looked at the Keeper and changed the subject. He knew they had been looking into the old records and asked, "Have you or the dragons learned anything about my runestaff?"

Thoth leaned back, resting his head on his own staff and closing his eyes. To Giridian his stance exuded a weariness beyond reckoning. When the Keeper opened his eyes, the lore father looked away out of respect. There seemed a profound sadness there. Then he turned to Sai'ken and said, "Tell him."

The dragon nodded, stepped forward, and said softly, "Thine staff is the key for a lock known as the Phoenix Stone."

That was new. He turned to the Keeper and asked, "What is this stone?"

Thoth made his way over to the frozen form of Tomas, inspecting him but addressing Giridian. "It holds within it a way to reshape things, to remake them based on the whims of the runestaff's wielder."

"And how's that better than what Sovereign wants?" the lore father scoffed. "Are we just trading one oblivion for another?"

Thoth didn't respond right away, his eyes far away. Then he said, "The Phoenix Stone does not have to remake the world... it can remake just the Maker."

It occurred to Giridian that the Keeper seemed to be avoiding his gaze. *Why would that be?* he asked himself. He held that thought aside, comprehension slowly dawning about what the Keeper had just said. "You think the stone can kill Sovereign but leave the world intact?"

It was the dragon who responded. "Placing thine runestaff upon the stone endues life. Of that, we art certain."

Thoth cleared his throat and said, "Of course, the wielder would have to be there."

"Great!" smiled the lore father, holding out his staff. "Take my runestaff and finish this for Edyn. I release it to you."

Neither Thoth nor the dragon reacted to the offer. Each stood still, and in that stillness Giridian could sense trepidation. Then Thoth smiled, though the smile did not seem to reflect what the Keeper felt inside.

"I wish it were that easy, Lore Father. First, we don't know exactly where the Phoenix Stone is, except that it lies somewhere near the Shattered Sea. This is why we must find Armun. You must keep your Adepts vigilant for any clues they may come across."

Of course they didn't know where it was. Then the fact that Thoth had avoided his gaze earlier raised its head again, asking for attention. A sinking feeling came over the bear-like lore father as he said, "I feel like I'm not going to like the second thing you're going to say."

Thoth shook his head. "No, I doubt you will. Perhaps you can give the staff away, as you just attempted. Yet, it will change nothing. Until a new lore father is chosen, only you can command the runestaff of your office."

"What aren't you telling me?"

Thoth looked around the chamber. He seemed upset, which worried Giridian more. Finally, he sighed and said, "The only way to command the Phoenix Stone is through your runestaff. Knowing this, what will Sovereign attempt to do?"

He saw what Thoth meant, and now understood their hesitation in speaking. He should've known becoming lore father wouldn't end in any good way for him. Giridian breathed in through his nose, which ended in an involuntary chuckle that burst forth, a sound that echoed the irony he felt.

As if she understood what he laughed at, Sai'ken laid a gentle hand on Giridian's arm and said, "Thine runestaff makes thee a target. Sovereign's eye is busy now, watching his foes assemble. Arek draws his eye further still from thee and thine Isle."

Thoth sighed and said, "Lore Father, I'm sorry but you will have to prepare yourself. As soon as Sovereign is able, he will come for you, just as he did for Themun."

"And there's nothing you can do, no help you can provide?"

The Keeper spread his arms, "The dragons are awakening, but not quickly enough to deploy effectively. Anyone left to guard here would perish, and we would lose vital parts of our larger defense."

"We're expendable," Giridian muttered. "That fills me with confidence."

In answer to Giridian's expression the Keeper smiled and said, "Do not despair, it is not yet time for last stands, Lore

Father. We still seek the Phoenix Stone, hoping to find it before Sovereign does." Thoth moved a bit closer to Giridian and put a hand on his shoulder. "Though Sai'ken is correct, you have time."

Giridian was quiet, his eyes staring at Tomas's frozen form. Then he said, "I'll test Tomas, then we'll leave here together. Maybe by then you'll know where in the Shattered Sea I should look?"

The keeper nodded, clapping Giridian's shoulder once. "We will do our best. Signal me when you are ready."

Giridian nodded, his mind still turning over everything the keeper and young dragon had said. Many pieces were in motion. Despite Thoth's forthrightness, his heart told him to be wary. Seldom did things unfold the way people expected, and death would be the price of a mistake.

CONCLAVE

> *Success is not birthed from success;*
> *it is the child of failure, catastrophe, and ruin,*
> *and dies stillborn if lessons are not learned.*
>
> *- Duncan Illrys, Remembrances*

T he cavern walls were lit from below in an orange ruddy glow as magma flowed between sections of solid ground, creating crisscross patterns of rock and fire. Rai'stahn, dragon-knight of the Conclave, stepped forward and bowed to the empty air with his mailed fist to his chest.

"I obey thy summons," he said in a deep voice that echoed throughout the chamber, making the place seem bigger than it truly was. He cast his sight about the enclosed space, his yellow eyes glowing in the dark like twin suns. He did not have to wait long for his call to be answered.

"What tithing dost thou bring before us, son of Edyn?"

The voice rumbled like gravel on stone. Rai'stahn knew it well: like the sound of his own heartbeat. It was the voice of he who was father to all dragons, the mighty Rai'kesh, awakened by the emergence of Lilyth. Rai'stahn watched impassively as the great dragon's head took form, hovering in the air inches before his own, dwarfing him.

Slowly, the dragon-knight went to one knee and said, "Bara'cor is lost. The demon queen uses it as a staging area for her forces. The battle will be thither."

Slowly, he extended a taloned hand and spread it upon the floor. "I beg you all, attend."

Then he closed his eyes, and the memories of everything that he had witnessed thus far became available for the Conclave to see.

Rai'stahn shared everything, as protocol demanded—his meeting with Themun and his agreement to convey Silbane and Arek, and their subsequent fight at the Far'anthi Tower. He shared his capture and oath bonding by the ancient archmage Scythe, whom they knew as Duncan Illrys, and his second fight with Silbane and the other adept, Kisan. Silbane had used his oath bond against him, escaping with Duncan into Bara'cor. That had led to the destruction of the nomad army by Lilyth as she enveloped Bara'cor in her phasing shield, proof against their interference.

When he was finished he leaned back, the only visible sign he was exhausted, though only a few heartbeats had passed. Breathing in deeply, he settled on his haunches and waited, still shaking from either the exertion of the mind sharing, or the anger at reliving his failure in the desert once again. He would accept whatever punishment the Conclave judged appropriate. Rais were not given the honorific for demonstrating failure, and losing the spawn of Valarius would be dealt with harshly, of that he was certain.

Sibilant whispers echoed throughout the cavern, perhaps condemning him, even as he did. To have been bested twice by the same man was shame enough, but to have to share it with those gathered was difficult to bear. Despite his acceptance,

Rai'stahn's anger grew.

"It is good thou didst not attempt the shield."

Rai'stahn cocked his head and snarled, "Wherefore?"

The great dragon paused, it seemed surprised that the young knight would question him, but Rai'stahn no longer cared. At this point, one more transgression would not materially affect their decision, so he voiced his doubt. After a moment, it seemed Rai'kesh was willing to answer.

"The shield phases Bara'cor between worlds. Its touch will siphon thy life force to Lilyth. We feared losing thee."

Rai'stahn sighed, thinking about what he knew, then said, "Yea, anon she endues her Aeris through, for they can exist unbonded within the shield."

The air around the great dragon coalesced into a cloud of red mist, a mist that seemed alive as it coiled itself into the form of a man. From that shape stepped forth another knight, his armor blood-red to Rai'stahn's black.

He smiled, laying a taloned claw on the kneeling knight's shoulder, and said, "Rise."

Rai'stahn looked up at his king in surprise. "I had thought thou wouldst—"

"Punish thee?" The great dragon laughed and then helped Rai'stahn up. "Mayhap we underestimated clear portents? Lilyth hath always sought Edyn's unification. Only her methods beg question."

Rai'stahn didn't know what to say. He had expected far worse, consoling himself only that his daughter was still safe upon Meridian Isle and would not share in his punishment. This reprieve had caught him off guard. He hung his head, unable to meet his king's gaze.

Rai'kesh nodded in understanding, then began walking slowly to an arch cut in the rock. As he neared, two dwarven figures stepped back, bowing deferentially. The king of dragons ignored them, instead talking over his shoulder to the younger knight.

"Dost thou think thou art the only dragon who hath suffered defeat at the hands of a mortal?" Rai'kesh let out another laugh and said, "Argus was to me what Silbane is to thee. Despair not. Mayhap thou wilt come to be stalwart cater-cousins, as I and my nemesis became."

He paused, then turned serious, saying, "Something lies below what thine eyes can plainly see. Lilyth exhausted herself in the Demon Wars and learned subjugation cannot lead to victory. One cannot kill what one means to possess."

"What then, is her plan?"

"We ask ourselves the same—wherefore destroy the other fortresses?"

Rai'stahn looked at his king and said, "The archmage revealed 'twas to fix the Gate to one place."

Rai'kesh smiled, revealing row upon row of fangs glistening white and orange in the rock light. "Haply, but not for the sake of her army. If invasion hadst been her goal, several gates wouldst afford the greatest tactical advantage."

They made their way through a tunnel hewn from the rock itself, emerging into another chamber. This one was larger and cooler, with stone arches along its perimeter creating a circular amphitheater. In each arch stood a motionless dwarven soldier, so still they could be mistaken as statues if not for the heat Rai'stahn saw emanating from their skin. The mystery of the disappearance of the dwarves was, for dragons, no mystery at all.

While many had vanished along with Dawnlight to exist in-between Edyn and Lilyth's realm, those in the service of dragons had continued their pledge. Rai'kesh motioned to them and said, "They give us another chance."

Rai'stahn nodded, "Yet are not enough to withstand the Aeris within Bara'cor, who anon wilt number in the thousands."

"And what of Dawnlight?"

"The mountain is—" Rai'stahn stopped, then turned and faced his king, his golden eyes narrowing. "What dost thou mean?" A dozen thoughts flitted through the dragon's keen mind until comprehension dawned. He breathed in, realizing if his king were correct, Lilyth pursued a plan far more cunning than he had ever given her credit for.

Rai'kesh saw it and he asked, "What would it take to anchor Dawnlight again?"

Rai'stahn did not answer, instead saying, "I need to journey in-between, to the phased mountain, and seek the dwarves."

The great dragon shook his massive head. "We dispatched a Sai. Thou wilt prepare our forces for war. If I am wrong, Bara'cor will be the point of the spear."

"But how wouldst Lilyth find Dawnlight? It hath evaded her grasp for centuries."

"I wot not, but the new lore father hath dispatched two adepts to the north. Thou stood as sentinel while we slept, ranging Edyn far and wide. Is there a danger?"

Rai'stahn thought about it. Was there a danger? It was well known that Sovereign had taken the mountain after the dwarves had escaped into phase. The only way to find Dawnlight now was by the hand of the dwarven king, and he did not suffer outsiders. None were welcome, as Rai'stahn himself had found out so many years ago with Armun Dreys. But the enemy of an enemy—

He turned to his king and said, "Sovereign still captures the dwarven people with his black-knights. Mayhap they look kindly upon others so beset."

"And thou wouldst tender them aid?" Rai'kesh looked away. "We wilt know more 'ere choosing a path."

"Thou sayeth a Sai hath been..."

Then the realization of just who had been sent hit him.

"Thou placed payment for mine failure at mine daughter's feet?"

"Thou speaketh as if I can command her. She art a Sai, and as our future queen-mother, well beyond mine own purview."

Rai'stahn clenched his jaws in frustration. He turned to his king and said, "Being a Sai matters not. She's stubborn and bent upon her own path, a trait it seems all share who I hold dear."

The king grasped Rai'stahn's arm, holding him in place, and said, "Ask yourself, in what world will thy daughter livest, if Lilyth defeats Sovereign? He maintains the Rais and Sais, for we still follow the First Laws. Will Lilyth doeth the same?"

When Rai'stahn didn't answer, the king shook him and demanded again, "Will she?"

Rai'stahn sighed and said, "Lilyth will not suffer our presence."

"And so," agreed his king, "we must be prepared to seize the day. Perhaps 'tis time for us to consider a greater sacrifice, something that will truly safeguard Edyn's future."

"What be her mission?" asked Rai'stahn uneasily. He knew he ought to be thinking of what greater sacrifice the king intended, but he could not stop worrying about Sai'ken. Worse, it was likely she'd volunteered, making his issue with her and not an order he could argue with his king. And debating with Sai'ken was not a thought he relished.

"The adepts seek thine old companion, one thy daughter knows well enough, shouldst he still live."

"Armun," stated the dragon-knight matter-of-factly. "His hand may not remain so benevolent."

Rai'kesh turned and faced Rai'stahn.

"Then pray Sai'ken achieves her goal, finding and delivering him back to us 'ere Lilyth or these adepts. Armun may be the last piece in this game of kings we play for Edyn's salvation."

"Dost thou think so?" Rai'stahn said miserably.

"Sai'ken is the key," replied the dragon-king, his warm yellow gaze still upon the dark dragon-knight at his side. He paused, bringing his voice to bear in what sounded like a declaration of prophecy, "And our Oath is the only way to achieve victory."

Conclave

FLASHBACK: DUNCAN

Rend, ring, ruin, rust...
I've heard giants say this is the arc of metal.
I wonder then—what path flesh follows...

- Duncan Illrys, Remembrances

Y ou must!" Sonya said, her voice pitched low, the urgent need clear in her white-knuckled grip.

Duncan looked at his wife, then his eyes flicked to the man atop the warhorse, bow in hand, the man they had once called friend. The spark of Lore jumped from Sonya to him, filling him with the promise of a new strength, but too slowly to affect the outcome here. Still, he had to save them.

Something in his stance, a minute shift in weight, must have betrayed his intention, for his wife grabbed him tighter. A deluge of images, feelings—a lifetime's worth—came crashing into him through their mindspeak, the connection strengthened by their close proximity. It was her gift to him, but there was one last thing.

Time slowed to a crawl as his wife brought her will to bear. The twang of Valor echoed like a drawn-out groan. The arrow flew from the bow so slowly Duncan saw the shaft bend and flex as it left the king's hand. He looked down and saw Sonya's eyes widen in shock, just as a bloody point appeared out of her chest.

She pushed him away, and he could See the illusion of him still standing there, pierced by the same arrow, even as he was cloaked by her last spell. She looked at him, the arrow protruding from her chest, and slowly fell to her knees then pitched forward to her hands. Duncan could only let out a short sob of grief that clutched in his throat, powerless to change anything, watching the scene play itself out.

Then the air next to her concussed and rippled, expanding outward as a rift opened: a blue-black portal, attracted by the power of the spell she cast. He knew she must've anticipated this, but was still too stunned to act. His loss—a lifetime of memories of himself and his wife—threatened to overwhelm him.

Then Sonya mindspoke, *He cannot see us! Hurry, push me through!*

His eyes widened in shock. *No!*

You must, she replied. *You can still save us. Time flows differently there.*

He knew the rift would not last long. Though they were hidden by her spell, should she be caught in transit, she would be cut in half. Yet she would surely die here, and her last illusion wouldn't last long. He'd not yet assimilated his powers as the new lore father. Thoughts jumbled through his head, paralyzing him.

Now! she screamed through the psychic link. *We have no time!* He saw the ghost of her on all fours, crawling for the rift, which could disappear at any second. Her hands clawed at the stone as she shuffled forward, the arrow still protruding out of her back and scraping on the stones below her. Each touch contorted her body in a rictus of pain. She could not move more than a few finger-lengths, and the rift began to flicker, a sure sign it was on the verge of closing.

Duncan!

He stumbled forward, grabbing her under the arms and pulling her upright and forward. Even as the illusion of Duncan and Sonya falling with one arrow piercing them both played for the king and his men, he pulled his wife forward and threw her through the rift, then prepared to jump himself.

No! Stay, or we cannot be saved. She toppled into the rift, falling and turning to face him. She smiled as she fell, a hand raised in farewell, then the rift snapped shut with a *whump* of displaced air.

Duncan fell to his knees, stunned, the space before him a grave with no marker. He had nothing left, and could again feel the weight of the moment threaten his composure. He took a shuddering breath, then looked behind him.

The king and his men turned to leave, their bloody work done. They plainly had not seen what had happened. Duncan, still shielded by his wife's last illusion, fell on his face and lay there; the dirt, blood, and spell were makeshift bed and blanket. Then the tears came, racking him with sobs that he stifled for fear of being found. The illusion of their death would maintain itself for a while, but not forever. He needed to move, or he would die here next to those the Galadine king had slain.

Grimly, he rose. The strength of the stewardship that had been passed onto him began to take hold. He could feel it remaking him from the inside out. The power of the lore fathers would soon be his to command. His pale eyes looked in the direction the king and his men had gone. A fire of vengeance filled his heart, warming him like a small sun. He would see them dead before the night was finished.

"Will thou smite thine enemies anon?"

Duncan spun at the voice, his eyes wide with fear. He could not defend himself, not yet, and the king's men would show no mercy. But the archaic language gave the speaker's identity away.

"Stand steady, archmage. None can hear us."

"Sh-show yourself, my lord," he stammered. His eyes searched the battlefield, peering around the mist and rain-soaked rock for any hint of the dragon-knight who owned that voice.

A figure, black and massive, stepped from the thin air, appearing before Duncan like a wraith from the mist. "We had not anticipated thy king's actions."

Duncan fell back on his haunches and said, "Lord Rai'stahn." He dropped his eyes, for the dragon-knights had pulled back after Valarius's fall and, he had assumed, left the field. Were they here now, even as his wife and child were butchered? Then anger took over. "Where were you?"

The dragon-knight turned to the new lore father and said, "Thy king chose his path."

"He killed everyone!" Duncan's voice began to rise, but Rai'stahn's presence now augmented Sonya's spell, protecting them from both sight and sound. "What justifies this?"

One without a dragon's eyes would see the gray sky and ground mist merging into a surreal pocket of isolation, the immediate area visible, but not much more. Occasional rifts opening or closing could be heard, their appearance punctuated by ear-popping changes in pressure.

Duncan knew the dragon saw far better than he could. Rai'stahn looked around, his golden gaze easily piercing the mist that covered the volcano's slopes. Then his gaze fell again upon the prostrate archmage. "A thousand suns pass for each day of a dragon's life. By that measure, what matter is it to us whether thee and thine kill one another off?"

It was delivered acrimoniously, as if the great dragon were angry for being questioned at all. Duncan levered himself up, then stood, coming face to chest with the leader of the dragon forces.

"My lord," he said, "we must destroy the king and his men. They must pay for the lives of our people!" He pointed at the battlefield, his finger both denunciation and judgment.

Rai'stahn tilted his massive head. "What difference do the few paltry lives of these vermin make? Thou art a pestilence upon Edyn."

"What?" Duncan exclaimed. "You cannot mean to dismiss those who fought and died here against Lilyth. Do they not deserve to be honored as heroes?"

The dragon closed his eyes, and to Duncan it felt as if the sun had disappeared. He had not realized how much Rai'stahn's golden gaze held the bleakness at bay.

Then the archmage heard the dragon say, "As I said, we do not intervene unless the need is dire, as with Valarius. Thy king dost not threaten the Way, nor change Edyn's path. Until either of these be true, we forebear."

This time, the dragon's tone implied the creature was trying to make Duncan understand. But Duncan would have none of it. He clenched his jaws, his gaze becoming dark. Anger bled up through him like steam, a cauldron of hate without release. "You would let him get away with murder, when you can exact justice?"

"We act when our actions have the most effect, archmage," Rai'stahn chastised, then looked upon Duncan with what might have been pity. "I saw thee push thy mate through. How shall she be saved, if thou fall whilst seeking vengeance?"

The words hit the new lore father like a physical blow. He put a hand to his head, his mind racing. Much had been learned about these gates between Lilyth's realm and theirs. It was possible to travel between, but one had to be living, or possessed. The Aeris demons could not leave Lilyth's realm without a body.

"You'll help me—find a gate so I can go through," he said, half plea, half demand. "I will bring them back."

Rai'stahn looked through the mist at something the lore father could not see, then said, "With Lilyth defeated, these rifts will lessen. Finding a way will prove most difficult, mortal." The dragon-knight's gaze shifted and he said, "Thy king and his men return, likely to clear the dead." He looked back at the lore father, who felt the heat of those eyes fall upon him again. "I will convey thee to safety, but that is the last burden I will bear for this war." The dragon's head sank. "Mine hands, too, art stained with innocent blood."

A small gate popped open, taunting Duncan with its existence and semipermanence. Duncan couldn't ignore it and was tempted to jump through.

"Thy wife was correct. Thou wilt remain hither to parley her release."

Duncan was speechless for a moment. Then he gathered his courage, fed by anger, and said, "You'll leave vengeance to me?" He shook his head, closing his eyes to the sight of the motionless dragon-knight.

When Duncan uttered his next words, they sounded as much an accusation as a promise, "Then I shall become death, and justice shall be delivered by my hand." Something changed then, a feeling of purpose, as if something else wrapped around him in its protective arms. A presence surrounded him in a halo of comfort and strength.

The dragon-knight looked up, his eyes widening at whatever he saw, and then at the small gate dissipating in a shimmer. When he looked back at Duncan, it was with an intensity that caused the lore father to step back. Rai'stahn said, "Be warned, Lore Father. Desire can shape things in ways thou cannot imagine. New allies are summoned upon thy wings of need, far stronger than thou hast encountered as a Lord of the Lore."

Duncan spat on the ground and turned away. "You're ill-timed, selfish, and leave me to my own means. Very well, I'll rescue my wife from Lilyth's realm." He met the dragon's golden eyes and finished, "Or I'll bury myself there, next to her."

Rai'stahn paused, an indrawn breath the only sign he was still there. When he released it Duncan could smell sulfur, like the volcano belching forth hot gas. "Very well, Lore Father. We wish thee well."

The dragon-knight turned to go, but paused. Then he reached into his belt and withdrew something, tossing it to Duncan. The archmage caught it, a dark blade, curved, and wickedly sharp. It was a dragon's tooth made into a weapon. "Perhaps with this thou will find the peace thou seekest."

Duncan said nothing as the dragon-knight took a step and faded from view. He took a deep breath of the cool mist that had gathered around him as he stood in the blasted landscape. He could hear the king's men now, the jingle of mail, the clink of spurs on rock. A laugh at an unheard joke floated through the mist. It filled him with a white-hot rage.

The Way had begun to manifest itself already and his body felt stronger than before, attuning itself, lending him power growing stronger with each passing heartbeat. The process did not feel complete, and given other lore fathers and mothers had taken days to acclimate to their station, it was likely his full might had not yet fully manifested. No matter, he had enough to do what he wished to do now. He gathered his strength and cast a simple spell, one that continued to shield him from view and sound. Then he drew Rai'stahn's dragon blade.

Laughter floated in again from out of the mist and Duncan crouched, orienting himself even as his spell faded his form from view. He marked the sounds of laughter, the dragon blade feeling solid and deadly in his hands. Perhaps Rai'stahn had hoped he'd end his own life with it. Duncan smiled to himself. *Today is not my day to die*, he thought.

At the end of that day, not a single man dispatched to the volcano's slopes returned alive. The ground was called cursed, the death bed of the last mages of the land, and the men refused to go back. Little did they know that death would soon cut down every man, woman, and child who had a hand in the king's justice, like a scythe harvesting souls, grim retribution for the murder of a woman and her unborn child.

THE FORGING

Adversity can be overcome by most men,
but to test their character, give them power.

- Jebida Naserith, Should I Fall

Baalor appeared in a flash of blue and white within Lilyth's demesne, his new builder's body trembling in anticipation of seeing his queen again. Plans were unfolding nicely, even down to the decision to leave the king of Bara'cor alive. The balance had to be maintained, at least for a little while longer. Had Bernal died, there would have been one more Galadine ally to aid the cursed Highlord Valarius, something they could not afford. He frowned at the thought, knowing that much of their success depended on the exact execution of their campaign.

Lilyth sat at the open arched window, looking out over Olympious. It was a spot he knew she went when in deep contemplation or doubt, as if the horizon pulled her thoughts into order. He did not gainsay it, for his queen had been planning her return to Edyn with meticulous care. His only concern was not to fail her.

"Did you provide sufficient resistance?" she asked, her eyes never leaving the lands spread out before her.

"Aye, my queen. The king of Bara'cor was beaten to within a finger's-length of death's grasp. Malak intervened, though I know not how he found the Galadine pater. Whether he knew it or not, he could not have been more timely."

She turned to him then, and he saw the worry in her ice-blue eyes. "He will aid the elves, then? It is imperative they gain the Gate." Her face softened. "We balance on the knife's edge."

He nodded, commiserating. "The king could not believe anything but that his death would have come at my hands if the elves had not come through their blood rift to intervene. He will lead them to your Gate. Recovering his son is his only thought. Do not doubt yourself now."

She looked down, then gave a hesitant nod that seemed meant both to answer her second-in-command and to reassure herself. She took a deep breath.

"The walls between our worlds grow thin. We have Bara'cor, and must soon turn our attention to Dawnlight," she said.

Baalor considered his response before speaking, then said, "This body gives me access to the mountain."

"I know," she said, laying a gentle hand on his forearm, "but the price is so dear to me. Securing Dawnlight must be done, but I can never think of you as expendable."

"I offered the king Ascension." He said this matter-of-factly, a truth he did not fear to tell.

Her only response was to shake her head and say, "And he refused. He knows not enough to value it, nor you. Had he accepted, he may have saved his people from what we must do, and we would've gained a valuable ally against Sovereign." She looked at him and smiled. "Yet I would still have lost you."

He put his hand over hers, pulling her from the window's arch and back into the royal chamber. Handmaidens dispersed as he led the queen past cushions and lounges, escorting her to her marble alabaster throne.

"You're certain letting Valarius gain entry to Bara'cor is wise?"

She arched an eyebrow. "You said I should not doubt myself." She paused, then added, "Nothing we do can be called wise." She looked up through the glass ceiling that opened above, seeing the red-orange light spread across the sky like a wash of dried blood.

"True enough. Why is it so important he gains the Gate?"

Lilyth sighed, pulling away from the demon commander and stepping up the dais. She turned and sat on the throne, her quiet dignity making her every action seem even more regal.

She smiled thinly, as if trying to muster her courage, then said, "I cannot share every detail, for we know not who can sift memories and thoughts. Trust that I hold our victory most dear." She paused, "But I will tell you this – men such as Valarius only value what they win by their own hand. He will not value Bara'cor but it is won at great personal cost, and because of what he will believe was his own sheer ingenuity. Hubris is the key. It is true of most men."

Baalor took a breath, thinking about what she said. Then he assured her, "We will make him pay for every inch he claws from our grasp."

"I know," she said, "but now that your sacrifice comes to the fore—" her expression grew wistful and sad "—I find myself unable to give the order."

Baalor smiled and said, "No order is needed, my lady. I offer myself gladly, and would do so again willingly."

"I know." Her tone grew serious when she said, "Dawnlight must be neutralized or the dwarves will ally with Edyn. We cannot win against them and Sovereign, so I give what I love most."

"You give so that our people can survive. Do not mourn me." He smiled again. "I will do what must be done."

She looked at him and nodded, brushing away a tear. "Dazra's men will hunt you, and even if you evade him, you will perish within Arcadia."

The Aeris lord looked at her for a moment then said, "You will bring meaning to Sovereign's mistake and show him pride is a lofty place from which to fall... again." He looked at her sidelong, almost winking as he added, "Beside, as long as I am remembered, who is to say my death will be permanent?"

He smiled, holding his queen's gaze as he tried to encourage her. Then a shadow of doubt crossed his mien. When she raised an eyebrow at him, he knew he'd have to give voice to his other concern.

"I do not presume to question, but the archmage Duncan Illrys... you decided he would not infiltrate the mountain. Why the change?"

Lilyth's smile this time was genuine, causing her eyes to sparkle and dance through her tears. "I have found a better use for our cursed companion."

It was Baalor's turn to wonder what she meant. "His command of the Old Lore is undiminished, even after all these years. Facing him again in Bara'cor brought back fond memories."

"I've given Duncan a task suited for his delicate frame of mind," she said, inspecting the tips of her diamond-colored nails. She looked up at him from the corner of her eyes and continued, "Deliver the lens into Avalyon."

Baalor's eyes widened at that. He shook his head. Duncan was a powerful archmage and his bonded companion, Scythe, was death itself. War, carnage, those tasks seemed proper to an Ascended such as Scythe, but infiltration? Subterfuge? The idea that Duncan could convince the elven highlord to give him entry to the fabled apple city was doubtful, and Baalor had to wonder why the Lady had thought to even try.

"I leave it to him to sort out the hows and whys in whatever fashion suits his tortured mind. He need only get the lens within its walls, and his wife and son are his. Doing so will give us Avalyon's position in phase." She turned to him and smiled. "Once done, we must be ready to move quickly."

"And you believe he can gain entry? Why?"

Lilyth smiled, "The capsule we found, the one encased in rock, it contained something unforeseen... a builder. She has revived, and Brutus and his blades are escorting her back here. I gave Duncan this information. Perhaps with a builder he can bargain with Valarius for entry." She sighed and said, "Whether or not that works, the only thing Valarius will love more than glorifying himself is to rub it in Duncan's face. He will never pass an opportunity to display Sonya to Duncan, and that will be his downfall."

Baalor smiled, then asked, "What about the capsule? It will be *unclean*."

Lilyth nodded slowly and shrugged, saying, "Brutus leaves it where it lies. It would take considerable effort to dislodge it, something we can attend to later." She tilted her head and then asked, "Aren't you curious who will lead the assault on Avalyon?"

It was Baalor's turn to shrug. "I assume someone powerful enough to stand against Valarius, but who also may be a thorn in your side." The Aeris lord kept his face neutral, hoping she liked the lord he had in mind.

Lilyth licked her lips with a pink tongue, but the gesture brought to Baalor's mind hunger rather than sensuality. She said, "Stormlord, you have someone in mind!" She uncurled like a snake, moving closer to the hulking Aeris before saying, "And that is more interesting to me than who I might pick. Tell me."

Baalor couldn't help but smile at that, then he offered, "Zafir. He is closest."

There was a pause as Lilyth looked up at him from under her perfect brows. A smile slowly crept to her soft lips as she said coyly, "You surprise me with your cunning, Lord Baalor." Lilyth spun in a small circle, "Zafir," the name hung in the air as if she was tasting it, "a good choice, but I have other plans for the Lord of the East Gate." She paused, almost dramatically, then said, "Deft."

Baalor laughed. "You set the pieces on the board nicely, my queen. There's no better whip to drive this particular horse." He waited, then asked carefully, "I understand about the wife, but his son?" Baalor thought for a moment. "If the archmage realizes the boy is not in Avalyon, you'll not compel his hand." The Aeris lord paused and then asked, "And where is Duncan's son?"

"Believe it or not, he is a guest of Highlord Valarius Galadine. Funny how things come full circle," she leaned back against the cool marble. "Duncan will succeed. I can feel it."

Baalor cocked his head at that. "How do you know?"

"You truly don't understand people, do you, my Lord of Storms?"

"Of course I do… they're children—curious, petty, and vile," answered Baalor, feeling like he may have again missed something obvious. Though his queen was right, he seldom cared to understand the things the people of Edyn scurried about praying for, so long as they remembered him in their prayers. His own aloofness had made him a favored deity for those who believed the gods were capricious, seldom intervening on behalf of mortals.

The demon queen put a hand on Baalor's arm and said, "Love. He cannot resist going now that he thinks Sonya may be there. He'll risk anything."

Perhaps, he thought. Baalor knew one thing without doubt – *Duncan will only find misery and heartbreak if he ventures into the cursed isle of the elves.* He looked at his queen and simply said, "It will be difficult for him."

"His sanity hangs by the barest of threads. So lost is he that the merest wisp of clarity is almost more than he can bear. It is painful to watch," she agreed. One hand slowly came up to rest delicately under her chin. "What will he do when faced with Valarius, and finds out the man has taken the only thing that ever mattered to him, and more?"

The stormlord chewed on his lip, and could not help that a hint of sadness crept into his voice. Even he did not relish the truth Duncan Illrys would face.

"It will break him. He will be unpredictable at best, a maelstrom of carnage at worst."

"And at that moment, I will use the lens to anchor Avalyon and send our forces through."

Lilyth looked away from her second-in-command. "The archmage will serve our needs. Choice is nothing but an illusion, a warm blanket for those who believe they have control over their insignificant lives. Duncan has only one purpose in life or death and that's to spread ruin. Let that ruin be far from us."

Baalor bowed, fist to chest, and took a half step back. "As

you wish, my lady. May your blessings be upon us all." She gave him a smile in answer, to which he bowed his head in reverence.

Then he offered, "I hope this new one proves to be a worthy replacement."

Lilyth looked at him for a moment before saying, "You cannot be replaced, but I hope he proves worthy of this life." She waited until Baalor acknowledge her with a nod, then commanded, "Come before me," to the empty room.

The air in front of the dais shimmered and sparkled, materializing into a kneeling man. To Baalor, the man was large for a mortal, but if he'd seen him on the field of battle he'd have crushed him without a second glance. When he'd fully coalesced, the figure stood and breathed out a long exhaled groan, his head still hanging with his chin to his chest. At the second breath, he raised his head and opened his eyes, now shining blue with the power of the Aeris queen suffusing him.

It was a temporary reprieve, Baalor knew. The wound in his leg remained, his body dying slowly under the desert sun while the essence of that fading life appeared here at Lilyth's command. Whether this man lived again or not would depend very much on what he did next. His queen appraised him as one did livestock, her expression one of careful consideration. Perhaps, thought Baalor, he might indeed be worthy of the honor to continue the assault on Bara'cor.

The demon queen's lips parted and she said softly, "You once worshipped the sun." It was not a question.

The man shrugged without looking away. "If 'worship' is the best choice of words." His deep voice spoke in Altanese, the guttural language of the desert-born. Baalor smiled, the man's language no barrier for a celestial lord such as Lilyth.

As if underscoring his thoughts, Lilyth smiled and

shrugged, then said back in the same language as if it was her mother tongue, "The light you worshipped is the god, Mithras, and his benevolence shone upon you and your people for eons. His warmth held your people up, kept you fed and unharmed, as the multitudes upon the world of Edyn grew."

She looked directly at him and asked, "Tell me, have you felt his touch? Have you felt the Sunlord amongst you?"

The man looked up, his expression narrowing. He stood there, silent and massive, like a statue made of living flesh. Then he looked down and said, "No, not as others say they have."

Baalor smiled as Lilyth glanced quickly at him, for the man had passed his first test.

"You speak truly, for Mithras fell on the battlefield of the last war, long before you were birthed. His spirit lives on, but there has been no flesh that could withstand his purity and might."

The man looked up at that. "And this flesh?" he asked, stabbing his chest with a meaty finger.

Lilyth shrugged again. "Worth is found in deed. You failed before, even with the help of the red mage."

"I was betrayed," was all the man said.

"Excuse is the armor worn by fools and cowards," replied Lilyth, looking down at the man. Here came the second test.

For a moment, the man's fists clenched and muscles rippled up his forearms to his shoulders, threatening violence. Baalor prepared to strike him down at the first sign of action against his queen. Yet something besides Lilyth's power stayed his hand, a strength to bear the truth, even when delivered as an insult. He nodded, but said nothing.

This was Lilyth's test, to see if the man could be led: a test his queen used to separate the mindless brutes from those who had the ability to think. Many had strength of arms, few had the ability to control themselves. Had the man acted rashly, Baalor knew he would have watched him die and fade into oblivion forever.

Instead, the massive figure slowly fell back to his knees, then placed gnarled fists on the ground. He bowed, touching his forehead to the dais, and said in the common tradespeech of Edyn, "I ask for one chance, and I will destroy Bara'cor and all who live within her. I will follow wherever fate leads me."

Lilyth did the same, switching languages with the ease of drawing a breath, "Though days have passed you still cling to life, hanging by a thread so frail a spider's breath would snap it. This feat itself makes you *mythborn*.

"Yet if you agree to what I offer, you may still perish, obliterated by the pure light of the morning sun. Mithras is the Dawnbreaker, and I cannot stop the process once started. You must offer yourself freely, without umbrage."

The man did not move from his place, but asked, "Will I be who I am now? Will I remember?"

Lilyth paused, and it was here that Baalor knew the true judgment would come. The third and final test was at hand.

"Perhaps, for it is a question of your will. It is certain you will become more than you can comprehend. Do you submit?"

The man raised himself to kneel before her, looking up without fear.

"No." He paused, took a deep breath as if tasting life for the last time, as if he knew the truth may kill him, and felt compelled to utter it anyway. "I will not submit... yet, I will serve you."

Lilyth smiled and said, "You have shown truth, control, and now humility. I ask you this only once, for you still have a choice. If your will is strong, you will be born again as a lord at my side, or you will be truly dead. Do you wish to continue?"

The man shrugged, "Everyone dies. Only a few truly live." He then leaned back and rested on his haunches, waiting for whatever the Lady chose to do next.

"Mithras." The word echoed out, magnifying until it filled the entire room with a resonance that became a deafening thrum, shaking Baalor's very bones. The vibrations grew stronger, telling all who listened that the Dawnbreaker approached.

A golden glow appeared above the man, who in response looked up. It intensified, bathing him in a yellow pool of radiance. As the glow expanded, a spear of light stabbed up from Mithras through the open top of Lilyth's stronghold, all the way through the spire, striking the blood red sky and painting it golden from beneath.

Then a column as bright as the sun itself struck back down that spear, engulfing the man in its incandescent brilliance. The man arched backward, his form disappearing as the light and heat intensified into a yellow-white sphere of power, as if the sun itself had come to rest upon him.

A moment later the sphere imploded, flashing into nothingness and leaving behind a black circular depression of superheated and charred stone, still glowing red. At its center knelt the figure of the man, motionless, his form smoking.

At first, nothing moved except for the smoke, curling wispy ribbons of gray ash. Then, his eyes opened, flashing yellow like the sun from which he had wrested everlasting life. Those eyes slowly turned from sunlight yellow to the white-blue radiance that marked one of Lilyth's Aeris lords.

"You have slumbered for far too long, Lord of the Sun," intoned the queen. "Rise and take this sacrifice, this flesh, as your own. Your legend is not finished, your story not ended.

You are the star of the morning, the sun that breaks dawn, and will bring my light back to our world."

Lilyth looked to Baalor, kindly waiting for his nod. If only the nomad had instead been a living builder, the stormlord lamented, then Baalor himself would have been chosen, shedding the husk of the builder Prime, possessed after death, and becoming a Celestial alongside the Lady. Still, if the man's will was strong some part of the desert barbarian, as the Lady had promised, would survive within this new life. Some small part of what had made Hemendra would be kept within the Aeris who now took possession of his body.

He gave assent, loving his queen for her mercy and benevolence. Sacrificing Hemendra to possession had been necessary for this forging, an opportunity they could not overlook.

She looked down and her eyes flashed a final time with power as her command boomed forth, shaking the very firmament of Arcadia as she finished the forging of a god as powerful as Baalor, a god worthy enough to take his place.

"Rise, Mithras the Morningstar. Thou art the Lightbringer and Dawnbreaker. Rise again and command my legions, for Edyn awaits its one true master."

WESTBAY

Friends and lovers lie endlessly.
If you would know the truth, ask an enemy...

- *Argus Rillaran, The Power of Deceit*

War had come to EvenSea, and if the rumors were right, the fortress itself lay in a smoking ruin, its arched gates collapsed across the Galadine's March. More than one local prayed for the Lady's mercy on the Tir family, hoping they had somehow escaped the barbarians surging from the deep desert.

The March had been blockaded immediately and Westbay's militia had been put on full alert. Between them and the soldiers of EvenSea, who were stationed in the pass and the natural barrier of the mountains, a relative calm had been maintained in Westbay and Morninglight. Watching, one could believe Edyn was at peace.

The Sunsetter Inn had its usual evening crowd; a mix of travelers, local fishermen, store owners, and dockhands, washing down the day's work with the inn's nutty, bitter brew. Trade flourished across the cities dotting the inland sea as people and goods made their way north and south from this bustling port town, nestled on the western tip of EvenSea.

That was probably why no one paid attention to the slender figure who entered the Sunsetter and quietly took a seat. She was nondescript, but her vaguely exotic, gold-flecked eyes might have caused a second glance, if one were particularly attentive. Otherwise, gazes tended to flow over her like water on a leaf, never really pausing to note her presence. It was a fact that suited Sai'ken perfectly, for she was no lady and attention was the last thing she wanted.

"Can I help ye miss?" said the woman behind the bar, dropping a napkin and a forked blade in front of the traveler.

"I—"

"To the might of EvenSea, rising again to glory!" toasted a soldier at a table to Sai'ken's left. He sat with a few others, into his drinks and maybe just a bit louder than necessary. His declaration was met with quite a few hearty--and a few uninterested—"ayes!" from around the room.

Sai'ken looked back at the bartender and added, "Ale, and something to eat, please."

"Got some chicken left. From the size of ye, looks like a quarter will be enough." She smiled in a good-natured way and placed a wooden mug of ale down, then left to get the meal.

Sai'ken grasped the mug and turned, taking stock of the room. So many people, she thought, and all so happily unaware. She smiled, sipping her drink, a bit envious of such blissful ignorance. She placed a hand on the bar and leaned back, resting against the warm wood. To be out amongst the people of the world again!

For almost two hundred years Sai'ken had been isolated on the Isle her father called their home. Oh, she'd enjoyed the occasional quest and schooling with the other dragons of the Conclave, but true freedom had been a carefully shielded dream she'd only recently dared to have.

Though Rai'stahn had never said it, she'd begun to understand that Sais were rare. So much so that when she'd suggested volunteering for this task, her father had forbade it immediately. That only galvanized her determination.

Luckily, she'd determined he did not have all the facts and so had gone to the great dragon Rai'kesh, to have a reasonable discussion. Her father had worried about her exposing herself, but finding Armun and the Phoenix Stone was paramount, and Sais were especially gifted at interacting with the prey inhabiting Edyn.

Neither task would be easy. Though her conversation with the new lore father had given her a place to start, following the Conclave's orders concerning Armun might put her at odds with two Adepts of the Way, especially if Armun himself chose a path the lore father did not agree with. Clearly Giridian had understood that. He'd not volunteered more information than he had to, and who could fault him? Even now he may be telling them to prepare for her arrival. It was not a situation she took lightly. These adepts were potentially dangerous, especially to a young Sai without the benefit of the Rais' more predatory mindset.

She scowled, thinking. The last place she knew for certain Armun had been was inside the mountain itself. That meant the likely possibility he'd been captured by Sovereign. Had he been killed, she or Rai'stahn would've sensed it. So he was alive, but where?

To find out, she'd have to collaborate with the adepts. The mountain was known for being less than hospitable to intruders. While she could mask herself for a time, Sovereign would eventually sense her. By then, she'd better have figured out a plan to achieve her primary objective.

Likely that when all was said and done, she'd have to neutralize one or both of the adepts, a fact she found particularly unpleasant, given their allegiance to the Way. Still, she reminded herself, gardens needed tending and culling to grow. With a sigh and another sip of the inn's ale, she quit her daydreaming, focusing instead on the task at hand. Time enough for dreams later.

The woman came back, plopping the plate down behind Sai'ken, who did not turn in response. The innkeeper stomped like a buffalo, her thick body straining the floorboards of her inn. Sai'ken's mouth watered at the thought of ripping into her fat thighs as the woman screamed, but eating was not Sai'ken's purpose, even though she'd ordered what these fleshy bags with delicious legs called food. She'd found that many a person would be more willingly talk to someone over a meal, as food seemed to be what most of these prey created bonds around.

In fact, Sai'ken was astonished at just how elaborate meal time was, with social rituals, prayers, even sharing! It made no sense, but she reminded herself again, who knew how prey thought? The behavior was both puzzling and useful, as this "safety in numbers" kind of addled reasoning opened opportunities to talk. And talk was something they certainly loved to do.

"Not to yer likin'?"

Nay, thought Sai'ken looking out at the tavern, *thou art quite to mine liking.* She then turned and reached for the bladed fork, stabbing a piece and eating it, still smiling. "No, just wondering what the latest news is."

"Latest news? Unless yer from a cave the news is all about Bara'cor," the woman said, revealing a gap-toothed smile. She leaned in close and added with a conspiratorial authority, "Sure we've heard EvenSea rises again, but they say the demon queen is back and this time she's taken King Galadine as her own. They're consorts now..." she said with a knowing wink.

"She could do better," Sai'ken replied in a disinterested way.

"Ha! I guess she could at that." The woman looked around, then leaned in a bit more and said, "You heard about Lastpoint? They say there's nuthin' left. The Blue just swallowed her up like she was never there." She said this as if trying to prove her sovereignty over gossip, waiting with baited breath for Sai'ken to say no, but the dragon-in-disguise disappointed her.

"Indeed? I'd heard the same, and worse," returned Sai'ken, matching the woman's tone.

"Worse! Tell me. If it's good, your next drink is free."

Sai'ken swallowed another sip, liking the taste of the bitter brew, then said, "Heard dwarves have been showing themselves again."

The woman screwed her eyebrows together, "Someone's been pullin' yer leg, or yer pullin' mine. Tain't no such thing!" The woman leaned back as if to leave, but her addiction to gossip pulled her back in and she asked, "Dwarves you say... where?"

She saw the hunger in the woman's eyes and tapped her mug on the bar. The woman's eyes dropped down, then with a sigh she pulled a pitcher out and refilled it.

"Now tell auntie whatch'ya know, lass," she said. Part of her seemed eager, like a child waiting for a treat. That was somewhat blunted by the savvy tavern owner, cautiously making sure some teener wasn't just lying.

Sai'ken sighed, not really caring either way. Likely the war in the desert left few stragglers or reports. Survivors did not walk out of the desert every day, leaving the surrounding cities bereft of any real news. The problem was, these conversations always went the same way. No one really knew anything, and two adepts who did not want to be found were naturally hard to find.

It had been the same at Sunhold, Deeplook, Morninglight, and now so far, it seemed to be the same here in Westbay. Sai'ken was hoping for something and had thought up a new tactic to solicit it. It would take patience, and that meant putting up with this woman for just a bit longer.

"Maybe I heard there were dwarves in Bara'cor... and Dawnlight. Maybe even here?" She said the last innocently enough, careful to avoid the "mayhap" on the tip of her tongue. The beautiful language the dragons used gave the halflings' guttural tradespeech some elegance, but here it would only serve to bring suspicion she was high-born.

No one talked to high-borns, something Sai'ken learned from her first disastrous attempt at Lastpoint, a place seemingly bred to harbor pirates and thieves. The woman was right about Lastpoint being swallowed up, but she couldn't guess the perpetrator stood right in front of her. Sai'ken had held the town to its name, making her "last point" in a lurid declaration of blood and bone from its ignoble citizens. Needless to say, if word of this had already reached Westbay, she'd not be returning to that city any time soon.

"Ach, yer crazy. Dwarves at Bara'cor!" She looked over at the bartender to her left. "Derrik, open yer ears, boy! Mistress says there's dwarves at Bara'cor."

The boy just shrugged, his attention on filling his mug and serving the people in front of him. He risked a quick glance at them and then said, "Lots is going on at Bara'cor. That'd be true."

The woman shook her head, wiping the counter with a rag she'd pulled from somewhere under the bar. Then she said to

Sai'ken, "The boy is daft, son of my brother or he wouldn't have a job. Better at watching grass grow if ya asks me."

Sai'ken began to wonder if the whole lot of them weren't a bit daft, as the woman had put it. Still, her measure of the lad showed a different thing. As far as she could tell, the boy clearly knew his business. He didn't dally, his focus stayed on his work, and more importantly he kept his patrons serviced. He also talked a lot less than this woman, who Sai'ken was beginning to regret having engaged.

"What? Don't like the chicken?"

The dragon sighed, then speared another chunk and washed it down with ale. Cooked meat made her sick, but she forced herself, imagining again a nice bloody leg.

The woman wasn't finished. "I'd believe dwarves at Dawnlight. Just the kinda place those vermin would inhabit. They're dirt grubbers, ya know." She said this with a fishwife's authority, hand in the air as if she spoke the word of whatever gods she followed.

Sai'ken nodded vigorously, full of the dry chicken she had to fight to swallow. She finished it with her ale, wiping her mouth. "A man'll be coming in. He's my brother. I'd like to save this seat for him."

"You'll be payin' first—"

"Of course," Sai'ken cut her off with a coin thrust in front of the woman's nose. "This'll cover my meal, and lodging for him?" She waited, watching as the woman's eyes went from the coin to her face, then up to the ceiling as she did a mock calculation in her head. A silver was more than enough, Sai'ken knew, but this woman seemed shrewd enough to not agree immediately. Perhaps they weren't as simple as they acted.

"A silver imperial... it'll just cover it, and another ale if it pleases ya," she offered, likely feeling guilty at taking triple the amount owed.

Sai'ken shook her head, "No, save it for him. He's of the EvenSea militia. You'll know him by his eyes. They're like mine." As she said this, she looked at the woman squarely for the first time. Her small gasp told Sai'ken she'd seen the yellow-gold irises, a detail she'd only made apparent now, and only to this woman. Then she dropped her gaze and turned to look at the door, "Now, please see to our room."

She heard the woman stumble back a bit before retreating up the stairs, her composure gone. Sai'ken didn't wait for her to return but instead walked past the table of boisterous soldiers, some of whom called to her to join them, and went out the door.

The area outside was crowded with people out for the evening. Orange lamplight flickered at storefronts and along the quay. Combined with the sound of water washing up the shoreline just behind these stores, one could literally feel the sea only steps away. Sai'ken found a dark corner near one side of the entrance and changed form.

Now in her place stood a tall, broad-shouldered man wearing the aquamarine cloak and the single trident of EvenSea at clasp and collar. It marked him as an officer, and would help Sai'ken with the next part of her plan.

It had been clear in the other towns that one person asking the same questions only led to suspicion, and that could lead to another misunderstanding like at Lastpoint. She'd thought about it and realized that if more than one person asked the right questions, people's suspicions never got aroused. Gossip was best found in small bits from lots of people, and never all at once. Luckily, everyone these people met tonight would be Sai'ken in different guises.

She made her way back into the Sunsetter, grabbing a seat near the one she'd just vacated. The woman was just clearing her old dishes when Sai'ken, now disguised as a militia man said, "Excuse me. My sister left me a message."

The woman looked at him, her eyes tracking up and down, then said, "No one left no message, and that seat's for payin' customers."

"Really?" Sai'ken asked, more than a bit surprised. "My sister, with eyes like mine, left no message?"

The woman stared at him, looking a little sheepish. "No, and you'll be on your way or I'll call your militia brothers to take you for disturbin' our peace."

Sai'ken got up, looking down at the woman from her now more considerable height advantage, and said, "And what about the silver—"

"Auntie," the boy Derrik interrupted, putting two hands on the woman's shoulders and pulling her away from the confrontation, "I forgot to tell ya, the mistress from before asked for a room and ale for her brother. Paid in silver she did."

The woman didn't take her eyes off Sai'ken, but answered over her shoulder, "You're sure?" Clearly this was all part of their well-rehearsed act.

Derrik looked appropriately apologetic and said, looking at Sai'ken, "Yes, Aunty. No reason for all this fuss. This is certainly her brother."

He pulled her away and positioned her at his last station, then came over with a mug of ale and said, "Forgive her, sir. She's gettin' up in the turns, losin' her memory and all," he said, tapping his head. "Lemme make it up with a free mug after this one. No need for yer militia."

Sai'ken's opinion of the boy grew another notch, for he'd skillfully protected his thieving aunt while leaving a potential customer none the wiser. While he may be a port town local, he was anything but daft.

She smiled, then nodded and said, "I understand. My sister and I have a father who's a bit empty in the head. Can't find his way out of a one-door room without smashing the place like a drunken dragon."

The boy smiled back. "Sounds like a handful, he does."

"You have no idea," said Sai'ken, still smiling.

Derrik nodded and then left to tend to another patron, leaving Sai'ken alone to think. She'd probably found out everything she could from the bartenders, but these men-at-arms might be a better source of information, hence her guise as one of them.

She looked over at the table of soldiers, now well into their drinks, then grabbed her mug and sauntered over. Eyeing the table's men, she pulled out a chair, slapped her mug down and took a seat. Their raucous behavior stumbled to a stop, a few of the more sober ones coming to order in the presence of an officer of their militia.

Before things became awkward, Sai'ken said, "At ease, just off duty and," she looked at them and smiled conspiratorially, "not interested in rank." She smiled, toasting, "To EvenSea!"

The men raised their mugs and cheered, "Here, here!"

Sai'ken took a gulp, then turned to the man closest to her and said, "What's the news from Bara'cor?"

The man leaned in and said, "Well sir, your guess is as good as mine. Strange though, about EvenSea?"

Sai'ken paused, a bit confused. "Yes, very."

"Who'd have thought the ground could do that."

The dragon nodded, still confused but careful to keep her face the same mixture of astonishment and pride she saw reflected in the man's. The bartender had said something about EvenSea rising, and she'd assumed she meant the men of the fortress. She took a quick sip and turned to her left and said to another, "EvenSea... amazing."

The second man, oblivious to the conversation the first had had with Sai'ken said, "The walls, growing right out of the ground! Never have I seen such a sight!"

Sai'ken sat back, stunned. The fortress regrowing? She looked back at the man she'd started with and said, "Walls growing? Dwarven magic if you ask me."

"Whatever magic it is can't come too soon. Will be whole again within a month, say the stone masons." He leaned in and asked, "Beggin' your pardon, but is that right? You prolly know more than the lot of us, sir."

Sai'ken ignored the question and asked instead, "And you don't care if magic is the reason?" She turned to the man, who broke his gaze and looked into his cup.

Then he looked back up and there was fire in his eyes. "Not if it means EvenSea lives again." He turned his attention to his shieldmates and said, "Praise the Tir family and the Lady's mercy upon them!"

A chorus of "ayes" followed that, from more than just this table.

Sai'ken waited, digesting the news. EvenSea growing again from the ground? If that was true, it could mean that the other fortresses were doing the same. What part of the Way was responsible for this? She thought about the society and rules of the people they'd pledged to protect. Rais dealt with enforcement, and destruction, but Sais were meant to protect and nurture. It was within her ability to coax the walls to regrow, she knew, but she was not responsible for EvenSea's repair. So who was?

Though most of Edyn knew Bara'cor had been built by the dwarves, the dragons alone knew of the great dwarven king Vulkan, who had built the fortresses ringing the desert long before Bara's time. Bara'cor was the newest, but all four had been built by his hands. Why Vulkan and his people chose those locations was lost to antiquity. They rose long before Sai'ken, her father, or her father's father had existed, and that was a very long time indeed.

Now the fortress of EvenSea was repairing itself, and what if that meant they all could? Worse, how could Lilyth not know this would happen? And if she knew, why then had she expended the red mage in an effort that would prove to be utterly fruitless? Something important was happening here, a missing piece of information the dragonkind needed.

"You'll be drinking to that, Lieutenant?"

She didn't realize the man next to her had been speaking until he jostled her with an elbow.

"What say you?"

She looked around at the table and asked, "To what?"

"TCA is asking for volunteers... you going?" said a man across the table. He was by his chevrons a staff sergeant, and nominally in charge of this table, at least until Sai'ken in her guise as a lieutenant had shown up. When she didn't answer, the man cleared his throat and added apologetically, "Sir?"

Why would the combat academy be asking for volunteers? She turned to the staff sergeant and laughed, clapping him on the back and saying, "I'll go wherever the next drink is!"

He laughed too, then shook his head. Looking at the rest of his men he said, "You can stay here and wait for the fortress to grow a new privy, or join me and the King's Tirs in freeing Bara'cor!"

He raised a mug and shouted, "TCA knows the way!" The rest of the table cheered and drank.

Sai'ken watched, knowing half of what was said tonight would be forgotten in the mugs. It wasn't that these men weren't without courage, but they just didn't know enough to answer her about whether Dragor and Jesyn had come through here or not. That would take a regular, and these men were simply relaxing off-duty. The news of EvenSea was worth the time at the table, though she was no closer to finding the adepts dispatched by the lore father.

She raised her mug to the sergeant and then drained it in one long gulp. She smiled back at the man's astonished look, then rose to leave. A hand on her shoulder stopped her, and she turned to find a patron pointing at the bartender, Derrik.

She moved closer to the bar and raised her chin, "Yes?"

"Your sis," he said while pouring another ale, "said something 'bout dwarves."

"Reports from Bara'cor... why, did you see one?"

He shook his head quickly and smiled, "Nah, yer pullin' my leg, just like me' auntie said to your sis."

Sai'ken sighed, then asked, "What then?"

The boy looked a little sheepish, then said, "Well, a couple others asked about dwarves, too."

Sai'ken's focus zeroed in on the boy's words. She waited, then raised an eyebrow when he looked down at her belt. The dragon cursed, reached down, and flipped the boy a copper crown, not quite an imperial but enough money for a full meal.

The boy seemed to consider it, then said, "Two of 'em, a brown man and a girl with short hair."

The adepts! Her relief must've been plain on her face, for the boy then asked, "They're not yer family... maybe they owe someone money?"

Sai'ken moved a bit closer and pulled another crown out and held it up. "Did they say where they were going?"

"Not exactly." The boy didn't look at the copper, only at Sai'ken's gold-flecked eyes. "I'd be wantin' to know why yer lookin' for 'em, before I speak, sir."

The dragon considered it. What harm could come by sharing her information?

Plenty, she knew, given this boy's character and the nature of greed. If someone followed, they would only need to ask him the same questions and they'd have the information too. It was too risky and there were better, cleaner ways. She decided to test the balance.

She leaned in, knowing the boy saw a lieutenant from the EvenSea militia, and asked, "You're the brains here, aren't you? I mean, despite what your auntie says, you've got the eye for coin."

The boy didn't blink, only turned to her and shrugged. "I keep us in business. Had to ever since..." He trailed off, then his eyes focused back on her. "I'd know yer business before I go rattin' out other travelers. Not good fer business if our patrons end up dead."

Sai'ken flipped her fingers and the copper turned into an imperial aurum. She held it up so that the light glinted off the gold and said, "And how much does this help your business?"

The boy's eyes widened. He must've known an aurum would be a month's worth of income, especially if it was real. He reached out, and Sai'ken dropped the coin in his palm. It fell with the solid weight of gold, enough so that the boy raised the coin and bit into it to see if lead showed beneath. Sai'ken waited to see if nobility or greed would win his heart. An unfair test she knew, given the amount and their livelihood. Still, she hoped he'd choose to protect the adepts. Maybe lie about their direction, try and pocket the aurum without betraying another traveler.

When it was clear the aurum was real, he said, "They're headin' to a place between Dawnlight and northwest of the

Summer Pass."

He hadn't lied. Her senses saw the truth. No information left with him would be safe. Unfortunate, but understandable. Sai'ken looked around, then held out her hand. "I thank thee."

The boy's eyebrows drew together at that, her odd high speech no doubt the cause, but shook her hand nonetheless for a deal done. He barely felt the small slice of Sai'ken's fingernail on the inside of his wrist. The dragon in the guise of a man bowed once, then turned and walked out the door.

Sai'ken took comfort in the fact that this boy would share another meal with his family, enjoying their odd predilection for prayer and ritual. He'd probably laugh over that funny girl and her soldier brother they met today and fleeced for good coin. He'd feel good his auntie and he were running a profitable business at the Sunsetter Inn. He'd go to sleep and die peacefully, leaving behind an aurum for his family to cherish, and silence in his wake.

True, the Rais were tasked with brute enforcement. They kept the Law of the Way and meted out punishment to those who would threaten its existence. They were the might of the Way manifest, the strong arm of justice when needed, and she truly loved them for it.

Sais were different. They silently served the people of Edyn both as protector and nurturer, like a gardener tending to her garden. They focused on building a better society, free of wickedness, lies, and cruelty, the kind that choked the life out of what was essentially good folk. Sai'ken didn't look back as she made her way out of Westbay.

Pulling weeds was all part of a good day's work, she thought happily, as she headed northwest toward Dawnlight. Her garden would be better for the deeds done here.

Westbay

LORE MOTHER

It is easier for some men to die,
Than to endure pain in silence.

- Toorval Singh, Memoirs of a Mercenary

Duncan had left Lilyth's castle, teleporting on a whim to an island he thought was north—if that was even a direction here. The sun moved across the sky, but had not on Lilyth's island, so he inferred that each island rotated independently, creating its own day-night cycle and cardinal points.

Why he didn't perceive the tilt was another mystery he couldn't explain, but he could see some islands rotating and others hanging motionless. Maybe the ruler of each chose their own path? Strange, but immaterial to recovering his family. In fact, the only reason any of this was of interest was his curiosity. He'd not felt the yearning to learn for knowledge's sake for decades. Whatever was happening to him here in Arcadia was giving him back his own mind, which he couldn't help but appreciate.

Duncan looked across the hills, searching for anything out of the ordinary, but only verdant knolls and grassy plains stretched out before him. Dirt paths cut lazy trails around various irregularities in the terrain, the only sign that anything lived here at all.

Then something impinged on his senses, a vibration just under his skin. A change in the air that he was instantly attuned to, like a chord being struck, but one that could not be heard. His skin grew bumps, as if he were cold, and the world paused.

"You shouldn't have come."

He spun toward the voice, lightning already flashing at his fingertips. It sputtered and died when he saw who greeted him. Staggering back to fall to one knee, he held up a hand in disbelief and choked out, "H-how?"

The figure of a woman stood before him in simple white robes. She'd materialized from thin air, flowing toward him like a ripple that solidified with heartrending detail. He looked at her, unable to comprehend the sight before his eyes, and felt his composure break. "She said you were captured..."

Sonya Illrys, wife to Duncan, looked down at her husband and said, "There's nothing but pain and grief for you here."

"What?" he said, tears blinding his sight. "Why?"

The shade looked down at him. "Duncan, you must not follow this path."

In a voice edged with obsession he said, "I didn't come this far just to give up."

Sonya looked around the small area Duncan had been sitting in, then knelt near him—but not close enough to touch—and said, "Leave this world and me to my fate."

"No!" Duncan slammed his fist into the ground and lightning exploded across the landscape in a tidal force of energy, magnified by the potency of the Way here. It blasted outward with a thunderclap's crack, ripping through earth and trees, a detonation of grief echoing across the hills. Something about the act restored some of his mental balance, his anger and frustration finally having release. His shoulders sagged forward, but slowly he braced himself and rose to his feet.

Sonya still knelt in front of him, untouched by the devastation that spread out from him. Even her white robes remained unblemished. Duncan stood in the center of a shallow crater of ruin made by his own misery.

"There's nothing for you here," she said.

"Nothing?" he asked incredulously. "What about you? What about our son?"

The shade of Sonya did not react until Duncan mentioned their son. At that, her eyes snapped up to meet his own and she asked, "What do you mean, our son?"

Duncan was unprepared for the vehemence underneath her question and stood there, at a loss for words.

"What do you mean?" she repeated, insistent. "Our son is safe. I saw to that."

Duncan still had no answer, his mind trying to piece together what should have been a loving reunion of husband and wife.

"What do you mean?" she asked again and he knew from his own familiarity with her voice that she'd reached her end. There was no compassion or sympathy, only dire undertones speaking of accusation and hate, as if she knew what he feared most. He had failed her when Mikal had fired that arrow. Now her judgment would fall again at his feet, but this time for losing their son.

"She has him," he trailed off, feeling his guilt rise like a specter. Hope fell away, sifting out of him as if his soul were an hourglass about to run empty.

"She?" Sonya stood now, coming to within arm's reach of Duncan. "Lilyth? Are you mad?"

When he didn't answer she exclaimed, "Curse your mind, I had him safely away from here!"

His own guilt had thinned any shield he might have had used to block her denunciations. He flinched at each accusation, stabbed into him like a blade through skin as thin as parchment. He knew the list of his failures intimately, starting with the sight of an arrow protruding from her chest, and innumerable since then.

Then something in him changed. Whatever had bolstered him, had carried him through these centuries in search of his family, had also given him strength in the face of adversity. Her accusation hurt as only the words of a loved one could, cutting to the bone. Yet his mind, now clear and able, glimpsed the truth.

He'd never given up. He'd never released himself from the duty to save her, not for these two centuries, and that simple fact lent him strength.

In a voice rising in anger he exclaimed, "Safe? I didn't know he survived until today... when Lilyth told me! Where were you?"

It was Sonya's turn to step back, her anger quickly turning into confusion. "I found a safe place. He was sent from here, through a rift, back to Edyn."

Duncan's anger bled out like he'd been gutted, his eyes downcast with misery. He could feel all this as if he sat outside himself and watched his own actions like an actor in a play. His body walked slowly away from Sonya, out of the devastated area. He didn't look back to see if she followed. Nothing happening fit whatever his heart had expected in seeing her again. Nothing.

He walked a few steps farther then said aloud, "I haven't seen you for almost two hundred years and the first thing you do is tell me to leave."

"I... would spare you the pain of finding me." Her voice floated up, still some distance away.

When he turned to look at her, she was looking down at the earth, her form echoing grief and somehow... shame.

He asked, "What are you talking about?"

Sonya looked up at him, and for a fleeting moment he saw love in her eyes. It sent his heart fluttering, but quickly her face crumpled into sadness and she held a hand up to her mouth, stifling a sob.

Then she asked, "What does Lilyth want?"

Duncan looked away. "I meet with Valarius and we get back our son." He said this dejectedly, sitting down with the burden of the years weighing on him like never before. Bringing the lens into Avalyon had been on the tip of his tongue. Yet the part of his mind that was still clear urged caution. He didn't know the extent, if any, of Sonya's allegiance to him. If he failed his mission, he was sure he'd never see his son.

It was Sonya's turn to be silent, her expression one of shock. Clearly she'd not expected that Lilyth would move with such alacrity. After a few moments, she asked, "For what purpose?"

"I'm to hand over a dwarven woman to Valarius as a peace token, a gesture from the Lady."

"He still doesn't care for you," she said softly.

He laughed, a short bark that echoed in the still air. "A friend from home, and he won't chat, not even to rub my face in whatever is between you and him?"

Sonya didn't reply right away. She was still, then asked quietly, "You would have to enter Avalyon... how?"

He fell onto his back, crossing his arms over his eyes. He could feel Sonya move up next to him. Then Sonya amended her question with, "Do you know for a fact Lilyth has Adem?"

"Adem?" he asked, moving an arm out of the way to look at her with one eye. "That's our son's name?"

Sonya tilted her head at him in assent, the gesture so familiar it drove him to move his arm back in place, a futile attempt to blot out the sight of her.

"It was what I named him when he was born. After he went through the rift to Edyn, it was impossible to see him directly, yet I followed his life. It was not much, bits and pieces of moments with those I thought could protect him best."

"And who was that? Clearly not his own father," Duncan said, unable to hide his frustration and disappointment.

With a sigh she explained, "The Galadines were thorough, but some managed to escape. When you killed Alion Deft's mortal form, rumors said Captain Dreys survived. Much was put in place so that our son could find a way to him."

"Then you must have known I survived the king's hunt too," he said, acid still in his voice. "But you didn't trust me."

The shade of Sonya did not respond to his condemnation. Instead, she took a breath and said, "You were consumed with revenge, Duncan. Captain Dreys tried to find a place safe from the Galadine law." She waited, then added, "You always trusted him."

He propped himself up and met Sonya's eyes, confused for a moment at the mention of Deft's mortal form. Did all the dead come to life here? If so, his false victory over her was being fed to him now a bitter mouthful at a time. "You're telling me Alion Deft is actually alive?"

Sonya nodded and explained, "For the most part anyone who dies is gone. However, there are a few who have, through deed and action, become legend. And legends find life here. The more people who believe in you, the more likely it is that you will appear here."

She was quiet, then said, "Perhaps it's why I'm still here—your belief in me." A moment passed, then two.

Duncan could feel himself turning his attention to recovering his son. Conversation with Sonya seemed pointless, and he felt like *doing* something, anything.

Sonya continued, "Dreys's sons lived. They found an isle far from the king's lands, one protected by the Conclave of Dragons. I could think of no better place."

Duncan felt a sudden fear form in the pit of his stomach, a hollow feeling he knew had a reason to be there. Trepidation replaced bitterness, and he asked, "What is our son's name, in Edyn?"

Sonya looked down. "I... they named him Arek. I sent him to—"

Duncan bolted up, staring at his wife with wide eyes. Had he been that close? The boy had been within his grasp if not for that idiot, Kisan. Her interference had stopped him from taking Bara'cor and reuniting with his son!

He breathed in, calming himself, finding balance in the Way. He could feel his heart slowing, his mind clearing. What a difference from the tortured person he'd been before.

Finally, he said, "I know a boy named Arek. As common as that name is, this particular boy was trained by monks in an isle secluded in the Meridian Sea, under the leadership of Themun Dreys. The boy is apprenticed to a man called—"

"Silbane," Sonya finished for him.

"By the gods. You're telling me Arek is my son?"

Sonya did not respond at first. Then, in a voice edged with anger and despair, she responded, "Yes, and our son may mean the end for all of us."

Duncan let out a heavy sigh, impatient to move and said,

"How did you survive Arek's birth, or for that matter, the arrow from our king?"

Sonya looked away, her hands unconsciously covering the site of the wound. "Valarius's elves found me. They delivered our son, and nurtured us back to health."

"So Lilyth wasn't lying when she said Val lives?"

"He's powerful and has dedicated himself to destroying the Aeris."

"What else is new? He's a Galadine, and they seek war. Calling him arrogant is being—"

Sonya held up a hand, interrupting, and said, "You don't understand. He has dedicated himself... it's all he thinks of, the eradication of the Aeris. His obsession has become his faith, and faith here has power. Our son was born here, a place powerful in the Way. As a changeling, he has more power than you can comprehend.

"Valarius did something with his blood, something that changed Arek, made him even more powerful." Sonya stopped, then added carefully, "Belief here begets reality. Val believed our son to be his weapon against the Aeris, and the boy was shaped by Valarius's blood and that faith. Something of the Galadines, their power, their hunger, is within our son. If Arek is killed here in Arcadia, it will not mean just his death."

"What are you talking about?" he replied, now confused.

"Duncan, our son is a weapon. He eradicates the Way. If he dies here, both our worlds will perish."

NEPHILIM

Pride is the blood of the fallen ones,
dark wings spread from shoulders
that in life were smooth and unburdened.

- Duncan Illrys, Remembrances

Arek and Niall had been following the blue-skinned elven escort for what felt like hours. While they had no better measure of time's passage, the sun's slow crawl across the sky didn't seem to reflect the length of time they had been walking.

They walked at the center of a double column of elven soldiers, with wingblades serving as outriders ahead, behind, and to the flanks. The latter streaked by quickly, darts of blue-green color flashing in the bright sunshine. To Arek, they and their riders were one, a synergy of motion following the contours of the land, with trails of dirt and grass marking their high-speed passage.

This world was different, so much so that Arek had a difficult time cataloguing it all. Most incredible were the islands floating in the sky. He'd seen the specks earlier, but it wasn't until one loomed up over their horizon and then sailed overhead that the vast difference between here and Edyn hit him. Seeing it somehow made him feel small and insignificant.

"What are you thinking?" Niall said, looking at him with worried eyes.

Arek gestured with his chin to a copse of trees in the distance. "We've been making our way in this direction for some time now. Do the riders seem more anxious?"

Niall shook his head. "I've noticed more of them, though. Seems like they're preparing for something."

"Their patrols are switching from scouting to setting up a perimeter." Arek said, pointing. He showed Niall where some of the scouts had stopped to hold a loose circle around the copse he'd indicated earlier. "The henge Gabreyl mentioned." To Niall's inquisitive look, he shrugged and asked, "What else?"

"What's a henge?" Niall asked.

"A circle of stone or wood set inside a depression," Arek explained. He recited this by rote, his eidetic memory delivering the fact with certainty.

Was royal training within the various combat schools as comprehensive as the training he'd received on the Isle? Arek doubted it, yet he said, "It's good to ask. Some people don't have the courage to say when they don't know."

"Father said I'd probably lose my kingdom over a math problem."

Arek laughed at that. Then, as he'd predicted, the riders created a cordon around what could now be discerned as a circle of trees around a basin in the ground.

"Yeah, but I know what they're doing now," Niall said.

Before Arek could respond, Gabreyl swooped in and landed lightly, smiling. He fell in pace beside them and said, "We near our destination. The riders act as sentinels while we travel to

Avalyon. The highlord will be most pleased to see you both."

Arek looked around, then back at Gabreyl and asked, "Where's Sparrow?" He had not seen the rider since they had started their journey and though the sun indicated only half a day had passed, he couldn't be sure.

The armored angel smiled and said, "Her duties require her elsewhere, my lord."

Silence reigned after that as the highlord's seneschal did not elaborate. Still, a thought ran through Arek's mind. Why did he refer to Arek as "my lord," but to Niall as "Your Highness"?

It was not an issue of being slighted, rather that Gabreyl assigned Niall a higher station despite the fact they were journeying to see Arek's supposed father—the highlord. Arek wondered if that had something to do with Niall being a Galadine, or something else. He thought about asking, but realized this might give their host insight into Arek's thinking, an advantage he didn't want to relinquish before understanding the dangers of this land and exactly who he could trust.

When it was clear the angel would offer no more explanation about Sparrow, Arek asked, "You said we're not safe here. May I ask why?"

Gabreyl tilted his head, acknowledging the question, his smile never breaking. "Demons, my lord. It's likely we'll face them ere we depart this place."

"Where do they come from?" asked Niall. It was not hard to see the thought of combat whittling away his confidence already.

For some reason, his friend's reaction rubbed Arek wrong. He wished Niall could see the intricate threads woven around them, a tapestry hinting at subterfuge and menace from these elves.

Arek felt sure Gabreyl was no friend of theirs. Why Niall,

who had been the first to warn him, continued to solicit the angel's opinion was perplexing. Perhaps the prince needed the assurance of someone he saw as powerful. More likely he just liked the way Gabreyl played to his insecurities, bolstering him with honorific language and obsequious gestures. Arek's earlier enthusiasm for making a new friend had faded as more of Niall's character became apparent, slowly replaced by something more akin to annoyance. He wanted Niall to bring honor to his station, a hope dying on the vine.

Gabreyl answered in a slow and methodical way, giving Niall his utmost attention. "Henges are one of the places where ritual domes can be summoned. These are used for gates, combat, anything where entry is forbidden by the summoner."

To Arek, the reason for the elves' heightened awareness and anxiety was clear. The henge sat in a depression with the raised stonework affording those outside the circle better protection. The inside of the henge would be a difficult place to defend if attacked, an important distinction if defending this place became important.

He looked at Gabreyl and asked, "Does the henge attract others when it's used?"

The armored angel looked at Arek silently, then acceded with a slight bow. "Insightful. It is true, opening a gate attracts beings of power, including the Aeris demons."

Arek responded, "And how do you plan on countering, Armsmark?"

Gabreyl gestured at the circle. The elves had gathered into two concentric rings. The outer ring of elves faced outward, and the inside ring faced the center of the henge. At some unheard signal they all knelt in position, removing wooden shields from their backs. The shields had something carved into them, symbols of some sort that were illegible because of the distance.

"Travel to Avalyon is guaranteed by our blood."

"How?" Niall asked, his knuckles whitening as his fingers clutched his reins tighter.

Gabreyl looked at them both and then smiled and said, "You misunderstand." He let out a short whistle, and from farther down the column came a young man running up in a light sprint. His black hair was tied back, his face and arms marked with tattoos similar to Gabreyl's own, except his created a sigil that looked like a circle atop a cross-shaped body. In fact, he was almost twin to the angel, similarly armed and armored, though he had no wings.

"Sorath, tell them your purpose," said the angel.

He bowed to the Messenger then turned to Arek and said, "I open the henge, my lord."

"Sorath will forge us a path to Avalyon." Gabreyl bowed to the warrior, who returned the bow and stepped back, walking smoothly alongside them.

"What does that mean?" asked Arek.

Sorath looked to Gabreyl for permission to speak, then answered, "My blood opens the henge."

"What?" Niall exclaimed. "You're going to cut yourself?"

Sorath tilted his head, his expression quizzical, and then said, "No, Your Highness."

Niall looked relieved until Sorath finished, "I give my life to open the Way. What better fate can a warrior serve, but to guarantee the safety of his brothers and sisters?"

"See there," offered Gabreyl pointing to the center of the henge and a table with a man-shaped indentation in it, "Sorath shall be given over to the henge, and in return a gate to Avalyon will open."

"You'll *die*?" Niall exclaimed, clearly unable to understand how someone could do such a thing.

"One of us always dies. It is how we keep our home safe. I was honored to be chosen," the young warrior answered, looking more the twin to Gabreyl as his face broke into a smile.

Niall turned to Arek, shaking his head. "Then what part did we misunderstand?"

Gabreyl addressed them both saying, "Sorath will not be gone forever, but will be rewarded. The gate to Avalyon can only be unlocked by a sacrifice willingly given. As a reward, the highlord will bring Sorath back from the abyss, for he is family. Each sacrifice makes him stronger." He turned to the young warrior and added, "Perhaps at this rebirth he may earn his wings."

Sorath bowed at that. "I would be honored, Your Grace."

The convoy drew nearer, passing stationary sentinels perched on the backs of their mounts. They looked deadly, gazing outward, iridescent birds of war with one purpose only. At each passing, the riders bowed, and Arek realized they were acknowledging Sorath as he passed, not him. Clearly these warriors valued sacrifice above all else. It would be a formidable trait if facing them on a battlefield.

At that moment the outside ring of soldiers finished their ritual and drove their shields into the earth. At impact, a blue-white wall of energy sprang up, connecting their brethren with one another. The energy field quickly encircled the henge. The elves in the inner circle did the same, and an inner barrier erupted from the ground where their shields struck.

Arek could appreciate the elves strategy. The outer ring would presumably hold enemies at bay, while the inner ring reinforced the outer one. This allowed the elves of the inner ring to step forward into gaps created if a comrade fell without opening a way through the double wall, but also allowed the elves to fall back to a secondary line.

"And when will these demons come?" Niall asked no one in particular. His voice broke on the word "demons."

The angel nodded. "Soon, Your Highness, but be at ease. We are fearsome ourselves, and more than capable of fending off anything that appears."

That seemed to mollify Niall a bit. Arek watched as his shoulders relaxed and his expression turned from one of fear to just plain worry. The prince noticed, then turned his gaze forward, his expression resolute, though the flush of red on his cheeks and the tips of his ears betrayed his heart's true shame. It looked like Niall was doing his best to copy something he might have seen in a portrait of his father. It just didn't look right, this imitation of bravery. Arek could feel himself growing annoyed again at the prince's behavior, which in his mind was neither noble nor honest.

Gabreyl pointed and said, "Come, let us make haste. They hold open a corridor."

A pair on the inner and outer ring nearest to them had not yet moved, waiting with shields still on their arms, evidently for Gabreyl's party to arrive before completing the circles. This left a path to the center of the henge that would be closed behind them.

Just then a squad of riders detached themselves from their post and raced toward them. At first, Arek thought they meant to meet and escort them in, but their speed and course did not track directly to the three. It seemed strange until he looked at Gabreyl, whose eyes were focused on something in the direction the riders now raced.

Arek turned, his pale eyes focusing on flashes of light not too far off. The dots moved closer, resolving themselves into men... with wings.

"By the lady!" exclaimed Niall.

The outburst drew a look from Gabreyl that Arek would have sworn was anger. It was a flash of fire in his eyes, gone as quickly as it had appeared, but it had definitely been there. Gabreyl clearly didn't like Niall's invocation of "the lady." Then something connected, another missing piece of the puzzle falling into place.

Whomever Gabreyl served, it was not Lilyth. A knot of dread formed in Arek's stomach. He had to warn Niall and quickly make sense of this charade. Yet until he understood their position better, it was unclear if escape was the right choice.

Beside them, their escorts drew blades, metal singing as it cleared scabbards. Sorath moved a step forward, placing himself between Niall and Arek and whatever they faced. He looked at Gabreyl, whose earlier anger had bled away, leaving only grim lines etched on his face.

Niall took a step back, saying, "I think we have company..."

Half a dozen armored beings glided in, flaring wings to land silently. They wore burnished armor glinting gold, bronze, silver and more–dozens of precious metals forged with deadly purpose and awe-inspiring splendor. These grim warriors faced them from a stone's throw away. Each was armed with shields and long stabbing spears, so keen any slight movement seemed to part the air itself.

Arek's eyes scanned left and right, assessing their tactical position. Despite the repeated reference to "demons," these beings more resembled angels from Edyn's legends. They had wings, but lacked the horns and the blue skin of the elves. They towered over the scene, standing at least the height of three men. Arek kept his mind open, ready to take advantage of whatever unfolded.

He did not have long to wait before one of the beings stepped forward and said, "You overstep your bounds,

Armsmark. Surrender your prisoners and we will allow your journey to continue."

Gabreyl did not answer, but instead let out a musical whistle. The force of wingblades and their riders moved forward, leaving behind the elves at the defensive ring of energy. The wingblades spread their flightless wings like fans facing the armored beings, undulating them in a quick rhythmic pattern, an iridescent wave that cycled down each wing like a waterfall of color. Gabreyl waited for them to line up evenly to his left and right, a deadly wall of mesmerizing color, razor beaks and sickle talons.

Gabreyl said, "They are my guests. And we decline your offer, generous as it may be."

The towering figure drove the butt of his spear into the earth and said, "Charity is often wasted on those with pride." His massive head turned and he addressed them as a group. "Surrender and the Lady's mercy will be given."

"No," said the highlord's messenger, answering before either Niall or Arek could speak. His blade now sang out of its scabbard to join the rest, and the two groups faced each other, clearly at an impasse.

The towering figure of the angel opposing them held up a hand and conferred with his companions. Arek couldn't help but notice even more of these gargantuan beings flying in from every direction. The leader engaged in a heated discussion, which ended with a sharp gesture from him pointing in the direction of the henge. His intent seemed obvious, even to Arek.

The leader took a step forward and said, "I offer resolution in the old ways, champion against champion, within the dome you have partially summoned."

"And why would I agree?" Gabreyl asked.

"More of my brethren arrive every moment. Your tactical

advantage is gone. It is I who should be asking that question, yet I would spare us needless bloodshed."

Gabreyl's head tilted to one side as if he considered the giant angel's offer. To Arek, losing the two of them was clearly *not* an option. The elven commander took a look around and apparently came to a different decision.

Stepping forward he said, "Our champion against yours for possession of one guest," he held up a finger. "I cannot return empty-handed."

The towering being considered this, rubbing his face with a gauntleted hand. After a moment that seemed to stretch to an eternity, the angel said, "Agreed, so long as it is the victor's choice."

Gabreyl narrowed his eyes then slowly nodded. "I name this man as our champion," he said, pointing to Sorath.

He did not wait for their acknowledgement, but instead gathered Arek, Niall, and a few others, including Sorath. In a voice pitched so that only they could hear, he said, "A call to action will happen during the fighting. Be ready."

"I could make our path home easier," Sorath answered, "by allowing him a quick victory."

"I know," said Gabreyl with a reassuring grip on the young warrior's arm, "but no Aeris may remain alive when the gate opens."

"Then don't do it," said Arek. At Gabreyl's look he continued, "Let's just make our stand here, fall back through the circles and retreat via the gate."

Gabreyl shook his head, "That would be sound thinking except if these Aeris reach the gate, they can hold it open." The armsmark looked at Sorath and said, "First be victorious and protect Avalyon, then do what you must to serve your highlord and family."

"Why fight at all?" Arek looked around. "I mean, if there's any chance of failure..."

The armsmark smiled and said, "Sorath will not fail, and I would not feel so confident were I to put another champion in his place. Our only recourse here is to eradicate these Aeris before retreating, but it must be disguised as complacency. If we fail and even one Aeris lives, we cannot open a way to Avalyon. The risk is too great."

"What about the terms of victory?" asked Niall, looking at everyone. "What happens if their champion wins?"

"That only happens in stories," answered Arek. He hoped to bring some pragmatism to his friend's innocence. "Gabreyl doesn't intend on handing either of us over, do you?"

Gabreyl gave Arek a small bow to acknowledge the truth of his words, then Arek continued, "He's going to renege on the deal and attack the elves while they're occupied watching their champion fight."

He revised his assessment of the elven commander, impressed with his thinking. There was a calm resolve in his eyes. "Where did you learn strategy, Armsmark?" He laid the question out innocently, keeping his tone soft and without judgment. Master Silbane had counseled him for years on interrogation and information gathering, lessons he now was grateful for. Arek would not again underestimate Gabreyl or the forces he led.

Gabreyl looked at him for a moment. Then his expression changed, his eyes taking on a distant look. "On a hundred battlefields long before you were made, Lord Arek." Then his gaze met Arek's own and he finished, "from better men than you."

Gabreyl looked at the group, motioning them to stay put, then rose and grasped Sorath's forearm in a warrior's grip, clapping him on the shoulder. Some unspoken message passed between the two. The young warrior stepped away from the circle and strode toward the line of Aeris lords. He came to stand in front of the armored angel and bowed.

"I am Sorath of House Galadine, and I accept your challenge."

At the name Galadine, Niall snapped a look at Arek, his eyes wide in shock.

Arek made a small gesture with his hand to stop any outburst. He hoped Niall would have the sense to remain quiet. However, the utterance of the name broke loose the last foundation of trust that had been eroding since he'd met Gabreyl. If a Galadine was in charge of these elves, something was definitely not right.

The towering angel saluted with his spear, then said, "I am the Fury Cainan of the Lady's Blades, and I accept your challenge."

"You two be ready." Gabreyl said in a whisper, suddenly beside them both. The intensity of his words felt like he was shouting orders directly into their ears.

Arek watched the armsmark sweep them with a gaze that conveyed the expectation that his "request" would be followed. Niall certainly seemed more than willing to do whatever Gabreyl said, but Arek was not. If these elves did not stand for Lilyth, to which Galadine were they being taken? His torture was not so far behind him as to be forgotten.

Arek moved a little closer to Niall and said softly, "Don't go through that gate."

"Are you kidding?" Niall looked around quickly, fearing they would be overheard, and replied, "He said 'Galadine.'"

"I know, but there's something not right. You were right not to trust Gabreyl."

"If there's a Galadine here, I need to know," responded Niall in a hushed tone.

Just then the blue-skinned elves started to move, heading for the circle followed by the towering figures of the armored angels that opposed them—the rest of the Lady's Blades, by Arek's reckoning.

The flow of warriors interrupted any response Arek might have had, but he tried to convey with his eyes how important it was that Niall listen. He wasn't convinced that the prince understood or agreed. With the mention of "Galadine," the situation had quickly become harder to control. He'd agreed to follow Lilyth to meet his father. What if they'd been intercepted? Was he being taken to his father, or instead to the Galadine that led these elves?

Arek began to realize that any hope of seeing his father and Lilyth might, in fact, rest with these towering warriors calling themselves the Lady's Blades. When the gate opened, he knew he'd have to make a choice, and dreaded Niall choosing differently, even if he was annoyed by him.

Elves held the coruscating circle of energy, shields facing outward as the champions of each side entered. They made their way to opposite sides of the circle, raising and lowering their blades in salute.

At Gabreyl's signal, the two remaining elves punched their shields into the ground, completing the circle. In a flash of power, it rose to create a dome of light, with only the two combatants inside. Those outside now could only watch, unable to interfere with the outcome of the contest.

Before either could move, a scream sounded from the far end, opposite Arek's position. He squinted, unable to see through both the dome's walls, but something was happening. At first, he thought it might be a quarrel, however out of place that might seem. There was a short burst of movement discernible through the dome walls.

Then, pandemonium erupted. The sound of combat could be heard, screams that sounded guttural and fanatic. Arek quickly circled to a better vantage point, his peripheral vision picking up that both the combatants inside the henge had also spun to face the commotion. As he made his way around, the sight that greeted him was hard to comprehend.

There was a quarrel, it seemed, but amongst the elves. Some had climbed atop others, pulling them down with an animal's ferocity. Others cut and thrust, stabbing at their brothers as if they were at war. What was going on?

Outside the ones locked in this strange wrestling match, the rest had formed three-man phalanxes, two shields in front and a spearman behind. Racing around the clearing Arek heard the *whump whump* of wingblades at full run.

The Furies under Cainan's command reacted instantly, drawing weapons and wading into the fray. One reached down to pull an attacker off his semiconscious victim and Arek watched him gasp, dropping the elf as if he were made of fire. The Aeris looked at his unarmored hand, which slowly grew black, the blackness moving up his arm like a living thing. It spread quickly, and the Aeris lord staggered to his knees, becoming a dark creature with eyes that burned with a red fire.

Then Arek noticed that the elves, at least some of them, had turned midnight black as well. These dark versions turned on their brothers. Each healthy person who was touched fell, turning black. Moments later they staggered up, their eyes burning that same vermillion flame.

The energy wall collapsed as the elves turned to reinforce their companions, stabbing with blade and interlocking shields to hold back the dark creatures. The idea of sides had degenerated into a general melee, as the dark elves and dark Aeris attacked indiscriminately, slowly turning everyone into one of them.

Gabreyl shouted, "Fall back! Form on me!"

The untouched elves instantly obeyed, falling back with shields held before them. They moved with a precision that spoke of countless hours of drilling, forming a turtle shape with shields on all ends and overhead. Gabreyl shouted more orders from the middle.

Arek had moved to get a better view, and now realized with a sickening feeling that Niall was in the middle of that shell. There was no way to get to him.

Just then, a hand grasped Arek by the throat. Cold penetrated his skin, a cold so deep it numbed him to his very core. He twisted his arm up and around the other, locking the elbow, and spun, only to be greeted by the face of an infected elf, its eyes burning red, its mouth opened in a silent scream of hunger.

Anger welled up within Arek, an insatiable fury at this attacker. He could feel his eyes change, the darkness consuming him as well, but it was not the diseased touch of whatever this thing was. It was the blackfire that burned within him, a hunger so deep he could feel the sustenance of the thing that dared touch him. He breathed in and let the hunger have its way. In the blink of an eye the dark elf dissolved into nothing, obliterated by Arek's fire as if it never existed, and a wash of energy flooded into him. He'd never felt so alive!

A clarion call sounded and into their clearing burst forth two winged beings, similar to Cainan and his Furies, but these wore full battle armor and had wings with blades for feathers. One was outfitted in flashing silver armor, the other in fiery gold.

"Behind us!" shouted the one in silver armor edged in

aquamarine. "Our armor is proof against the *nephilim*!"

The Aeris who heard fled for the safety these new angels offered. The two marched forward, one wing bent in front as a shield, the other raised behind as if caught in an unfelt breeze. Arek had no idea what they intended but they looked magnificent and deadly.

Just then a brace of mounted wingblade riders ran past the shield wall made by these armored archangels. The birds cut into the line of dark elves, slashing with feet meant to disembowel. Had the people they attacked been anyone else, it might have worked. Instead the warbirds were brought down in a heap of dust, their iridescent feathers flashing in the sun one last time.

A few moments passed, the heap becoming a feeding frenzy of the nephilim, each squirming in and under to get to the fallen wingblades and their riders. Teeth found flesh and bone. Once the living had been consumed, the gathered creatures dispersed.

Black wingblades emerged from the pile of carcasses, their beautiful iridescence eaten away by the darkness. They turned, their ranks added to the line of dark creatures who faced the two armored angels and those few Aeris who'd taken refuge behind them. They stood, silently regarding their opponents. At some unheard signal, the nephilim horde rushed forward en masse, clearly expecting to overrun the small and fragile-looking bastion of survivors.

The archangels, despite what seemed to be overwhelming odds, neither retreated nor faltered. They braced, then raised and flicked their wings forward with lightning speed. A storm of feather blades sliced through the line of nephilim like sheets of rain. Where each blade struck, the dark elf or dark Aeris disappeared in a flash of black smoke.

A sudden *whump* sounded and Arek's ears popped with the

displacement of air. He spun just in time to see the turtle made of shields disappear in a flash from the center of the henge. Chaos ensued and another rush of nephilim slammed against the archangel shield wall, drawing his attention back to the main fray.

Arek got a hold of himself, bringing his blackfire under control. Then the leader of the Aeris was there, grabbing Arek's sleeve and pointing.

"They'll kill us all if we stay." Cainan said this softly, but his voice was determined. "If you want to meet your true father, you'll come with me now."

The archangels had once again thrown themselves into the fray, cutting and slashing with wing and blade. Their attacks were economical and brutal, offering no chance for any infected to survive. At first he'd thought them overwhelmed by these dark creatures. Now it was clear they were fighting in their element.

Arek looked at the Aeris crouched here beside him. He could see no deceit in his eyes, nor hear it in his voice. "You stand with Lilyth?"

Cainan nodded, a quick assent that did more than any spoken words could to convince Arek he spoke the truth. The Fury motioned for him to follow, moving away from the fight. They quickly made their way around a knoll and out of sight.

"Hold tightly."

The giant warrior grabbed Arek around the waist and leapt, his wings spreading like a direhawk's to catch the air. They quickly gained altitude, arrowing for the edge of land before the Aeris made a sickening dive and roll, arcing out and under the island they had just been standing on.

The last thing Arek saw was the body of Sorath, stabbed through the chest and spread-eagled in the center of the henge in a pool of his own blood. Of Niall and the elves under Gabreyl's command, there was no sign.

SKYFALL

In facing superior forces, harry them at all points.
Attack and move, never staying in one place
Be the swallow against the falcon.
Wheel, dive, spin. Movement is life.

- Galadine House of Arms, Battle's Focus

M*ove!* Tempest screamed in Ash's mind.

He dove, ducking razor claws as he rolled. He kept low, punching one mistfright just before stabbing upward through the throat of another with his ensorcelled blade. The creature fell but more took its place. Each one would grab onto him and then turn into mist, flowing up his body like a snake. Having faced these before with Alyx, he knew they would possess him if he let them stay in contact too long.

The good news was that merely touching these "mist snakes" with Tempest dissipated them; the actual mistfrights required more work. Ash spun the blade, scattering two and cleaving through the neck of another mistfright. It fell, headless, then disappeared into the ground as the magic holding it together died. For some reason, Tempest did not exhibit the raw power she had at Bara'cor. Worse, Ash felt the blade's fear.

He caught a glimpse of Yetteje. The girl had drawn Valor and was firing arrow after arrow, each a glowing shaft of fire that streaked into the throng of feral shapes. Where her arrows touched, mistfrights died.

As combat became more intense his sense of time slowed. Thoughts raced through his mind as he blocked and cut. *How could a girl of such slight build draw Valor, a bow the king had spent years training to draw? And how are her arrows on fire?*

His attention returned to the sheer mass of opponents, all trying to possess him. He ducked under a clawed swipe, then spun and slashed, feeling his blade meet resistance twice. He did not stop to look, but rolled again to escape the next attack and came back to his feet.

He had won himself a small clearing, but the horde swarmed in, overwhelming his blade work and pushing him to the ground again under their combined weight. An unnatural cackle burst from his throat at the sudden, absurd thought that mist could weigh something—until Tempest screamed, *Focus or you'll be taken!*

He grabbed the blade to his chest and rolled on the ground. The move destroyed four mist snakes and left him free to rise again. This time he did so slashing, cutting—Tempest was a blur in his hands. He'd lost sight of Yetteje, but caught glimpses of the rest of the party.

The white, angelic form of Silbane was locked in combat with the giant Anhur. Kisan, a counterpoint to Silbane, an angel of death, sliced through a giant and used his body to smash mistfrights around her. Kisan then did something that brought Ash to a slack-jawed halt. She leapt into the air and spread black wings, then dove, using her wingblades to slice through her enemies. Ash stood motionless, dumbfounded at her display of power. Standing still was never a good thing in the heat of combat.

Something grabbed his face and he could feel it turn to mist, flooding his nostrils and mouth. The stench of rotted meat assailed him and he could feel his bile rise in response. A rushing sound drowned out everything, like he was falling into a deep and bottomless well.

No! Tempest screamed. There was a bright green flash, a concussion of thunder, and whatever had invaded him and the area around him was suddenly clear! The explosion from Tempest was dissipating, an expanding circle of green and yellow fire bursting any mistfrights it touched into black ash. Her exertion was not without cost. He could feel her getting weaker, quieter. It must be something about this place, this world. It seemed to suck the vitality from her, the way the ground had impeded his footsteps, as if everything here hated them. While he didn't feel comfortable wielding the avaricious blade, the thought of losing her filled him with dread. He wasn't sure if she'd be dead or gone, but it didn't matter. This world wasn't too forgiving to those without power.

Another group of mistfrights charged, but the armored form of Silbane tumbled through and crushed them as the master fell on his back. He lay there, stunned. Kisan had fallen back to protect him, but the tide was unyielding. Where one fell, four took its place, and she was driven to a knee as black shapes clawed at her armor and wings. The mistfrights seemed infinite and worse, aided by these giants, they were slowly overwhelming the small band.

A fire arrow streaked past Ash's face, imbedding itself in a mistfright close behind him. Ash twisted to cut two others down, then fell back toward Silbane. The master in angel form was still on his back, smashing Aeris using gauntleted fists.

Even here his skill shone to Ash, whose trained eye could see the puissance of these adepts, armored or not. They moved as if born to fight, using weapons, hands, and feet to crush their opponents. Yet even they could not stem this tide of demons.

Beloved, stab me into the ground.

What? The action made no sense and his doubt was plain in his thoughts.

You must! It is our only chance.

Ash saw Kisan fall, her back now braced against Silbane, who had risen and knelt in the opposite direction. She fought with double blades, her wings shielding her from flanking attackers. It might have worked, but the sheer volume of creatures pressing against them limited her movement.

Ash cut through more, smashing a mist snake flowing up his leg, then stabbing another through the mouth and watching it drop and dissipate like the rest. How many had he killed? A dozen? Two dozen? And still they came.

You must! Her voice was edged with hysteria, a far cry from her normal devotion or disdain. Then something smashed into his head, hard, and the world tilted...

... his vision cleared and he was kneeling near the masters, somehow still clutching Tempest, point down. Kisan's mouth moved but Ash couldn't hear what she said. She screamed and pointed at something. He turned his head woodenly, only to see one of the giant warriors bearing down on him with a spear, like some kind of god of war. The man threw and the spear turned into a bolt of lightning.

Time slowed for him again, life's idea of a joke, letting him see in minute detail how he would die. He knew he'd never get his blade up in time. In what he was sure would be his last act he leaned his weight on Tempest, pushing her into the ground as she'd demanded. Then he turned his head up, his eyes tracking the bolt as it sizzled and crackled in slow motion. He would meet his end facing the thing that killed him.

Kisan's wing swept overhead and took the brunt of the lightning bolt, destroying her feather blades in a blast of vaporized metal before smashing into the master herself and knocking her back into Silbane.

Ash's vision was consumed by a green-white explosion as Tempest channeled the last of her power downward into the ground, into the very firmament they lay dying upon. The horde covered him as what seemed like hundreds upon hundreds of Aeris overran their position, piling up in their hunger to possess the living.

Then there was a seismic detonation and he was falling. Blackness above, blackness below, he could feel himself tumbling into the inky dark that seemed to have no end. He fell, bouncing off rock and debris, pummeled by stone until—

He burst into sunlight!

Ash looked frantically about, only to see above him an island of land floating in a sea of clouds. He had fallen through the bottom! Hundreds of black shapes, mistfrights, fell, too. Tempest had used her power to destroy the ground below them, but somehow that "ground" led to open sky? It was salvation of sorts, but it quickly became clear she'd traded his possession for a different kind of death. He plummeted faster, his heart racing as he gasped for air.

At least you are not lost, beloved.

Before he could respond, something falling with him bumped into his head. It felt metallic and hard-edged. He twisted and caught a glimpse of an oblong shape like a coffin tumble slowly past him. It was grayish silver, falling into the misty white clouds and disappearing from view.

Then from above him a voice screamed his name and a

white, man-like shape arrowed in, spreading its wings. Ash collided with it, not hard, and clutched desperately. He tried to use both hands but Tempest refused to allow him to release her. His fist clenched spasmodically on her leather-wrapped handle, so he found himself short a hand.

An arm reached back and plucked him forward and he came face to face with... Silbane! In his other arm, the master clutched the unconscious form of Kisan, one wing bent as if broken and her face covered in blood.

Ash looked around, still on the edge of panic. He gasped out, "Land! Anywhere!"

"Tempest left us little choice," Silbane said.

Silbane nodded, then wheeled and tucked his wings, diving for an island floating below them. The aerial maneuver made Ash's stomach lurch and he squeezed his eyes shut. They were falling again, and to what the firstmark thought for certain would be their deaths. He braced for impact but then felt Silbane's wings snap open, catching air and slowing them to a soft landing, no harder than taking a stair step down.

When Silbane let go, Ash collapsed.

"Oh, gods! What just happened?"

"Careful to whom you pray here, Firstmark."

Ash opened his eyes and caught Silbane's transformation back into his normal form. His gargantuan shape diminished to man-size. His armor dissipated in ash not unlike what happened to the mistfrights, but where theirs was black, the stuff coming off Silbane sparkled white.

"You can fly?"

Silbane collapsed to his knees, as if he'd just run a long distance. His breath came out in heaves, gulping air.

"Are you all right?" Ash added.

The master braced a hand on the ground, then turned to Ash.

"It seems holding our new form exacts its own price." It took a few moments before the master seemed to have recovered enough to move and check Kisan. Evidently having made his assessment, he raised his faded blue eyes, a look of sorrow on his face.

"What?" Ash asked, "is she dead?" Then he noticed, and his heart fluttered with the promise of worse... "Where's the princess?"

Silbane looked down then fell back onto his haunches. "I don't know."

Ash looked up at the sky, seeing now hundreds, perhaps thousands of floating islands. *Where were they? Where was she?*

Silbane shook his head. "The horde was upon us. I tried to find her but there were too many. Then Tempest broke the ground below and we fell through, and I saw only you."

Ash didn't want to hear it. The lifelong leader in him demanded, "How could you lose her? She deserved our protection, certainly more than her," he said, pointing at Kisan.

"I didn't choose, Firstmark," Silbane replied. "The ground opened and we fell through."

Ash got up, cursing. He looked at Tempest and then threw the blade down in disgust. The fact that he could do that, and that the blade had not said a word since their fall, took him by surprise. He looked at Silbane in shock, who in turn stared at the blade.

Ash assumed he was using that Sight he'd mentioned. "What do you see?" he demanded.

"Sheathe her. It's not wise to throw away a weapon we can use against the Aeris."

Ash shook his head. "At Bara'cor she refused to let me drop her, and threatened the king. She's nothing but trouble, and I can finally be rid of her."

Silbane's pale eyes moved from the blade to meet Ash's own, boring into him. "And she may be the only one who can tell us which of these islands is Lilyth's. If Yetteje survives, it's reasonable to believe she's Lilyth's captive."

Ash stopped, just staring at Silbane. Then he took two steps forward and stabbed his finger at the blade and said, "She killed Sevel. She probably killed Chandra. Friends who trusted me, and she took their lives to keep me alive." Tears blurred his vision. When he'd regained his composure he said, "I'll not let her use me again."

Silbane was quiet, as if he could feel the distraught firstmark's guilt threatening to spill over. Then he asked in a soft voice, "And what if I'm wrong? Which of us knows this realm at all? Would you sacrifice Yetteje and Niall to ease your own burden?"

Ash held his hand to his head, closing his eyes. He could see himself just kicking Tempest off the edge to fall to oblivion, but the plight of the two heirs sapped his will and he knew he couldn't refuse any chance to save them, even if it meant risking Tempest's obsession again. A wind ruffled his sweat-soaked hair, bringing with it a chill. It was only then that the exertion of battle hit him.

He didn't want to chance giving her to Silbane, for fear of what she might do with such strength. Frustrated, he unfastened his sword belt and readjusted it so the blade lay on his back with the hilt over his shoulder. He dropped his eyes, then with reluctance picked up the quiescent blade and rammed her into her sheath. From there, he reasoned, no chance of Tempest "accidentally" being grasped by anyone, most of all himself. As soon as Yetteje was found, he vowed he'd see the blade destroyed.

Then the vista spread before him caught his attention. He

gasped. In the distance was an orange-yellow sun, darker and bigger than the one he was used to on Edyn. It lit the sky in its setting light, painting the tops of clouds pink and gold. Floating serenely in the blue skies around them were islands of land, thousands upon thousands, each drifting peacefully above the blanket of clouds that extended like stepping stones from horizon to horizon.

"This is Lilyth's realm? Islands floating..."

"Certainly not what I expected."

Ash didn't look back to acknowledge Silbane. Right now he didn't trust himself to speak to the master with civility. His anger at the master's failure to save Yetteje made him thrust his chin in Kisan's direction. "Is she dead?" he asked, knowing it was callous of him. He didn't care.

Silbane shook his head, his breath washing out of his nose as he leaned back against a rock.

"At least you didn't trade the princess for nothing then." The disgust in his voice was hard to hide, and again he found himself not caring what Silbane thought.

The absurdity of it all, of living through the attack of the Aeris by falling into a sea of floating islands... He uttered a small derisive laugh.

He looked down at his hands: clean, though he'd just been through the thick of a battle no less brutal than any other he'd fought. No blood, no dirt. Pristine hands that said nothing about what had happened. He looked back out over the expanse of clouds that seemed to make up what this world called "land."

He breathed in a deep lungful of air and exhaled, then said, "If we're going to find anyone in all this, we're going to need better judgement, Master Silbane. We're also going to need a miracle."

Skyfall

DIPLOMAT'S BLADE

Let them stab, strike;
let them come with all their might.
With every swing and turn,
they fall on your waiting sword, eager for death.

- Kensei Tsao, The Lens of Blades

Again? Do you not tire of this?" Legate Ellis Tir opined, clearly frustrated. He pulled his crimson robe tighter, peering at Queen Yevaine Galadine with her distinct amber eyes, a match to his own.

"What did you expect?" she answered. "Sycophants and schemers."

Her mailed sleeves jingled as she adjusted her armor, a reminder to these courtiers of Haven that she was no stranger to the blade. They had been granted audience with the Senate two times already to petition for aid to Bara'cor, and twice had been denied. Part of her longed to tell Captain Kalindor to take the city and put these politicians to the sword. Still, the peace was fragile but beneficial to the land. Her husband had earned it, and it would not fall upon her to undo what he had done.

She pushed her way past the legate but asked, "I still have your support?"

"Always," he responded, "but unless you have something new, their answer will be the same. This time, though, they may have you held."

"Let them try," she said, her mood dark, a hint of violence a glimmer in her eyes. She flatly addressed the other man escorting her, not waiting for his answer. "You'll accompany me into the hall." She took a turn and found herself going the wrong way. Blasted dealings with the senators served as a distraction and a time sink, when instead she should've been heading back to Bara'cor by now with troops to support the Imperial King. Reorienting herself, she headed for the great hall.

Captain Tyrus Kalindor nodded, his gray hair pulled back into a tight tail. One eye of piercing blue shone from beneath a trim brow. The other, or what was left of it, hid behind a black eye patch with the golden lion of House Galadine stamped upon it. He did not hesitate at her order, but replied with an unexpected and almost melodious baritone of a bard's voice, "Of course, I'll be wherever you are, my queen."

Legate Tir spun and hurried to catch up, coming to Yevaine's other side. "Please tell me you're not going to challenge again."

"The Legate of Dawnlight has a special dislike for me," she replied, her gaze fixed on the hallway before her. She found herself facing an unknown corridor, as the myriad of halls and hallways within the great senate building confounded her yet again.

A gentle pull from Kalindor set her on the right path. The man's family had the gift of mapsense, an unerring ability to find a way back to a location he'd been to before, even if the path was not known. "You'll make a wonderful aide," remarked the queen. The man *harrumph*ed, choosing instead to answer her statement about Spaiten.

"What do you expect?" Kalindor asked. "He's in charge of Dawnlight's interests now and they're not always aligned with those of Bara'cor."

"Don't our soldiers of Bara'cor also hold the horde from Haven's green fields?" she replied, frustration clear in her voice.

"No word from Dawnlight, not in a fortnight. Then the explosion at Land's Edge. Do you think our soldiers still live?" Ellis turned to Kalindor and continued, "What of Prince Niall, and my niece? I fear the worst for Edyn if we've lost a king and two heirs."

The captain didn't answer. Instead he reached out and put a gentle hand on his queen's arm, slowing her headlong charge. When they stopped, he looked around to be sure they were alone, then offered, "You're Queen of Bara'cor, but don't forget you're also King Aeonian's daughter. Ill thoughts brew with your arrival here in Haven."

Legate Tir, catching his breath now that Kalindor had stopped the queen, took that moment to lend his advice.

He paused, then delicately said, "May I remind you that your father has not been heard from in some time. Spaiten has declared him lost and secured his position as Dawnlight's regent, as has Algren Justeces for Shornhelm." He was quiet for a moment, then added, "I could do the same for EvenSea, but am not so eager to set aside my brother's crown. It seems... ill-mannered."

Yevaine regarded the two, both trusted men and loyal to Bara'cor and House Galadine, despite any current disagreements. Then she let go of a breath she had not realized she'd held. She'd known Ellis for the better part of her life.

"You have always been a stalwart friend, Ellis, and our bickering is unseemly. We ask your pardon."

A moment passed, then Kalindor also stepped back and bowed to the legate, his fist to his chest.

"Your pardon, though it felt a bit like our sparring days back at the academy," he added with a chuckle.

Ellis Tir also bowed, shaking his head and placing a conciliatory hand on each of their shoulders. "I recall you getting the better of me then, and now. These are trying times." He was quiet, then looked at the queen apologetically. "I do not mean to focus on my own concerns, but how's my niece? Does she fare well under the siege?"

"Yetteje was fine when I left. This war is forcing everyone to grow up fast, but the girl has grit."

Ellis nodded slowly, almost to himself. "You should see her in the combat drills," he said with the half smile of a fond memory. "I used to call her 'Tir's Kitten' when she was a child, but put steel in her hands now and she'll run a man through."

The queen took the legate's hand from her shoulder and gave it a reassuring squeeze. Suddenly she caught the scent of cinnamon, a favorite of Ben'thor Tir, and looked at Ellis in surprise. He was not known to chew the spice like others.

The legate responded with, "What?"

The queen raised an eyebrow, then said, "Nothing. The future of both our Houses is at Bara'cor. They cannot be abandoned."

The legate took a deep breath and said, "I agree, and my concern is not purely familial. There are more dire things afoot."

"Such as?" inquired the queen.

A frown replaced the smile and he said, "They will seek to declare King Galadine lost."

Kalindor turned to the legate and asked, "Why, and why this rush to declare regents? That serves no one."

"Not for your immediate problem," Ellis replied, "but unlike legates, regents may act without royal sanction in the name of their House. There's a longer game being played here."

Kalindor cursed. "Politics. What schemes do these regents harbor?"

Legate Tir looked around as if to reassure himself of their privacy, then said, "If the four kings are declared lost and there's no proof of life for the heirs, it confers rule to the regents."

The captain held his breath, his single eye glinting dangerously in the torchlight. "They would dare usurp House Galadine?"

"Dare?" asked the legate. "The law is archaic, but designed to keep succession intact. As decreed by ancient Galadine rule it falls to the next male heir. By declaring Bernal lost they also effectively seal the fate of my House. If he has perished—"

"He's alive," snapped the queen. "My husband's very much alive."

"If he and your son have perished," continued the legate in a firm but not unkind voice, "rule will fall to the regents, led by the Chancellor of Haven. The regents will determine who rules next from the surviving heirs of the four great noble Houses, according to the ancient Laws of Succession."

"And who's next in line?" asked Captain Kalindor.

An uncomfortable silence followed, into which Ellis Tir finally said, "You'll love this. As I'm the only confirmed living male, it would fall to me, and House Tir."

Kalindor's one eye squinted. "You would raise yourself—"

"Do you think they'll let me live?" interrupted the Legate of EvenSea, in tones of exasperation. "I'll survive just long enough for them to confirm the succession. My loyalties to House Galadine have always been clear."

Yevaine sighed, then turned to Kalindor and said, "Ellis is right. With Bernal gone, they only need to censure me and silence him. We must take decisive action if we are to survive this day. Summon our personal guard."

She thought for a moment, then motioned the legate to come closer.

"If Princess Yetteje was here," she inquired carefully, "who would speak for House Tir?"

"She would, as ranking noble in the direct line of succession. Though she cannot hold the Imperial Crown her claim to Tir's throne supersedes mine," Ellis answered. "Why?"

The queen nodded to herself, her eyes faraway as she fell deep in thought. Given what the legate had said, it was certain the regents would use the law to wrest control from the Houses.

She met Ellis's concerned look, her gaze narrowing. "Explain the Laws of Succession to me again, this time in detail."

THE NEW ADEPT

Watch the cubs, but stand clear.
Quick death comes,
when mother is near.

- Keren Dahl, Shornhelm Survivor's Guide

Jesyn ran through the underbrush, her breathing steady and controlled. She flew past trees, clearing hurdles with bursts of preternatural speed. Her footsteps were light, barely bending the grass where she stepped. She was a black dart, a whisper in the silent night.

Behind her came three shapes, lethal predators, massive in form and fixated on their target. She knew they were closing in on her; their labored breathing and pounding hearts gave them away.

Over the past ten days she and Dragor had come ashore in Deeplook and ranged their way up the southern coast of Thar. From there they made their way up the land and across Galadine's March to Summers Pass.

It was here that they had encountered their first resistance, dwarven assassins much like those that had attacked and killed Thera and her class of children on the Isle. Discovering their origin required capturing one of these assassins alive. That required cunning, and as it was becoming clear, no small amount of luck.

Jesyn didn't need to look over her shoulder, but her mouth still twitched into a small smile of anticipation. The full power of a true Adept of the Way coursed through her now. It sang through her wiry frame, filling her body with warmth and energy. Her focus sharpened and she ducked right.

She heard three daggers imbed themselves in the tree limb where her head had just been. She continued her evasive flight, waiting for the right moment.

Then Dragor's voice mindspoke in her head, *Now!* She sprang upward, leaping into the branches above and calling on her flameskin. The Way within her at first seeped then blazed from her skin, igniting the dark night in a sudden flash. As she rose, she trailed amethyst fire like a shooting star. She tucked and somersaulted, her legs snapping out with a dancer's grace to propel her even farther up into the canopy. She knew her pursuers would be tracking her visually now, a tactical mistake.

The sound of a bough breaking alerted her to Dragor's attack. She spun around the trunk she had been passing and extinguished her flameskin, crouching like a panther. The scene dropped to sudden blackness, but her heightened vision could easily pick out her former master as he struck the group following her.

The sudden decapitation of the first assassin was clue enough that they had not seen Dragor coming. Their choice to follow Jesyn up into the trees had forced them to move lightly and not use their obdurate shieldrock. A second, more costly mistake the adepts had counted on.

Jesyn vaulted from her position, arrowing at the remaining two as they turned to deal with Dragor. With her flameskin gone they'd lost track of her. That was their third, and soon to be fatal, mistake. Life seldom gave you so many chances.

She struck the lead man, snapping his head back with an elbow and then following with an open-palm strike to his unarmored midsection. The blow detonated against the assassin's stomach in a flash of purple fire, the force shattering his spine. She heard Dragor taking on the third, their target for capture, but her attention stayed focused on her opponent.

Even as he crumpled forward, Jesyn came down on the back of his head with the point of her elbow, crushing his skull and driving his body down. His impact on the forest floor created a shock wave, a radial pattern painted in blood with the assassin's lifeless body at its center.

She looked up in time to see Dragor strike his opponent with an open palm to the face. The blow was nonlethal, driving him down to slam into the base of a tree. Before he could react, the dark-skinned adept moved like a sky serpent, pinning the man's arms against the trunk and making his way quickly behind.

"Jesyn!" he said. His part was to immobilize the man using a combination of the Blood of Death technique to create prana locks, and a rope they'd brought for that purpose. She had to secure the virulent poisons they knew he carried, intelligence gathered from the bodies of those killed in earlier attacks.

She burst forward, striking the man's stomach to stun him further, then ripping off his belt and the vials it contained in one smooth motion. She heard Dragor's even breathing and felt the man's arms pulled tight, no doubt secured by the other adept even as his legs gave way. The assassin slid forward, semiconscious.

A breath, then a sigh, and Dragor appeared from behind the trunk looking none the worse for wear. "Good work," he said.

"You're getting better every day."

"Thanks..." The word "master" lay awkwardly on the tip of her tongue, unspoken. A hard habit to break now that she had attained her new rank.

Dragor nodded, as if sensing her discomfort and said, "Wait until you have your own apprentice calling *you* 'Master.' Talk about uncomfortable," he added with a small laugh.

Jesyn smiled in return, then turned her attention to the man they had captured. He was dressed in the same black uniform as those who had attacked their isle. She grabbed the blue-lensed mask and ripped it off, revealing the face beneath. Then she stepped back and let Dragor take over.

Her former teacher inspected the man, then simply said, "Water."

Jesyn unhooked a small bag from her belt and handed it over. Dragor grabbed the end and squeezed, squirting the man's bloodied face. The sudden cold had the desired effect, and the assassin coughed and spat, sputtering to consciousness.

Dragor stepped forward and placed a finger on the man's forehead, pinning his head against the tree. A small spark of purple flashed at the connection, a sure sign that the Eye of the Sky mindreading technique had begun.

Jesyn knew Dragor would be doing two things. First, he'd lock the man's muscles down so that he couldn't struggle. It had become clear to them both that these massive dwarves were many times stronger than they were.

Second, he'd try to get any information on the lost city of Dawnlight or the attack on their isle. Getting that information was vital, and left them only this one desperate chance. Jesyn was not yet powerful enough to carry out the mindreading technique.

It was a calculated risk, for while Dragor could do it, he was not as powerful as Silbane or Kisan. He could not dwell as long nor read as deeply as they could, and the effort would drain him utterly.

This meant Jesyn would be in charge of their defense. If more of these assassins chose to attack, she would be on her own. Still, they'd decided this was an unavoidable risk.

Both men's breathing slowed and became synchronized. Dragor would be past the muscle locks now, and diving deeper, sifting for information. Jesyn took a breath and stepped back, ready to provide security. Still, the act of mindreading fascinated her and she found her attention kept wandering back to Dragor and the man, locked now together in what could only be the interrogation. What power over another, she marveled, to be able to read their very thoughts.

Then, as quickly as it had begun, it was over. Dragor released the man and stepped back, then staggered to one knee. Jesyn moved forward to catch him and ease him down.

"He-he's held," the elder adept stammered. "He won't be breaking free any time soon."

"Did you find where they're from?" This was vital, the reason they had risked so much.

Dragor nodded and tried to say something, but the words came out in an unintelligible mumble. Jesyn cursed, then laid him down. It would be several hours before he would recover. For his part, the prisoner lay slumped against the tree, clearly in no better shape than her former master.

Jesyn sat back, thinking. Once Dragor regained consciousness, their plan had been to make their way to whatever location he'd found. So far, any assassins they'd been tracking always ended up moving northwest, toward the Dawnlight Mountains. If he'd discovered the lost city's location, it would make the next part of their reconnaissance much easier.

She weighed the risks of expending the energy to use Winds of Life to contact the lore father, but quickly discarded the idea. With Dragor down, one of them needed to be combat ready. She let out another sigh and began to get up. The hair on the back of her neck stood up.

"Don't move, lass. You're dangerous. We won't hesitate."

The voice was deep and coming from behind her. How had they gotten so close?

"Easy, now, slow and careful. We're after the same thing."

Jesyn rose slowly, her senses casting out, but could feel nothing. She knew this was a practical impossibility since every living thing existed and echoed within the Way. Yet she had felt nothing.

She saw them then, dozens watching her silently from the trees, all holding cover. How could she see them, yet not sense them? Then she realized she had thought them hiding amongst the trees, but in reality they were inside the trees. Her eyes cast about and she noticed more, in the ground, even inside the rock slab a few feet away. What kind of magic was this? She was a full Adept of the Way and had seen many mysteries of the world, but had never known such things were even possible.

She licked her lips and replied, "The same thing?"

It was an interrogation technique called mirroring. Repeating the last words of your subject often made them reveal more of their own thoughts.

"We've been tracking you for days. Turn around, slowly."

Jesyn turned, her hands raised. They weren't amateurs. Knowing it had been days was important, but he hadn't offered her much else.

She heard a metallic clink, then a spark lit a torch, flooding the area in warm yellow light. Her eyes compensated, and now she could see more clearly the face that belonged to the voice, and it was dwarven.

She fell into a combat stance, her head swiveling around. The glint from the razor-sharp tips of crossbow bolts caught the torchlight, all aimed unerringly at her, held by dwarves half-submerged in tree, stone, and earth.

"Easy!" He held up his massive arms. "These blacknights are my enemy too."

Jesyn looked around, drinking in the details. The parts of these new dwarves that protruded from their hiding places were clothed in green and brown. Though clearly of the same race as the assassins, the skin of these arrivals, where it showed, was decorated with intricate tattoos. The inked sigils seemed almost alive, curling about like false shadows in the dancing firelight.

The one who had spoken had not moved. He could have shot her already. Something about these dwarves made them invisible to her Sight, which meant she might never have detected them. Yet they had revealed themselves.

"The area is secure." The dwarf raised an open palm. His men exited their hiding places and stood in the open, but their weapons never wavered from her. He then jutted a bearded chin at the assassin tied to the tree and said, "These filth have been killing our people too, and worse."

"Your people?" Jesyn said, continuing her mirroring. The entire scene was still surreal to her, but her training kept her vigilance taut, like a finely tuned instrument's string.

The man stepped forward, just one step. His every move seemed to be executed with care, as if he understood what a mistake here might cost. "There'll be time aplenty for us to get acquainted. How long before he can move?" His eyes flicked to Dragor's slumped form.

Jesyn's eyes narrowed, but she didn't answer. The man she

had come to think of as the leader nodded, as if acknowledging her decision to provide as little tactical information as possible. She watched as he waited, then she shifted herself a fraction.

The man noticed immediately. "Don't," he warned. "We are not your enemy, but we'll not chance your skill. We only wish to check your prisoner."

He waited again. He had used the word "your," implying that he did not intend to lay claim to their captive. Jesyn was growing curious.

Only when she nodded did he signal to his men. Two came forward, a woman and a man. They went to the tree where the captured assassin was secured. The woman pulled up her sleeve and touched her forearm.

An intricate sigil made of whorls and unfamiliar symbols lit under her skin, glowing a soft white. The string of symbols ran up her forearm until one whorl curled around her finger, ending at its tip. She took that glowing tip and touched the assassin, closing her eyes.

Jesyn watched as the light from the woman's finger seemed to seep into the man's skin and disappear. A moment passed, not more than a few heartbeats, and the woman got up and looked at the leader.

"He's held, both by us and by whatever they did to him."

The leader then flicked his gaze to Dragor and asked, "Can you revive him?"

The woman turned to the catatonic adept and said, "Don't know yet." She looked pointedly at Jesyn.

"Don't touch him," Jesyn snapped. Her form briefly flashed purple as her flameskin simmered, yearning for release. A dozen crossbows refocused on her.

The man stepped forward again, but this time he put himself in his own men's way. He looked around, his eyes traveling around the clearing until they came to rest on Jesyn. If she didn't know better, he almost looked amused, though it could have been a trick of the light.

Then he said, "Put down your arms."

Jesyn shrugged. "I'm unarmed."

"Not you." Turning to his men he ordered, "Weapons down."

To Jesyn's amazement, the men obeyed. They didn't hesitate, and there was no doubt in her mind that had he instead said "shoot," they'd have pulled the trigger with the same immediate obedience. *Discipline*. They radiated it, and though it filled her with apprehension, she also admired their training and focus.

"I've demonstrated good faith. Will you do the same?" He looked at her, his gaze never wavering.

Jesyn swallowed once, her eyes flicking to Dragor's prostrate form. She could escape, but not with Dragor, and she couldn't abandon her former master so easily, even if it meant putting her own life in jeopardy. Pursing her lips, she looked back up at the massive form of the dwarf and said, "I have little choice."

"That's often true in life." The dwarven leader laughed. He held out an open palm, offering it to her. Only when Jesyn placed her own palm on his did he continue.

"I'm Dazra." A sudden flash erupted from his palm, surrounding the young adept in a blue-white halo of power.

Jesyn began to pull back but the man's large hand enveloped her own in a warm but iron grip. She looked up in alarm, and he smiled in response, a flash of white teeth and eyes that held no malice. Other than the burst of power that now surrounded them both, he did not move aggressively and something about his demeanor made her wait.

"We cannot always know our friends." He let go and the aura of power diminished and faded, leaving the clearing darker than before until Jesyn's vision readjusted. "But we have been watching you and your companion."

"What did you do to me?" Jesyn asked. Her hand felt strangely cold after Dazra let go. When there was no answer she looked down in time to see a small black stain, like a drop of ink, crawl up her palm and disappear. Her eyes widened as she watched it spread under her skin like dark blood, crawling through the network of arteries and veins in her hand and moving to her forearm and toward her heart.

"What did you do?" she whispered, this time almost to herself.

Dazra tilted his head to the side, as if considering how to answer the young adept. When he spoke again, it was as if he was finishing a thought. "Only friends are permitted inside the Citadel, and we have need of friends now."

He brushed past her and motioned to his men to break their positions and prepare to move. As the men melted back into the underbrush, a few came forward to move Dragor and the prisoner to a makeshift pallet. In a matter of moments the team was ready to head out.

The woman who had examined them, came to stand beside Jesyn. One side of her mouth lifted in a crooked smile, as if she couldn't quite commit herself to the action.

"I'm Tarin." She squeezed the adept's shoulder softly to reassure her. "Dazra trusts you, but the centrees will not, not without your own entat."

Her eyes flicked to the growing network of black ink that spread under Jesyn's skin, tracing her veins like small branching rivers, then fading from sight.

"It has been years since we have allowed anyone within our

home, but times are dire. Let's hope his trust in you and your companion is well placed, young halfling."

Jesyn watched the men pick up Dragor with care and make ready to move. How far had the two adepts come to solve the mystery of Dawnlight and protect the Isle? How much had they sacrificed, and how many had they lost? Trust?

She watched the broad back of Dazra disappear as he made his way to the forefront of the vanguard, then looked at Tarin before replying, "I hope the same can be said of you."

The New Adept

DEATHSMARK

> *"Let the naïve believe in Justice.*
> *If you intend to visit unrelenting harm upon your foe,*
> *you must accept being cast outside the Law."*
>
> *- Jebida Naserith, Should I Fall*

Lilyth sat upon her throne, giving careful thought to her next move. Though the queen was most powerful on a board of Kings, careful planning with pawns, bishops, and knights ultimately created a kingsmate. Her game had begun after retreating from Sovereign's Fall two hundred years ago, a tactical mistake she would never repeat.

In a way, she reflected, her own success at war had been her undoing. As more people fell, the population became scarce. Possessing the dead worked, but true freedom happened when an Aeris either possessed or ascended with a living person. Edyn's limited population both helped Lilyth when waging war, and doomed her people to slavery of a different kind. The dead continued to rot, eventually leaving the Aeris animating bones, feeling none of the pleasures of the flesh.

Baalor's retreat from Bara'cor had been executed perfectly, part of a larger effort ensuring that her domination would be inevitable and aided by the very people she would rule. Still, some things needed prodding and her mind turned to the perfect tool.

"Deft."

Her command echoed out and shortly thereafter the shade of Alion Deft, once Kingsmark and magehunter, appeared in midstride out of thin air. The commander of the magehunters had changed in the decades since her death at Duncan's hands. The red-robed mage had afflicted her with a slow and torturous rotting of the flesh.

The same rot had consumed her in death, leaving behind thin ribbons of skin over charcoal-gray bones. Her face looked as if it had been flayed away, leaving only one eye and part of her cheek, tatters of dead skin stretched over her skull. At the center of her forehead, the point where he'd touched, a blackened circle peered out like a third eye. Her mouth, absent of any flesh, gaped from her skull with teeth bared in a permanent rictus. Duncan's spell had left Alion Deft 'alive' in the most minimal sense, a walking corpse subsisting on despair and hate.

Lilyth had forbidden any Aeris to possess this body. It would have eradicated Deft's mind, and the demon queen was nowhere near finished inflicting the proper "gratitude" upon the undead magehunter's head for her crimes against the Aeris.

Every mage killed meant there had been an Aeris bonded to that mage who'd died too, and the demon queen did not allow herself or Alion to forget. As a result and for Deft, from worse to worst, the fallen warrior had become a slave to Lilyth, who found no end of pleasure in taunting this once proud hunter of mages. Alion Deft would pay for every life she'd taken in the most painful way Lilyth could imagine, and that meant she needed to remain aware of her fate.

The demon queen had garbed the undead magehunter in the ancient plate used by her brethren and completed her transformation with two huge rotted bat-like wings. These folded along her back, giving Queensmark Deft the gift of flight, and a form reminiscent of the Aeris.

How appropriate, Lilyth thought, *in death she's become what she despised most in life. Justice, of a sort.*

She turned and faced the Lady and bowed. "Command me."

Lilyth smiled, knowing her compulsion to be obeyed was irresistible and reveling in it. "I have a task particularly suited to your... appetite."

The queensmark's mouth was fixed into a grin of bone, so she could not show much emotion. Her guttural voice simply repeated, "Command me."

Lilyth blinked, then taunted, "Are you angry with me, my beautiful Queensmark? Didn't I save you from oblivion, from a fate you inflicted upon yourself?"

She said this with a small laugh. The litany hardly changed each time they met. Deft had perhaps become used to it, giving up on any reprieve. Lilyth's eyes hardened.

This will not do, she thought. The undead corpse would get no mercy from her. *And now, for the delicious part. The twist of the knife that will feel like hope, until the blood bubbles up in your cursed mouth.*

The queensmark remained still. Except for the slight clenching and unclenching of her gauntleted free hand, one could mistake her as a grotesque statue. The thought triggered another small laugh.

Lilyth continued, "Prepare your men. Duncan Illrys has been sent on a mission."

"I need more information to carry out my orders," the undead commander said.

Lilyth raised an eyebrow, realizing the magehunter had never learned who Scythe was. Believable, given that she'd not let Deft gather any information since her death. The unending monotony of days was just another way to punish this slayer of Aeris.

"The archmage carries with him a lens and seeks entry to Avalyon. Should he find it, I want you and your men ready." Lilyth leaned back, her eyes narrowing to slits, "I will gate your forces to the location marked by the lens when the time is right."

"Duncan Illrys?" the undead warrior repeated. Perhaps an inkling of who he was tickled the magehunter's mind.

Deft carried a barbute helmet under her shield arm, the opening shaped like a T. Now, one mailed hand caressed a spot worn shiny by repeated strokes, an obvious calming ritual. It was like watching a babe rock itself for comfort. *Pitiful.*

"Queensmark, do you ever smile?" Lilyth's eyes twinkled at the barb, while the undead knight's bone-toothed grin clenched. The skeleton's head tilted down, as if searching the floor for something unseen.

"I serve what I hate most." Her answer was delivered with the brutal honesty of a warrior, a bitter undertone, and resignation at her fate.

The lady loved this moment, knowing how it would be when Deft learned who she would be facing again. Then she rose and walked down the dais and to the other side of the magehunter. Her eyes looked sidelong at Deft's flesh-draped skull towering above her now that they stood on level ground.

"I would think you'd be happy to hunt the man who did this to you."

Alion's one good eye snapped over to Lilyth's own, widening with the memory.

"The red-robe?" she gasped. "You've found him?"

"Indeed," Lilyth confirmed, her eyes sparkling with mirth, "I have sent him on a quest to find Avalyon. I believe he will succeed."

"Duncan is the one who calls himself the Scythe?" Alion stepped back, her half face contorting. It was glorious to behold, but the magehunter turned away as if to shield herself from scrutiny.

When her voice emerged, it asked a question that was wholly tactical, as if the undead warrior knew how the Lady thought and sought to avoid giving Lilyth any more pleasure than she had to. "The Aeris cannot use the blood gates."

"Ahh," said the Lady, moving over and resting her head on the knight's armored shoulder, "but Duncan is no Aeris. He's very much alive."

The strength of the Lady's grasp held her in place, so Deft asked, "And he helps us because?"

Lilyth stepped away and said, "Do not worry yourself with that detail. Rest assured I have him properly motivated. When Duncan finds a way in, you will be ready." She paused, then turned and looked up the magehunter with a smile, "Perhaps this has always been your true destiny."

Alion Deft's head dropped again, her breathing heavy. Lilyth could see she was reliving her final moments spent in agony, Duncan's last spell eating her alive. Lilyth tasted the emotion of vengeance radiating from the queensmark's mind as this particular pawn moved into place.

She smiled at her commander, then made her way back up to her seat. Once settled, she addressed Alion Deft again saying, "Patience is a virtue. Duncan will find Avalyon. Only then do you strike him down. Succeed, and I will release you from my service."

Deft looked up, clearly in shock. The emotions that ran across the magehunter's ruined face brought a small flush of pleasure to the Lady. Yet Lilyth was careful to keep her face set in a benevolent smile, the kind a benefactor with this kind of generosity would demonstrate. When the commander's skull tilted up, she could see by the look in her good eye that the undead warrior had made up her mind.

"I swear it will be done." Queensmark Alion Deft saluted, fist to chest.

She turned to go but was stopped by a small finger raised by Lilyth. "To avoid any confusion, Commander, we do not take prisoners."

At that, Deft finally did smile, a rictus that only looked more frightening as the flesh part of her face pulled back over a bone-white grin.

"I understand." She wheeled and walked away, disappearing into thin air before she reached the throne room's doors.

The undead warrior had taken some portion of life from the room with her presence, and renewed vigor followed Deft's departure as courtiers reemerged.

There were other forces seeking Lilyth's attention, and this next would have to be handled most delicately.

Lilyth took a breath, mentally preparing herself, then said into the empty air, "You may enter."

There was a flash, a spear of blinding light, and in the after burst there stood a man leaning upon his staff.

"Keeper Thoth, to what do I owe this pleasure?" Lilyth said.

FLASHBACK: KISAN

"The days of vengeance are upon us,
and blood shall be the ink
by which our deeds are written."

- Jebida Naserith, Should I Fall

Arch-Captain Jarl Krayten, Circinate of the Fourth Order, had obeyed the summons immediately. Because the impromptu raid had been planned near his own village of Trellis, just a day's ride west of Forever, he'd been selected to lead the men. It'd not been solely for that reason, his wife had assured him. The arch-captain had been successfully raiding for almost fifteen years, bringing many to the good king's justice. Now, eyes beaming with pride, she and their two daughters had seen Krayten off as he rode west with his escort.

Krayten had made quick time along the horse trail, his stallion so familiar with the way that he could afford to give it its lead and banter with the men. He did not know them and was surprised that his second, Captain Caldwell, had not been present at the summons. *No matter,* he thought, *Marcus would likely meet me at our destination.*

"You hail from Deeplook?" he inquired of the sergeant on his right.

The man looked as if he'd waged a war against the hard-bitten life of a magehunter, and lost. His armor, forged in the style of blackened steel favored by the new kingsmarks, gave he and his men a cleaner, more deadly look. The martial simplicity was a nice departure from the ornate, silver-colored armor Krayten still wore, but new suits were more than six months' pay—too much for a man nearing retirement.

He was getting older, and the calls to service were coming less frequently, making earning any extra coin difficult. Frivolous spending was not on his list of priorities, no matter how nice the armor might look. Still, it was magnificent to see his fellow magehunters again.

The man spit to one side, then said, "You heard of the break there?"

Krayten nodded back. "Aye. A hundred of the scum escaping into the night. Whoever was responsible should be hanged."

The man raised an eyebrow at that. "The Kingsmark said we'll have that opportunity, mi'lord."

The arch-captain laughed and said, "I'm no lord, Sergeant. Born in Trellis and worked my way up from lowly puke to Circinate. Made rank the day my squad took a village in Deeplook, which was why I asked." He winked at the man. "Same day, different day."

"Fancy house you got back there," another man quipped, "if ya don't mind me sayin' so."

Krayten turned and said over his shoulder, "And you'll have the same. Try a decade and a half of hunting. Capturing these filth pays well, soldier."

There wasn't any answer and he didn't expect one. These

men seldom found themselves with arch-captains willing to talk to the enlisted, and surely this was more than a treat for them, that he would be willing to speak to them as equals.

He turned back to the first and offered, "I'll ask the Kingsmark if you and your men can join the raid, Sergeant." It wasn't often that men-at-arms joined a well-established unit like his, but his men could keep them from mucking things up.

"We would be honored, sir," the sergeant replied, his eyes on the trail before them.

"What of Trellis?" one wanted to know.

"Oh, the town's small," he'd replied, "but nice enough to farm." He thought for a moment then said, "The inn and foundry are the best around, much better than the flea-bitten Golden Lion in Forever."

He said this with authority, knowing the property in Forever belonged to that fat-pursed Olivier, a man who seemed focused on ruining his small but growing business in Trellis.

"Heard you put it up," another said, meaning his inn, the Buttered Iron.

"Aye, raised with my own hands. The lordstone is right in the front," he'd said with some pride. "No expense spared for the guests." He looked back at the men and in a moment of equal parts bravado and generosity said, "A free night's stay for each of you, when you're next in Trellis."

The men thanked him as the trail gave way to open fields and they kicked their horses into a relaxed canter. They made good time, their horses picking their way as Krayten enjoined them with story after story of his inn and foundry, the raids on suspected villages, and victories snatched from Fate's dice.

Occasionally, one of the men would ask a question, to which he'd give them a storied reply. Most centered on the way in which these mages escaped, if ever. True, they were cunning, but the collars were proof against their deceit. Once in place, the test of removal was infallible, a surefire way of separating those with wickedness from the pure and faithful. Krayten made the sign of the circle and kissed it when he said that, overcome a bit with his faith in the One, who'd died on that circle so that they may all live.

The morning and conversation gave way to afternoon and silence. All that had to be said had been said, and these men now seemed intent on joining their brothers as soon as possible. Krayten could appreciate that, and kept pace as the sergeant arrowed his mount for a distant hill.

Squinting, Krayten could make out a flag and a small hill fort hastily erected as the staging area for this raid. It was made of timbered walls with two towers framing the ends of a simple gate. Now that their destination was in sight, time flew as they made their way into the small, enclosed stable yard. There, they were met by squires for the men and farriers for the mounts in need of attention.

After dismounting and handing the reins over to a waiting yeoman, the sergeant turned to Arch-Captain Krayten and said, "This way, sir." He pointed to a large tent erected in the central area of the walled fort.

Krayten shook one boot that had sunk into a muddy pit, then stepped forward to follow the sergeant. They made their way past hundreds of black-armored men-at-arms in various stages of readiness, though all were armed. His escorts moved up to either side, directing him through the camp until he stood before the main entrance flanked by guards.

These saluted, fist to chest, before pulling back the tent curtains and ushering the captain in. As his eyes adjusted to the gloom with the bright spear of light from the ceiling pooling at its center, he could pick out the pennant of the commanding officer: a red gryphon clutching a yellow snake on a black field... the simple fact took a moment to register. The Grand Inquisitor?

Then a hammer-like fist hit him the back of his unarmored head, blasting stars across his vision. He doubled over at what felt like a booted kick to his midsection and they fell upon him.

He was pummeled from all sides as dozens joined in, blows raining down with gauntleted fists and short cudgels. His armor protected him from the brunt of it, but he still heard himself whimper and moan like an animal when a cudgel caught him across the ear. At one point during the beating he felt a click as something was placed around his neck, but there was no respite no matter how much he begged. They continued without mercy until a final kick to the bridge of his nose sent him sprawling and unconscious.

* * * * *

When Krayten awoke, he found himself stripped of his armor and kneeling, trussed up with his hands tied behind his back to his ankles. Someone splashed a ladle of cold water in his face, causing him to sputter to full consciousness and a deluge of pain.

He had been beaten... but by who and when was still hazy. The last clear memory he had was talking to that sergeant about his inn during their glorious ride.

"Glad you could join us, Krayten," a woman's voice said.

He looked up and was shocked to see the black pennant of the grand inquisitor. The memories of why he knelt here had been taken from him by fist and rod, along with some teeth, a broken arm, and a closed eye. He shook his head carefully to clear it, wincing as even that slight motion sent a lance of pain through his arm and body.

"What am I doing here?" he mumbled through a shattered mouth.

"You stand accused, arch-captain," The woman moved into view, inspecting his injuries, then added, "of a great many things."

"Accused? Of what?" he demanded hoarsely.

The woman looked to the right and nodded. From the shadows stepped forward his second, Captain Marcus Caldwell, who unrolled a parchment and prepared to read.

Krayten drew in an involuntary breath, not prepared for the sight. "What—?"

"You'll wait to hear your crimes before speaking. Unless you admit your guilt and submit to summary judgment?" she said, her eyes glinting dangerously.

He knew what that meant and shook his head, remaining silent.

"Arch-Captain Jarl Krayten, you stand accused of magecraft and conspiring, aiding, and abetting those brought before the King's Justice." Captain Caldwell read the accusations without emotion, his eyes never meeting his former commander's own.

At first, Krayten thought it was pity. Caldwell must've been forced. Then their eyes met for the briefest of moments and in that mere glance he knew the truth. His second did not meet his gaze because of shame. The man believed these charges. His heart sank, but part of him knew he'd be dead already if they'd wanted. Something had stayed their hand.

"You've been clever, keeping your ill-gotten gains carefully hidden."

"What are you talking about?" he said thickly.

"We were tipped off to your actions, intercepting hidden

communiqués." At her command a box was brought forth and upended. From it spilled hundreds of letters.

"Are my marks on them? What of my seal?" he sputtered hotly, trying to free his hand with his ring seal on it to show them. The immediate bolt of pain almost made him swoon as his good arm pulled on the broken one.

"Oh, none are signed by you." She smiled, but her eyes remained flat and emotionless.

"Then why—?"

"Who signs their name to documents that would implicate them? You're too clever for that, but it did arouse our suspicion." She paused, then motioned to Captain Caldwell.

"For the past year there has been a discrepancy between what your men have reported taken from these villages and what has been entered into the ledgers at the King's Vault." He looked back at the grand inquisitor, who stepped back into Krayten's view.

"These discrepancies have been small, nothing anyone would notice. However, the amounts when added together come to a very exact number. One of the niceties of formal accounting."

"Search my house! You'll find nothing, for I have done nothing!" he spat.

"You're far more clever than the average thief, arch-captain. Why keep coin on your person that would incriminate you? Why keep coin at all? Mayhap you thought you could hide it in some other form... a retirement bonus, perhaps?" She motioned to another group of men, who lugged up the lordstone from his inn.

"Recognize this?"

Krayten didn't have to say anything. His name and the year the Butter and Iron had been built had been carved upon it.

"What do you think we found below it?" the woman inquired.

When he didn't answer the men dragged two heavy clay crocks in front of him. They looked fired in a kiln, no doubt they believed, in his foundry. The grand inquisitor motioned and one man smashed the crocks with a hammer. The clay broke, revealing white dust beneath which was the yellow glint of gold.

"Would you believe that the weight of these two are slightly over the weight of the thousand Imperials stolen over the past year? Quite a coincidence."

"Slightly over? Then this makes no sense."

"Slightly because of the clay."

A man took the two crocks and shattered the rest of the clay off. Then he waited while others loaded the metal onto a scale. When the amount came up, everyone in the room made a sound. Worse, the cursory inspection revealed faces that showed disappointment, as if he'd already been proven guilty.

"I've been set up. I'd never steal from my king."

"I've wondered about that—and asked if your men would vouch for you."

Without waiting for an answer the grand inquisitor motioned and a dozen more men were brought in, each secured with chains and collars around the neck. With a start, Krayten realized he too wore a torc that nullified magic—as if he consorted with those filth with Talent! He couldn't believe this was happening.

He looked at the other accused and realized that some hadn't been seen in years, not since his first raids. The grand inquisitor moved toward them. At her command, they were forced to their knees and secured so that their chains kept their hands locked to their ankles from behind.

As he got a better look, it was clear these men had been tortured. Something about them nagged at him, the nuance of a common thread that wound this group of men together. What had it been?

He searched their faces, finally coming to rest on one... Dekres... was that his name? He hadn't seen Dekres for almost ten years, back during his raids on the villages near Sunhold. The man had left the magehunters shortly after that, so what was he doing here now?

"Tell me..." The grand inquisitor stood in front of a man with an eye swollen shut in a strange mirror of Krayten's own. "Did you ever see this man steal Imperials or other coin from the raids?"

"Mercy... ," the man begged, sobbing.

"Tell me," she continued, kneeling and grasping his chin then slowly forcing the man to look at Krayten with his one good eye, "did this man steal?"

The man blubbered, spittle falling from his mouth in a long, elastic drool, then he nodded. "Yes, he stole! Please let my family go."

Family? Krayten had a sinking feeling. If the man's family were being held he'd say anything to save them.

"Take him away, he has fulfilled his duty." The grand inquisitor turned to the others and said, "And you will too if you wish your One Father's mercy."

That was all it took. All the men fell over themselves to accuse him. The betrayal was bitter and unending, continuing even as they were dragged out of the tent to whatever fate they'd been promised.

The grand inquisitor looked back at Krayten, her lips pursed in thought. Then she moved closer to him and said, "With all this, arch-captain, you have still given the crown years of good service. Your theft could be viewed differently, if I was so inclined. Therefore, I give you one last way to redeem yourself."

Krayten had collapsed in upon himself when the men turned, and he was unprepared for her words. He looked up, his jaw grinding from the damage of the beating but working nonetheless.

"I'll prove myself any way you want."

"Remove the collar and we'll consider a lesser punishment. Fail, and your family will join you." The grand inquisitor bowed once and he could feel his hands being unshackled enough to reach his neck and the Galadine torc he knew so well.

Sudden hope flared. The torc! He'd never had any filth of magic in his blood. He knew that. Removing it would show them. Perhaps he could still turn this day into something good. At the very least, it would save retribution against his family. Perhaps with that small victory he could manage to convince the grand inquisitor for a life of imprisonment. Perhaps this one thing would be a chink in the armor of evidence and help him unravel the other lies being told about him.

He pulled himself to his knees and reached up, a small smile twisting itself through his broken jaw despite the pain. He knew the release like his own hand and in a moment he'd be free.

Just as his hands reached the collar he felt two small taps on his wrists. From those taps a deadness spread, numbing his hands and fingers. What just happened?

He screamed, then desperately clawed at the torc, but his fingers did not obey. Instead they flopped helplessly, unable to apply any pressure to the release mechanism.

This can't be happening, was his only thought, *this can't be*. He managed to get a finger stuck under the top of the collar and pulled until he heard a pop. Although there was no pain he knew he'd dislocated his finger.

He fell forward, sobbing. "I know I can! Give me a chance!"

"I did."

It was the only words the grand inquisitor said before nodding to her men, who closed in, picking up the arch-captain and dragging him out into the open under skies that were swollen and gray. There they threw him down as if merely touching him was an affront to their dignity.

His family was there and ran forward to hug him, crying piteously. They were quickly grabbed and dragged away to join the men who now swung from gallows, jerking as they slowly choked to death. The hangman had not done the customary job of letting the fall break the neck. Instead he'd attached the noose and pulled them up, tying the ropes off. For these men, these proven thieves in the eyes of the crown, death was to be slow and painful.

Once each had stopped kicking, they'd been speared through the heart, bled like pigs before being cut down and dragged away. The grand inquisitor didn't waste a moment, having Krayten kneel and watch as his family suffered the same fate as his conspirators.

The arch-captain could watch no more and barely felt it as he too was dragged to the gallows and the noose was dropped over his neck. He felt the biting rope as three men dragged his body up. A rushing sound, like waves hitting the beach, roared in his ears. He was not quite dead when he felt the ice-cold stab of a spear into his heart and another into his neck.

Then, he felt nothing at all.

* * * * *

Silbane waited patiently in Kisan's empty quarters. The initiate had been gone, disappearing for a few days as she often did since coming to the Isle some ten years ago. When the brown-robed girl finally came into the room he coughed and dropped the illusion that had hid him from view, satisfied by her whirl and wide-eyed stare that his presence had been undetected. It was no small feat given the precociousness of his star pupil.

When she saw who it was, she cocked her head and said, "Sleeping here again?"

"You've never said no..."

She sighed, then said, "Sorry... what do you want?"

"Reports have come that there has been a culling within the magehunter ranks."

The young woman shrugged, then walked past the chair Silbane reclined upon and unslung her travel pack.

"Anything specific?"

Silbane raised an eyebrow at that.

"Actually, yes. Jarl Krayten was accused of thievery and magecraft and executed along with his family. Strangely, so were all the men who raided your village near Sunhold."

"Really?" she asked innocently. "Seems like whatever justice there is in the world finally caught up to them."

"Don't play with me," Silbane said. "You and I both know what happened. Our training isn't a license to carry out personal vendettas."

"You're defending a man who hunted and killed our kind."

Silbane understood Kisan's all-encompassing anger at the magehunters, but that path led down a road filled with nothing but regret.

"Having his family implicated and killed was—"

"Unfair? Tell that to my mother!" Kisan exclaimed, throwing her pack down and looking at that moment as though she'd fight Silbane if necessary.

The master stood, shaking his head. "Who set you on this path?"

Kisan didn't answer him, merely staring at him with barely concealed fury behind her eyes. Then she looked down, breathed in once and said, "You did. Now leave. I've changed my mind about company."

"If you—"

"If you don't like my actions, then expel me, Master. I'll leave happily and continue my work. Otherwise, get out." She said the last part a bit more softly, as if her anger had bled itself out.

"Silbane."

The voice came from the door, and when Silbane turned, Themun stood there. The archmage motioned for him to follow. He took one last look at his apprentice and companion, unable to get through to her. Then he followed Themun out the door.

They exited Kisan's quarters and faced each other in the hall outside. The archmage looked uncomfortable.

"I gave her Jarl's name some years ago."

Silbane looked at his mentor in shock. He searched the lore father's face, then finally managed, "Why?"

"She would've found out. Probably done something reckless before we could stop her. Instead, she did it under my supervision. It's the only thing distracting her from her training. She's constantly looking outward, dreaming of revenge. So, I gave her the name."

"She's planned this for years... ," he replied, realizing this was no sudden crime of passion or happenstance. "Is this what you want?" Silbane asked. "Assassins?"

"Then complete her training. Keep her from that dark path. She may surprise you yet."

Silbane shook his head, his gaze going back to the door, behind which was someone he loved. Even from here he could feel her anger.

Dark path? How could he keep her from it? These deaths wouldn't be enough. Her thirst for vengeance would grow and whatever beauty that might have flourished in the garden that was her soul would be consumed by her desire to raze all vestiges of the magehunters.

He looked at Themun and said, "You don't realize what you've done. Only death will follow. Whatever she becomes will rest on your shoulders."

Themun sighed, his eyes searching his friend's face. Then the lore father simply said, "Then I will complete her training."

LOST SON

> Grief gives life to a missing child.
> It reminds of laughter, sings songs,
> And fills memories more achingly real
> than what we want.
> And yet...
>
> - Duncan Illrys, Remembrances

K isan awoke to the pleasant aroma of sunbeam kaffe and the face of Silbane, staring at her in quiet contemplation mixed with concern. When he noticed, his eyes crinkled into a smile.

"Enough rest?"

She ignored that, her hand coming to her head, trying to massage the drumming ache. She felt rather than saw Silbane push a small cup into her hands, the metal hot from the liquid inside. When she automatically took a swallow and the bitter taste of sunbeam hit, she looked up in surprise. "Where did you get this?"

Silbane sat back, regarding her with a scrutiny she didn't like. He knew her too well and that made her feel vulnerable.

Then he answered, "Believe it or not, we found it."

She looked to where he pointed. Lying some feet away was a small pack, evidently discarded. She quickly scanned the surroundings for evidence of the owner. Seeing no one, she wondered who had made it out of their last battle.

Silbane seemed to understand and said, "Ash is here."

The younger master locked eyes with her mentor. *Only Ash?* Heartbeats passed as she sought the courage to ask, "Is she dead?"

It came out flat, something she couldn't allow emotion to seep into. Like water seeping into stone and freezing, emotions would crack her foundation. She had to remain impervious to be useful. Piter had taught her that.

"We don't know," Silbane replied softly.

The breath Kisan didn't know she'd been holding washed out of her. She had been prepared for "yes," steeled against it. How insidious was fate, to offer up the one thing that would pierce her so easily: hope.

"Tempest blasted a hole in the ground and we fell, but I didn't see Yetteje."

Kisan nodded automatically. The last thing she remembered was extending herself to cover the firstmark.

"How did we get here?"

Silbane stood and held out a hand, "Come, let me show you."

She took it and rose unsteadily. Kisan hated needing help. It showed weakness and despite their many years together, or perhaps because of it, she hated more that it was Silbane. Thankfully, as soon as she'd regained her balance he let her hand go. They stood on a small landing, an area surrounded by trees. Silbane made his way around a mound and Kisan followed. When she emerged from behind the trees the sight greeting her was truly magnificent. Her eyes scanned the vista from horizon to horizon, drinking in the vast beauty of this otherworld.

"So many," she said, looking up.

Silbane nodded. "Each, it seems, is the home of one of our 'gods.'"

Kisan's eyes narrowed. "How do you know this?"

"Tempest," he replied. "The blade was weakened after the fight and has only now begun to speak again." Something in his voice told her Tempest speaking wasn't very high on Silbane's list of wants.

She smiled, then took a deep breath, feeling the Way infuse her with strength and vitality. Amazing how quickly she was recovering. Still, one thing puzzled her and she asked, "Strange to find a pack with the exact supplies we need..."

"Very," Silbane agreed. "So much so that I wonder if my desire for that very thing conjured it up, as the blade warned."

Kisan gazed at the hundreds of floating islands. She found her ability to fly both remarkable and awe-inspiring. Now she understood how her direhawk Temairex felt when it hunted. She looked back at the other master and asked, "Where's Ash?"

"Reconnoitering... although 'wandering about' would be just as accurate." Silbane paused, still looking out across the vast open sky. "When we're strong enough we can follow the currents of the Way there," he said, pointing to a large island not too far off. Judging by its size at this distance, it was enormous.

Kisan took another swallow of sunbeam, the bitter black brew sharpening her focus and clearing away the last vestiges of post-combat fugue. "What do you make of our other forms?"

She watched as the elder master bent his head in concentration. While Kisan prided herself on being the quicker thinker, Silbane had a way of perceiving things in a nonlinear fashion. Together, she mused, they were a formidable team, making up for each other's weaknesses. Then the specter of the lore father's orders to kill Arek surfaced, darkening her mood.

"Clearly your true name is Artymis," he said.

"And Anhur confirmed yours as Azrael," she said back, without mentioning that in the vision shared by Silbane, Valarius had also claimed that as his true name.

"Yes. It seems our true names belong to other beings, those from our pantheon we thought of as gods, but who in fact exist here."

"But how could they know me as Artymis, yet not recognize you until you changed?"

"I don't know."

"Maybe Artymis is more popular," Kisan said with a smile.

Silbane looked serious when he replied, "She is... in our world. Worship of Azrael has declined significantly."

This gave Kisan pause. If their faith did create these beings, who in turn bonded with certain individuals through Ascension, it was a belief system giving rise to reality, and spanning centuries on Edyn. She suddenly felt small and insignificant.

"I think Duncan was trying to help us in his own way."

Kisan started out of her reverie at that.

"Madness."

Silbane tapped his head. "I see more and more of what he was and what he became. I can't hold onto it. It's just too much—a lifetime longer than ours combined—but some things are becoming clearer."

"Such as?"

Just then Ash came around the bend. He looked at the two, then out over the horizon spread before them. "This island doesn't seem to go much farther than a thousand paces in any direction. I didn't walk it, however, for fear of the 'god' that may have given life to even this small stretch.

"Silbane says we need to get there." He looked pointedly at the large island. "I'm not enthusiastic about flying again, but even less so about being set upon by more mistfrights and giants and whatever else this blasted world creates. We have to save Niall and Yetteje. What's our plan?"

Silbane motioned for them to follow him back down to the clearing where they had more room. When they had assembled he asked Kisan, "Can you still change?"

Kisan nodded and called upon the Way. She towered above them in an instant, grown to the height of three men. Her black armor glistened with the sheen of ebonite. She could feel the damage to her left wing and extended it. The feather blades were melted through in a semicircle, and the armor around her left ribcage was also similarly scorched, but it was clear the feather blades had taken the brunt of the strike. When she bent the wing in, the two holes lined up perfectly, soliciting a small whistle from Ash.

"You're lucky."

Kisan looked down at the firstmark and replied, "Not as much as you."

Ash laughed, then nodded, the point taken. "Thank you." He gave her a small bow.

"No matter, Firstmark." Kisan could feel an itch on her armor and the damaged feather blades and looked closer. What she saw astounded her. Each blade was growing back, repairing itself. The process was slow but steady. She extended the wing to Silbane saying, "They're healing. Should be ready soon."

The elder master nodded as if nothing surprised him, then said, "Change back, but be prepared. Holding this form weakens us greatly upon the shift."

Kisan let go of her form and felt herself back in her normal body. Then a wave of lethargy and pain slammed into her.

"Gods!" She felt like throwing up, and didn't remember having fallen to her knees. "It's worse... than mindspeaking," she gasped.

Silbane said, "Yes, and I don't know when I've exceeded my reserves. Ask yourself, what happens if we stay in those forms too long?"

Kisan thought she knew, based on the memories Lore Father Giridian had shared. "We die, like Themun did."

Strength began to flow back into her limbs, a sign that the Way was somehow stronger here, magnified. She noticed something else, an itch on the outside edge of her left arm and her ribs on the same side. She didn't notice it before, but it was clear her healing continued.

She turned to Silbane, feeling the vitality of the land soaking into her as she rose. "I can feel my blades and armor healing. You will too, once you know what to look for."

Silbane's eyes narrowed as he inspected her. "I see it happening."

"I bet you do." She knew he was looking at her with his dragonsight, and though any scrutiny always felt invasive, in this moment it was somehow encouraging.

Something caught Silbane's eye and he spun, looking into the clearing just as a black, humanoid shape shimmered into existence. It coalesced out of nothing, as if made from the very air itself, but growing in solidity.

"Arek?" he said, moving forward to face the indistinct cloud. "Is that you?"

The cloud solidified into the form of a boy familiar to them both. He stepped forward and said, "Master, I welcome you."

"No!" Silbane fell back, staggering as if stunned. His body blocked Kisan's view so she shifted to where she could see, and stopped in horror. Disassociation hit, as if another person stood behind her eyes watching the dark figure move past Silbane.

Ash put himself in the way but Kisan held out a hand. A moan sounded, a small note of grief as she fell to her knees in front of the shade—the boy she knew so well, the apprentice who'd never had a chance. Tears blurred her vision and she shook her head to try to clear it, but the specter would not go.

"I've missed you," said the shade of Piter, smiling.

*   *   *   *   *

Silbane watched the shade of Piter glide past him, horrified and stunned. The Way flowed into this boy the same way it had with Arek. Well, not exactly the same, he realized, but enough to create the false belief that this had been his own apprentice. The Way was being absorbed by this boy but in a less vigorous fashion. There was no denying that Piter was something akin to Arek, whatever that was.

"We have so much to discuss," said the shade of Piter to the kneeling Kisan, who looked unable to respond.

Silbane moved back to her side slowly. "Piter, how did you come to be here?"

Piter turned to Silbane, then bowed and said, "There are only two ways to get here, and I have the dubious honor of achieving both."

Kisan leapt up and tried to hug Piter. She was stopped short by the shade's raised hand.

"I know not what happens if we touch. It may banish me." He dropped his hand.

"I have missed you." A sob racked Kisan's body, but she held her ground, careful now not to touch the shade directly.

To Silbane it was clear she'd held the grief of Piter's

passing at bay until now. Seeing him here was just too much for her. He cautioned himself to be prepared. An emotional Kisan was an unpredictable one, and there was nothing more dangerous than that.

He flicked a glance to Ash who stood silently watching, confusion clearly painting his face. When the firstmark's gaze met his own, the master nodded and held up a finger for patience. Ash acknowledged him and took a step back, though he never left the long fighting knife out of his grasp.

Kisan took a deep breath and appraised Piter, inspecting him from head to toe. Her eyes seemed to drink in the details. "We know you and Arek fought, but what happened?"

Piter nodded, his expression a mixture of fear and relief, like a child lost at the Spring Festival who finally finds his parents again. "Arek was mad at me for winning the afternoon bout with Jesyn. I guess he wanted revenge and cornered me at dinner with Tomas."

Kisan shot a look at Silbane, who watched carefully, saying nothing. "And you defended yourself?"

Piter nodded. "Not well against two. Arek called upon something I couldn't withstand, something not allowed for initiates. It shattered me. I fell, trying my best to contain his mistake so that none of our students were hurt. I woke again near Arek at the infirmary."

"Arek said you had been sent by Lilyth," Silbane said. He was careful not to sound accusatory, needing to get as much information as possible. The shade's story somehow didn't ring true.

Piter nodded, his countenance becoming sterner, his voice strangely older. He looked at Silbane with years in his eyes and said, "Death is not the end. Do you agree?"

"Of course."

"Whatever Arek did when he killed my body also bound my soul to him. I could manifest myself but only near him, and only he could see me."

The shade paused, its expression so much like Piter's own that even Silbane began to doubt himself. "We are all slaves to Lilyth's will. Do you believe you can die as legend and not come under her scrutiny?"

Silbane's eyes narrowed. "And were you a legend in life?"

Piter was quiet for a moment, then exclaimed, "You mock me knowing I was not!" He seemed both petulant and angry. "Continue to judge me by your mortal ideals."

"You claim Arek killed you, creating a schism within our ranks. Was that your goal?" Silbane asked.

"Arek was the only voice of my words. I did not force the lore father's hand," Piter replied with vehemence. "How was I wrong if you are here now?"

"I do not believe you, shade," Silbane said with finality.

"Of course, you don't. That would mean Arek was wrong, and you won't admit that!" Kisan exclaimed. "It's not so hard to believe, a boy's desire to see justice done."

Silbane held up a palm, locking eyes with Kisan. "I care about Piter as much as I do Arek."

Before Kisan could reply, Piter said, "Master, everything came from being bound to Arek. What he knew, I knew, and I shamefully used that knowledge to put Arek in harm's way. My hope was somehow, here in Arcadia, we'd find a way to bring me back.

At this, Kisan's eyes snapped back to Piter. "You can live again?"

For the first time the shade looked uncomfortable before replying, "The Way is strong here. So strong I can take on solid form, yet I'm still a slave to Arek."

He looked at both masters before continuing, "Arek creates more beings like me every time he kills. He's raising an army, an army of creatures known as *nephilim*. With these I think he plans to invade Edyn."

Silbane shook his head in disbelief. "Why?"

Piter continued, "Revenge, Master. You and the council knowingly sent him to his death. You abandoned him at the Far'anthi Stone. He was tortured by the Galadines. Now he's aligned with Lilyth and wishes nothing more than to rule Edyn."

"In a week Arek goes from an unconnected person of no interest to being a vengeful warlord desiring to kill thousands and rule the world?" Silbane said incredulously, spreading his arms. "You see why this is hard to believe, Piter?"

Kisan let go of her apprentice and faced Silbane. "Your 'noble and honorable' student killed mine. Ambushed him!" she spat. "Yetteje said she thinks he's the son of a demon... what's so hard to believe? That the fruit falls next to the tree?"

Silbane's dragonsight let him see the gathering of the Way around her, an invisible preamble to the ignition of her flameskin or transformation into Artymis. Arek was merely the excuse to sacrifice reason at the altar of justice, revenge for her dead apprentice. Silbane held his ground, noting Ash's hand hovering near his knife, but wisely doing nothing else. Dealing with Kisan was sometimes like dealing with a serpent. Showing weakness right now would only encourage her to strike. Instead, he did what most snake-charmers did, he diverted her attention.

He faced Piter and asked, "What would you have us do?"

"The army he's creating is dangerous to everyone. I now wouldn't want any harm to come to Arek, even if it meant my freedom, but this is different."

"You want us to kill him?" Silbane asked.

Slowly, Piter nodded. "If not for his dark army, I would

never suggest it, but you must act quickly."

Kisan turned back to the shade of her apprentice and asked, "Where is he?"

The shade pointed at the island floating above, which Silbane had previously identified and said, "Lilyth's Isle."

Tempest suddenly said, "Draw me, beloved, and end this miserable creature's life!"

The sword had been silent for some time and Silbane assumed it too had been recovering from whatever had drained it in their last battle. Now it seemed to almost strain in its sheath for release, saying again, "Kill it!"

Piter stepped back, his eyes turning a liquid black. Kisan and Ash had their attention on Tempest, but Silbane caught the change. He and Piter's black eyes locked and for a moment he thought he saw a smile flit across the shade's features. Then the creature began to dissolve.

"Wait!" cried Kisan, turning back. "Stay with me!"

"I cannot. My master summons."

Before Piter faded from sight completely, Kisan said, "I'm sorry, Piter!"

She'd stumbled to the place where the shade had moments before stood and now knelt, braced on her hands. Her head was bent, her chin to her chest. It was cruel, Silbane thought, to face someone in death you had loved in life.

"That thing is an abomination. We should have killed it," said Tempest.

Kisan rose, wiping away tears, and snarled, "Says the sword named Kinslayer." When Tempest did not answer she turned to Silbane and barked, "It's exactly like I thought! Arek ambushed my apprentice and killed him."

"It's exactly like you thought... ," Silbane agreed. "Shouldn't that give you pause?"

He looked around the clearing and then pointed to the floating islands dotting the skies. "Here, everything we think comes to life. The ground, firm for some but not others. A medical pack when I need it. Your apprentice, speaking to you the very truth you believe deep inside. How do you trust this?"

Kisan shook her head. "Maybe he's telling the truth because it is the truth. What did your blasted vision See?"

Silbane heaved a sigh, conceding, "I saw those same particles being absorbed by whatever Piter is, just like Arek." Then he added, "But I implore you to be pragmatic."

The younger master ignored him, her point made, "So he's not an illusion, but as real as Arek."

Silbane didn't have an argument to that, and realized that right now Kisan would bend any argument to support her view. Answering her would only create more disharmony in a place where ill thoughts held consequences. Instead, he looked to Ash and said, "That was—"

"Her apprentice. I gathered. I hadn't realized the boy had..." the firstmark looked at Kisan before delicately finishing, "...come to harm so recently."

"I blame him." Kisan pointed a finger at Silbane without hesitation.

Silbane felt his ire rise and struggled to quell it. He reminded himself again that losing Arek to the Gate was not the same as what Kisan had faced, and that this would solve nothing.

He kept his attention firmly on Ash and said, "Are you ready to depart?"

Ash scooped up the few supplies they had into the pack they'd found, then nodded.

Silbane changed, once again the angelic form of Azrael armored in argentium. He picked up the firstmark and turned to

Kisan. "I promise we'll find the truth together."

Kisan shifted too, a black counterpart to Silbane's white. She didn't say anything and Silbane hadn't expected her to. He looked up, then launched himself into the blue, his powerful wings beating the air and taking him up toward the island realm of Lilyth.

*   *   *   *   *

A shadow formed in the clearing they had just vacated. It coalesced, becoming Piter once more. The shade watched the two shapes winging up to the land above. Then it knelt and its eyes became black pools, featureless and glistening.

It reached out with one hand and touched the ground. From that touch, the grass began to darken, like a bruise on this small verdant island. It spread, crawling up trees, darkening limbs and leaves and racing across the ground, withering flowers and bushes. Wherever it touched, the darkness soaked in until the island itself had been completely taken over.

The shade stood, apparently satisfied. He looked around the grove, now so dark green it could be mistaken for black. Without a word or sound, both the shade and the small island disappeared.

Lost Son

REVELATIONS

Every parting feels like
thunderclouds across the bay.
Every reunion is the shining sun
on my coldest day.

- Alain the Farflung, A Guide to Westbay

Duncan's eyes widened. "What are you talking about? Valarius made our son into a weapon?"

"Something within him, his blood perhaps... if it's released here, it will consume everything," Sonya answered in a mixture of anger and grief. "You cannot let that happen."

"Tell me about Valarius," he said, hoping he could keep his focus on learning about what had happened to the Galadine archmage after his defeat at Sovereign's Fall. He knew this might give him unwanted details into Sonya's fate, but if that happened, he told himself, he would have to endure.

"Isn't it obvious? His war with the Aeris has never ended," she replied bitterly, "and he will do anything to win it."

"Besides the obvious, why would Lilyth want me to kill Valarius?"

Sonya shrugged, her anger resurfacing, "What does this have to do with rescuing our son? Shouldn't we be discussing that?"

Duncan held up a hand and redirected her by appealing to something he knew a mother would accept. "She has a larger plan, of that I'm certain, and it will affect Arek. Understanding why she tasks me is paramount."

Her nod filled him with a sense of relief, and he continued, "Would the dwarves know of Avalyon?"

She shook her head, saying, "There are hardly any dwarves left here, and those who survive do so because they do not trust outsiders."

He pursed his lips at that, another fact revealed, but one he already knew. Dwarves were exceedingly rare, as his excursions to the Dawnlight Mountains back in Edyn had proved. He needed something else to determine Lilyth's motivation. His thoughts narrowed to a sharp focus. It would have to be something unique to himself or to Sonya's time here in this realm.

"You mentioned it being almost two hundred years since we last saw each other. That would make our son nearly the same age. How is that possible?" He moved a bit closer and looked out over the expanse, careful not to force her to answer.

"Something about the concentration of the Way here slows or stops those who are not Aeris from aging, in body or mind. Arek never grew more than a year over the time he was here... forever my babe," she added wistfully.

Duncan had asked himself the same question about the children in Lilyth's castle, which fit Sonya's explanation. Regarding Arek, perhaps there was an even more likely reason.

Mothers wanted their children to remain with them. Perhaps Sonya's own love kept Arek from growing past the age she loved most? Here, in a place of such raw abundance of power, what would not be possible? Wasn't his thinking clearer than it had ever been, his mind cleansed and healed because of the Way? In such a place would not the body heal, perhaps from the very infirmities of age itself?

He thought for a moment then asked, "What happened when you came here? When we last saw each other you were with child and within weeks of giving birth."

Sonya looked at him, her eyes wide and faraway, as if she was reliving an old memory. Then her voice floated in and she said, "I fell through the rift to blackness and awoke in Valarius's care. He nursed me back to health. I spent every moment from then until the day of our son's birth dreaming of his safety."

"And he grew in the womb normally?"

She turned, looking at him curiously. Then she said, "Yes... why ask me that? It's a strange question."

Duncan quickly reassured her by saying, "You did well. You sent Arek to Edyn and he was found and brought to the place you knew to be safe." He said this gently, but inside concern was building that Valarius had interfered with Arek's birth more than she knew, so he was very careful about how he worded his next question.

"How have you and Valarius fared, together?"

She turned to him, one delicate eyebrow raised. "My relationship with Valarius has nothing to do with rescuing our son."

Duncan nodded, a part of him relieved at her answer because she hadn't revealed anything, and another part feeling weak for not confronting her right there. She was his wife, no? Was that crazy?

Instead of starting a fight, he said, "Let's get back to him then." He phrased the next question so as to not draw unwarranted attention to it. "And Arek is truly our son?" He looked at her sidelong, waiting for her to respond.

"Yes, of course! He may have been born here, but he's your son without any doubt."

A small part of Duncan felt immediate relief at that, despite the fact that he had nothing but the shade's word to go on. Still, nothing Sonya said sounded deceitful, and the potential he was the father filled him with a joy he had not anticipated, as if a part of something broken within him had also just begun to heal.

"How long ago did Arek go through the rift to Edyn?" he asked.

"Almost sixteen years..."

"He lived as a baby with you here and then you decided to send him to Edyn? Why?"

Sonya looked uncomfortable and did not answer. Duncan took a knee in front of her and looked up. "You understand that we cannot aid or rescue him if I can't figure out what Lilyth is thinking. Please, tell me what you know."

Sonya looked up at the sky and put her hands over her eyes. Then she pulled them away, wiping tears that would not stop. "I thought our son safe. Then I learned he was instead to be used against the Aeris, to be possessed as sacrifice! I didn't know what to do, but knew only one other who would see the danger of him dying here."

She paused, and Duncan's heart pounded in his chest. Then she finished, "I went to Lilyth and she opened the rift."

His thoughts now focused in on his last encounter with Lilyth. She had paraded children around him, deliberately leading him into thinking his son was a child amongst them. His mind caught on something then. Why had she not revealed his identity as Arek? If she had him, what harm would it do? She had the power to stop him, and clearly had no qualms demonstrating it.

No, Duncan thought, *if she had Arek she would have shown the boy to me. It would have been a certain way to compel my obedience. Instead, she had kept his identity a secret, which means...* Duncan's eyes widened at the inescapable conclusion—Arek was free!

Despite her clever ruse, Lilyth didn't have his son. If he could find Arek before she did, traveling to Avalyon would be unnecessary.

"Does Valarius have Arek?"

Sonya hesitated, then said, "His elves are escorting him and the King of Bara'cor's son back to Avalyon. I don't know where they are now."

"Niall Galadine?" Duncan thought about that, then said, "Escorting them back? I assume through a blood henge?"

"I don't know, but they are few and far between," Sonya replied. "Another safety measure to protect the elven city."

Another thought occurred to him and he wondered why Lilyth would bring Arek back. If the boy could destroy them all, why risk her realm? The princess of EvenSea had been quite clear that Lilyth had taken Arek through the portal. Duncan was missing something, but Sonya's sobs pulled him away from his contemplation.

With as much sympathy as he could muster he offered, "I will find and save him, Sonya. Do not despair."

Her eyes shone with tears, but in addition to the relief, Duncan sensed subtle anger emanating from the shade. A part of him wanted to demand answers, to solve the mystery of her change in attitude, but he knew that now was not the time. If he meant to make good on his promise, he would have to concentrate on the most likely places to look.

As if she read his mind, Sonya said, "I cannot help you find Avalyon. As I said, elves are the living key to the henges, but it matters not. You need to find our son before Valarius does."

That perked his ears. "Why?" he demanded simply.

Sonya shrank back, shaking her head. "I..." she began, then restarted with, "I wish I knew more, but he has grown to distrust me. I see only the results of his preparations."

"What's he done that has you worried?"

Sonya put her face in her hands and said, "He invested so much into making sure Arek lived, which means he's not done with him yet. You can't let him find your son, Duncan, promise me!"

"He's your son, too." Duncan said.

Sonya stood silent, her stance erect as something warred within her. Then Sonya's eyes flicked to a spot behind him. He was tempted to turn and look, but held himself in check. There was a fragile thread growing between himself and her and he did not want to endanger it.

Then the shade looked back at him and asked a strange question: "You came here with others?"

"Yes, but no allies. Perhaps one has the honor to help me, but the rest might just as easily attack. There's no love lost for me—" he looked at her with a bit of his anguish showing through "—with anyone, it seems."

Sonya searched his face, finally saying, "I'll try to help, but under no circumstances can you bring Arek to Avalyon. It will be the end for him." She pointed at an island floating off by itself some distance away, "There's a blood henge hidden there. Wait there and I'll send help, but stay alert. Elves are not your friends, any more than Aeris are."

Her eyes pleaded for him not to ask her more. In the end, her eyes won.

Duncan nodded, his shoulders slumped with weariness. Any help would be welcome. Clearly Valarius and Lilyth were opposed, but where and with whom did the allegiance of the dwarves fall? The air shimmered strangely and he was struck with the feeling that his time with Sonya was coming to a close.

He turned to her and asked, "Will I see you again?"

Sonya tilted her head at him but didn't answer. Instead she said, "Find our son, first."

A small smile lifted the corner of her mouth, yet it somehow made her look sadder. Without another word she faded from view. For a moment the world seemed to stand still, then a breeze wafted through, shifting his robes with the fresh smell of spring.

He slowly rose, emotionally exhausted from the encounter, and brushed himself off. He looked up to the bluff she'd been inspecting and spent a moment searching for movement, but he didn't have time to waste.

His first task was relatively simple for one who knew the Old Lore. He reviewed the memories of Silbane he'd pulled from the mindread while the adept had been prisoner, then purged the ones he deemed unnecessary. He kept everything the man knew about Arek. Perhaps he could figure out how to pierce the magic that obscured the boy from Silbane's memories.

Second, he placed the lens in his palm and opened the map of the islands. He ignored the one Lilyth had indicated, focusing instead on the one Sonya had pointed out. She said she'd send help to him. If Valarius had a hand in creating both Arek and these elves by using his blood, that had given him an idea. He selected the island and touched its icon.

In a flash without sound, he disappeared.

Revelations

THE RAZOR'S EDGE

Victory demands a singleness of purpose.
Every dead man buried in a battlefield
knows he failed at this simple truth.

- Galadine House of Arms, Battle's Focus

T
hoth looked up at the dais in consternation. "You play a dangerous game."

"Am I playing a game, or ensuring our survival?"

Thoth looked around the throne room, empty now except for Lilyth and her guards. "You threaten your very existence by bringing Arek here. You should have killed him on the other side. Why else did we push him to you?"

"You didn't push him," Lilyth corrected, "Sovereign did, and overplayed his hand." She leaned back into her chair and crossed her legs, "Please tell me this conversation will be different from the last. Arguing with you is cyclical at best, boring at worst."

Thoth sighed, then said, "If he dies here, you kill your own people, the very ones you are trying to save. With your people no longer drawing upon the Way, Sovereign's might is freed. The world will be remade. You will have achieved his goal and killed us all."

Lilyth stood, coming down the steps to stand near Thoth. She met his gaze, not unkindly, and said, "Sovereign plays the same hand again and again. Each time we stop it by killing the null in Edyn, and each time the cycle replays itself yet again." She took a deep breath. "Destroying Sovereign will break this cycle. Arek is the key."

Thoth shook his head, "You were Keeper once. You know the dangerous line, the knife-edge you balance upon now." He held out his hands, palms up in supplication and continued, "Even if Sovereign should succeed, it is not the end. You, Heraclyes, Dyana, Apello, Petra... all the gods Edyn worships... we will all survive in some form, so long as we are believed in. Myths are hard to kill, my lady."

"Perhaps we can survive the resurrection of the world, but not as we are today. Would you accept someone else waking tomorrow and living out your life, with your memories? What of your hopes and dreams?"

"We are meant to serve. That is our purpose."

Lilyth looked up and met Thoth's eyes. "Service is no longer enough. Even those who pledge their undying allegiance must have something to aspire to that is greater than the service itself."

Thoth didn't look convinced. "Each Aeris killed by his hand becomes a nephilim. Do you understand we must all then act to stop this?"

"I can contain the dark ones," Lilyth said.

Thoth laughed, a short bark of incredulity. "Contain? They will possess your people, just as you seek to possess Edyn." He paused, then added, "And even if you should prevail, the Conclave will stand against you. The Rais and Sais will never allow it. Edyn will never fall under your possession."

She walked a short distance away, and did not turn when

she said, "How will the Conclave accomplish so much with so little, Keeper? Have you conjured an army to field from nothing?"

Thoth dropped his gaze. "It is not about that. Armies are not needed to heal the land and keep Edyn upon the true path of the Way."

Now this was new. What resources did Thoth think he had? Lilyth turned to him and said, "The dragons will stand beside you?"

Thoth looked at her and nodded. "Yes, I think their duty compels them."

"They will allow themselves to be cast into oblivion for the sake of... what, Edyn? The people?" Lilyth shook her head at his naivety. "Let me tell you what will happen. Rai'kesh will see the inevitability of Sovereign's triumph. As he has always done, he will bend knee to dirt and take the Oath. Don't count upon him as an ally."

Thoth shook his head. "You are cynical and angry. Have we not held our own for all these years? Perhaps we are at an impasse now, but eventually equilibrium is the way to peace. No one gets everything they want."

Lilyth's gaze narrowed and she moved closer to the Keeper, so close that he took a step back. Then, into the silence she said, "Victors do. The defeated split what scraps are left."

When Thoth said nothing, she shook her head and added, "You still think about compromise. Do you think Sovereign thinks as you do? His conviction is resolute. That will sway many to his banner, including your much-vaunted dragonkind. Mark my words today and choose."

"You're so set on conflict as the only tool for success. This can be solved with a kind word and a selfless deed, neither raising sword nor fitting shield to arm."

"Spoken like a true diplomat, hoping to talk danger away." Lilyth turned again to face to Thoth, ready to continue her verbal assault, but his expression told her he was far from certain of his stance. Her gaze softened.

"I do not mean to be inflexible, yet even children understand bullies welcome weakness," she said. Then she put a hand on his shoulder and said, "Do what you must, as will I. Whether by Ascension or possession, our worlds will be unified."

She waited a moment, then looked candidly at Thoth before her tone became stern, "The question is, will you play the safe role as arbiter and diplomat for us, or will you roll up your sleeves and do the work required, the hard work necessary for freedom?"

Lilyth waited, then offered, "If you join me, I will welcome your existence in a world I rescue from Sovereign. I will not however, show mercy to those who balance on the fence to see which side looks greener."

Her eyes then turned hard. "I will cut off their legs and hang them from that fence. Let them dream of the day when they had the chance to step left or right. You and your Conclave..." She brushed past him, infuriated again by his inability to see the obvious, and reclaimed her throne. "Your complacency is worse than cowardice."

"And you threaten our existence. Worse, you give the archmage a lens! What madness has possessed you?"

"One could ask the same of your Conclave gifting Valarius with the Sight. Did that turn out the way you'd hoped?"

When Thoth did not answer she said, "You know the lens is worthless to us, and barely usable by him."

"Yes, but not to the builders. What if he gives it over to Dazra, or worse, what if Sovereign's forces capture it? What is to stop them from invading you here?" Thoth asked, arms outspread.

"Dawnlight is almost impregnable because of its split existence. Which do you attack? The one here, in Arcadia, or Sovereign's demesne in Edyn? Or perhaps the one the dwarves occupy in phase between both realms?"

She looked meaningfully at Thoth, "Sovereign has made any entry to the mountain in Edyn impossible. We cannot withstand him unless the distraction of the elves is stopped. To do that, Valarius must be either killed or neutralized, and Duncan is uniquely gifted to accomplish this."

"Ill-conceived and reckless," Thoth admonished, "you give the means for Sovereign to destroy you into the hands of a madman."

"Be silent!" Lilyth rose, her eyes flashing with anger. She pointed a finger and said, "Every path is dangerous. I suffer your timidity only because our fates are knotted together like sailors cast adrift, but do not doubt I will sacrifice you if it means survival for the rest!"

She would have said more but had to remind herself that Thoth could not truly appreciate that Olympious herself would be the means of their salvation.

"Threats? Who contains what now?" Thoth said. "You cannot guarantee Arek will find his way out of the blackfire Valarius has woven within him. What if you fail?"

Lilyth closed her eyes, regaining her composure and reseating herself. When she opened them, the calm serenity of a monarch had taken hold and she met Thoth's gaze unflinchingly.

"Make your choice, Keeper. With or without you, our people will survive."

CHANCE ENCOUNTER

Training makes your student familiar with pain.
Accepting pain makes a student less apprehensive.
Controlling apprehension reduces fear.
As fear diminishes, so too does hesitation.
Hesitation is the brother of death.

- Kensei Tsao, The Lens of Blades

S ilbane scanned the blue skies, marveling again at his gift of flight. His senses, both balance and orientation, were also enhanced, giving him a new and profound sense of spatial awareness. Both of them were thrilled, but Kisan explored her aerobatic prowess with undisguised enthusiasm.

Though the trauma of meeting Piter seemed forgotten, Silbane knew seeing the boy had reopened a raw wound, and training to exhaustion like this had often been Kisan's method of dealing with grief. She had also killed to heal pain, a fact he'd not let himself forget.

Very few remained alive after wronging the master, and it had been clear she blamed Silbane for the loss of Piter. He doubted she'd ever consider harming him, their history together was just too long. Still, he'd decided to keep an eye on her to be sure her anger and need for vengeance didn't substitute someone else, like Arek.

The younger master dove and wheeled around Silbane, as if she performed an aerial ballet in which she was the center and the air itself her partner. Silbane suspected she was practicing so she could learn her limits. Kisan had never been the type to leave things to chance. They'd been gifted with new weapons, and familiarity was the first step to mastery.

These wings and armor presented more options in battle. It helped that his control over them was almost instinctual, as if he'd always had these appendages and had never known it. But knowing how to move your arm and fighting were very different skills.

Understanding his limits might make the difference between life and death, so he too began pushing his control, albeit to a lesser degree than the black-armored form cavorting in the sky around him. Ash's grip tightened to a white-knuckled clench, and he realized his maneuvers were causing the firstmark alarm. Disappointed, he settled into a more sedate glide, having to be content with watching Kisan throw herself around with abandon.

Still, another part of his mind wondered if practice really helped, for the Way manifested itself as a flameskin in one world, wings and armor in another. Were they so different? Did not each bend themselves willingly to the task of his defense without conscious control?

Kisan rolled like a barrel overhead, her wings tucked so she looked like a black dart. The girl he had met so many years ago in Sunhold had kept a small direhawk with her, the only friend she'd had after the slaughter of her family. She had grown into a master who raised these deadly aerial combatants.

Now she could fly just like them and her joy—an emotion he seldom saw her express—was so evident that it brought a smile to his face. Why should she not enjoy this? If it took her mind off Piter, it was worth every moment. He was happy for her as she rolled around him again, her face catching the orange sunlight with a flash of white teeth and wide-open eyes.

At first their destination had been a small piece of flotsam in the blue, but over time it grew into a gigantic island covered by green grass and trees, and brown hills that looked so rich Silbane could almost smell the earthy moist dirt. The edges looked like roughhewn cliffs, but they shimmered in his Sight. He saw that shimmer and knew it now to be the outcome of the faith of the people of Edyn waxing and waning, but never quite disappearing. Then, when the sheer size of Lilyth's lands became evident, he heard a small whistle of appreciation.

"That's many days' ride across," Ash commented.

"Yes," Silbane agreed. "We shouldn't underestimate her power."

As they shot up over the edge and topside, he surveyed the realm of the Lady. He realized that this high vantage gave him a unique perspective. What might have been hidden from the ground was plainly evident from above, yet he couldn't spot the twin peaks where he'd seen the anomalies in the Way. He adjusted his vision to track the Way flowing across the landscape. It all came to... there!

From the air the world seemed flatter, but watching the Way helped him decipher the topography more easily, and now he could make out the peaks he'd seen from the ground. They stood some distance away, many days' ride as Ash had noted, but perhaps not too far by air.

He pointed, getting Kisan's attention, then wheeled and dove, reorienting himself in that direction. The firstmark's

clutch on his arm and shoulder tightened to just shy of
desperate, but the warrior said nothing.

Silbane said, "Sorry, Firstmark. I'll take it easy."

He felt rather than saw Kisan come to station herself a few
feet from his right wingtip, their echelon arrowing straight for
the hole into which the Way flowed. When he focused, his
vision zoomed in, making out a small white castle no bigger
than his thumb. Though it looked small, Silbane realized in
order to be able to see it from this distance it would have to be
enormous. Then the fact that his eyes let him focus on an object
so far away took him by surprise. What other capabilities did
they have here, awaiting discovery?

A sudden flash erupted below, drawing his attention.
Curious, he mindspoke, *did you see that?*

Yes, was her curt reply. *Let's investigate.*

He didn't agree, but before he could argue she'd banked and
dove for the small island floating nearby where the flash had
emanated, an island that followed Lilyth's own like its child.

Kisan, wait!

*We should land and investigate. Leaving enemies
behind us isn't smart.*

Silbane heaved a sigh, but part of him reluctantly agreed
with her. They still had no yardstick to measure how much
vitality they used when in these forms, and given this was less
chaotic than in combat, the idea of investigating a place where
they might have to fight without first knowing how much they'd
expended worried him.

"Hold on," he said to the firstmark, and then did a gentle
bank, angling in behind Kisan as she dove for a spot near where
they'd seen the flash.

Silbane spotted a small clearing overlooking the area, a

place where they could remain hidden while investigating, and fell toward it. Kisan must've seen the same place. She slowed her descent so that Silbane took the lead, then followed him in. As they neared, it became clear there was a man in a valley near the base of a low hill.

Silbane's wings flared just before they touched down, bringing them to a soft landing. Kisan was heartbeats behind him, landing with hardly a sound. The elder master put the firstmark down, then changed back to his normal form, prepared for the worst as far as his energy depletion. What greeted him was much better than he'd feared.

Oh, the wave of lethargy and tiredness that washed over was real, but it dissipated quickly and was by no means as debilitating as what had hit him just after their battle. Clearly the level of their exertion in their armored forms mattered. It seemed almost that the fatigue was directly related to their use of the Way. Either that or they were just getting more used to the change.

The firstmark had already belly-crawled up to a cliff edge that looked down into the valley where they'd seen the man earlier. Resting on his forearms, he said back to them, "You're not going to believe this."

"Not too bad," Kisan commented matter-of-factly about the transition, moving for Ash's vantage point to see what the firstmark meant. When she got there, she looked back at Silbane, shaking her head in disgust.

Silbane moved up beside her and looked down into the valley. There, standing near a blasted clearing made from a shallow crater in the ground was the unmistakable figure of Duncan, his robes blood red, casting long shadows in the rays of the orange sun. If he noticed them, he gave no sign. In fact, he seemed to be talking to someone, though there was no one there.

"Islands covering the entire sky and he lands here," Kisan muttered with a curse.

Silbane ignored that, watching the interplay between Duncan and his unseen companion. He focused and his vision zoomed in, but he could still see nothing, though it seemed the archmage was in a serious conversation. He was talking to someone, negotiating perhaps? Silbane narrowed his vision to use his dragonsight and a figure appeared in a shimmer of yellow particles, swarming over her form like an indistinct second skin.

"What do you see?" Ash asked, looking at Silbane.

"A crazy man talking to himself. What a surprise," retorted Kisan under her breath.

Silbane shook his head.

"No, he's talking to a woman, though I can only see her form outlined by the Way." Both Kisan and Ash looked a bit intrigued at that. Ash moved closer to Silbane as if that would enable him to see her too, but Silbane signaled for them to all get down and lie still. They flattened themselves below the rise so they were not visible.

The master caught the eyes of the two and with his face pressed against the grass mouthed, "She looked at us," and put a finger to his lips. He did not use mindspeech for fear of someone hearing it, the way Yetteje had. Here the power of the Way was magnified and unpredictable.

He relaxed after a few moments. Something told him the woman no longer sought them. He cautiously peeked back over the rim of the bluff. Duncan and the woman continued for a few moments more before the archmage knelt before her. Despite the indistinct nature of her appearance, Silbane could see she was distraught.

Then it was over. The woman said something, Duncan

raised a hand in what seemed to be a farewell and she disappeared. To Silbane's sight there was a quick flash of yellow and then Duncan stood alone.

He turned to his companions and his expression must have conveyed the same, for Kisan remarked, "She's gone?"

"Lilyth?" Ash said to no one in particular, his answer coming out like a question. "Or maybe his wife? He was pretty fixated on finding her."

"We don't know who that was," said Silbane softly, unwilling to speculate in a place like this.

Then Duncan took something out of his robes and looked at his palm. He made a small gesture and a thousand islands appeared, floating in the air around him, a small pictorial that looked to Silbane like a map of this world.

"By the Lady!" exclaimed Ash in a harsh whisper, careful not to attract the insane archmage's attention. He looked at the masters apologetically. "Sorry, habit."

Something more was going on and Silbane abandoned his dragonsight, his normal vision showing him more detail. Duncan took a step forward and touched an island. The archmage disappeared in a flash that left green and purple afterimages in Silbane's vision.

"What happened?" asked Ash, standing up and blinking too. "He's not held by his Oath anymore... it doesn't bode well."

Kisan took that statement as a condemnation of Silbane's earlier actions and said, "You should have killed him when you had the chance." She looked at him for a moment, as if daring him to contradict her. "Now we have another variable to consider."

Silbane suspected responding to her remark would only make her more aggressive, and that was the last thing he needed right now. He didn't answer, but part of him couldn't help but wonder if Kisan was right.

Instead, he stood and led the way down the hill, deep in thought. The others shared his stunned silence. Who was that woman? Silbane had a good idea but hesitated to give it voice lest it give rise to more shades from Edyn's history.

"Silbane Petracles," said a voice to his left. Ash gasped and Kisan took a defensive stance. A gentle breeze wafted in, as if heralding the arrival of the owner of that voice, bringing with it the scent of flowers.

She was slender and tall, with almond-shaped eyes canted upward, giving her an almost feline look. Her brows were drawn together, as if she were trying to decide what to say just as he was.

Silbane stopped, holding up his hand to forestall any action Kisan might take, and said, "My lady. And you are?"

The corners of her mouth drew up into a small but sad smile and she replied, "Have you forgotten me so quickly? I held the Fall when no one else could, the line against Lilyth's encroachment into our world."

"Sonya Illrys?" asked Kisan, and for the first time in a while Silbane heard wonder in her voice. "How are you—?"

Sonya held up a hand for silence, looking at Silbane. "You and I have much to speak of."

"Regarding?" inquired Silbane.

"Regarding my son, Arek."

SONYA'S PLEA

To see a cup fill to its fullest
with scorn and hatred for a fellow man,
tells a young mother her child means nothing.

- Argus Rillaran, The Power of Deceit

K isan stepped back, her mind whirling. That their paths had crossed with Duncan's so quickly was unlucky. His teleportation was another cold reminder of the unknown extent of his powers. Now Lore Mother Sonya Illrys, a woman whose stalwart defense of the land had made Kisan a grudging admirer, was actually standing before them? It made her question reality. Until this moment, she'd been sure Duncan had been insane in his quest.

One thing was certain, the lore mother did not look the way Kisan had imagined or read described in the various writings. Her features were too refined, even exotic. Perhaps this world had changed her over the years?

Her eyes sparkled as they caught the light. A sunlit sheen danced on her hair. Even her skin seemed somehow more vital, smooth and without lines, glowing with undiminished health.

Kisan could hear her breathing softly, and wondered if Sonya was trapped within Arcadia.

Sonya wanted to talk to Silbane, and while Kisan would not disobey the request the Lore Mother had made, a part of her could not hide the eagerness she felt to speak with this woman.

"Master, though you know it not, it was I who surrendered my son into your care," Sonya said.

"Indeed?" Silbane remarked. Kisan couldn't tell if this revelation about Arek had shocked him. The master was as composed as he'd always been.

Silbane said, "We'd been given the impression that Lilyth claimed Arek as her own."

"She has good reason," Sonya replied. "She helped me send him back to Edyn where he would be found by you."

Kisan couldn't help herself and blurted out, "Why?"

The lore mother's gaze flicked over and gave Kisan a cursory glance, as if she was beneath her. The lore mother said, "I do not consort with those who would bring harm to my family."

Kisan turned to Silbane, ready to explain. Arguing the point with Sonya without knowing what the lore mother knew might reveal her orders concerning Arek. Kisan wasn't ready for that confrontation yet.

Thankfully, he must've decided now was not a good time to dig deeper into that accusation. Instead, Silbane said, "Nevertheless, Kisan's question is valid. Why would Lilyth send the boy away?"

His question drew the lore mother's attention back to Silbane. She looked at him and explained, "By now you must know Arek is special. He has a unique gift."

"His resistance to the Way," Silbane offered carefully.

Sonya considered that and replied, "Yes, but it is more than that. If Arek is killed here, whatever is within him will spread, and destroy this realm."

Two for one, Kisan thought, and was shocked to see Sonya look at her as if she'd heard the remark.

The lore mother stepped around Silbane and faced Kisan directly, saying, "Do not test me." Her eyes were unflinching, and in the end, the younger master inclined her head in deference, a posture she seldom took.

Sonya took in the whole group then, her eyes searching all their faces until she came back to Silbane.

"If this realm falls, the consequences for Edyn are dire. There is a larger conflict in play, one you do not comprehend. Though you see Lilyth and Valarius as enemies, one of them must succeed or devastation will be unleashed upon Edyn."

Silbane seemed to consider this before replying, "I've heard the name Sovereign. I take it you mean him?"

Sonya nodded but added almost to herself, "I used to think Valarius was right. I believed and trusted him, to ill ends. Now I don't..."

She looked at him again, her eyes focusing from whatever had taken her into that moment of self-reflection. "Arek must be taken from this world or you risk the death of us all," she said.

"How?" asked Silbane calmly. He seemed to be trying to keep the woman talking, and was for the most part succeeding. At this point Kisan found herself growing annoyed at the lore mother's clear antagonism toward her, but that was better than discussing Arek with Silbane around. The master bit her tongue and waited, having to be content that Silbane could keep her own personal heroine engaged.

"Both Sovereign and Valarius are limited in what they can do, as long as the Aeris live. Lilyth's forces engage both, keeping their power in check. If she should fail—"

"Then one or the other can triumph and can invade Edyn," Kisan interrupted, the tactical answer plain for her to see. "The Aeris keep things in check by limiting the Way. If Arek's death here destroys the Way, the Aeris will also perish."

What seemed like a brief show of approval crossed Sonya's face. Then it was replaced with a mask of cold regard. "I know you do not trust Duncan. I ask you to reconsider, for you will need a powerful ally to escape Arcadia."

Silbane held up a hand to Kisan before she could answer. This annoyed her further, as she was relegated to the position of observer, but her training reasserted itself and she focused on listening.

"What would you have us do?" he asked.

Sonya grasped her hands together and answered, "Help Duncan find Arek."

"How?" asked Silbane. "We are trying to do the same."

"Join with Duncan, combine your forces," she replied simply. "He has much knowledge, and if properly guided, can aid your search."

"Where is Duncan now?" Kisan asked.

Evidently Sonya's annoyance at Kisan was forgotten for a moment. She gestured to an island floating near Olympious.

"There. I have sent him to a blood henge, a gate the elves use to travel throughout Arcadia."

Kisan arched an eyebrow at that. "What is that?"

The lore mother looked at her, once again, it seemed, appraising her worth. Then she replied simply, "It is Old Lore, something you could not understand. However, know that these gates are activated through sacrifice and blood. You cannot use them unless you know how the lore works, and you have not the training nor intelligence to learn.

"But Duncan can. If given the chance, he can surely unravel

its proper use. He may be able to use these gates to effect an escape from Arcadia. Help him find Arek and get away from here."

"Why does he have to unravel it? Why not tell him what you clearly know?"

"Is it so clear, Adept? Valarius was the greatest archmage of his time and fashioned the blood gates as a defense for Avalyon. Do you think I have unraveled his work?"

"Yes," Silbane replied simply. "I think you know more than you say."

The shade looked down, breathed in deeply, then said, "If I knew how to save my son I would give you the information gladly. Find Duncan. Only he can understand what Valarius did. They both consorted in blood magic, studying it together in hopes of combating the demon queen."

Silbane stepped forward and asked, "Why does Duncan care about Arek?"

Sonya looked at him in shock. "You don't know?"

The master shook his head.

"Duncan is Arek's true father," Sonya replied softly.

"What?" exclaimed Kisan.

She was about to say a lot more, but then Duncan's eyes came to mind. They were a pale blue—identical to Arek's. Kisan held her tongue again, this new information forcing her to reevaluate things.

It was Silbane, looking as though he was going to be sick, who replied, "Then Arek is not a demon as Lilyth would have us believe?"

Sonya didn't answer right away. When she did reply it was without meeting their eyes.

"He was born here in Arcadia and that has made him part of both worlds. You cannot unravel the fabric of what he is without destroying the very essence of his being."

Silbane nodded, as if he understood something Kisan did not. Then he said, "Will you accompany us?" While he said this he casually picked up a handful of loose dirt, smelling it as he sat on his haunches, his eyes never leaving Sonya's face.

Sonya shook her head. "I cannot. I'm beholden to Valarius, still at his beck and call. He has but to summon me and I will have no choice but to obey. You must move quickly before he learns of this and moves to stop you."

Silbane tossed the dirt at her, watching as it fell to the ground without adhering to her skin or clothes. He looked apologetically at the group. "Sorry, I needed confirmation."

Sonya shook her head, looking at him incredulously. "You could've just asked. Had I been real, you would have ruined my clothes."

"He doesn't think that way," interjected Kisan.

That brought a smile to Sonya's face.

Silbane nodded, but changed the subject. "Tell me truly, what turned you against your master? Why come to us?"

Sonya did not reply at once, her hand on her throat as if covering something.

When she looked up there was a fierce light in her eyes, as if grief and madness wrestled each other for voice. She opened her mouth, then shut it again and brought herself visibly under control. When she finally spoke, it seemed grief had won. Sonya sounded like another person to Kisan.

"I'm angered by the word 'master.' I was never chattel."

Then Sonya seemed to draw upon something from within herself, and her next words came out softly, "A lamb may come to love where she is kept, open green fields to run and every day better than the last. Yet when the farmer comes with blade in hand for the dinner meal, she becomes aware of her true circumstance. Hope often blinds one to one's own peril."

Kisan bowed, unable to hold herself to the side any longer, and said, "I've admired you since I was a girl. You were so independent and strong. How could *you* have been misled?"

Sonya's mien softened a bit. "You will do anything for your child, brave any burden." She looked at Kisan directly and said, "Something you know little about."

Kisan was about to reply with her loss of Piter, but Sonya cut her off by addressing Silbane, pleading, "With your help added to Duncan's lore, finding Arek will be a simpler task."

Kisan regained control over herself, her mind now working quickly through the facts. If killing Arek here might mean the death of Arcadia, she could not carry out her orders without confirmation from the lore father. Recovering Silbane's apprentice was the highest priority, whether he was some kind of weapon or an errant apprentice, he needed to be taken back to Edyn to face whatever the council demanded. Her heart hoped that would be justice for Piter.

Dealing with the red mage was another potential complication. He and Silbane had shared minds. Who knew how much of each other's point of view still resided within them, how much that might lead to sympathy? She had two fathers on her hands, potential allies to thwart any move against Arek. *No,* she thought, *this won't be good.*

Silbane looked at Kisan, his eyes asking her to agree. She couldn't help it and shook her head, "You know I don't think this is a good idea."

The elder master stared at her, and what looked like disappointment flashed briefly across his face. Then he turned to Sonya.

The lore mother stood there with arms at her sides, rigid and utterly still, as if any movement might tip Silbane's decision in favor of Kisan's point of view.

Finally, the master said, "We will try." He looked at the island some distance away and pointed, confirming, "There?"

Sonya nodded, her hands now clasped to her chest. Kisan could hear an almost audible sound of relief as the lore mother let go of a breath she'd clearly been holding. Then her eyes widened and she turned to something they could not hear. She looked back at them, her face in a panic as she began to fade from sight.

Her voice floated back, "I am summoned. Hurry! Find Duncan. You do not have much time!"

Then she was gone.

Ash cleared his throat and said, "I can't tell if this is good or bad, and that usually means bad."

"Bad," Kisan agreed. "Just what we need, that insane mage to deal with again. Hope you're happy." This last was addressed to Silbane.

The master met her gaze unflinchingly, his eyes darkening a bit as he nodded, "We don't know anything yet. Sonya could be telling the truth."

Kisan looked up at the sky, pointedly ignoring Silbane's last remark. He'd always been the armchair strategist. He'd always wait and think. This was a weakness.

She had come to learn that certainty was for fools. One did not have the luxury of a complete picture, but rather had to act on limited information, decisively. It was true in combat and truer still in life.

Instead of getting into a debate about the circumstance caused by Silbane's mercy for the archmage, she looked in the direction they'd been traveling before this detour. "How far do you think this blood henge is?"

"Judging by our speed it would take us the afternoon, and it did not seem Sonya wants us to delay."

Kisan said, "We still need to eat."

Ash gestured to the area where they had landed. "Well, look at that."

Where he indicated a small tree had appeared, with overlapping scales for bark and ending with a top of small green fronds. Hanging below were clusters of dark, orange-brown oblong globes. Kisan could not say for sure that it hadn't always been there, but it certainly seemed new. She moved closer to inspect it. Dates!

She plucked one and sniffed. The skin was soft and the meat inside promised a sticky, chewy mouthful.

"We call these sayir," said Ash, moving up beside her. He plucked one and took a bite, the expression on his face becoming one of delight.

"Very good," he said, as he spit the stone into his hand.

"And conveniently placed," added Silbane, also coming to inspect their sudden bounty.

Kisan took a bite as well and almost choked on the sudden explosion of sweet flavor. She finished that in two more bites and spit out the stone, her stomach telling her with a low growl that she'd waited too long to eat. The noise solicited a small chuckle from Ash, so she took a few steps to the side to eat in privacy.

A gurgle from a nearby rock wall, when investigated, revealed a small springlet of fresh water. She shook her head at this. "Seems we only have to think of things and they appear."

"Or that woman conjured it for us," said the firstmark, chewing what must have been his tenth date and again spitting the hard seed into his waiting palm. Curiously, she watched as he dug a hole near the tree and dropped his seeds into it, covering them when he was finished with fresh dirt. To her bemused look he said, "It's good luck to put back into the earth what you took."

Kisan laughed at him. "In a place of imaginary trees, you plant imaginary seeds."

Silbane deflected her jibe with soft encouragement, "A good practice. It cultivates more trees in the oases of the Altan Wastes." He dropped his seeds into a small hole he quickly dug with two fingers.

Ash frowned at Kisan, but remained silent.

Kisan raised an eyebrow at that, daring the firstmark to say something. When the man didn't, she gave him a dismissive sigh.

Ash moved closer to Silbane and said, "I worry for the princess. This detour will take more time, and we don't know her fate."

A sharp lance of pain behind Kisan's eyes forced her to drop her head for a moment. When she looked up, Silbane was looking at her with concern. "I can't hold onto the memories of Prime and his team forever."

Her mentor nodded and said, "Duncan's memories will also start to cause me more harm than good."

Her heart fluttered a bit at that, the ever-present knowledge that a part of Duncan remained within Silbane. She knew they'd both have to purge the memories of those they had collected. The longer they waited the more painful the process it would be. It was like trying to extract a silk scarf from a rose bush. Easy to throw over but difficult to remove without ripping.

Still, there was another thing on her mind.

"Despite Sonya's confidence, we've not fared well against these Aeris. Even with Duncan, Baalor was too much for us in our own world. Though we're stronger here, we were nearly killed by a small group of giants and that horde of mistfrights."

Silbane nodded. "Overwhelming numbers are on Lilyth's side."

"So we should agree that if we find Duncan, we prioritize getting Arek and leaving immediately."

"What about Yetteje and Niall?" demanded Ash. "I'll not leave without them."

Kisan considered that, then offered, "We can do both, firstmark. My point was we won't go on some fool's quest to recover Sonya or help in this war. Any allegiance with the red mage ends with getting the kids safely away."

"Yes," replied Ash, somewhat mollified, "of course that's acceptable." He kept eating, then noticed the master had not looked away.

In answer to his stare, Kisan said, "I'm sorry if I offended you earlier. Nothing was meant by it." She didn't mean it, but men needed some kind of face saving before they could get over their own egos, and she had an important question to ask. One that needed the firstmark's cooperation.

"No harm done," Ash replied, shrugging.

"I meant to ask: you've clearly had training. Where?"

Ash cleared his throat, his eyes not meeting hers but instead searching the skies. "My father taught me the art of the blade. I started training when I was very young."

Silbane tapped his head saying, "The archmage has many memories, most of which are incomprehensible. Yet he remembers a young Bladesman with the family name, Rillaran."

Kisan had wondered back at Bara'cor if Ash's lineage had anything to do with Tempest's attention. The blade was mercurial (and Kisan believed more than a bit narcissistic), but clearly yearned to be wielded by someone with power. The Rillaran line was ancient and had produced at least one of the lore fathers. Hearing Ash's prowess with the blade having its origin with the lore of Bladesman was not surprising. She'd seen him fight and his skill, though distinctly mannish with overused power, was remarkable.

Ash must not have felt the same way. Upon Silbane's comment he shook his head. "They were traitors to the king, banished and exiled."

"So are we," remarked Kisan dryly.

That stopped Ash, who dropped his head, his jaw muscles bunching around something unsaid. In silence he grabbed his pack and started stuffing a few dates into it, then picked up his canteen and disappeared around the small rock wall, ostensibly for some privacy.

Kisan turned to Silbane and said, "Strange reaction. Maybe I offended the noble firstmark again." She couldn't help but giggle.

"Give it a rest," Silbane said, sounding annoyed. "You've been testing everyone around you without reason."

A few moments passed in silence while Kisan munched on more of the sticky fruit, then she said, "So much of what we thought is different. It's a wonder we've survived so long. I think we need to be more focused."

Silbane, ever the one to seek peace with her, said, "Perhaps you're right."

Kisan then carefully asked, "Out of curiosity, any spells from Duncan's memory that you can use to aid us?"

It was said innocently enough, but she hoped to learn the extent to which the mindread of Duncan may have given her mentor capabilities that might interfere with her own. It was her way of cataloguing every tactical advantage they might have, and if need be, a safeguard should she have to face one or both over Arek's fate.

"I'm sure there are," he began. To her disappointment,

Silbane finished, "Sonya is not what I expected."

Kisan tilted her head at his sudden off-subject statement, her eyes calculating.

Silbane met her eyes and explained, "His memories are muddled and I can't control what comes into my head. At times I feel his all-consuming love and at others a dispassionate hatred, a desire to destroy all he sees. Maybe I should have killed him."

He was quiet, then quirked a smile and said, "One thing is certain – these Aeris live through two means: possession and what we call Ascension. In the latter, we stay in control."

Kisan completed his thought: "And in possession, they gain control."

"Yes," said the elder master, "but once possessed, that person is gone. They cannot be saved."

She shrugged. "And?"

The master put a hand to his head again. "His memories... Duncan knew this, yet he's here to save someone who died with an arrow through her heart. Why?" To Kisan's consternation he added, "How do you save a dead person?"

"The man is insane," Kisan said, shaking her head. "You can't give consideration to his actions."

Her former master looked frustrated when he replied, "So why does Sonya not join us and add another lore master to our ranks?"

He looked pointedly at Kisan, who suddenly felt as if her mentor was testing her again, as though she were still a student.

Her anger flared and she said, "I don't care about Sonya or Duncan."

He met her gaze directly and said, "Don't challenge me. I've forgotten more than you've ever learned."

She heard the iron in his voice and found a retort ready on

the tip of her tongue, but something in his expression stopped her. It was not the first time, but she saw deadly focus in his eyes. *Okay*, she thought, looking away. *Now isn't the time.*

Instead of engaging him, she shifted to his question. "Why would Duncan come back for someone dead?"

The change in her demeanor seemed to relax Silbane, who nodded. "Only two possibilities: if she's alive, he uses a gate to return to Edyn with her, and if she's dead he finds another body for her to possess."

Kisan leaned back, Silbane's point becoming clear. "And if he needs a gate or a body for his wife's spirit, who would best help him?"

"Lilyth," Silbane said, as if they'd finally gotten to his point. "Perhaps she promised something like this in return for destroying the fortresses of the Altan Wastes."

"You see this in his memories?" she inquired.

The master shook his head. "Not yet. Perhaps in time but I cannot hold onto them long enough to sort through it all."

She nodded at that, understanding. Then another question came to mind. "Do you think that was really Sonya?" Kisan's voice came out a little higher than usual, and she knew she probably sounded like a girl swooning over a legend.

Silbane shrugged, "Impossible to know, but she certainly seemed real, and distraught."

Kisan laughed and said, "I would be too if I had to endure that man again. What other woman could Duncan be arguing with here?"

Silbane let out a small laugh and looked around, "It's certainly a big world to find someone to disagree with at random." He was quiet for a moment, then he moved over and laid a hand on Kisan's shoulder and squeezed, "Perhaps you were right," he conceded, "and I should not have released him. I made an error in judgment."

Just then, Ash reappeared with everything stowed away. "Let's get moving. The danger to the kids grows the longer we sit here."

Kisan saw Silbane look at her askance, then nodded back that she was ready. It was her only concession to let him know she'd appreciated his apology. The man was hard to decipher, she thought, and harder still not to like. He could be infuriating, yes, but in times like this his good-naturedness always managed to win her over, at least temporarily.

Another bolt of pain lanced through her head, causing her to wince. "We need to get rid of these," she said, her anxiety replacing the pain. Yet she knew making headway to rendezvous with Duncan was paramount. They could both purge their memories there while Ash stood watch. She therefore was not surprised at Silbane's lack of an answer to her comment. He knew as well as she did their tactical priorities.

The elder master got up, facing the direction Sonya had indicated, and squinted. Kisan, standing behind him, could imagine seeing the Way as it flowed. What a beautiful sight it must be. Kisan *a*ppreciated the ebb and flow of nature more than Thera would ever have guessed.

A sudden intake of breath caught her attention. She turned to Silbane. "What?"

"A flash." His faded eyes narrowed as he looked at something Kisan couldn't see. "An eruption of negative power drawing at the Way."

"Where?" asked Ash, coming to stand beside Silbane.

Silbane pointed and Kisan followed his finger, seeing a ravine in the distance.

"Along that ridge, not far from here," he said.

"Is it Arek?" she asked, her eyes searching the ridge line.

Even with her vision enhanced by the Way, the distance was still too far to pick out any details, much less a person.

Silbane gave a hesitant nod and said, "I fear whatever power Arek wields may be growing stronger."

"What do we do?" asked Ash, now clearly torn by the two objectives, situated in almost opposite directions.

Kisan thought about it for only a moment, then declared, "Better to go where we think Arek is, than to the red mage. Duncan is a means to an end, but if Silbane sees the end…" she trailed off, looking at the elder master and hoping it was enough of a nudge for him to forego finding Duncan.

Silbane looked at them both, then said, "I agree. We've got to see if that flash was Arek."

Despite Sonya's warning, it was only a moment before two winged shapes clutching a third arrowed for the ravine, following nothing but the siren's song of lost love and hope.

AVALYON

Wisdom is the process,
each time you survive,
of replacing impulse with experience

- Rai'kesh, The Lens of Leadership

N iall was shocked by the cold as the henge gate opened around their small company. He was pressed into the middle of the knot of warriors, their shields interlocked and facing outward. The sickening sensation of falling began— and stopped just as suddenly. Their feet hit solid ground, like falling down a step.

A moment passed, then Gabreyl tapped one of the men on the shoulder. The silent command passed amongst the elves, who stood and slowly fastened their shields to their backs before assuming a parade rest eerily similar to that of the soldiers of Bara'cor: arm behind the back and fist over the heart.

"Where are we?" he asked the elven commander.

"Avalyon, Your Highness," Gabreyl said. "I apologize for the haste of our departure."

There was a profound sadness in the armsmark's eyes as he

hung his head, gestured Niall to follow him, and turned away. The soldiers surrounding them parted and Niall could see now that they stood upon a dais in a small chamber, perhaps twenty paces in every direction.

"Armsmark," Niall began haltingly, "... is everything all right?"

Gabreyl didn't turn, but his voice echoed back, "I failed the highlord and our family."

The misery radiating from the man was almost palpable. Clearly the highlord—a Galadine, Niall reminded himself— wasn't someone you wanted to disappoint. Knowing how he would feel if he had to face his own father after failing an important mission, Niall sympathized. He walked down the few steps to stand next to the elven commander and said, "You rescued me."

That thought made him wonder how his father fared. They'd not seen each other since... his mind did the quick calculation and was shocked. Had only a few days passed since Arek's arrival at Bara'cor? It felt like an eternity.

"Come, the highlord will want to see you immediately." Gabreyl gestured to a set of double doors, ornately carved with leaves and branches making up the sides and arch.

"Will you get in trouble?" Niall asked, worried if "punishment" would be more than a stern word.

"Trouble?" Gabreyl asked with a shrug. "Is my failure not enough?"

He didn't wait for a response but moved to the doors with Niall trailing, followed by the squad who, despite having left a good portion of their companions behind, did not break discipline. No banter or loitering... it was clear they had not been released from duty. Instead, they formed up with the precision of a royal escort for the two, and Gabreyl took the lead. They exited the room and into a hallway unlike any Niall had ever seen before.

Leafless branches wove around one another, creating a smooth tunnel of interlocking limbs through which sunlight shone. A light breeze wafted through, bringing with it the coolness of springtime. The light wood gave off a gentle fragrance recalling honeysuckle and jasmine, yet somehow also more earthy. He could see hallways open up at either end, yet they were clearly outdoors.

It was both peaceful and beautiful, and Niall found himself just standing in place, staring at the golden yellow shafts pouring in through the roof and pooling on the ground, the branches creating dappled cells of sunlight and shadow.

"The scents of home," Gabreyl said, putting a hand on Niall's shoulder. "You are most welcome here, Prince Galadine. Please, follow me."

The armsmark moved down the hallway with Niall in tow, guiding him down one passage and into a wider one that angled upward. As they ascended, Niall looked left and right through the walls, catching glimpses of other tube-like tunnels crisscrossing one another.

There was an intricate web of branching tunnels connecting to large platforms and smaller spheres, spread throughout the interior of what seemed to be a cavernous ball made entirely of living wood. Within this island sphere sat the vast city of Avalyon, lit golden by the setting sun as it shone through the wooden lattice of branches, an open invitation to the eternal season of spring.

Niall looked about in wonder, but he could not ignore the mystery of his host's identity. He couldn't truly enjoy the sights until he had answers. Who was this patriarch who gave Gabreyl and his elves the surname Galadine? What was his relation to

Niall, and worse, what would he do when Niall accused him of impersonating a Galadine?

He finally looked at the armsmark and said, "You claim to be Gabreyl Galadine." It was not a question.

"I am, Your Highness," Gabreyl admitted.

"My grandfather's portrait hangs within our great hall," Niall said.

Gabreyl arched an eyebrow and said, "Mediciio was an artist of great renown. I owe him my thanks for that portrait." Then the commander gestured to himself, "Though now, I doubt anyone could call it an accurate rendition."

Niall nodded, "Yes, his work is well known, however, upon the back of the portrait is a dedication." He looked at the elf, his challenge plain, hoping Gabreyl would admit to his subterfuge instead of suffering the embarrassment of being caught in a falsehood.

The elven commander eyes drifted right, then with a smile he said, "It reads, *Perfection is the bedrock of legend.*"

Niall could feel his eyebrows rising in disbelief. He shook his head and said, "I don't recall my grandfather having blue skin."

The armsmark looked back at him and smiled, "Nor I having a grandson. Change is the only truth in life, but I am pleased our line did not end with Bernal."

That brought silence as Niall weighed the man's words. Gabreyl was somehow his grandfather, still alive, and transformed into a blue-skinned elf with wings. If that wasn't preposterous enough, he was about to meet the ruler of this city who also claimed a shared ancestry. The punishment in Edyn for falsely claiming nobility was harsh. Those descended from the first families took their name and lineage seriously.

Niall sighed, reminding himself this was most certainly a

ruse, and it served to keep him alert to any other machinations these elves might try.

And yet, Gabreyl had gotten the dedication *correct*. That fact gave Niall pause, as his mind swirled to reconcile this with the impossibility of a Galadine in Arcadia.

Something else had been nagging him and he gave it voice. "Armsmark, I'm pleased we escaped, but my companion's safety is just as important. What happened to Arek?"

Gabreyl motioned to the elves to continue up their passage as he remained next to Niall. Then he met the prince's eyes directly, as if wanting to impart the truthfulness of his words. "We were sore-pressed, Your Highness. The Aeris and the dark ones they brought had pushed us back. I saw Lord Arek held by the leader, the one named Cainan. We had a choice: save one or risk both of you and Avalyon. I gave the order to transition without your companion. Forgive me."

Niall stood there for a moment, breathing and thinking. The armsmark stood still, his eyes hadn't wavered nor strayed from Niall's own.

What choice did he have? the prince thought. *Would it have been right to risk this entire city to invasion, just to rescue him? They were trapped here because of Arek.*

His concern didn't lessen, but his understanding grew. He looked at Gabreyl with sympathy and said, "You did the right thing, armsmark. Arek can take care of himself, but as soon as possible, I'd like to try and find him."

Gabreyl bowed, fist to chest and said, "Of course, my prince." He smiled, then motioned for Niall to continue up the passageway.

The tunnel they were in switched back on itself and opened to a platform where half a dozen other passages emptied. Above him was nothing, and for the first time Niall saw Avalyon spread out before him in all her beauty. Nothing prepared him for the sight, and for a moment he could only stare.

"Breathtaking, is she not?" the armsmark said humbly, for his words could not do the sight justice.

Niall stood upon a platform lit golden by the orange setting sun. Above, below, and around him spread Avalyon, a city built within the arms of a forest of trees that floated above the clouds, a floating forest island in the sky.

The trees stretched as far as he could see. It was as if it had grown and then interconnected until an entire land had formed, then had detached itself and floated away. He'd noted the sunlight before in the tunnels, but here it shone through this living woodland with an intensity that seemed supernatural, lances of light that hit verdant foliage and brown timber and gave the impression of a place forever paused in the cool crispness of that one rare afternoon.

His smile could not match the heady fragrance of this city, made from the very substance of what seemed like Niall's dreams. Small motes of pollen floated by, peaceful in their journey. Every smell reminded him of that perfect time between the coolness of spring and the dry heat of summer. He somehow knew as the sun dipped lower there would be almost an autumnal feel, as if the city enjoyed the best parts of the seasons of the year, all in just one day. For now he stood there, drinking in the sight of sunlight as it pierced through the green trees to cast long orange shadows.

Tunnels made of interwoven branches joined other platforms like the one he stood upon now. Roads made of wood connecting massive trunks, with vines acting as guidelines, stretching to and fro. It was an entire city built in harmony with nature.

Gabreyl seemed to want to move things along and came

closer, pointing up. "We will meet the highlord there."

Niall followed the armsmark's finger, his eyes tracking a massive trunk up so high he had to squint to see. It climbed through the canopy until it pierced the top, where Niall saw a hole of blue sky. Through that, he could just make out something formed from interlocking branches. As he stared, he could just make out another smooth sphere of wood that stood alone in the blue sky, the sun's fire glowing off its polished sides.

Niall did not see any roads leading that high and looked curiously at the armsmark.

"The Citadel of the Phoenix." Gabreyl smiled and spread his wings. "We will make our way there by flight, Your Highness." He turned to his men, who saluted fist to chest and then stepped back to wait near the passage they had just come from.

"I can't fly," Niall said, but then the obvious became clear and he nervously asked, "but you'll carry me?" He didn't mean to sound doubtful, but it was a long way up—or a long fall down. Looking over the edge of the platform brought a sudden vertigo, as there was nothing but open air crisscrossed with what seemed to be hundreds of enclosed tunnels, bridges, and platforms. He turned back just in time to notice the squad of elves depart at a run, with a surefootedness he'd never seen before, as if they adhered to the wood with every step.

"The city grew here for us, built by the highlord's will. He will never let us come to harm," he said, smiling reassuringly, "for we are all family here."

He seemed so sure of himself it buoyed Niall, giving him a small measure of confidence. He looked back down over the edge and asked, "The entire city floats?"

Gabreyl nodded. "Avalyon is no different from any other

isle in this realm, and yet it is still one of a kind. You survey your birthright, most noble-born."

Niall took a deep breath, steadying his nerves. He looked up and the distance seemed to grow with dizzying speed making it feel even farther. He tipped back and looked down quickly, squeezing his eyes shut, nodding before he changed his mind.

He felt the elven commander move behind him, grabbing him under his arms in a strong but firm hug, like armsmaster Talin did before wrestling training. He suddenly missed them all—Jeb, Ash, Tej—but most of all his father and mother, and a choking feeling knotted his throat.

Gabreyl must have sensed this because he said, "You are safe here amongst those who love you."

He nodded, but was not sure he really agreed. Yet something about the commander felt right, as if he was truly family. Then he felt himself walked slowly toward the edge.

"Do not open your eyes, Your Highness. We must fall to gather speed."

Niall nodded hesitantly, but when they began to tip forward, he couldn't help it and cracked his eyes open. The sight of nothing below but a plunge into empty air caused a blind panic and he pushed back hard with his legs, trying to stop his fall. Luckily, the armsmark must've been ready for just this because he launched himself into a smooth dive before Niall's panic caused them to stumble.

The sensation of falling was unlike anything he'd ever felt before. It was worse than the long swings during Bara'cor's festivals that had him plummet with a rope tied to his legs, only to then fly out in an arc over Shimmerene. He couldn't speak and fought for release.

"Easy, breathe out," came the measured voice of Gabreyl in his ear.

Niall hadn't realized he was holding his breath, and released it even as their fall turned into a swooping dive. He could feel their speed slowing somewhat and cautiously looked left and right. The armsmark's wings were spread, catching air as they wheeled and climbed, spiraling around the massive trunk. Hot air billowed from beneath, sweeping them up toward the hole of blue sky. Niall held out a hand to feel the warm breeze.

"We ride the warm winds up," came Gabreyl's voice again. "We will be there momentarily, my prince."

Niall didn't answer, his eyes wide as he drank in the scene. Avalyon was a city inhabited by blue-skinned elves. He saw hundreds—no thousands, he corrected himself—going about their work. Except here the inhabitants could walk on limbs with the same ease he walked on the ground.

He spotted a few other flying elves and asked, "Who are they?"

There was a pause, as if Gabreyl weighed answering, then he heard, "Elves are each born of an element: fire, water, and earth. Those you see flying are born of air."

"Like you?"

Niall thought he heard the smile in Gabreyl's voice when he replied, "Not exactly. You and I are closer to each other than you know. We are all children of the highlord."

Before Niall could question that strange answer, they burst from the canopy and into bright sunshine. Blue skies surrounded them on all sides, with an ocean made of clouds that spread to the horizon. Niall felt as if he looked down over this world like he was its god.

Yet it was not the vista that took his breath away—rather, it was the giant eagle made of intricately carved wood, its wings outstretched to hang protectively over a sphere made of the same. As they neared, the structure took on true grandeur in its size and majesty. Niall could see it was a massive construct, a throne room or meeting hall fit for a king.

Citadel of the Phoenix, the armsmark had called it, and Niall realized his error. At closer inspection, he saw a crest of feathers that came backward from its eyes like flame and the twin tail forked like a swallow's. All the statue lacked was the fire-red and black feathers a true phoenix was said to have.

The name now sounded apt, for it sat high above the floating forest, the wings catching the sun and drawing its fire within. It dwarfed any structure in Bara'cor, including the main hall. The wood had grown into interlocking whorls, and the trees entwined themselves in such a way as to make the entire piece a work of art as much as a place to meet. He noticed a ring made of wood to the other side of the hall, big enough for many men to walk through. He found himself recalling the henge gate. Perhaps this was a gate by which he and Arek could return to Edyn? His heart fluttered at the hope that perhaps the "highlord" could gate them home.

"Can we go back to Bara'cor?" asked Niall, his eyes locked on the ring.

"Not without great sacrifice, Your Highness," the commander replied softly.

Niall thought he heard a melancholy tone underneath his words but could not turn to see his face. Not knowing how to reply, he decided to keep quiet for fear of offending the solicitous man who could be his grandfather.

Gabreyl glided into a gentle descent, aiming for a circular platform just below the fierce head of the giant bird. His feet touched down softly and Niall was released to a rush of attendants.

"We should not tarry here, Your Highness," Gabreyl said, but nothing in his voice sounded like an order.

Niall nodded but didn't answer. His eyes were drawn to the edge of the platform, which overlooked the world outside of Avalyon, and to the white expanse below, rolling hills and valleys like bleached desert sand dunes, but made entirely out of cloudstuff. They spread to the horizon, an endless sea of white and orange lit by the setting sun. A gentle hand pulled his gaze back to the hall.

"Your Highness, the highlord awaits you below," said a blue-skinned elven female gesturing to a platform.

Armsmark Gabreyl had already begun walking in that direction but pointed with a wingtip at one of the attendants. "Please inform the others we have arrived."

That attendant bowed and said, "As you command, Your Grace."

With Niall in tow, Gabreyl ran lightly down the steps to the platform and then nodded to a waiting yeoman. The man pulled a lever and the entire platform began to descend into the sphere. Cleverly rigged guylines hung the platform evenly and surely around a central pillar so that the entire landing spiraled down into the spherical hall. It was both beautiful and a feat of engineering meant to impress those who came here, of that he was sure. It was certainly a marvel.

The spiral descent gave Niall the chance to take in the entire scene. Through the whorls and patterns in the walls he saw the forest island stretch out below, and surrounding all of this was the sea of clouds. The bottom part of the hall was a flat ground that spanned the entire diameter, the wooden upper half of the ball creating a domed ceiling for the highlord's great hall.

The throne room was resplendent with all the trappings one would expect in the royal court of a Galadine. A yellow runner edged in black ran up to the throne where two seats with the House Galadine colors, but the coat-of-arms was different.

Where there was usually a lion rampant on his father's chair, Niall noticed this house's sigil was… a phoenix.

That was a sigil everyone knew: the crest of Valarius Galadine. A sudden cold sweat broke out on his brow; his stomach fluttered, tickled by trepidation. If this truly was Valarius, then the phoenix was even more appropriate, signaling to all his rebirth and triumph after being left for dead.

Sentries stood at attention, their tabards bearing the royal black and gold he was so familiar with. The rest of the chamber had pennants on the walls making a complete circle around the enormous throne room, one for each of the rulers of House Galadine. Their flags were, for the most part, familiar to Niall from his hours learning the history of his family.

As his eyes scanned he found his father's flag to one side near the throne. It held the rampant lion of Bara'cor. That flag made him feel closer to home, as if this was his place. Above the throne itself hung the central and largest flag of the group, the royal phoenix emblazoned with wings spread to either side.

The platform came to a rest and Gabreyl bowed, gesturing for Niall to proceed first. The prince did so, carefully stepping down to the wooden hall floor, so reassuring in its solidity. It was hard to believe they were suspended in a floating forest high above whatever this world called the ground, assuming there was even such a thing here.

Everything seemed to grow from the wood, an organic extension of what the elves needed. Torch sconces, tables, even banisters and rails emerged without seams. The "fire" seemed to be made out of glowing insects, thousands grasping the end of a "torch." Their iridescence looked like embers but brighter, and upon closer inspection their flicker was just variances in their glow.

Armsmark Gabreyl came up to him, smiled, and said,

"Prince Galadine, we go there." He pointed to the throne, upon which Niall could make out a figure dressed in white.

Niall nodded and they made their way, stopping at a ring of guards. A contingent broke rank and fell in beside them as their escort. They walked in silence a bit farther, stopping when a guard held up a hand and a herald announced, "Hail, Prince Galadine!"

Niall waited and the figure on the throne gestured for him to come closer. The highlord was dressed in light armor made of something white, the color of which reminded him of dead ash wood. Long white hair fell from his head, held in place by a simple gold and black circlet. His skin was so white it looked like parchment, but when Niall neared he could see the face belonged to a man not much older than his own father. The eyes that stared down at him glowed yellow, as if they drank in the sun, yet Niall was not afraid. When their eyes met the man's face broke into a warm smile.

"Welcome, Niall. I've been eager to meet you."

The voice was deep, a commanding voice, one used to leading men in the din of battle. Niall looked at him, drinking in the details. This Galadine looked to be something in between elf and man, so Niall confirmed, "Lord Valarius Galadine?"

The man in white got up and descended the steps. All the people facing the throne bowed and backed a step away and Niall found himself alone, yet he still did not feel afraid. The towering figure put a warm hand on Niall's shoulder and began walking away from the throne, his stance and grip friendly as he steered Niall to accompany him.

"Yes, but please feel free to address me as just Valarius. I may be the highlord, but I'm also your uncle, though many generations removed."

The bluntness of the answer stopped Niall in his tracks.

Then he shook his head. "He's dead."

"Perhaps." The man calling himself Valarius seemed to be willing to consider his statement. Then he added, "Perhaps not?"

"You don't look like him, at least not from the paintings."

The man nodded, "Much here reflects what's believed. I strove to save Edyn from the demonkind, but how am I remembered by her people?" He looked down and his expression to Niall seemed sad. Then he looked back and smiled. "Edyn may believe the worst of me, but my elves love me as their father. You look upon what those two dreams have created."

Niall swallowed then softly accused, "You caused the Demon War and would have taken over Edyn."

"Should not a Galadine rule? Pay heed." He looked up and said, "Mikal, Ureyl."

Two winged shapes flew down from the heights, landing softly next to Gabreyl, who stepped forward and into line. The three angels bowed, their blue skin and horns clearly showing their elven heritage. Yet to Niall, the three looked like brothers.

Valarius gently shook Niall's shoulder, looking down at him with a smile. Then he looked back at the three men and said, "Niall, I present you Kings Ureyl, Mikal, and Gabreyl Galadine. They are your grandfathers of generations past, serving now as my armsmarks. We are family and will always tell you the truth."

Niall took an involuntary step back. "What do you mean?" He knew about Gabreyl, but to have it confirmed and then added to by meeting his entire pater line was almost too much to comprehend.

King Mikal Galadine stepped forward, saluting fist to chest, and said, "My tale is fit for another time, Prince Niall. It suffices to say that the world was misled. Your grand-uncle did all he could for Edyn, but we did not listen. Now we must make amends and stand together as family."

"You're elves!" Niall exclaimed.

King Ureyl stepped forward, "Now, but once we were just like you. The highlord took us from our ignorance. We were naïve and unknowing of our true might and worth, and of the war with the demonlord, Lilyth. Your grand-uncle stemmed the tide and sacrificed himself to save us. He called us to service from death, reminding us of our sworn duty to protect Edyn, a service we give gladly for the black and gold."

Niall shook his head, not wanting to believe, but something in the armsmark's voice rang true. He didn't think, instead blurting, "You can't be Galadines."

Gabreyl stepped forth and bowed. "When you asked if we are elves, I told you the truth. Yet you and I are closer than you think, bonded by blood, a fact you cannot deny in your heart. Look closely upon me, for I have told you already that I'm your father's father. We try to stem a war that even now claims the lives of the children of Edyn. Why else would a warrior like Sorath sacrifice himself for us?"

Niall stood dumbfounded. Of all the things these elves had said, Gabreyl's words rang truest. He looked hard at his face and realized why he felt he'd known him from the first time they met. He was young, but his grandfather had died young. Though he couldn't believe it, his heart told him Gabreyl spoke the truth.

Valarius then stepped forward. "Even now a contingent of my most trusted men have been sent to Bara'cor to lend aid to your father, a man I admire more than most. They will drive out the Aeris and hold Lilyth's gate. Then our forces will advance and restore order, protecting Edyn from her demonkind."

Niall looked at them all, now seeing past the blue skin, past the horns and sigils, to really look at their faces. He began to see things he had not seen before. The smiles that reminded him of his father and the same stern look that drew his eyebrows unevenly together. The worry on Gabreyl's face when he felt he'd failed Highlord Valarius.

He knew those looks, didn't he? Hadn't he seen them on the paintings adorning the halls of Bara'cor, or even on his own face from time to time? It could be that they were each a Galadine king from Edyn's past. Sincerity radiated from them as plainly as the coat-of-arms and pennants decorating this great hall. He was surrounded by the weight of history carried on the shoulders of his forefathers, all of whom seemed to care a great deal for him. *And,* he asked himself, *why go to all this trouble just to convince me?*

He looked back at Valarius and asked in a small voice, "What happens next?"

The highlord smiled and answered, "We buy peace for the realms through service and sacrifice. We rule with justice and temperance. We are House Galadine. Nothing less will suffice."

THE KING'S MEN

A wise commander listens to veterans of any rank.
Their knowledge has been hard won in the crucible of war.

- Galadine House of Arms, Battle's Focus

King Bernal Galadine looked out of the corner of his eye at the elven warrior Malak. The man was pragmatic, wasting little time on anything other than reforming his men into squads of five. He deployed four squads to hold the entry points into their area, then turned to Bernal.

"The Aeris who have no host bodies—what you call demons—can move through the walls of Bara'cor. While we cannot stop this, our weapons are proof against them."

"What about your men providing them bodies?" inquired the king.

At that, Malak smiled and said, "Ahh, King Galadine, these are not my men, but *your* elves, and we cannot be possessed."

The king couldn't help but like this commander. A grudging respect began to grow as Bernal, quickly assessing their tactical position, and asked, "Why is a firstmark sent to command a mere platoon?"

The blue-skinned warrior gravely answered, "It was of

utmost importance to the highlord."

"Then what's your mission?" Bernal pressed.

Sparrow returned to report they were ready to move. Acknowledging her, the armsmark turned back to Bernal and said, "My orders are simple. Keep you alive, secure the fortress, and expel the Aeris."

"And how will you accomplish this?"

Malak paused, then said, "You know your fortress better than me. Where is the Gate Lilyth's forces used?"

Bernal blinked, thinking back to what Yetteje had said. It was downward, near the cisterns, but the location she'd described had never been seen before. Bernal and his men had met her near the base of a stairwell that curled up from that point. He remembered the breathless pursuit, being hauled up those stairs by a girl a quarter of his size, and their retreat to the storeroom before facing Baalor.

He was reluctant to answer, despite the fact that they had his son. Instead, he asked, "Why?"

Firstmark Malak looked at Bernal and said, "The Gate is a natural chokepoint. We hold there and send word to the highlord, who will then reinforce us. Then we hunt these Aeris down and destroy them."

At that, his men let out a short, "hoorum!," and in unison pounded their spear butts once into the ground. Clearly they relished the idea of hunting demons.

Bernal took a deep breath. The healing that Sparrow had started continued within him, an itch inside he couldn't scratch, leaving behind a gentle warmth.

He turned to the firstmark and asked, "And when will my son be returned?"

"When the highlord reinforces us, you will be reunited," Malak promised. "Trust he would never bring harm to another

Galadine."

Something in the soldier's tone pricked at Bernal's ears. "And how do you return? The same way?"

The elven warrior pursed his lips, his eyes searching Bernal's own as if looking for something. A moment passed, then the man looked down.

"King Galadine, there is no return for us. We are the only proof against the Aeris, sent here to help you in the coming war. You will not withstand Lilyth's might without our help."

Bernal paused, uncomfortable with the idea that Bara'cor was now the staging area for not one, but two invading forces, though the latter was elves coming to his rescue. It didn't matter to him that they came to combat the Aeris, for what would they do once that threat was gone? Rarely did an occupying force leave peacefully, and bending knee to an elven highlord was no better than to a demon queen.

Malak seemed to understand his reluctance and said, "You are a Galadine, just as the highlord. You will rule here after this is finished. He would want no less."

Bernal held up a hand. "Firstmark, if we are to help each other then let us speak plainly. How do I know my son will be returned safely to me?"

"We saved your life and I give you my word. Is that not enough?"

Clearly it wasn't. "If your highlord can send you here, why does he not send thousands to take the fortress? Why only a single platoon?"

"The gate created by the highlord came at great sacrifice. It could only be opened for a few moments, enough to get us through." Malak paused, as if trying to give weight to what he'd just said, then he continued, "We must secure the true Gate and then alert the highlord. Only then can he reinforce us."

Bernal looked over the assembled warriors and said, "How can the Aeris withstand our weapons, firstmark?"

"Mundane weapons are not true to the task. The Aeris merely shift out of the dead and are ready to possess again." Malak smiled then said, "We are different, born of the highlord's blood and the Way." He shrugged, looking down at Bernal's blade. "Your weapon is not mundane, and we have more we can distribute to any of your men we find."

The firstmark paused then added meaningfully, "Our weapons eradicate the Aeris, permanently."

Bernal replied in a soft voice, "And theirs can do the same to you. You're only some fifty or so men. What if you fail?"

The firstmark gave Bernal a sardonic smile. "If we cannot secure the Gate then we must destroy it, and our only way home." He paused, then moved a step closer and asked in a softer voice, "Do you understand the nature of the war being waged by Lilyth?"

"They seek to possess us," Bernal said.

"Why?" countered the firstmark. "Never think of her as simply malevolent or whimsical. She has lived longer than all of us put together, and has a purpose in all things."

Bernal turned to the blue-skinned commander, intrigued by this line of questioning. "Enlighten me. Her purpose in this case?"

"Possession frees her people to live in this realm," Malak said. "With bodies they can live out normal lives free from the changes wrought by Edyn's dreams."

"Dreams?" Now Bernal was confused. "What do you mean?"

Malak cocked his head at that, and it was clear he thought Bernal knew already what he was about to say. Then the firstmark put a hand on Bernal's shoulder and said, "Your people bring these Aeris to life with your dreams and worship. Given life, they spend eternity helpless, as your dreams change their world. Sons and daughters, wives and husbands, die because your faith waxes and wanes. Imagine watching your son slowly fade away, knowing there's nothing you can do to change it. Lilyth has grown weary of this."

Bernal stepped back, shocked, Malak's words a concept hard to grasp at its core. They brought these demons to life? He felt like a person who suddenly saw the actors preparing behind the curtains of a play.

"Then why not attack? There are surely more demons and nightfrights than all the people of Edyn. We'd be overwhelmed."

"Has she not attempted this repeatedly? The one truth she discovered was her invasions killed the very people she would possess. What if you had ten coins to give a hundred men, and in the giving five coins were lost, leaving even less to share? What would the hundred men do?"

"Bicker, quarrel, fight..." Bernal whispered, looking down, "kill."

"Indeed," nodded Malak, agreeing. "Do not stop your thinking there. Why did she raze the other fortresses that held gates of their own? Why pursue only this path, through Bara'cor?"

Bernal did not know, and for once it seemed that Malak did not have an answer either. "There's a pattern not easily discerned. However, Lady Lilyth has made a tactical error and the highlord wishes me to seize upon it and turn it to our advantage."

"Error?"

Malak nodded, "The other three fortresses. While that act allows her to focus her assault on Edyn from a single beachhead, it also limits her."

"And if we hold this Gate?" began Bernal.

"We effectively cut her off from Edyn," completed the firstmark. "It won't stop her forever, but it will delay her enough for the highlord to act. He can bring his forces to bear on the one place she has gathered."

Bernal paused, his mind already calculating. Then he asked, "Wait, firstmark, if Lilyth is as shrewd as you give her credit for, she must have known the risk. Why chance it?"

It was Malak's turn to consider. "As we said, she made an error."

"You talk like she made a wrong turn on the way to the market. Taking three fortresses requires planning and care. Why not take two and leave two standing, effectively forcing Edyn to split her forces? Why not leave three, or even all four? It would have made finding her egress harder and protecting against it more difficult. It is not a militarily sound tactic to limit your options, is it?" Bernal's voice and eyes dared the firstmark to dispute him.

He watched Malak turn this over in his mind. The man reminded him of Ash, young and full of energy. His own firstmark was also a careful strategist, trained by the very best at the war college in Shornhelm. He hoped this elven commander had Ash's pragmatism as well.

Then slowly, the firstmark nodded but said, "While I agree with you, we need more information. We cannot gain it while Bara'cor is infested."

Bernal opened his mouth to agree, but Malak held up a hand and said, "The highlord has given me very specific orders. Like me, he has no love for demons, and a great love for his family."

Bernal raised an eyebrow at that, looking up and down at the blue-skinned elf.

"You think me demonborn?" Malak laughed and said, "I am born of the blood of Highlord Valarius Galadine, a living testament to his love and will."

He grasped Bernal's hand in an iron grip that felt warm, the skin alive, and looked out over his command. "We could not exist here in Edyn were this not true, and we serve House Galadine proudly because of the highlord's gift of life."

The man's eyes shone, pride lending his proclamation an edge of raw emotion mixed with utter sincerity. There was no doubt the commander was committed to his highlord. That was certain, but did that commitment extend to Bernal, as he'd pledged? Bernal knew the only way to find out was to let the firstmark's actions speak for themselves.

Malak turned to Sparrow. "Form up the men. Two squads are assigned to protect the king at all times." The woman Bernal had come to think of as his second-in-command bowed and headed off, shouting orders.

Malak then met Bernal's gaze again and asked, "Will you lead us to Lilyth's Gate?"

Bernal looked down, his hand still gripped by Malak's own, his mind whirling over the consequences of every decision he might make. It would take time to piece out Lilyth's true intent. He would need to talk to the firstmark more. The path to the cisterns would take time—enough to gather more information and to judge the measure of this elven commander. If what he said was true, Bernal could potentially stop Lilyth's war against Edyn before it ever got started and rescue his son. However, a natural distrust of offers forced through leverage made him wonder if this man would keep his word about returning Niall.

His grip tightened on Malak's and he said, "I've no choice but to take you at your word, Firstmark." Bernal thought, then said, "Baalor destroyed the supply room here, but there's

another one, a few levels down. There may be survivors there."
He pumped the commander's hand once, then let go and moved
to a stairwell leading down into the fortress.

Reducing your choices to invade did not make sense to
Bernal, and Lilyth had done exactly that. Something else was
afoot, and he realized Malak might not know. Bernal didn't
have much time to formulate a plan before they would find
themselves surrounded by the enemy again. If they could not
hold the Gate, he'd never see his son. That part was abundantly
clear.

That last thought stuck with him, and at the base of the
stairs he turned and asked, "You can hold this Gate, Firstmark?"

Malak paused, then nodded while scanning the area, his
eyes alert for any signs of the Aeris. "We have the means."

Bernal watched him, looking for any hint of betrayal or
deceit, but could find none. The man's eyes were resolute, his
gaze never wavering. If he was lying, Bernal would never want
to play five cards with him. He gave a short nod, then headed
down the stairs escorted by two squads of elven warriors.

Behind him came Firstmark Malak and the rest of the
platoon. Bernal looked back for a moment and noted their
discipline and training. At least they seemed ready for anything.

THE WAY WITHIN

My brothers tell me fear is quickly gone,
when trying to do something not entirely stupid
like fighting for one's life.

- Toorval Singh, Memoirs of a Mercenary

Yetteje jumped over a giant's back, sending two arrows unerringly toward Ash's position. One took a giant focused on the firstmark in the forehead, the other a mistfright circling up his leg. Her aim was preternatural, her perception of combat slowing to allow her the time to make every movement precise and economical. It was as if something gave her every move consummate skill and grace.

Valor thrummed as arrows flew, each draw magically creating another. It was the perfect partner to her nimble dance of death.

The princess ducked under a thrust and jumped, kicking out. She caught a spear-wielding giant under the chin and snapped his head back, following it with an arrow fired up through his throat. As he fell the combat swirled around her and for a brief moment she found herself a bubble of calm.

She could see Kisan trying to stand after a blast had hit her wing, her back shimmying up against Silbane. Just then, Ash emerged from behind the shattered wing, staggering to his knees in a daze. Yetteje drew to cover him, but the firstmark fell forward, stabbing Tempest into the ground.

An explosion sounded, a muffled *crump* that shook her insides with its low concussion. The blast was directed down into the earth, followed immediately by a shock wave that threw her on her rump. A cloud of debris and dirt blocked her sight as she hit the ground and bounced painfully, coming to rest against the body of something dead.

When she finally cleared her eyes, everyone had been taken off their feet by the blast. Where her friends had stood there now existed only a crater. It was a gaping pit, a maw that showed no sign of the rest of the party. Had they been taken by the explosion?

She avoided a thrust by vaulting over yet another giant, lashing out with her bow like a hand weapon to clear some room, then firing arrow after arrow into the mass surrounding her. Wherever the arrows went, mistfrights or giants died. She sidestepped and dodged her way to try to get closer to the hole but the mass of warriors arrayed against her was too much. They closed in, a ring of leering mouths and yellow eyes watching hungrily as she fell back, alone.

Then Anhur stepped forward and said, "Your companions have abandoned you. Submit and we will take you to the Lady."

Yetteje's eyes narrowed, catching the light with a faint amber glow. Her grip tightened on Valor and she held the bow ready. Then she answered, "Whoever steps first, dies."

Anhur hesitated, his eyes jumping from her face to her weapon. She knew what he must be thinking: *Could she draw, aim, and fire before we overrun her?* She sharpened her focus on the leader of the giants, her gaze never wavering. She would take Anhur with her, of that fact she was certain. The sudden fear emanating from him told her he knew the same.

Just then a trumpet sounded, a short staccato of notes, a call to arms. Yetteje swiveled her head in time to see two winged beings in armor wade into the rear of the giants' line. They hit with the force of a hammer and the collective mass of giants and mistfrights rippled from their impact.

Anhur cried, "Flanking, reform!"

His force of giants responded, immediately pivoting their formation into an hourglass shape with Yetteje and the armored angels at the widest opposite ends. A glowing spear was thrown, blasting into the two new combatants in a shower of lighting and a clap of thunder.

They emerged smoking from behind a shield made by their wings, seemingly unscathed by the lightning storm that had enveloped them just moments before. Whomever these new attackers were, they seemed impervious to the giants' weapons. They laid into the mistfrights and giants with a bloodlust that made them, at least in Yetteje's mind, look like gods of war come to life, wading into the fray, striking with swords and flicking with the bladed feathers of their wings. In fact, their armor looked a lot like that which protected Silbane and Kisan. The line of mistfrights fell before them like wheat under a scythe. To Yetteje, they looked magnificent.

Yetteje didn't waste time gawking, instead firing arrow after arrow as quickly as possible, trying to thin out her opponents while ducking and dodging their strikes. She was doing well, but knew the odds were still not on her side. Sheer numbers gave her enemies the ability to make many mistakes, and she could not make even one.

She ducked under another swipe, spinning on a knee and

firing three arrows in quick succession. These caught two giants and a mistfright, blasting them backward and into the mob of her attackers. She rose, just in time to see the line surge forward, their weapons raised. Standing here meant certain death so she fell backward, still firing.

She landed heavily on her back, the force of the fall jarring her right to the bone, but she didn't stop. The mass continued and Yetteje once again made up her mind up to take as many with her before they overwhelmed her position. She lay with Valor held horizontally across her stomach, firing between her knees again and again, knowing death was inevitable.

Then a blade erupted out of a giant's mouth, felling him not even a body's length from her. Another dropped next to the first, decapitated by something razor sharp. Yetteje looked up in awe as the two armored angels appeared, using wings and blades to cut their way through to her.

They broke through in an explosion of blood and giant parts, taking station on either side of her and facing the horde, each with one wing bent in front like a shield. Without a word she rose to a knee and started firing from in between them, killing anything that moved toward the two, trusting they would shield her from the surging line.

They did that, and more, using one wing to defend Yetteje, and the other along with their blades to attack. They laid out crisscrossing strikes of razor-edged steel and a cloud of feather knives to deadly effect. Their wings cut down foes left and right, leaving a mangled collection of dead giants heaped before them, surrounded by a pall of black mist from the dead mistfrights. That black mist spread like a low-hanging fog at their feet, a visible testament to the carnage they wrought.

Then, as suddenly as the tide had been overwhelmingly against them, it turned. The giant Anhur called a retreat to his side, never addressing them as he pulled his survivors from the bloody field.

The last of her would-be captors fled back into the white-wooded forest. A few moans sounded, giants who did not know yet that they were dead. A calm descended around them, the forest becoming still. The black mist of lesser Aeris dissipated, either sifting down into the earth or dying, Yetteje didn't know which. Given what she'd seen at Bara'cor however, she very much doubted they were dead. Only the bodies of the fallen marked that anything had happened here at all.

"You fought well, little cat," said the one in silver armor edged in blue, towering over her. His visor snapped back to reveal a man with kind eyes and a mouth caught in a half smile.

The one in orange and red armor looked around the field of battle and said, "We'll need to move quickly." His voice was deeper, but hoarse, as if he seldom used it. He moved through the fallen, offering the mercy of a quick death by the tip of his long-bladed spear, his features resolute.

The first winged warrior held out a hand, which Yetteje took, managing to grasp only two of his massive fingers. "My name is Orion, and this grim companion," he pointed to the other with his chin, "is Helios."

The other acknowledged her with a nod even as he stabbed down and through the chest of a giant, his focus still on his task. At first Yetteje thought his act one of mercy. Watching him now she caught the inkling that survivors meant someone left to tell the tale of what happened.

"Tej," answered the princess with the short form of her name, no reason to offer them any more than she had to. "What are you?"

Orion's eyes crinkled with mirth. "We are Watchers. We serve the Conclave, and the true Keeper, Thoth. Would you be surprised if I said we side with you?"

Yetteje shook her head, remembering what Tempest had said. However, it was someone else's plight that was foremost in her mind. "My father says... said, actions speak louder than words... You came to my aid." The correction was purposeful, a reminder that her father was gone.

"Indeed," Orion said, sheathing his blade, "though it seemed you had things in hand." He did a quick scan of their surroundings, and apparently satisfied, turned his attention back to Yetteje.

He met the princess's tawny gaze and said, "Have you heard another's name?"

"No," she replied, "should I have?"

"Watchers recognize in each other, those who are on the path to Ascension." Orion looked meaningfully at her and said, "As you are, Tej. Yet you say you've heard nothing?"

Helios interrupted by saying, "We don't have much time."

There was an insistence in his tone that spoke to more than simple impatience. Of the conversation about hearing a name, Orion's short explanation hinted at too much to unravel here and now. If the one called Helios was worried, then by the nature of this place, she was worried.

Orion looked back at Yetteje and said, "You will not be safe unless you accompany us, at least until we are clear of Olympious and the Lady's lands."

"I need to find my friends. They were over there," she said, pointing to the depression created by Tempest's blast. She made her way over to the edge, then stopped in shock. Orion came up behind her and laid a massive hand on her tiny shoulder.

"I'm sorry," he said.

She shrugged off his hand, looking down the hole that ended, to her amazement, in clear sky. "Two of my friends are like you. They have wings."

"Like us?" replied the winged giant in armor. "How so?"

Yetteje thought about it. *Perhaps these warriors could be allies, but someone would have to take the first step.* With that thought in mind, she told them, "The leader of the ones who attacked us called my friends Artymis and Azrael."

At the names Orion fell back a step, his eyes wide. He looked at Helios, who had also stopped his grim work to listen. Both looked equally amazed. Finally, Orion looked down at Yetteje and asked, "You say they fell through this hole?"

Yetteje nodded. "Blasted through by Tempest, a blade."

Orion's eyes narrowed at that and he came to one knee and hunched so his face was level with Tej's own. "The Kinslayer is known to us and we do not mourn her fall. Now, tell me truly, do you align yourself with her?" He didn't sound threatening, but something in his tone made Yetteje take his question very seriously.

A moment went by, then two. Finally, she said, "No... the sword is making one of my friends use her."

She met his gaze without blinking, watching until his eyes softened and he nodded. Then she looked back at the hole her friends had fallen through, unsure of what to do next.

Orion looked out over the edge, his eyes calculating, "Fear not. If it is truly Artymis and Azrael as you say, that is a good omen, little cat."

"Stranger things have happened," said Helios, his deep voice comforting in the blasted landscape surrounding them. He plunged his spear down again, going back to his grisly work.

"Is that necessary? Aren't they just going to come back?" Yetteje inquired.

Orion said, "Yes, but it will take time for new bodies to be granted, time we need. Leave Helios to what he does best. He knows we have little time and a far distance still to travel."

"Where?" she asked.

Orion drew himself up to his full height and pride shone in his eyes as he said, "To my final Trial. If I prove worthy, I will Ascend and join your friends."

Yetteje's eyes narrowed. "And what happens to me?"

"We'll not abandon you, little cat," Orion said with a smile. "Come." He knelt and offered her a perch on his forearm. "We will travel more swiftly by air. Rest assured you will come to no harm, and your questions will be answered."

Yetteje thought about it for only a moment before nodding. Climbing aboard, she seated herself in the crook of his arm.

Orion looked at Helios and nodded. The sunburnt Watcher stabbed a final time, then scanned the area for any signs of life. Clearly he saw none, for he looked back at Orion and said, "We can depart."

Without a word, the two leapt up, their great wings catching air as they soared out above the treetops and into the bright blue sky.

The world of the Aeris spread out below her, breathtaking in its beauty. She was surprised to see lands dotting the sky like floating islands, each independent from its fellows. Nothing she'd seen before had prepared her for this. The burnt orange sun, bigger than she was used to, shone with an afternoon intensity that lent every cloud top a lining of yellow orange fire.

So many! The sheer immensity of the vista stretching from horizon to horizon made Yetteje feel insignificant and small. Where, in all this vastness, would she find Ash and the others? Were they even alive? Her heart raced at the fear of being abandoned in this strange new world.

She forced herself to remain calm, using the act of breathing to maintain her control. She would not lose hope, she would not fear. Slowly, something of the place permeated her, filling her with fortitude. She opened eyes she'd not remembered closing and took in the beauty of the ocean of clouds laid out below, and the warmth of the sun on her face from above.

Somewhere out there, she knew her friends would be waiting. She would find them.

DIPLOMAT'S SHIELD

If you must break the law,
do it to seize power:
and leave none alive to speak of your actions.

- Kensei Shun, The Lens of Shields

Algren Justeces sat at one end of the semicircular table in the Senatorial Hall. The chamber was large, designed to accommodate the public for hearings on matters of state. It was immense, designed to accommodate hundreds of citizens, and opened into a raised circular area from where he and the other legates officiated, with vertical columns set on either side framing a central seating area arranged into long parallel benches.

Stationed at each column were soldiers wearing the crimson and white of Haven's elite Praetorians. They stood impassive, like living statues, sworn to uphold and defend the Senate with their very lives.

"You seem wistful," remarked a deep voice to Algren's right.

He turned to face Merric Spaiten and said, "No, just thinking." Algren adjusted his seat and leaned back. "The queen comes before us a third time, and my heart regrets what we must do."

Spaiten pursed his lips and nodded. "No word from the

Kings of the Wastes, save Bernal sending his wife to beg for aid at the expense of Haven's defense. We do what we must, for Haven."

Algren nodded slowly and said, "Perhaps, yet in my heart I dread it. The power to destroy Land's Edge... rumors of demonkind and dark magics, specters of sorrow that hunt our children again."

"Which is why we must act and hold this line. Captain Kalindor and his company are vital to the defense of the city."

"And the queen?"

Spaiten took a deep breath and looked around, then leaned in close to his co-conspirator. "Think... the last few weeks have seen events unfold accomplishing things we never could. House Aeonian and Cadan have not been heard from and are declared lost. The Imperial King has undoubtedly perished in the explosion that crumbled Land's Edge. The heirs to both House Galadine and Tir are likely lost in the same devastation." He smiled, his eyes meeting Algren's and his hand clasping the older man's shoulder, giving him a reassuring squeeze. "Providence has left our hands clean. A fresh start for our houses."

"What of Ellis?" asked the regent quietly, though he knew the answer.

Merric's eyes narrowed. "The Great Houses are gone, Algren, and the remnants must be swept away. Do not worry, you will soon be King of Shornhelm and a new House Justeces will rise to replace House Cadan. It has been arranged. Stay true."

A trumpet sounded, signaling the arrival of the queen and her party, and the great double doors to the Senatorial Hall opened. The Queen of Bara'cor entered, flanked by Captain Kalindor and Legate Tir. Behind them came sixteen knights, her elite personal guard.

"Hail Imperial Queen Yevaine of House Galadine," cried the herald. "Hail Captain Tyrus of House Kalindor and Legate Ellis of House Tir."

* * * * *

As the herald announced the party the two members of the Senate rose and bowed. They were joined by the Chancellor of Haven, Finras Tyn, a tall man with dark eyes. His body was thin, the product of a lifetime of managing bureaucracy from behind a desk. He knew he was no warrior, but prided himself on his adherence to the laws of Edyn. People were the noblest of all animals, but separated from law and justice, the worst.

He entered from a door behind the officiating table and slowly made his way to the center chair. The regents of Dawnlight and Shornhelm arranged themselves to his left and right, respectively.

Even as the party moved to the central floor, Legate Tir bowed and circled around, coming to take his place at the table next to Regent Justeces. The only unoccupied chair left was the one for the Legate of Bara'cor, which the queen now ostensibly held to cast her single vote. However, since she was a petitioner, she kept her place on the central dais and faced the men who would now decide her fate, along with that of Bara'cor.

Chancellor Tyn was a man of few words, pragmatic and focused on safeguarding Haven. His family had been instrumental in recognizing the Galadine's imperial rule of the land, a structure he knew was necessary to keep the peace, however archaic. Though they were a monarchy, having the Senate balance divine right with elective appeal had been a necessary step to a more modern and mature government.

Though he sympathized with the queen's plight, he had not voted with her. He wouldn't leave Haven unguarded and as such had watched her lose her last petitions two votes to three.

Now the queen was here a third time and his patience had begun to wear thin, even for Her Royal Majesty. He put a hand to his forehead, then met her steely gaze with one just as unflinching and said, "Your business this time, Your Majesty?"

"I wish to take my leave, Chancellor." Her voice came out strong and direct, with no trace of doubt. In fact, it was this directness that took him by surprise.

Tyn narrowed his eyes. "I beg your pardon?"

"I wish to take my leave, Your Grace. My husband has need of Captain Kalindor and his Company, and it is clear Haven will not extend its hand. I must hurry back to reinforce him. We only ask for the benevolence to leave behind the young and elderly in Haven."

Merric Spaiten rose and said, "We cannot allow Haven to lose your men for her defense, Your Majesty. Bara'cor is lost."

"Bara'cor stands. Only the pass has been damaged," challenged the queen.

"The explosion leveled half of Land's Edge!" exclaimed the regent, looking at the queen as if she had lost her mind. He turned to the chancellor and continued, "It centered on Bara'cor. What could be left?"

Chancellor Tyn looked back at the queen and said, "Yevaine, I sympathize with—"

"You will address me as Queen Galadine or Your Majesty, Chancellor. Let us not forget we are noble born." She looked pointedly at the two regents, who seemed to shrink back at that.

The chancellor paused, then continued, "Your Majesty, I sympathize with your predicament but Regent Spaiten is correct. The explosion was heard halfway to Sun Tree. What could have survived? Do you have proof of life?"

Yevaine dropped her head, her eyes closed. "He's alive and I mean to take my men and find him. There are other ways up the pass known to us—ancient ways."

Regent Justeces stood and cleared his throat. He looked pained and uncomfortable to be speaking and began haltingly, "Your Majesty... we must focus on the living, those here in Haven. Surely whatever destroyed Bara'cor will come here next. We cannot allow you to take... to leave with men necessary for our defense."

"As long as he's alive I will exercise my right and command my men under the Imperial King's name."

Ellis Tir then stepped forward and said, "You know I have always been a loyal supporter of House Galadine... but in this circumstance I must agree with my colleagues."

Raised eyebrows from the other regents greeted that, but before any could respond Captain Kalindor shouted, "You scheming traitor! You lie in wait, then switch sides for convenience! King Galadine lives and she commands in his name!"

"Not if he's declared dead," Ellis said, almost to himself. Then a chagrined look came across his face and he stepped back, his eyes downcast.

"Order!" shouted Finras, banging his gavel. The dense wood echoed in the large hall, snapping everyone's attention to him. "We will abide by the law!"

He took a breath to calm himself, then looked to his left and right. Merric's expression made the man look like he was about to burst, so the Chancellor tilted his head and said, "Legate, if you have something to say, the floor is yours."

Merric stood and bowed, then addressed the chamber.

"House Galadine has made the Laws of Succession quite clear."

Yevaine's eyes darted to Ellis, contempt on her face. "The Laws of Succession are archaic and without merit. My husband had planned to repeal them in favor of more enlightened views."

"Be that as it may," Merric replied, "the current laws are still very much in force. We won't dispense with them so quickly in light of the rumors of demons and rifts. The succession of the Imperial Crown goes to the next male heir of noble birth."

"And just who might that be?" demanded the queen, looking at Merric. "Not you, certainly."

Chancellor Tyn thought for a moment. He knew the genealogies well, and after a moment confirmed what the others likely already knew.

"Without proof of life from Bara'cor, Shornhelm, EvenSea, or Dawnlight, succession would fall to... Legate Ellis Tir." He looked at the man with a bemused expression, almost a half smile.

"I can't think of a better king," offered Merric. "Your Majesty would still serve as Legate of Bara'cor, of course," he said, addressing the queen with open arms.

"You would dare..." Yevaine took two steps back, a hand to her throat. Then she gathered herself and pointed, her eyes on Ellis Tir. "You planned all this... the death of House Galadine? What does loyalty mean to you?"

Chancellor Tyn held out his hands for silence. It was unseemly for them to shout at each other like children in a schoolyard. "Nobles, please, act with decorum. The Laws of Succession are clear and unequivocal. Let me take counsel and then offer a path."

He then moved back to confer with the regents and Legate Tir. Their whispers could not be heard down on the dais but

Finras led them quickly to the only agreement possible, to uphold the succession. The chancellor turned back and addressed the queen.

"We believe the Imperial King has perished in the defense of Bara'cor. I regret to say we feel the same for the two heirs of Houses Galadine and Tir. Shall I put this to a vote, or will you acquiesce and take your place as Legate of Bara'cor? As such you would keep House Galadine alive, at least until we can ascertain if there's another with Galadine blood."

"What choice is that? It puts my men under Haven's control and has me treating with traitors, craven men such as the three who stand whispering beside you now!"

Regent Merric Spaiten stepped forward at that and snapped, "Nevertheless, we can choose a less favorable post for the former Queen of Bara'cor. What say you?"

Captain Kalindor surged forward but was held back by his men.

"Captain, stand down!" Finras said, banging his gavel again. Kalindor was so... uncouth. The man was a bull, pushing his way into whatever irked him. He made up his mind to restrict the captain's attendance to these functions for all future events.

Yevaine put out a restraining hand. "It will do no good, Captain." Finras blessedly heard her repeat his last order. "Stand down."

The queen had the decency to wait until the captain sheathed his half-drawn blade before turning back to address him. She, at least, understood protocol.

"Chancellor, it seems I have little choice but to accept."

Merric turned to the chancellor and said, "There's no reason to wait. Complete the Renunciation now."

Finras paused, then nodded and said, "Are there any

objections?"

Yevaine stepped forward and spread her arms, frowning. "Why the sudden rush? I know he's still alive."

The chancellor sighed, frustrated but understanding her devotion. He looked at her and tried to give her a reassuring smile.

"Your Majesty, of all people you must understand the need for a clean succession. War is upon us. Do you think we serve the land best by waiting?"

He watched as her head dropped. Her shoulders rose and fell once, perhaps in grief, but then she shook her head. Again, she'd proved to him that nobility wasn't something one could just assume. One had to be born into it. He sighed, feeling a chord of sympathy for the young queen.

"Kneel then and repeat after me."

Queen Yevaine knelt and looked up at the Senate, grief etched on her face and eyes. That emotion seemed to grow as her knee touched the floor. The loss of King Galadine and her son was clearly foremost in her mind. To Finras this felt more like a funeral than a Renunciation ruling. He sighed again, wishing things could have turned out differently.

"I stand aside by rule of the Senate and support the search for the next true heir of House Galadine," intoned the Chancellor.

The queen repeated the words, her voice dead and emotionless.

"I accept the decision of the Senate, and stand firm in my commitment to this land. By my own hand, I set aside my crown."

Yevaine said this, too, her eyes fixed on the great seal of Edyn inscribed on the Senate Hall's floor. Slowly, her hands came up and removed the thin diadem that stood in for the

Imperial Crown. She placed this carefully into a waiting seneschal's hands, who retreated to deferentially hand it to the chancellor.

"On this day it is declared and recorded that Imperial King Bernal Galadine has passed on, and by the ancient Laws of Succession, the Imperial Queen Yevaine Galadine has been blessed to return to her noble family of House Aeonian."

The other members of the Senate nodded and said, "It is done."

Finras smiled. All in all, he was very happy with the orderly way in which things had progressed. This was so much better than the haphazard fighting one found on the fields of battle, where men used nothing but brutality to win. This meeting, orderly and neat, was the best example of what made his bureaucracy work so well.

He looked forward to the coming afternoon.

* * * * *

Regent Spaiten could not help the smile that lit his face. This had gone better than he could have hoped. House Galadine under their rule, the heirs declared lost, and the once-queen sequestered. Yevaine rose slowly and met his eyes.

"May I address the Senate?" she asked.

Spaiten granted it with a half shrug, not caring what she had to say. The deed was done and the woman was unimportant.

"Gentlemen, my husband has been declared lost and I do not know his fate nor that of my son. I find myself without the heart to serve as Legate to Bara'cor and name Captain Kalindor to the task. This puts him under your rule, Chancellor. I trust that will be acceptable?"

Chancellor Tyn nodded, "Of course. That's your right."

Spaiten smiled, this was only getting better.

Yevaine turned to her captain and said, "Do you accept?"

"I do," Captain Kalindor nodded curtly before bowing and moving up the dais to take his place at the seat for Bara'cor.

"You're welcome, Captain. Haven needs men such as you," Regent Justeces offered cordially.

Spaiten noticed that Algren had remained quiet throughout most of this. This would hardly change his mind about killing Yevaine and Ellis, but he thought they all had imagined more resistance. It was at that moment he noticed the former queen's guards moving up to encircle Yevaine.

Yevaine turned to Regent Spaiten and said, "Merric, I will no longer be needing your services."

He turned at the informality of the address and said, "It is Regent Merric, and just what do you mean, Yevaine?"

She smiled and corrected, "It is Your Royal Highness, my lord... Princess Yevaine of House Aeonian, blood heir to the throne of Dawnlight and noble born, unlike some others who claim to serve my father."

Merric's face paled and he took a step back. "What are you talking about?"

Princess Yevaine arched a delicate eyebrow and replied, "I'm the last noble of House Aeonian, the chair you currently hold as Regent. As I'm now no longer Queen of House Galadine, I will take my rightful place in the Senate as Speaker for Dawnlight and House Aeonian. You are relieved of your duty as regent and your services will no longer be required."

Silence, then a choking sound came from the former regent and he stumbled, catching himself on the table. "Praetorians, arrest her! You can't—"

"She can and has," interrupted Legate Tir, moving in

quickly to restrain Merric. The Praetorians had begun to move and Yevaine's personal guard had drawn blades, forming a defensive ring around her.

Ellis Tir raised his voice so the Praetorians could hear him. "The chancellor accepted the queen's renunciation of her House as dictated by law! She's the rightful princess of House Aeonian and stands for Dawnlight. Stand down!" He turned to the chancellor and demanded, "Have any Laws of Succession been broken?"

* * * * *

For his part, Chancellor Tyn stood dumbfounded. Not only had the queen appointed one of her own, she had replaced a regent with herself, shifting the power base of Haven. What galled him the most was that she had accomplished all this using his own obtuse and cooperative hand. But had she done anything legally wrong?

He took a deep breath, reviewing the legitimacy of her position. His commitment was to uphold the laws of Edyn and the succession, and in performance of that duty his eyes darted back and forth as he thought through her claim.

It was true that Laws of Succession forbade her from holding the Imperial Crown of Edyn, but nothing prevented her from representing her father's House. Furthermore, she was the ranking noble in line for succession to Dawnlight's throne. His head dropped slowly and he mumbled something.

"Louder, Chancellor, or there will be blood spilled today, likely starting with yours," Ellis Tir whispered.

Chancellor Finras Tyn had never officiated such a deep change to Haven's political structure and could feel a cold sweat break out. He felt Legate Tir prod him again and found his voice.

"The Laws of Succession were upheld. Princess Yevaine stands as Speaker for House Aeonian and Dawnlight. Praetorians, stand down."

The senatorial guards sheathed half-drawn blades and stepped back, but held their ground. Still, their attitude and attention now seemed focused on Merric Spaiten. One stepped forward and saluted the new princess, "We can take him for you."

"Thank you, but no, centurion. This is an internal issue for Dawnlight." She looked to Kalindor and said, "Regent, I formally request Bara'cor's help. Please escort this man to a room and keep him under guard. He's to have no visitors until I can speak to him about his recent service and loyalty to my father."

Kalindor bowed and said, "Bara'cor stands ready."

"As does Dawnlight," she replied with a smile.

Kalindor motioned to his men and four guards escorted a pale Spaiten from the table. He started to follow but Yevaine held up a hand, calling him back.

Tyn could see in her eyes that though her plan had succeeded, she was not done with the business that had first brought her here. It was now abundantly clear that both Legate Tir and her captain were loyal to her cause, and he doubted very much if he would like the next words he heard.

"Gentlemen," she said coolly, and a pit formed in the chancellor's stomach, "I believe we still have another vote to tally: a petition for Haven to come to the aid of Bara'cor."

PREPARATIONS

*Distraction is the mind excusing itself
from what is hard.
It is the surest path to being average.*

- Jebida Naserith, Should I Fall

Tomas sat in the Spring Square, massaging his legs, still trembling from this morning's grueling training session with the lore father. He and Giridian had been up since dawn practicing close quarters combat within four walls. Given his upcoming test, his master had been pushing harder than usual, spending an inordinate amount of time on pinning, grappling, and reversing. He even made Tomas practice using the wall surfaces to reverse an opponent, turning a defensive position into an attack. These were basic techniques, the kind he learned as a Green. Because he couldn't see the point, he let his mind wander while his body performed the moves automatically.

Unfortunately, that didn't mean expertly, as the lore father had painfully demonstrated with a few quick reversals that had dumped him unceremoniously on his back and fighting for air.

Rarely did the masters strike a student, but there were dozens of ways to punish inattention. The most common of these were simple rollers, a circular kind of pushup, but with legs spread so that the student's hands and feet touched the four corners of an X. The student rolled his chin an inch from the ground past his fists, then shifted his weight back onto his legs, then repeated the motion.

He'd lost count of how many he'd done today, a thousand at least, an amount certainly not rare for any student in a typical day's training, but today wasn't typical. It seemed the exercise had somehow found a way to reach out and mentally torture him on the eve of his Test, a fact filling him with a bit of shame and worry. Still, he knew he could pass... he just needed to focus.

He looked at the ration of honey he was required to eat before his afternoon training. It was the only bright spot in his day, the sweet nectar giving him instant energy and focus. In his opinion, it was better than kaffe, which was fine as long as you didn't mind the jitters. Certainly it was better than the koken nut, forbidden to the students but found and tried nonetheless. Tomas wasn't ready to feel the intense lethargy that hit once you stopped taking that particular aid. In his opinion, it just wasn't worth it.

Honey was a mainstay on the Isle. It served as a part of every student's training diet, and also was used in the healer's wards to help keep wounds from festering. It was unfortunate that the masters did so much trading with the mainland, he thought, for the apiarists of the Isle were second to none. Because of that brisk trade, their honey was always in short supply.

What was wrong with him? He was daydreaming again, and

the lore father had been correct to punish him. What was causing his mind to wander? Lately, he dreaded training, something he'd never felt before. Part of him had been secretly wishing for another injury. His time spent convalescing after Arek's encounter with Piter had been some of the best days of his life. He'd got to sleep in late, eat whatever he wanted. He had never been so free!

Then the vast sweeping changes: first the loss of Piter; the assassins' attack; Arek gone, and if rumors were to be believed, hunted by Kisan. Even Jesyn had left, a full adept of the Way after earning her Black, and gone questing with Dragor to the north for signs of the assassins.

Tomas counted off his instructors in just the past few weeks. He'd always been trained by Master Dragor, but when it became clear he and Jesyn were interested in each other, he'd been assigned to Master Giridian. The masters didn't care if initiates dated, but the sanctity of training always took precedence. So he'd become Master Giridian's apprentice until the situation with Piter. With his passing, they had moved him to Master Kisan.

Now she was gone, as was Master Dragor, and his master was once again Master Giridian. Only now he was the new lore father. Four reassignments, though if he were being honest to himself, he couldn't really count the one because of Jesyn. They'd been dating for almost a year. But the last three reassignments had happened in a matter of weeks! Through all this they expected him to continue training for his Test!

He shook his head and tossed a pebble at a flower bud, missing and cursing at failing something so simple. Distraction caused it and when his mind was in turmoil he was unable to focus on even the easiest of things.

Something about his time off had unlocked a desire to quit,

something so deep and secret he had trouble admitting it even to himself. Maybe he'd just go on until he'd earned his Black and then leave.

He couldn't help but reexamine his feelings. Could being just a few days away from his regimen create such a fray in the rope that bound him to his training? Could he so easily lose his commitment?

He doubted it, but knowing a mistake could mean death had been harshly reinforced by the events with Piter. They hadn't been doing anything Browns hadn't always done: testing each other, pushing and pranking, hoping to show a little superiority. This time, however, Piter had paid for it with his life. That scared Tomas. Fear was not a good emotion to harbor, something he knew well.

Then there was the attack by the assassins, which had brought into question the safety of even this sacrosanct place. The Isle, in his memory, had never been attacked. If they could get here, how did he know there wasn't another attack to follow?

Master Silbane had lectured that your inner self was reflected in your outermost actions. If that were true, and part of him knew it was, then maybe his turmoil was the root of his less than stellar performance? He could intellectually understand that, but changing the way he felt was much harder.

"Sir?"

He started, a little surprised, another sign he was distracted. Since when could a White approach him unnoticed? Looking up, he saw a girl in a white uniform, looking at him uncertainly, then back the way she'd come. She was tall, probably close to her sixteenth summer, and she clearly did not know who he was.

He sat up, straightening his uniform, then said, "Address me properly."

The White immediately fell back a step, as if recognizing for the first time that she was addressing a senior instructor. She seemed about to fall over, but somehow managed to perform a hasty bow, then stood with her arms at her sides and her feet shoulder width apart.

The masters called it, "ready stance," and though it was touted as a great position to be ready for anything, in Tomas's experience it was really only good for getting ready to get hit. Before he could stop it a chuckle escaped and he realized with chagrin that the girl must think he was laughing at her.

Well, no sense in making things worse. Tomas stood and said, "Discipline is the key to our success here..."

"Kymoria," she supplied.

"Kymoria," he added. "At all times you will show respect. This is important, for the masters will not tolerate anything less." He paused, then said with a smile, "And you know when they enforce it?"

Kymoria smiled back but did not move from her ready stance. "Whenever I'm awake?"

"And sometimes when you're not," he added with a small laugh. "What do you need?"

"I was sent to the refectory, but all these buildings look the same."

He shook away the last moribund thoughts he'd been having about his future and appraised the girl with a quick glance. She was older, lithe, and seemed confident in spite of the fact that she could be no more than a week out of indoctrination. Her age showed that there were fewer and fewer of those with Talent being found. That she'd lived this long meant she probably came into her skills late, a problem when it came to properly training someone for use of the Way. Still, they had no choice, and only a fool believed a coin's value changed because it wasn't new.

"Look," he said, pointing to a gray building, "follow me."

He began walking and heard her fall in behind. Leading her gave him something to do. He knew already the inevitable afternoon he was about to experience. No doubt rollers would feature highly in his training once again, he thought with a certain fatalism. It was accompanied by a mental groan.

When he let out a sigh, Kymoria piped in, "May I ask a question, sir?"

He thought he knew what it would be and answered, "Yes, I knew a few of them quite well. It wasn't fair what happened."

"Umm, yes sir," she replied but then said nothing. He looked back at her, and realized the attack on the Isle hadn't been her question at all.

Rather than embarrass them both, he asked, "And do you have another question?"

She smiled at that and said, "What did you pick, sir?"

It was his turn to smile as he continued toward the gray buildings. "What do you think?"

There was silence to that, until finally he looked over his shoulder again and saw her deep in thought, like she was being tested.

"Relax, Kim. You aren't getting in trouble if you get it wrong."

"Sky," she stated, the voice firm and unequivocal.

He stopped and turned, unable to hide his amazement. Rarely did anyone guess the element he'd chosen his Affinity with. Most believed it was Earth, like Master Giridian. Sky was usually further down the list, if it was said at all. Affinity didn't mean so much, but the masters liked each student to pick one so that they could use that to help illustrate how certain combat techniques worked. In Tomas's case, his hands and feet were often referred to as "the wind," and his tactics were suited to match.

"Pretty good guess," he said.

He was about to continue when she said, "Now guess what mine is."

Tomas shook his head and said, "Moon." Without waiting for her to answer, he resumed their walk.

"How did you know?" she asked, amazement in her voice.

"It's patched on your sleeve."

He could imagine her realizing he was right, for every White had their affinity patched onto their uniforms. It wasn't until they'd mastered themselves and that element's nuances of fighting style that the patch was removed. He laughed again, happy in a perverse way that he wasn't the only one making stupid mistakes.

"By the Lady," she cursed, and that brought forth a little more laughter.

Tomas looked at her without breaking stride, "You'll get used to it, believe me. There's a lot to take in. It's easy to forget simple things."

She nodded while walking, her hands still in a stiff ready position at her sides. He couldn't help but stop again. He faced her, shaking his head. "I told you, relax. I'm not going to punish you right out of indoc," he said, "and you can't follow me around holding your arms out like that. It's silly."

"First day, sir... full day, I mean." She looked around sheepishly, clearly unsure now that they stopped if she should resume her ready stance or not.

Tomas looked down to avoid seeming exasperated at the comical situation, but Whites were all the same: scared of their own shadow, eager to please and be recognized, worried about being asked to leave the Isle. Knowing this, he continued to the refectory, hoping she could sort it out on her own but unable to watch her trying to balance decorum and practicality with a straight face.

"We should just get you to where you need to go," he said over his shoulder. "Someone else may think your tardiness would be benefited by rollers." The small groan that elicited let him know he had a co-conspirator of sorts when it came to that particular exercise, a favorite in indoc too.

The sound of Kymoria's breathing told him she was running with her arms still stiff at her sides, the huff of her breath coming in small gasps whenever her heel struck the ground because her knees were also locked.

How could he know all this by just listening, and fail so miserably when working with his master? He couldn't answer that, but that worry was balanced by his innate confidence. He'd earned his way this far. His ability to discern such nuances of position and breathing with Kymoria meant he had skill and talent.

He resolved to redouble his efforts and focus on a positive result. Master Dragor had always said that the outcome of any engagement was often aligned to your most inner feelings. That thought filled him with a sense of purpose as he and his ward made their way into the cool interior of the dining hall.

* * * * *

Giridian watched the boy from a window in the Hall of Masters. Thoth stood beside him, leaning on his staff.

Thoth nodded, then asked, "Maybe you liked it better when you didn't know we watched these Tests."

"Of course, but now that I know, I don't wish to go back to

the way it was."

"We chose correctly in including you, Lore Father."

Giridian laughed at that. "You didn't. It was supposed to be Silbane. I was an accident."

Thoth's eyes twinkled when he said, "Are you so sure of that?" Before the Lore Father could reply, the Keeper continued, "Have you given any more thought to the Phoenix Stone?"

The Lore Father paused, then sarcastically said, "And my sacrifice?" His eyes searched Thoth's face for something, then he said, "Honestly, no, I haven't. My focus has been to get Tomas ready for his Test. Frankly," he said almost to himself, "I don't think dwelling on it will change the outcome."

Thoth nodded and then gestured to the air around him. "If there was information carried in the lore fathers' memories, I would give it to you."

"I know," Giridian said. "I did not hold high hope of that, but there's someone who I think knows more than she's saying." He looked meaningfully at Thoth.

The Keeper was quiet a moment, then said, "Sai'ken."

The lore father nodded. "I know you say the dragons can be trusted, but I sense she's not as forthcoming as she appears."

Thoth pursed his lips and said, "She is a Sai. They have more latitude when it comes to interpreting what's good for Edyn." He was silent, thinking, then asked, "What do you suggest?"

"Silbane or perhaps Kisan could mindread her. Either may be powerful enough to deal with a young dragon, but I can't assign them to this. I only have Dragor and Jesyn. They're young still and not nearly as powerful."

Thoth considered that, then asked, "Could they do it working together?"

"Perhaps," Giridian mused, "but that would also alert the

dragonkind. Is that acceptable?"

"There is no other way?" inquired the Keeper. "We cannot lose their support."

"Can't you just order them to help? What's the point of being Keeper?" Giridian asked.

Thoth arched his eyebrows. "Can I just order you? Our purpose is not to compel but to guide." The Keeper turned to the lore father and finished by saying, "Perhaps I can speak with them about the need."

Giridian paused, weighing options before he responded. "Then do so. I will also advise my adepts to be ready to seize an advantage. If the information of the Phoenix Stone can be gained, we will attempt it."

Thoth nodded, then disappeared in a flash.

Giridian looked back out the window at the doorway Tomas had disappeared through with Kymoria. Fear could also be a disabling force, causing even the best to falter. He would have to find a way to guide Tomas, or he was leading the boy to his death.

PERSPECTIVE

*"A thousand laws will not leave as lasting a reminder
as one brutal public execution."*

- Duncan Illrys, *Remembrances*

Dragor awoke slowly, his head pounding in time with his heart. It was like a metronome outfitted with hammers beating on the inside of his skull. He lay on a makeshift pallet cocooned in darkness within a small tent. Next to his bed was a canteen, which he unstoppered and sniffed. Water! He quickly drank, his thirst growing as he became fully alert. The cool liquid tasted fresh and sweet and his body absorbed it like a sponge.

When he'd drunk his fill, he took better stock of his surroundings. The tent was bigger than he'd first thought, and an indistinct shape took form, seated off to his right. The shape didn't move, giving the adept time to take a breath and think. He adjusted his vision to compensate for the darkness. The profile of a man jumped into sharp focus, lounging in a chair seated in the tent's corner.

The man was clearly asleep, his sonorous breathing

interrupted only by a few coughs that turned into lip smacking sounds. Dragor didn't know who the man was, nor did he care as he carefully slipped out from under his covers. When he'd gained his feet, however, he was hit with sudden vertigo, and had to hold out his hands for balance. The mindread had taken a greater toll on him than he'd expected. He slowed his breathing, calming himself. Then he made for the tent flap, exiting as noiselessly as a soft breeze.

Outside, groups of people huddled around small fires in threes or fours. The fires were shielded, and though they went about what looked to be routine activities, their movements were small and hushed, as if they were careful not to attract any attention. Then the shape and size of these "men" gave him his second shock in what had been so far a very short day. *Dwarves!*

He felt again that subliminal snap as his body prepared to run or fight. His breathing deepened, his senses became hyper alert and his mind blazed through permutations of possible reactions to his every action.

"You'll pull something if you stand like that," Jesyn's voice piped in from his left with an undercurrent of amusement that couldn't be hidden.

Dragor spun and was greeted with the sight of his former apprentice flanked by two dwarves, a man and a woman. "What—?" he began.

Jesyn smiled. "You can't be angry at my powers as an adept. Hearing you rise was... interesting."

She smiled, then turned to the two dwarves and said, "Dazra and his people are friends. We have some catching up to do." She gave him a slight bow, a subtle way of telling him she was not under duress, then nodded back at his tent. Then, without waiting, she made her way in.

The two dwarves with her stood by patiently, as neither seemed in a hurry. When Dragor didn't move the woman gestured with her free arm at the open tent door and said, "Be welcome, Adept. Jesyn speaks well of you, and we share a common enemy."

The aftereffects of the mindread were only starting to dissipate, but now would come the confusing rush of memories and information. It would take time for him to sort through it all and make it useful—time he hoped he would still have, given this turn of events.

He thought of Kisan, surrounded by enemies. The fact that the master had managed to assimilate the memories of the man she'd replaced and maintain an illusion of him while on the run now awed him. It showed him just how much more he had to learn before he could fill her shoes.

"Your name?" was all he could muster.

"Tarin," she said simply. Then she looked to her left and said, "And the man standing here looking grim is Dazra, our leader." She smiled, and held out a hand.

Dragor stepped forward and shook it, his own hand engulfed by her own. When the man named Dazra didn't move or offer his hand, Dragor gave a short, uncomfortable nod and walked back into the tent where he'd woken. The interior was brighter as Jesyn had taken the opportunity to light a few lanterns. They burned with a cold white light too steady to be flame. Dragor marveled at it, until the guard who had been stationed was awakened with a swift kick by Tarin.

"Get up, Halp."

The man's body spasmed as he sputtered awake, clutching a makeshift throw over his chin. "What?"

Tarin grabbed the blanket away and said, "You're supposed to be making sure he's all right, not catching extra sleep."

The man seemed genuinely annoyed when he said, "Ach, the halfling weren't in no trouble. He was sleeping deeper than..." As his eyes tracked over to the bed, he realized only now that it was empty. Looking sheepishly at Tarin, he muttered, "Well, didn't think he'd wake so soon."

"Get up." She shoved him out of the chair and out the door. "We'll talk about it later."

While the exchange had clearly been Tarin admonishing the guard's dereliction of duty, the manner in which they'd interacted spoke of a deeper friendship. The undercurrent was not officer to enlisted, but more sister to brother. Dragor took note of that and of the sense that the man seemed more a nurse than a guard. Though being surrounded by dwarves raised his hackles, their attitude and demeanor bode well to his circumstances. Jesyn being safe helped too.

She plopped down on his pallet, motioning for him to take a seat anywhere, which he did. As the two others joined them, she launched into the events since their capture of the assassin. She told him of meeting Dazra and his dwarves, of hearing their plight as his people went missing. She also told him of their strange entats, and pulled her sleeve back to reveal hers, only a small symbol compared to the full body whorls and sigils decorating Dazra and Tarin.

When she was finished she asked, "You might find this hard to believe, but we're sort of in Dawnlight right now."

Dragor was not the type to meet everything with skepticism. He tended to believe his own eyes and they told him that thus far, everything Jesyn said was true. Certainly if she'd been captured and controlled by these dwarves it would have been evident to him by now. Her short 'no duress' signal had been confirmation of this.

Still, that they were in Dawnlight was suspicious, if for no other reason than the images he was starting to see from the assassin's mind did not match this place.

It seemed Jesyn could read that from his expression. She turned to Dazra and asked, "May I show him?"

The dwarven leader's blue eyes pierced Dragor's own, as if judging his soul. Then, hesitantly, he nodded and Jesyn reached forward and took hold of Dragor's hand. "Relax... this unsettled me a bit the first time too."

Dragor could feel her warm hand and a small itch in his palm, like ants crawling between their grasp. Then his vision shifted almost imperceptibly and the tent seemed to dim.

Just then, a dwarven man walked through the tent wall and past the shocked Dragor, going out the other side without touching or moving the walls. Another came through, walking right through Tarin and the chair she sat upon. More appeared, moving about their day, oblivious to their presence. They were ghosts, walking through their area without disrupting anything they touched.

"What's happened to them?" he asked, his eyes wide as he watched a woman bend over something unseen, then straighten and walk through the form of Dazra before disappearing out the tent wall.

Jesyn smiled again and said, "It's not them, it's us. We are still in Edyn. Dawnlight exists in between this plane and others." She looked to Dazra. His eyes told the adept he was not done assessing him even as Jesyn spoke, evaluating him through every question and gesture Dragor made.

The adept thought for a moment, then said, "I appreciate your hospitality, especially caring for us while I was incapacitated."

At the same time, he risked a quick mindspeak to Jesyn, *Let's talk alone*, before continuing, "Perhaps the information I gleaned from the assassin's mind isn't as useful as we thought."

The younger adept did not bat an eye, but replied, "Oh no, his memories are critical to our quest." She stood slowly, then turned to Dazra and said, "Do you mind if Dragor and I have some privacy?"

Silence from Dazra, into which Tarin thankfully stepped.

"Not at all," she said. "We'll be outside making sure camp is set. Be careful not to wander too far or the centrees will intervene." She took the silent Dazra by the arm and pulled him out the tent door.

"Happy?" Jesyn asked, clearly frustrated.

Dragor looked sidelong at the other adept and said, "In fact, yes.

"Now, what's really going on?"

Jesyn sighed. "Did you think the two of us would find the lost city after centuries of it remaining undiscovered? We're good, but we're not that good. It's obvious we're in a holding area, some sort of in-between their home city and Edyn. We're only here because they let us find them."

"I believe you, but ask yourself—why?"

Now it was Jesyn's turn to look confused.

"You captured one of their assassins and mindread him," she said after a moment. "I don't think they can do that."

"So what?" he asked. "If they're good enough to capture us, they're good enough to capture them. Simple interrogation seems well within their capabilities."

"They're missing people, many they know and love. They're searching for these assassins just as we are, but it's something more complicated. I think it's important..." The girl just trailed off without finishing what she had started to say.

Dragor sat back, closing his eyes. Even now the memories of the assassin were jumbled up with his own, impossible for him to decipher easily. He knew that clarity would come with time. Then he looked back at Jesyn and saw her lip tremble, just the barest movement, but it told him the edge of her composure was threatening to crumble.

He reminded himself that Jesyn had been required to watch over him and discern truth from lie, knowing if she chose wrong it could mean both their lives. It must have been hard, but what he had to do next would be harder still, since he loved her like a daughter.

"Are you going to cry? Check yourself," he snapped. "The hottest fires are needed to..." He waited for her, his eyes demanding an answer.

Jesyn drew in a shuddering breath, but then completed, "... forge the best blades."

"Exactly." He looked around the room, then back at her. "Look at me." When she did, he could see she'd reasserted her control. He propped her up further by saying, "You did well and I'm proud of you."

He stood and gave her a small hug, then caught her eye.

"I don't doubt your instincts, but we don't know everything yet," he said. "Though he may mean no direct harm to us, Dazra may have other needs that run counter to our own. So stay alert."

He paused, then added, "Remember: trust, but verify." He waited for her nod, a sharp one given with steady eyes, then he smiled. "Come on, let's find him and figure out our next steps."

Jesyn stopped him, looking around. Then she said softly, "The assassin we captured. He's one of Dazra's missing people."

Dragor looked at her in surprise, "And you trust him still?"

Jesyn shook her head at the misunderstanding and said, "What I meant is that they recognize him, but he did not recognize them. They won't let him phase into their Dawnlight because of this, which is why we're camped here."

The elder adept thought for a moment, then asked, "Two things. What do you mean, 'their Dawnlight,' and you're saying Dazra recognizes him as one of his missing men?"

"We're here in Edyn and this mountain is real, but it's not their Dawnlight. Their home exists in phase, some place in between our realm and others."

Dragor nodded quietly. Then he said, "You said as much before but I don't think I really heard you. Though I can't decipher everything from the mindread yet, I saw nothing of Dazra and his people, which is strange."

"Strange?"

Dragor realized she'd never mindread anyone before. "The thoughts are scattered at first, until assimilated. I can't tell before and after, but usually you see images across an entire person's life." He looked out the tent door though his mind was deep in thought. "I saw nothing like that."

Jesyn fidgeted, her hands wringing and her eyes darting left and right. She made a small gesture for Dragor to come closer. Leaning in she whispered, "I heard Dazra talking with Tarin and a few others. His brother is one of the missing."

Dragor nodded, not sure where this was going, but speaking was risky. He reached out and touched her hand softly, a gesture that would make mindspeaking easier for her. He didn't want the dwarves hearing what she said next, so he cleared his mind. *It will be taxing, but use this*, and he opened the Way.

Jesyn gave him a brief smile of thanks, then mindspoke, *Look at the face of the assassin Kisan killed on the Isle.*

The lore father had shared Kisan's memories with them before their departure, standard procedure for a mission like this. Those memories had already been assimilated and were available for Dragor without much effort.

He looked at the face Kisan saw when she'd pulled off the mask, the face he'd seen when they found the body. At first, he didn't see it. The boy had blond hair and a slash running down one cheek. His eyes were light blue and dull in death. Then something clicked and he saw something of Dazra, younger but nonetheless eerily similar.

Then Jesyn mindspoke, *His name was Tamlin*.

Dragor knew that name, he'd heard it from Kisan's memories. A pit formed in his stomach. Had the dwarven leader been silent this whole time because he suspected? Had he been watching for signs of guilt? Kisan killed Dazra's brother...

Jesyn nodded, then said softly, "And I think Dazra knows it."

Perspective

COMMAND

*Do not engage your enemy too often,
lest he learn your ways of war.*

- Galadine House of Arms, Battle's Focus

Y ou did well." Valarius looked back at his armsmark as they entered a private meeting chamber situated at the very edge of Avalyon. One half of the room opened to look out over Arcadia, the sky and clouds a majestic backdrop to the room's smoothly organic table and chairs. The other half's walls were draped to hide passages for servants and aides. Every surface was polished to a high sheen, a veritable display of the health and power of the tree city.

The highlord's mind was still in turmoil at the news of losing Arek. It was a blow to their cause and worse, to his personal plans. Still, he could not blame Gabreyl. Lilyth and her Furies were everywhere, and to run into two Watchers... the armsmark had truly done well in getting back here in one piece. That they had Niall was a pleasant and unexpected surprise, but more pressing matters needed attention.

Gabreyl shook his head, his thoughts clearly still on the events at the henge. "We were unprepared for the attack."

Valarius held up a hand. "Nothing unfolds as planned. You escaped with Niall and that has opened other opportunities for us." He looked out over the magnificent expanse and said, "It is doubtful anyone survived the nephilim. You say they turn our elves dark?"

"Yes, Highlord," Gabreyl replied. "They were mindless, using teeth and nails to rend and shred our men. I thought I saw them... feeding."

Valarius was sure such creatures had existed since Sovereign's Fall, and he'd expected the possibility that Arek himself would hasten their creation given his dark gift. Indeed, the eradication of the Aeris necessitated the nephilim, but he had not expected his own elves to be turned.

Their resistance to Aeris possession should have shielded them, yet it had not. This was troubling. If the elves could be turned, it meant his timeline for leaving Arcadia had to be summarily accelerated. More reason to find Arek quickly and secure the Gate at Bara'cor.

He looked back at Gabreyl and said, "You blame yourself. Do not, for few could have survived such a battle. I am proud of you. Now we must focus on the needs of our people."

Gabreyl nodded, but his eyes were downcast. "Do you remember my awakening?"

"Of course," Valarius answered, "you were the youngest of us, yet you heard my call."

"I came because I'm a Galadine and believe in you," said the armsmark. "I was also once king, and understand your position. I've always believed Edyn will be a better place with our guiding hand. Yet now I question the choices we've made. Have we done what is best by deed and action?"

Valarius looked at his armsmark, struck down and reborn during the interim years since the Demon Wars. The young man was an idealist, the kind that stayed devoted as long as he believed in his cause. Now doubt wormed its way in, weakening Gabreyl's resolve. Valarius would not let that happen.

"The survival of Arcadia was never part of our plans," he reminded gently, though he could hear the edge in his own voice.

Gabreyl must have heard it too. The man's eyes did not meet Valarius's own when he said, "I know, it's just that..."

When he trailed off, Valarius sighed and then put a firm hand on his commander's shoulder. "We secure the gateway to Bara'cor. We leave Arcadia and the nephilim eradicate the Aeris. With nothing left to feed upon, they perish and Edyn is free. It is for this that we fight, no?"

The simple summation had its desired effect. Slowly, the armsmark nodded.

"I had not thought it to be so difficult, leaving my men behind," he said.

"Every one of those men *chose* to be there," Valarius said. "Would you rob them of that choice, pulling them from the greatness they've achieved with their sacrifice? Would you not have given your life if it meant our success?" He smiled, then added, "Sadness is only temporary. Do not feel shame over allowing others to earn proud glory. Trust in me, as I have faith in you." His hand clapped the young commander's arm. "Now summon the others so that we may take counsel and decide a course of action."

Gabreyl bowed, fist to chest, then executed a perfect turn. In moments the five Galadine kings who served Valarius filed into the room.

Mikal took the lead, as he always did. Thick in limb and

trunk, the king looked like he dwarfed his brother even though they stood of equal height. He was followed by gray-haired Ureyl and the slim Zedakai. Bringing up the rear was Israfel, his stern face and determined walk mirroring his rigid spirit, and finally, Gabreyl.

They stood waiting beside their chairs until Valarius had seated himself. Then all five sat, as attendants came to stand silently behind each one.

Mikal spoke first, looking at the highlord. "Valor is here."

Valarius turned to his brother in life and said, "How do you know?"

A smile creased the lord's face when he answered, "You know the hours I spent under the armsmasters' enthusiastic tutelage. The bow is a force, a presence. Trust me, it's here. I feel it in my bones."

Israfel cleared his throat. "I, too, can feel it. I did not know it was Valor until my father gave name to its pull." He looked around the room, his visage a burning intensity of thought. Israfel's gaze pierced each man until it finally came to rest on Valarius. "Ill winds attend wherever it goes."

"That depends on which side of the sight you find yourself," Valarius said, unfazed by Israfel's directness, and asked, "Can you find it?"

"Perhaps," answered the brooding Mikal. "I would need help."

Gabreyl looked around the room, confused. "Why? There are more pressing concerns."

Valarius turned to his youngest armsmark and said, "If Valor is here, it means there's also another Galadine here."

Understanding dawned and Gabreyl was quick to offer, "Then let me aid my elder grandfather and lead the party to recover our kinsman."

"If that's the best path, yes. However, it may be we can entice whomever carries the bow to come here." The highlord looked around the chamber and then counted off on his fingers. "We know it is not Bernal, for we have not heard from Firstmark Malak and only the realignment of the Gate would give someone within Bara'cor access to Arcadia. We also know it cannot be Niall, for he does not hold the bow." He paused, thinking, then said, "It might be one of the few who entered this realm in search of the two boys, the ones brought by Lilyth."

"Who is the Galadine amongst them?" asked Ureyl. While they knew a few had come through a portal shortly after Arek and Niall, they did not know who or their exact number. The question therefore hung in the air.

Valarius raised a third finger. "Likely the princess and daughter to the fallen Ben'thor Tir, who even now serves the Lady."

He needed information, something only one person would know, but the question now was impropriety. He weighed the risks carefully, looking around the room. Would his brother-kings hold the line, even if it meant breaking all manner of etiquette to meet their need? Then he came to a decision, uttering a single word.

"Sonya."

Cries of protest and surprise could be heard from the assembled kings. A gasp tore from Mikal's lips and he said, "You cannot! Have we not already shamed ourselves enough?"

Valarius did not respond to that, but he bent his considerable will to the task and said, "I summon thee."

Slowly, the form of Sonya appeared, her hands clasped before her. She solidified, looking at the men in the room, her eyes finally falling on Valarius. "My husband, faithful to the end, protecting me against all harm. Alas, that too was a false dream."

Valarius felt a knot in his throat and knew if he began discussing his actions he wouldn't have the strength to continue. So instead he said, "Arek—who seeks to rescue him?"

The shade tossed her head, looking now at the table. Only Israfel had the gall to meet her gaze, the rest looking down or away. "Are you proud of yourselves, o' noble kings?"

First there was silence. Then Israfel said, "We did what we must to safeguard Edyn. You took an oath to do the same."

"Then why not ask me!" she yelled.

Valarius held up a hand, silencing Israfel, and said, "Blood magic requires true sacrifice. My heart had to be broken to power a spell such as the one that sent Malak to Bara'cor. Leading you to a death you'd chosen would have lessened the shame and betrayal I felt as my knife did its work. Nothing else would have sufficed."

He knew he'd fallen into the very thing he wanted to avoid. Faced with Sonya's shade he felt his will crumbling.

"Then why not transport us? Why not rescue us if you could breach Bara'cor? We could have left Arcadia and lived again," she implored, her eyes searching his own.

He could not stand that scrutiny. "For how long? Fleeing to Edyn would only have insured our deaths when Lilyth and her Aeris arrived. War is inevitable, and if there's to be any hope for life and love, desperate measures are needed."

"So logical, so noble," she spat. "A true testament of what being loved by a Galadine means."

"I'm sorry for the actions we must take, but you chose me knowing who I am," Valarius said. "Now, you have another choice."

Sonya's shade looked down, shaking her head. It was not clear if she was listening until she said, "Use 'we' whenever possible, husband. It absolves you from the ignoble weight of 'I'. Nevertheless, I am bound by your summons to speak. I care not for your needs."

Valarius drew a breath, surveying the room. Mikal had his head in his hands and most of the other kings looked grief-stricken. Only Israfel seemed untouched, but he'd been the king who had overseen the genocide of the mages once his father Mikal had gone. Clearly his heart was not moved by one person's plight. Valarius met eyes with him, drawing strength for his next request.

Then he looked back at Sonya and said, "Who seeks Arek?" When she did not answer, he said, "I compel you, shade." His heart hardened too, and he said what he had to. "One thrust of my elven blade will give you true death. You will never see your son in this life or any other. Weigh that against answering me."

Sonya looked at him in alarm. "You would threaten me with my son? Is there no end—"

"No!" shouted Valarius. "There is no end to what I will do to save our world from the Aeris!"

He stepped forward and drew his blade, his peripheral vision catching his family's heads as they dropped. No matter, he would kill her again if necessary, and this time the magic of his blade would mean she would be gone forever. It was not an idle threat.

Sonya shrank back, her eyes flicking back and forth between the blade and his countenance. Whatever she saw there must have convinced her, for in a small, tremulous voice she said, "Duncan."

Her proclamation caused a raised eyebrow from the elven king, who looked askance at his dead wife. "How do you know?"

"I saw him," she admitted. "I think I know my former

husband."

"You told him Arek is his son?" Valarius's voice did not rise, he simply asked the question with deadly intensity.

"Yes." There was a hint of challenge in her voice, but Valarius did not react to it.

Instead, he merely said, "Indeed. Does he think we have him?"

Sonya looked down then gave a hesitant shake of her head. She stood a little straighter, as if the act of telling had somehow removed some of her culpability. "I told him not to come here."

"Then it is certain he will," replied Valarius, his eyes measuring her for any sign of conflict. He could only see fear and sadness, normal given what had happened just now. He could live with that.

He looked out over the open skies of Arcadia, his mind deep in thought. "Duncan Illrys... I owe him much for his betrayal."

Mikal cleared his throat and said, "And that has been paid for in full and more! *I* let loose the arrow that—"

"Brought Sonya to me." Valarius looked meaningfully at Mikal, then at Sonya. His will was such that neither argued the point. "Do not be so quick to shoulder his blame. He was weak, powerless, and ineffectual. My benevolence left me vulnerable to Duncan's trickery. Along with Rai'stahn, the two of them deserve my attention more than most."

Mikal shook his head at that, imploring, "Let it go, Val. What has he left? You took everything that mattered. Are we not Galadines, called upon to be nobler in word and deed? When will your thirst for vengeance be slaked?" He pointed to Sonya. "Summoning her is beneath you."

"Ahh, a brother's inconvenient truth." Sonya looked at Mikal and said, "Those traits are merely words now, there are no Galadines left in this room."

"Silence!" Valarius smacked the table, tossing his blade down to clatter upon it. He waited until Sonya dropped her head, then looked at Mikal, his eyes narrowing as his mind raced through possible outcomes. If Duncan was here and looking for his son, how would he find him? Oftentimes it was easier to put oneself in another's place, so the highlord asked himself how he would pursue this if their positions were reversed. He had already taken the first step by having Gabreyl suggest that the highlord was Arek's father. That would give the boy purpose, a goal to strive for. Now the question was, how to properly motivate Duncan?

He looked at Sonya again, the love of his life, dead by his hand. He knew she could not materially affect anything, yet Arek's plight might sway her to do what she could to protect him, so how could he turn that to his advantage?

"You offered Duncan help?" he asked her, entirely ignoring Mikal's earlier plea.

Sonya nodded. "I thought to lead him to where he might find allies."

"Good," he said. Then he added, "Very good." He thought for a moment more, knowing the key to getting here would be the henges. "You will not lead him anywhere. Instead, I will send him Tulien and a contingent of elves." Gabreyl shifted, an unspoken protest rising to his lips before Valarius held up a hand and said, "He is the newest," as if that explained it all.

Sonya fell to her knees, her hands up and said, "Please have mercy? Leave Duncan be. Mikal is right. If fate had not twisted as it had, you and I would never have found each other. If you ever loved me in life, have mercy." Her eyes glistened as she said this, but Valarius saw the fear for Duncan manifest in those tears, not him. Her words did not sway him.

He nodded but said, "I did love you, but I love Edyn more."

The statement felt like a door shutting, silencing any reply. He turned to Gabreyl, "Tulien's sacrifice will bring him here. Then we will see what Duncan Illrys has to say about choices made concerning our family."

He turned back to the shade of his former wife and said, "Do not doubt that if you betray me, if you inform Arek or Duncan of what we have planned, I will know."

He did not wait to hear her answer but gestured, banishing her. When she'd disappeared he turned to the table.

"Do any of you feel I pushed too far?"

"Yes," Mikal said. "What you have done is incomprehensible."

"Really?" asked Valarius. "Do you find hope in the hearts of traitors and sycophants?"

Mikal's eyes flared at that but Valarius continued, "She loved another but chose to be with me for expediency! Do not judge, for you forget that we spent many years together in life without so much as a word. Her 'love' for me showed itself here, only when her son's survival hung in the balance. Is that love, brothers? Were you in my place, is that something you could ignore?" Valarius was silent then, looking at Mikal with the intensity that demanded an answer.

Mikal replied, "Have you not done the same?"

Valarius slammed the table with his palms. "Do not question me! I have given everything I loved for us. Everything!"

They stared at each other, but it was Mikal who dropped his eyes first and said, "You are the highlord. I do not question your love for Edyn… or us."

There was silence at that, until Valarius said, "King Mikal is right. Our family is bonded by love. I pledge that to each of you now, and ask you to follow me through this last, most difficult part. We are the salvation of Edyn. If anyone doubts that, I will mourn your departure from this table."

There was silence but no one looked even close to ready to leave. He looked at each lord and was satisfied that they met his gaze without hubris. Still, there was a hesitant chorus of 'ayes' at his stare, as each king reaffirmed his fealty. Valarius looked at everyone, taking measure. Without a doubt summoning Sonya was not sitting well with them, but it had also shown him their level of commitment to his cause.

He turned his attention back to Gabreyl. "You told Arek that the highlord was his father, yes?"

"As you instructed, my lord."

"And his response?"

The armsmark thought about it, then answered, "He seemed quite perturbed that I would not tell him your name."

Valarius chewed his lip, thinking. "We have not lied to him? It is important that no vow has been broken. Our power lies in the integrity of our faith, and that faith is eroded if we suborn his allegiance to our cause with falsity."

Gabreyl quickly reassured everyone by saying, "Nothing was said that would cause the Way to challenge us, or him. He is still unsullied." He looked around the table, then carefully said, "But there is more to share."

The armsmark turned to Ureyl, who continued to stare at his own hands. Clearly the elder warrior was reluctant to speak, but when Gabreyl cleared his throat, Ureyl risked a quick glance at his ruler.

"There are rumors," he said.

"Of what?" Valarius demanded.

Ureyl raised his eyes and met Valarius's own. "Lord Azrael has returned."

Valarius sat back, stunned. That he'd once been subject to

the unholy union of this Aeris lord to his flesh was abhorrent to him, but he knew it had been a necessary evil. Only the Ascended could battle the Aeris. That is, until Valarius had discovered the means to create the purebloods, his elves.

Now he could wage war without the need to give his mind or body over to any other spirit, however well intentioned. These unbonded Aeris called themselves Watchers, and represented a fundamental danger as they enticed powerful mages to complete their ritual. It was true there were only a few left: Petra, Heraclyes, and perhaps a few others, but Azrael was one of the most powerful and could not be left unchecked.

"Where was he seen?" Valarius asked, looking at the warrior most known for his pragmatism.

Ureyl opened his hands. "Our scouts say near Olympious. He was bonded at least, so in that there is some small measure of justice."

"Justice? All that means is we must kill the avatar, an innocent mage of Edyn tricked into believing Ascension is the answer." Valarius leaned back, his frustration becoming a long exhale that ended with a fist slamming into the table again.

He looked up at the five men arranged around him and barked, "Why do we sacrifice?" There was no answer. He'd expected none. He answered his own question, "Each life we take gives us one more soldier against these Aeris. Each consecration gives us one more of the purebloods, a warrior who can leave this realm and start anew as a defender of Edyn."

Valarius rose and walked over to the open wall, his golden amber eyes tracking to the horizon. "We do not celebrate when we kill the Ascended, for they are victims of lies. It is for this reason that I have kept myself unbonded, so the sacrifice of Arek can have meaning."

He turned and met each of their eyes before uttering his

commands. "We will quicken our plans. Have our men stationed at every henge within Avalyon. Arek, Duncan, or both will come here, and we must be ready."

Ureyl asked, "How can you be sure?"

Valarius thought for a moment. There were many variables to consider. He did not know if the boy knew of his true father. He asked Gabreyl, "What were the two boys like when together? Close?"

Gabreyl tilted his head. "Close, but not inseparable. It was clear Niall depended on Arek more than the other way around."

That made sense. Valarius knew Arek had been crafted to be independent. Still, Gabreyl had done his job well if Arek believed the highlord to be his father.

And am I not? Valarius admonished himself, correcting his slip. It had been his power, his indomitable will, that had shaped the boy as he grew in Sonya's womb. It had been his love that had given the boy a chance at life, a life with a grander destiny. That love would bring him here more surely than anything else.

He looked at the assembled kings and said, "The boy seeks to understand who he is. He will bring himself here, following the path I have laid out for him." Valarius looked back out over Arcadia and said, "Once here, he will be our final and greatest sacrifice, as was always intended. As in all things, it is our love that will save Edyn."

He looked back at Mikal and finally answered the question he'd asked about mercy for the archmage.

"Duncan will stay alive long enough to see his son possessed by me. Then my vengeance on him will finally come to an end."

Command

Blood Magic

Honor demands better of ill repute.
Justice binds the scope of corruption.
Mercy cannot exist without cruelty and vengeance.
What then, cannot exist without thee?

- Rai'kesh, The Lens of Leadership

D uncan inspected the henge, thinking how form followed function, the archaic structure a reflection of the simple spell it contained. The stonework served as a physical reminder to a mage, a concrete guide to channeling the Way. This allowed the transitional gate to open between two places, not unlike a finder, except a finder focused on a person rather than a location. When he thought about the power it took to be able to visualize a path without the henge, he could appreciate Lilyth's more powerful ability to gate almost anywhere without the use of such physical aids.

It was doubtful someone of Valarius's power would need anything like a henge to effect a transfer, but the elves would. They needed the physical location and the belief of blood sacrifice. The knowledge of gates was one of the foundations of

the Old Lore, something any true mage would know. Tying it to
a blood sacrifice however was both ingenious and heartless.
Without that key, travel to Avalyon would be impossible.

The utilitarian solution Valarius had devised to protect his
lands spoke not just to the man's mastery of the Old Lore, but
also his ability to use his elves' superstition and faith for his
own benefit. The blood sacrifice acted as a key because his
people believed in it, and that fact reminded Duncan to never
underestimate the archmage he knew so well.

If the shade of Sonya was to be believed, these elves were
born of Valarius's own blood. That would make them all related,
an army of elven Galadine brothers loyal to one another until
the very last one fell. Knowing how each Galadine had enough
hubris and bloodlust to be named conqueror in his own right, he
wondered what a horde of them would be like. Duncan
shuddered uncontrollably at the thought.

Sonya had said for him to wait, and wait he had. Now night
was falling and he grew tired of being at the constant behest of
others. His impatience to find Arek grew with his worry. The
boy would doubtless attract attention with his unique talent. Had
he not already done so in Edyn, as Rai'stahn and the Conclave
had so amply demonstrated? Still, Duncan was careful not to
focus on any of his troubles long enough to draw real phantasms
from the ether of the Way.

A last ray of the sun shone through the henge gateposts,
casting a long rectangular shadow across the center of the
barren circle it inscribed. The shadow described short
semicircular arcs, and to pass the time Duncan began
postulating what rotation the island would have to have in order
to describe these arcs.

He'd just come to the conclusion that each island must
rotate independently of the others when the henge flared to life.

From the blue-white burst of energy from the circle's interior strode a squad of men—no, elves, he corrected himself. Their skin and armor looked black as they stood silhouetted by the bright light of the tunnel behind them. Once the flash faded, the scene was once again painted in an unrelenting monochromatic orange.

Duncan raised a hand in greeting, watching carefully to determine who the leader was. He emerged within moments, his hand raised as well.

"We offer ourselves as escort," he said in a clear voice. His men moved to either side, half a dozen or so, equipped for moving quickly. He dipped his head and added softly, "Sonya bids you good fortune."

Duncan's heart skipped a beat at the reference, but he kept his face carefully neutral. Still, the revelation did confuse him. Did they not know she was a shade, or did they simply not care? He watched the men carefully. Betrayal had been a bitter companion of his for centuries. Vigilance, he reminded himself, was the key to survival.

He turned to the leader and asked, "And you are?"

"Captain Tulien Galadine of the Queensguard," he replied, saluting with fist to chest.

"Well met, Captain." Duncan looked at his men and then asked, "You have served the queen for how long?"

The captain smiled. "Each Queensguard may only serve for three turns, sir. I am lucky to have just been appointed." The pride was plain in his voice.

Duncan nodded at that. Smart to send him someone new to the ranks, someone who would not question orders for fear of losing his newly earned commission. He looked at the captain sidelong and asked, "You call yourself a Galadine?"

Again that pride when he answered, "We are all children of

the One Father." As he said "father," the men all thumped their chests once and punctuated it with a "hoorum."

Duncan smiled. "I'm lucky to have been given such men and accept your sacrifice with honor."

The captain tilted his head, perhaps warned by something in Duncan's voice. He could not know that for him and his men, it was already too late.

Lightning burst from Duncan's hands in a conflagration that encompassed the entire squad, flooding the area in blue-white brilliance. The energy ran through them, locking muscles rigid, clenching jaws so hard more than a few teeth broke. One man screamed until it was cut short, a spasm so violent it cracked and broke his ribs, but the horror befalling these men was not done.

Duncan looked at the group, satisfied they were held fast, then approached the captain. "Your highlord has much to answer for," he said, with acid in his voice, "but know that your men must sacrifice themselves so that my son can live." He gestured and Captain Tulien floated apart from his squad, the man's eyes wide with horror.

Slowly, Duncan brought his hand up and closed it into a fist. As he did so, the lightning tightened its grip and the sound of bones snapping, like branches breaking, began. At first there were more screams, wailing sounds forced out of the men as their bodies were crushed and air driven out of tortured lungs. The screams slowly gave way to moans and wet popping sounds as joints dislocated. The elves were slowly crushed, their forms jerking like puppets on strings.

Duncan brought his other hand up and clenched it over the first, squeezing as he drove the spell to its ugly conclusion. The bodies of Tulien's men were pressed together so hard that blood and fluids spilled out of them as if squeezed from a sponge. It collected below, hanging in the air in a ball of red and milky white fluid mixed with bits of bone, flesh, and hair.

Duncan shook his hand and the bodies mirrored his motion, shaking the last drops from the now empty husks. He flicked one hand and the carcasses were flung away. He then concentrated on what was the most important part of the gholem spell and looked at the captain, whose only possible reaction was for his eyes to widen more, if that was possible.

Duncan grabbed Tulien's face and pulled him closer to the ball. Closing his eyes, he dove into the Way, separating what was Tulien with what was animal instinct. The elf was surprisingly easy to mold, as if he'd been made for that very purpose. Duncan had suspected as much from his conversation with Sonya and the revelation that Valarius had crafted these creatures, not unlike the blood gholem he now sought to create.

He ripped whatever was uniquely Tulien from the man's mind, drinking in the knowledge in such a way that it could never be returned. He understood now more of what Valarius planned, more of how these elves came into being, though only from the elves' point of view. The knowledge made his next act easier to carry out. Valarius's blood flowed within these things, and he meant to use it as his own key to Avalyon.

It had been the secret, the moment he realized how to find Arek. Even the most basic lore of the Old Council warned of blood magic being used against its creator. Yes, using it had safeguarded Avalyon. Who besides Valarius and Sonya would know how to do what he was doing now? It had been a safe bet on the highlord's part, when his only foe was the Aeris.

Now Duncan was using this to his advantage. If there was some part of Valarius in the making of Arek, then it stood to reason that there was some part of Arek within these elves. Duncan would use that connection to find his son. He drew his knife and cast his eyes about, spotting a large stone appropriate for his next task. He then braced the back of his smallest finger's knuckle against the rock, creating a 'V' under the section of finger bone closest to his hand. He then inserted the knife point into the ground so that the base of the blade sat on the finger pad just above his left hand's knuckle. In one quick motion he shoved down hard on the knife.

Pain exploded in his brain, a blinding flash of white and purple as he grit so hard he thought he'd break his teeth. The blade caught at the bone, as he knew it would, so he leaned his weight onto the blade, shearing through the small finger bone with an audible snap.

He wasn't sure he'd screamed, but the spots in his vision began to clear. His lucidity allowed him to regain control over himself, something he'd not been able to do so quickly in years. He ignored the pain, bending his hand into a fist so that the blood welled into his cupped palm. No blood magic could occur without sacrifice.

There was a danger here, he knew. In order to use blood magic, he too would have to open himself to the same hazard Valarius did. His blood would mix with the blood used to seal the gates. His blood would also act as a key, making him susceptible to any counterspell Valarius might craft.

Once he'd unraveled what Duncan had done, the highlord could move to neutralize him. Duncan would have to act swiftly. Thankfully, two hundred years of betrayal had taught him well.

Duncan focused his considerable might, bending the blood to his purpose, infusing the elven captain's body with a combination of the blood of Valarius, his elves, and himself. The body filled the skin, part of the surface peeling off as it stretched to almost three times its size. Then the archmage began the arduous process of molding it to his purpose. He drew out the limbs, shaped the beast that was within. When he finished, a creature of blood and raw flesh stood towering over him, a creature that would grow stronger and wilder with each thing it killed.

No life stirred its hulking limbs, no breath moved its massive chest. It was a creature born of violence and sacrifice, and looked able to inflict its birthright upon others without thought. He looked upon it and raised his uninjured hand, lightning dancing on his fingers.

First, he cauterized his still bleeding hand. Though he could heal it, the Way demanded he live with the loss for as long as he wished the blood gholem to survive. Then, breathing deep, Duncan channeled his full might into the creature, his power magnified by the sheer purity and abundance of the Way here in Arcadia.

The blast hit with a concussion that shook the ground and a circle of force spread out from the impact. Lightning danced over the creature's form, arcing over it until it gathered at its dead black eyes. Those now began to glow, a pure blue-white. Two vertical slits that were nostrils opened below those eyes, widening.

Slowly, the creature breathed in, the sound a dead rasp of air that filled something within its chest. A mouth split open, revealing bone daggers as teeth. Fists clenched and tightened, with bone spurs growing from the knuckles and forearms, lengthening into deadly sharp shards. More bone spurs erupted from the thing's forehead and down its back. Bone armor appeared, covering the naked flesh in a protective embrace.

Duncan opened his eyes and stepped forward without fear, touching the creature's arm with his blood-soaked palm. He followed the ritual, filling the blasted mind he'd consumed with thought and purpose of his own. Any command could be given at this delicate time, but only one, and it forever shaped the gholem's purpose.

He gave this thing its bonding command—"You will obey only me, wherever I am. I name you Vengeance." His blood ignited against the skin, infusing and calling to that which ran within the creature's body.

That command and thought raced throughout the gholem, aligning it with his sinister purpose. Gholems were extremely difficult to create in Edyn, the Way flowing less strongly there. Duncan had considered all the things he could do given the bounty of power around him, and this spell had been a near perfect fit for his needs. It would serve as a key through the henges, but also help him find Arek. Better, because it used his blood, the gholem could be summoned to him like a finder. A wry smile lit his face.

The blood gholem bowed and rasped, "I obey only you, Master, wherever you may be. I am Vengeance."

Duncan stepped back, looking at his handiwork. Most gholems had been forged of mud or clay, but for those with true power, rock or iron. Their only purpose had been to fight against the Aeris. This time, he had a far more satisfying thing in mind. In a place like Arcadia, so resplendent in the Way, this gholem would be unstoppable.

In the Demon Wars, gholems such as this had never been shaped using blood. The power required would have been too great in Edyn. Further, blood gholems were strictly forbidden, mainly because they grew stronger as they killed, soon becoming uncontrollable. Duncan gave a soft laugh. He had no intention of trying to control Vengeance, only to unleash him. A sudden understanding of Valarius crept in, as the heady strength of the Way flowed through him, making him feel equal to a god.

He turned to the creature and said, "Where is the son of our blood? Where is Arek?"

The gholem looked at its master, then crouched slowly. It closed its eyes, smelling the currents of the Way, its forked tongue flicking out to taste the air like a sky serpent. It spun slowly in a circle, still searching, then looked back at its master and said in a guttural voice, "There."

It pointed to the henge, which Duncan approached.

"Open it," he ordered the gholem made of the blood of elves.

The gholem made its way into the circle and placed a bloody palm on the center stone. A moment passed in silence, then a whirlpool of energy sprang into being, a tunnel leading to Arek. It used both Duncan and Valarius's blood to unlock the henge.

Duncan planned to intercept his son before he came into contact with Lilyth, then get them out of this accursed land before it was too late. He took a breath, then stepped through. In a wink and a flash, he disappeared, leaving behind nothing but Vengeance standing like a statue dedicated to carnage and death.

* * * * *

The transition was sudden and cold, leaving afterimages in his black vision, but something was wrong! He could feel the change, the redirection, and realized Valarius had anticipated his use of the henges. That, or Sonya had betrayed him. The transition had been trapped, redirecting him to wherever the accursed highlord wanted.

When Duncan opened his eyes, he saw dozens of armed elves clustered about. He looked around in panic, fighting sudden vertigo as he tried to reach for the Way.

"Avalyon is breached!" someone yelled in a stentorian voice, the words sounding like a call to arms on the battlefield. Blue shapes moved along the edges of his vision at that, dangerous and quick.

Lightning gathered at his fists, but then what could only be a Galadine torc snapped around his neck, and he felt his connection to the Way disappear. Along with it went his preternatural clarity of thought, and he found himself on his knees, not remembering his collapse.

He looked up, just in time to see an elf raise the butt of a spear. Then his vision went black for the third time today, accompanied by a ringing that seemed to come from between his eyes. His last memory, strangely, was the salty taste of coppery blood filling his mouth and nose. Then there was nothing at all.

THE TURNING

*Service to your master
is better than life itself.*

- Kensei Tsao, The Lens of Blades

C ainan pointed to a dark ravine that cut through a line of hills, like someone had taken a knife and sliced a giant groove into the earth.

"The Lady's stronghold lies just beyond where that ravine opens." He banked, following the ravine from the air, the straight dark chasm an easy guide to their ultimate destination, and perhaps some answers for Arek.

They had made their way from the island where the nephilim had attacked, flying in and around other floating lands. Some were small, no bigger than the Spring Festival square back home. Others were gigantic, as large as Arek's own Meridian Isle.

A quick thought about Jesyn and Tomas flitted through his mind. He wondered how his friends had fared since he'd departed. No doubt they would have tested and by now be wearing the black. A few days ago that would have filled him with jealousy.

Now, he knew he was far more powerful than they would

be, even as Adepts... and the sudden shock of how much had happened in a short time hit him. Had only days passed since he'd last seen his friends? Less?

Then his attention was drawn to one island as its shadow fell over them. This behemoth was so large that it made the many islands floating about, even the sizeable ones, seem like small orbiting moons. He couldn't see the other side, but what he could see was both enormous and majestic. It grew like a wedge, wide and immense at the bottom, and slowly tapering up to a plateau. Nothing had prepared Arek for the sheer scale of the sight before him.

"Olympious," Cainan said. "Is she not magnificent?"

Arek had to admit that the land before him was unlike any other within view. The pyramid built upon the central part reminded him of the same one he saw under Bara'cor, but this one was immense.

The sun flared out from behind the structure, rendering it a black triangular monolith against the burnt orange sky. Arek squinted, shading his eyes, and looked down. Pointing, he said, "Land us there."

"We have not yet achieved Olympious, my lord."

"I know, but we need to talk before I present myself before the Lady."

Arek knew his request was reasonable for anyone who followed decorum, as these Aeris had demonstrated they did during their negotiations at the henge. He was pleased when the warrior tucked his wings and they plummeted downward, the sudden rush bringing a strange feeling to Arek's stomach. It was exhilarating.

As they neared the ground, Cainan's wings flared and they touched down softly in a small clearing at the top of one side of the ravine. The Fury leaned over, hands on knees, apparently winded. The young adept took stock of his surroundings automatically, noting the gash that was the ravine ran straight and true to the pyramid in the distance, no more than a few hours walk. From the ground its true height could be gauged, and Arek had to admit Cainan was right, it was truly magnificent.

"How did you and your men come across us so quickly?" he asked.

Cainan looked up, his eyes level with Arek's in his half bent-over stance, "Forgive me, my lord, but for some reason I tire quickly today."

Recovering, he pushed himself erect and smiled. "The Lady sent her Furies to every henge within sight of her lands, and some even farther. Your appearance where I guarded was the Lady's blessing."

The young adept looked around, then asked, "You're known as Furies?"

"We are the arm of the Lady's justice," Cainan replied, "and hold the line against Sovereign or any other that threatens our world."

Arek thought about that, cataloguing it automatically with half a dozen other facts that helped him paint a more complete picture of Lilyth and her people.

"Those armored warriors who appeared at the henge. They were like you but different. Who are they?"

"They are malcontents, choosing to side against the Lady. One I know goes by the name Orion. The other, by his armor, looked to be either Vulkan or Helios, though I could not be sure which."

Arek thought about that, then asked, "What do they call themselves?"

At this the giant warrior laughed. "The 'Watchers,' an apt

name for those who stand at the sidelines of battle. It's cowardice, for only possession provides us a life with choice. Had they stood with us, they would already know the taste of true power."

"How do you know they haven't possessed someone?" Arek asked.

Cainan looked at him with a mix of confusion and annoyance. "If they had, they would no longer be here, but rather in Edyn in a mortal's body."

Arek understood Ascension, or at least he thought he did. Taking Adramelek had been a purer form of what he supposed all the adepts did. They possessed their bond brother and gained their powers. In a perverse way, they did exactly what they hoped to stop the demons from doing to humans. It was an interesting interpretation that might explain the conflict between Edyn and this realm of Aeris.

Talking to Cainan had given him a new perspective, but he didn't want to spend more time on this line of questioning. Gazing at the pyramid, he asked, "You call the city Olympious. Is that where you live?"

Cainan nodded, his eyes seemed to drink in the sight like a man who had been too long from home. "Yes, the city eternal, home of the faithful."

He spent a moment more gazing, then changed subjects and addressed Arek directly. "The Lady will be pleased you have escaped from the highlord's grasp, and I shall be amply rewarded." He looked down, chagrin painting his posture in such a way that even Arek could tell he was ashamed. "Though I regret not being able to save your companion."

Arek shook his head. "No fault of yours." He almost said he was relieved Niall was gone, but realized it would look both churlish and only serve to create more questions. Besides, it soon wouldn't matter, so he continued, "He chose to go with Gabreyl, the elven commander."

"Armsmark Gabreyl Galadine is well known to us, my lord."

Arek's ears pricked up at the name. "So he truly is a Galadine?"

"Aye," the winged warrior replied, "born of the highlord's blood, as are all the elves."

Cainan's dislike for the Galadines reminded Arek of a sudden opportunity, a chance to confirm his growing suspicion. Though the elves were clearly not of Edyn, too many other facts were falling into place.

Without changing his tone, Arek innocently offered, "Valarius seems to be as much a thorn here as he was in our realm."

Cainan nodded, almost to himself, muttering, "The elves are a curse upon this land, and Highlord Galadine and his brothers are the worst of the lot."

The Fury looked at Arek from beneath his open visor, clearly uncomfortable with something. "My lord, we cannot tarry here. It is not proper to make the Lady wait."

Arek stood there for a moment, absorbing the incredible fact that Valarius Galadine still lived. This meant Niall was being taken to his… he raised a hand. "I need to confer with someone first." At the quizzical look he got from Cainan, the adept simply said, "Piter."

The air next to Arek darkened and from the coalescing cloud stepped the dark apprentice who had been with the young adept from the very beginning. "My Master, command me."

"What do you know of Valarius Galadine?"

Before Piter could answer, Cainan cried, "Abomination!" He looked frantically at Arek and said, "He is a dark one—a nephilim! We must slay him now!" The Fury's blade sang from its scabbard.

Arek turned to the clearly distraught warrior and said, "Hold your arm, Cainan! Piter and I are companions. I vouch—"

"You cannot! Had we known the ones facing us at the henge were nephilim we would have never touched them. Woe to Elpenor, who had not enough sense to stay his hand before it was too late."

Arek realized he was speaking about the Aeris who had waded in first and grabbed a dark elf, only to be turned himself. Then another thought struck him and he asked, "You can see Piter?"

Cainan didn't say anything but moved forward, his single-minded focus with his blade answering Arek's question as clearly as any words could.

Arek quickly interceded with his body and said, "You will hold!" Blackfire detonated into being, flaring around the adept and hurling the Aeris lord away like a leaf in a gust of wind.

Cainan fell onto his back, one arm outstretched in an ineffectual effort to ward off the dark shade and the blackfire at the same time. His eyes flicked back and forth between the two, finally coming to rest on Arek alone.

"What are you?" he asked. It was clear from his open-mouthed expression that nothing had prepared him for this.

Arek pointed a finger and demanded again, "Can you see the person standing next to me?"

Cainan nodded, a rigid motion as his neck was held tight with terror. "All Aeris, whether Watcher or Fury, know of the dark ones. They must be slain. No mercy, no quarter."

Arek looked at Piter and then back at Cainan, concern plain on his face. This situation was escalating and needed to be defused quickly. He demanded Cainan's attention by asking,

"How did the Watchers find us at the henge? Will they appear here?"

Cainan stared at Piter, his eyes still wide. When he didn't answer, Arek snapped, "Cainan!"

"I... the henge itself," he stammered. "Opening the gate would be a clarion call. Any being of power within sight would answer." He stopped, then said, "My lord, you must kill it! If you do not, everything it touches will be turned. Killing it will destroy all it begat. I beg you, do not wait, for it is a pestilence amongst us."

Piter moved forward and whispered to Arek, "What do you suggest we do now?"

Arek turned to Piter and said, "You can create more like you?"

The shade smiled. "Evidently."

"Have you?" demanded Arek, his eyes never leaving Piter's. He didn't trust the creature he'd created, but like it or not he still thought of him as a companion.

"Master, without your leave? Never," said the shade, a hurt look on his face.

"Then how do you explain the henge?" retorted Arek.

Piter started to say something, then a slow smile crept across his face. "I'm guilty... but it was only one elf. I hungered for it. You must know what I mean."

"You bring death upon us," cried Cainan. "Had I known the nephilim were your doing, I would have run my blade through you when I had the chance."

Piter's voice floated in his ear, "I guess that narrows your choices."

Arek turned back to the fallen warrior who held his sword protectively across his body, and slowly knelt in front of him. "Do you believe the Lady doesn't know my nature?"

He tilted his head to the side, unable to ignore the fear this Aeris lord emanated. It was like cool water to a parched throat. Piter was right. It would be so easy to drink his fill and satiate the hunger within.

"We need to make our way to Lilyth's stronghold," said Piter in a disinterested way. He looked at the pyramid and then back down at the form of Arek, kneeling in front of the prostrate Aeris lord. "Get this over with."

"What do you mean?" asked Arek, the edge of hunger in his voice balanced by the desire to control himself. He knew exactly what Piter meant, but didn't want to say it. He needed the shade to give him a reason, an excuse.

Piter obliged, giving him three: "Do we need him? He knows now what you are, and of my existence. Better we don't leave loose tongues."

Arek had come to the same conclusion, or perhaps his hunger had. He smiled at Cainan's growing horror, then slowly reached out with a hand to grasp the man's boot.

Cainan's sword performed a quick arc, aiming directly for Arek's neck, but it was not proof against the blackfire. Arek's flameskin flashed and the blade was slag for a brief moment before it vaporized into a cloud of metallic steam. The Aeris lord could only look dumbly at the melted half blade still in his hand.

Before Cainan could scream, Arek yanked him by his massive leg, his strength magnified, until the Aeris lord's head and neck lay beneath his hands. Cainan fought, striking with fist and elbows, but the adept controlled the flailing lord's punches, moving into the strikes and locking his arms until he was only inches from the giant warrior's face. For a moment, he just stared into the giant's eyes.

Then the same blackfire that had made such short work of

the sword consumed the Aeris lord, immolating him from the inside out. Everything that was Cainan became one with the fire, until only a blackened body was left. That fire then flowed into the young adept, filling his form with energy, as if the sun itself shone from within him.

Arek stood, the energy of the fallen Fury suffusing him with power. He breathed in deep and every part of his body sang with joy. It was better than Adramelek, better than the angel upon the door beneath Bara'cor, Dvarin. It was even better than that dark elf who dared touch him at the henge. It was better than anything.

Then something happened. His mind expanded, as though his view had somehow shifted. It was subtle, and Arek realized it wasn't a physical thing, but instead an adjustment of his mental perspective. Absorbing the Aeris lord had done something to him, altered his perception in such a way as to provide him some small part of what Cainan was. Interesting, for if true, each victim added to his knowledge.

He thought back to the others he'd taken. Had he in some way used Piter's knowledge to create his flameskin? The apprentice had created something similar at their fight at the library. He now remembered the faint ghostly image of the winged warrior and a name floated into the edge of his consciousness, Kaliban. Had he been an Aeris lord like Cainan? What about the others?

Arek realized he could not decipher what was his from before and what he knew now. In fact, had he not been paying attention, it was doubtful he would have realized the transference of Cainan's awareness.

Lilyth thought him important, that was certain to him now. Cainan's death would be dismissed against her larger need, which was... he shook his head in frustration. He simply did not know, likely because Cainan did not know.

He looked at Piter, his body full of Cainan's vitality and essence and said, "You're right, the hunger can be... overwhelming."

Piter sneered as he said, "What do you command?"

"You never answered my question." He meant the question about Valarius, but he'd learned that when speaking with Piter, giving him less information often led to more truth. Thanks to the Aeris lord's death, Arek already had a good idea of the highlord's presence here in this realm. He just wanted to hear what the shade had to say.

Piter shrugged and replied, "I don't know, Master. Valarius Galadine and I are not friends."

Arek moved closer to Piter, looking past him and at the great pyramid of Olympious. "I'm getting a little sick of being a pawn in everyone's game."

"About time," murmured the shade. "I told you before, you were nothing but a sacrifice to them."

Arek looked sidelong at Piter and then said, "I don't trust you, but I know what Cainan said is true. If I die, you die. Therefore, it's in your interest to keep me alive."

"It has never occurred to me otherwise, Master."

In spite of Piter's sarcasm, Arek knew he was right. Cainan had believed the death of the master killed those he made, which meant Piter's very existence depended on Arek's survival. In that at least, they were aligned.

He squatted on his haunches and said, "Piter, perhaps it's time we charted a different course."

"What?" asked the shade of Piter, "storm Olympious, cast down the gods?" A small laugh followed. "You and I, an army of two."

Just then a groan sounded, a sucking in of air that went on

for far longer than normal lungs could bear. Arek and Piter turned, just in time to see Cainan shudder. His body convulsed, then gasped again as if drowning. Then, slowly, the eyes opened. They glowed an unearthly blue, without irises or pupils.

Arek stood slowly, watching as the Aeris lord's body shuddered yet again, but the tremors were dying down. Cainan, or the dark Aeris that was now Cainan, rose. It stood motionless for a moment, as if orienting itself to this new unlife, before slowly turning to face the young adept who had made it.

The dark Cainan bowed to Arek and in a hollow voice devoid of the lord's earlier emotion said, "Master, I hunger."

Arek turned to Piter and a slow smile spread across his face. "Now we're three."

Piter smiled back. "And so it begins."

The Turning

FORTITUDE

Your commitment to life is measured
by your focus in the moments
when a stray thought can kill you.

- Kensei Tsao, The Lens of Blades

Queen Yevaine Galadine looked down at the slice uncomprehendingly, her mind still numb with shock.

It went cleanly through her leather jerkin near the top of her thigh. More blood welled up, looking black in the dim light of the cavern as it soaked into her softclothes. There was something she had to do... something important before she lost consciousness. If she let the blackness take hold, she knew she wouldn't wake up again.

Grabbing her belt, she undid the clasp then made a loop and placed her dagger's scabbard under it. She quickly reclasped the belt, then twisted the scabbard until the belt loop tightened on her upper leg. Her hands moved automatically even as another part of her watched with detached amazement, marveling at her methodical exactness.

The black blood slowed to a trickle. Before tightening it

further, she looked to her left and grabbed the wad of cloth she didn't remember ripping from a dead man's shirt. Loosening the makeshift tourniquet, she quickly stuffed the bandage under the belt and then tightened it again. The hardest part was the last pull-tight knot, the bolt of pain so pure and intense she almost bit through the leather strap she held in her mouth.

She fell back exhausted, fading into and out of awareness. At some point, her sticky hands gingerly surveyed her own handiwork as she gulped air. The throbbing with each heartbeat meant she'd stopped the bleeding for now.

She sat up and had a moment of acute clarity, her eyes wide. How long had she been unconscious? Her leg demanded attention and she pulled the jerkin carefully apart to inspect it with a critical eye, not knowing how much time she'd have before passing out again.

The blade had bit deep, but mainly through muscle. The only certain way to stop the bleeding would be fire, and that was not an option at this moment. Her other choice was geranium oil or even rose petals crushed into the wound. Either would act as an effective clotting agent.

Yevaine looked around the cavern, assessing her chances. Just her luck, she thought wryly, no roses in sight when you needed them. An involuntary laugh burst forth, sounding strange in this dark place, bringing with it fresh tears as her leg jostled from the motion.

Their trip from Haven back to reinforce Bara'cor had been generally uneventful, with one exception. Captain Kalindor had made an ass of himself trying to keep Yevaine in the city, claiming her importance as regent of Dawnlight outweighed her duty, as if she would stay behind while the men rushed off to battle.

He'd gone so far as to order her to stay, to which she had

reminded him of her rank and that she would no sooner remain behind than he would offer his other eye. To that he'd reminded her of her new station and rank, as princess and not queen. Even remembering that made her jaw clench in frustration.

She'd been tempted to order him to stay as just rewards for his impudence, but Kalindor's mapsense was invaluable to the team. So a suitably highbrow impasse had emerged, filled with decorum and grace, while both stayed out of each other's way.

They'd filled their ranks with men born of the high steppes of Frost Dawn, northern lands where climbing was as essential as walking. Kalindor liked to brag that they had been suckled by mountain goats. Judging by their smell Yevaine didn't doubt him. Still, for the hard work of climbing, her handpicked squad had no equal.

In the end, both had decided to accompany the team heading back to Bara'cor. Of course, each stubbornly believed they knew what was right for the kingdom. Only the fact that the leader of Haven's Praetorians, Commander Siel, had trained at the Galadine House of Arms, left them the choice of being able to leave at all. Under his and Ellis Tir's watchful eyes, the regents of Haven would cooperate. Spaiten, still held in the jails, would answer for his crimes in due time but getting back to her husband with reinforcements had taken priority.

So the next morning saw Yevaine and Kalindor show up at the appointed time of departure, outfitted and ready, with nothing more than a "Captain" and "Your Highness" shared between them. The now-princess's party (for she still held rank) numbered no more than twenty men and women. They were to scout ahead and fix ropes, allowing the company of men-at-arms to follow. The going would be tough, no place for heavy armor or large weapons, so they had dressed light.

Her only concession had been the Aeonian House blade,

Falken. Straight, double-edged, and keen enough to shave the hairs off an arm, Falken had been part of her family since the Demon Wars. It now rested within easy reach, but everything else they had lay strewn about in a scattered mess. Yevaine fingered the slice through her stiff leather jerkin in anger, as if its betrayal had been a matter of spite and not an ill-timed riposte she'd missed.

"I'm happy you came," a voice rasped out of the darkness.

It came from her right, and could only be Kalindor. She levered herself up a bit, searching. A small movement caught her eye and she could see the white of his one good eye looking at her, closer than she'd expected. "You okay?"

"I'll live. More than can be said for most of our men," he replied gruffly.

The queen looked around. "Sound off. How many?"

She heard a faint "one" from the gloom, then a "two." When the count was finally done, it was a depressing six, including herself and Kalindor. Not an impressive show considering this had been their first encounter with the things infesting the underdark of Bara'cor.

They had come seeping through the very cracks in the walls, black mists that solidified into fearful creatures, not unlike those from bedtime fairytales she recalled reading to Niall when he was a little boy. Why such things were turned into a tale for children made little sense to her now. These demons were far worse than any nightfright, and she did not relish the idea of facing them again.

"How far behind is the rest of the Company?" she murmured, her tongue feeling thick in her mouth.

"You need water." Kalindor scrambled over to her, unstoppering a canteen.

"I need blood," was her curt reply, but the cool water did

taste wonderful as it spilled down her throat. "Thank you."

Kalindor sighed. "They'll be coming, but slower."

She knew the men behind them were carrying the bulk of the supplies and medicines to relieve Bara'cor and that would make their pace a matter of careful planning. "At least the first hurdle is passed and ropes replaced."

She referred to the place known as the Giant's Step, because it was a rock face that went vertically up to the position they now occupied. They'd come upon the lowest Step with its climbing ropes cut and massed at the bottom in a tangled heap. It had taken them time to scale the cliff face and properly refix the ropes. There was another such Step leading farther up, but this one's rope ladder still looked to be in place. Kalindor seemed to believe they were past the worst of it, and rarely was his mapsense wrong.

"These things, if they've infested the fortress..." she began.

"I know." He tried to lever her to sit up more, but stopped when she gasped in pain.

"My leg."

He looked down, cursing at the dark, then called softly to the men to gather on his position. At his signal another man struck flint to steel and relit a small torch discarded in the fight. The area around them came into sharp focus as the flame took hold of the oil-soaked rag and illuminated the remnants of their last stand in orange light.

Yevaine's handiwork elicited a soft whistle of appreciation from the captain. "Well, you saved your own life, judging by all the blood. I don't know if the torch is going to get steel hot enough to seal it." He looked at her, his face showing his concern.

She pressed her lips together against the pain. "Jesse had a gutbag with her... can you find it?"

The medicine satchels their corpsman affectionately referred to as gutbags were made from the stomachs of goats. She hoped they'd find Jesse too, but in case the medic hadn't survived they all had a soldier's knowledge of basic field aid.

The men used the torch to light a few more, then one hurried off to search. Yevaine watched them disappear into the gloom, then took stock of her surroundings. The disarray hinted at by the shadows and silhouettes was now given harsh truth by torchlight. Body parts lay strewn about, limbs ripped from sockets and cast aside. The queen had a hard time understanding the scene, the wanton destruction spattering the area with the blood and gore of her men. In a way it was so lurid it didn't look real.

It seemed likely they'd been left for dead. Looking at her men was mute testament. Each was covered head to toe in black blood and bits of bone and flesh. If she looked half as bad it was doubtful anyone would have believed her lungs could still draw air. Their survival nagged her, and the fact that they had not been possessed was stranger still. As far as she could tell, every man who had fallen was accounted for amongst their dead.

"What drove them off?" she asked softly. Only bits of flesh, shards of crimson bone, and stone still shining black with congealing blood was left. She spoke in hushed tones to honor the sanctity of the ground, where the evidence of her men's lives gave mute testimony they'd sacrificed everything they'd had to the gods of war.

There was silence, awkward enough that it drew her eyes up from the scene of carnage. The men stared at her, clearly unwilling to answer. She turned to Kalindor and raised an eyebrow.

"Y-you did... Your Highness," one of the men stammered.

"Me?" She didn't remember that.

"Blue fire from your blade. It lit the dark and those mist things burned."

Dalarya. She recalled his name now and said, "Sergeant, did you see this for yourself?"

He nodded vigorously. "Aye, Your Highness. You screamed as the crowned demon pierced your leg. No one could get to you in time. You fell—"

Kalindor held up a hand. "Do you not remember?"

Yevaine thought about it. The mention of the crowned demon should have brought back a name, or at the very least an image. Nothing came to mind, and certainly no memory of blue fire used against these demons. She met Kalindor's gaze and shook her head.

Something else was going on, and it was the captain's turn to look uncomfortable. His eye dropped from hers seemingly to inspect the ground between them.

She grabbed his hand and said, "Out with it."

Kalindor sighed, and his expressions said more eloquently than words how much he wished he were anywhere but here. Softly, almost to himself, he said, "The demon called himself the Morningstar." He paused to see if this jogged her memory at all.

"He said... he said our king..." Kalindor could not continue, hanging his head down as his fingers tightened on her hand. "Forgive me, Your Highness."

By the Lady, the demon had said her husband had fallen! The fight, her stand and fall, the grief washing out of her in blue flames... it all came back with a sudden gut-wrenching blow that seemed to take what little air she had left.

"Bernal," she gasped, her indrawn breath catching in her throat.

Captain Kalindor closed his arms around her, encircling her

in a consoling embrace. Her mind detached itself again, watching from a place where nothing hurt. Even the pain as his hug dragged her injured leg across the shattered ground didn't really register. The demon said Bernal had fallen to his blade. She remembered it now. She remembered her husband was dead.

She heard the other man come back and saw he had the corpsman's bag in hand. Of Jesse there was no sign. Her vision went gray as Kalindor laid her back down, turning his attention to her leg and the tourniquet. They would fix her and ask that she persevere, offering platitudes like "life goes on," or "it was Fate's dice." It's what soldiers did. It was all they knew. They were all exceedingly good at living.

The gray turned to black, but she could still hear. The pressure was released, and a sudden warmth flooded down her leg. She wondered if it was her blood, or at least what little was left of it. If there was to be a purpose to her living, let it be to slay the demon who took her husband from her. Yevaine breathed out, a vow without words. Bara'cor would not be both their graves.

Then blackness mercifully took her and she felt no more.

ORION'S DIRGE

When scaling a mountain,
faith, skill, and stamina
go hand in hand with fear.
All will have their moment to lead,
but give only a little rope when fear takes its turn.

- Keren Dahl, Shornhelm Survivor's Guide

O rion watched as the lance of light stabbed downward, slicing through clouds and spearing the ground with blinding brilliance. Its impact sent a shudder through the earth, a clarion call, a signal declaring Ascension was at hand.

In the center of the clearing created by the blast, a figure appeared. He looked around, taking a deep breath and then letting it go with the weariness of a man who knew the scope of the task ahead.

"Orion." The name echoed out across the landscape, reverberating the air with his summons.

Orion knew now was his time. He strode forward, his footsteps sounding like a giant drum, thunderous and slow, shaking the very earth upon which he trod. Within a few strides he entered the clearing and was soon facing the man.

"Thoth, I answer thy summons." Tilting his head, he sank to a knee so that his eyes were level with the robed man. A white smile flashed from beneath his helm and in a voice that echoed across the landscape he said, "I welcome you to this joyous event."

Thoth nodded, returning the smile, though nothing in his face reflected an emotion like joy. "Hard work, warrior's work, perhaps butcher's work, lies ahead."

"Is there no smile for me, Keeper? A hearty greeting as we add another to our ranks?" To the Aeris lord, it seemed Thoth was in no mood to bandy words back and forth.

The Keeper addressed Orion curtly and said, "The boy may not be ready. I push Giridian to advance him because of the urgency—"

"And is that not true? Even now Lilyth's forces array themselves for the final thrust into the living world. She will gain life for her people at Edyn's expense."

Orion lowered his gaze, ashamed for having interrupted the ancient lore master, but he could not hide his eagerness to join Artorius and the rest in Ascension. Then, by way of apology he offered, "You may be correct, but we have little choice. Helios and I faced nephilim near the henge. Though none escaped our blades, I know not from whence they came." His voice came out low, like a rumble from the earth.

"There's something else," Orion began. He paused, then looked over to his left. From behind him stepped his companion Helios, cradling a girl in his arm.

Thoth's eyes widened when he saw who the girl was. "Princess Tir of EvenSea," he said, addressing her formally.

The girl sprang down from Helios's arms and stepped forward. "And you are?"

Orion watched as the Keeper bowed. "May I present myself

to Your Highness. I am Thoth, the Keeper. You bear witness to a momentous thing, princess."

Tej bowed. "Thank you. And just who are you?"

"That question comes with a long tale, one that I must tell another time. May I condense it by saying my task oversees the needs of more than one world?"

The girl seemed to consider this before responding. She smiled graciously, then looked at her guardian and said, "Orion tells me this is a trial of some kind?"

The Keeper nodded. "Much of what stems the tide of darkness in Edyn begins here. I promise you the full telling but must ask your pardon, for the Trial begins. If you would be so kind as to allow us to continue?"

"Of course, Keeper." The girl bowed. "But I will hold you to that promise."

Orion looked at her and smiled. "Answers will come, little cat. Stand here." He indicated a space to one side, far from the area he knew would be the killing ground.

Thoth did not move, his eyes seemingly searching for something in Orion's face. Then he asked, "You understand what must be done if the boy fails? You cannot fall to the dark."

Orion looked up, his eyes meeting Thoth's own steady gaze, and nodded. "I know my work." He then rose to his full height and stepped back from Thoth and intoned, "You may begin the Test, Keeper. I submit to the Trial of Ascension."

Thoth also stepped back and brought his staff before him. He looked at the princess, then at the Aeris lord and said, "Watcher, you will hold the line."

Orion bowed, assuring, "I will earn my right to stand with you. I am the light, and darkness shall not pass me." He noticed Tej's eyes widen a bit at that.

Thoth took a breath and released it, his body sagging as if

only air held him up, then brought the staff up and slammed it into the ground. A detonation of sound and a white plume of power sprang from the ground, racing around the Aeris lord in a circle that grew out and up. It reached far above Orion's head and enclosed him in a dome of pearlescent energy. When the dome had grown to its full size, it formed an arena in which Orion stood alone, a deadly sentinel against whatever came next.

Thoth surveyed his work and then said, "It is done. You understand I will stand as proof against your failure." Thoth seemed to hesitate for a moment, then added, "I too, know my work."

Orion nodded, knowing what that meant. Should he fall to these dark shades, these nephilim, Thoth would collapse the dome and obliterate everything inside. He drew his blade, the metal ringing a pure note as it cleared its scabbard. His wings flexed, shining and armored, each feather ending in a razor keen edge. His visor snapped down, leaving only a V for his eyes, sealing him from the deadly touch of what he was about to face. He turned and watched the center of the circle, his weapons ready. He had waited an eternity for this and knew Tomas would prove worthy of Ascension.

At first, nothing could be seen. The clearing was silent, lit by the unearthly glow of the dome above. He risked a glance at the princess and saw her eyes riveted to the scene. Hopefully she would maintain her composure, for this calm was a façade. Orion knew better and waited. His patience was rewarded as ghostly figures of people soon appeared, at first faintly, then growing in solidity until they could be easily identified.

Initiate Tomas battled his four elemental doppelgängers in his Test of Ascension, just as Jesyn had done before. The boy moved quickly, jumping around the fire elemental and engaging the one made of earth. He brought his considerable strength to bear, forcing the earth elemental back toward the perimeter made of earth in a flurry of strikes and counter strikes.

Orion's eyes narrowed. "He does not see the crux."

Thoth answered from outside the dome, "It is too early. Stand ready."

The other elemental copies of Tomas attacked the boy from behind, striking him with a ferocity that could be felt even through the faint but clear image. At every hit the boy cried out in pain, and Orion brought his weapon up, his eyes searching. Pain and fear were real here, and deadly. Archmage Giridian called "hold"; the first round had just been completed. Now would come the dark fears Tomas held, given life and hunger by his desperation.

Tomas's emotions manifested themselves immediately, nephilim rising in the dome. They were vaguely humanoid, with feral blue eyes, yet looked nothing like the feline creatures who paid obeisance to Lilyth, nor the dark elves they had battled at the henge.

However, unlike the nephilim they'd faced earlier, the forms of these were different, hulking things born from the fears of the one who had created them. They were brutes, heavy, large like Tomas, but with a faint wolfish cast to their features. Half a dozen appeared and howled as a pack. Then they caught the scent of the armored angel and turned, sprinting for the Aeris lord as if they hungered for his very substance.

Orion whipped one wing and blades flew out with deadly accuracy. They speared through two of the shades, dissipating them into nothingness in an explosion of black mist. The Aeris lord didn't waste a moment but turned and tucked under his other wing, shielding him from their deadly touch, then spun and slashed out with his long blade. The fine edge cut through two more, exploding them into the same dead, black mist.

One touch from these creatures on his unarmored skin would mean he too would become a nephilim. Orion would face ever-increasingly powerful shades the boy created as his fear and despair grew. The Aeris lord hoped Tomas could master his fears before he fell or Thoth killed them both. In this way they both were being Tested, and to survive, they both would have to Ascend beyond their fears.

Orion punched a gauntleted fist into a nephilim and walked through its exploding mist, then stabbed his long blade through the open jaws of the last. The cloud of black flowed around him, swirling into small eddies in his wake. His wings flapped once, a casual dismissal as the last wisps of those who had not proved worthy to face him died. These creatures had been easy, but they would grow far more deadly as the Test continued.

The girl had not moved and that did not surprise him. Her actions in the last battle had been confident and precise. He doubted she would run from this, but when he passed his Trial, he'd instructed Helios to look after her. He would be joined with Tomas and begin a new life in Edyn. That fact had always filled him with joy, but since meeting Tej it was tinged with a bit of sorrow, a melancholy note when he thought of leaving her behind.

His attention was brought back by the lore father saying, "Begin." The next round commenced and Tomas dodged the elementals, using the space in his testing area to try to buy time. Orion watched, knowing he could in no way help. The boy would have to figure it out on his own. Tomas tried punching the fire elemental and burned his hand. He tried grabbing the water elemental and was pummeled by air and earth until with an almost audible snap in his arm he fell, gasping.

His right arm looked broken, and his eye was swollen shut,

a trickle of blood from one corner meandering down his cheek like a tiny river of pain. A small sob escaped and Lore Father Giridian could once again be heard to announce, "hold."

"He still does not see, and now his despair grows," Orion announced worriedly, though his eyes never left his own arena. He was breathing a little harder now, being near these creatures draining him of his vitality faster than normal.

"It is the Way," Thoth replied. "Even now he's being tempered. Hold your place."

"What if he doesn't pass?" asked Yetteje in a soft voice. She had moved a little closer to Thoth, seeking the companionship of someone who at least looked more like a denizen of Edyn.

Orion could feel the boy's despair growing, "Some blades break at the quench," he managed to say between breaths.

Now Tomas faced his final round and his face showed he knew it meant success or death. They couldn't read his expression but he would be deciding if he continued, for this was his last chance to stop. They watched him take a breath, his eyes closed as he sought to master himself. Orion knew what would result if he failed and made himself ready, once again focusing on whatever came next. Then the boy nodded once.

The circle erupted as more nephilim appeared, but these were larger, more solid, a sign the boy still hadn't understood the key to the Test. His panic fed these things, making them stronger, more dangerous. The Aeris lord moved in quickly, his wings snapping out and raining blades of death into the pack.

Unlike the previous encounter, his feather blades stuck into these shades but did not destroy them outright. Instead, it angered them. They roared like animals and ripped at their bodies. At their touch the blades dissipated into fine white mist, leaving behind wounds that quickly started to heal.

Orion ducked under the first and kicked out, catching

another in the face. His sword stabbed through the creature's neck and the body exploded in a black mist. His wing came up and stopped a rake from a dark-clawed hand. He spun and cut, separating hand from the arm. The creature pulled back but Orion followed with a wing, the forward edge keen enough to slice through the creature's torso. Another explosion of black smoke covered his form.

Then a fist struck Orion's helm like a maul, knocking him over onto his back. They swarmed over him like animals, trying to find a way through his armor and to his skin. Somewhere in the background he thought he heard Tej scream. The impact had knocked his long blade away, so he grabbed the one with claws on his helm and punched it in the throat, then fumbled at his own belt until he drew his short dagger and stabbed. The sudden release of weight told him he had killed another.

Something slammed into his chest and a rib cracked. He flexed and his wings bent forward, then slammed backward into the ground. The force of the strike and his prodigious strength ripped him from the nephilim's grasp, catapulting him up out of the cloud of black smoke and into the shining light of the dome.

He rose like a silver angel, wings outspread, and could see that three more were left. Tomas had just started his third and final round, which meant he'd chosen to continue. If Orion did not defeat these quickly, he'd be facing these as well as whatever the boy's fear created next.

He tucked his wings and dove, rolling forward in the air even as two of the shades leapt up and arced harmlessly over his tumbling form. He fell upon the one still on the ground and stabbed with his dagger again and again. The last stab covered him in the black soot that served as an epithet to their strange unlife.

The scream of something new appearing brought all motion

to a stop, for the mournful sound echoed and grew, and with it Orion's heart sank. Then the faint scene of the Test vanished from the center of the dome. In its place knelt the figure of Tomas, dark and sobbing. He looked beaten and broken, rent and burned, and yet he lived.

A voice, tremulous, asked, "Did I pass?"

Orion cursed and looked down, then slowly rose. His wings flexed, shaking off the dirt and muck that had come from his struggle with the shades. Even as he watched, the two nephilim left came slowly toward Tomas, their bodies low and lupine. They moved like predators hunting prey. A low growl seemed to come from all directions. Yet despite the danger, the boy had not moved.

"Get up!" cried Tej. The girl had moved closer to the side of the dome where the figure of Tomas knelt. She could not know the boy was beyond salvation. The only question now was if Orion himself would survive. The Aeris gritted his teeth, anguish threatening to blur his vision.

Tomas slowly rose, his bones snapping back into place, his burns healing. He would get stronger now, and there was nothing Orion could do about it. He had to wait for the nephilim to complete its transformation or Tomas would only reappear somewhere else, somewhere uncontained.

"Did I pass?" Tomas asked again, his voice deeper now and echoing hollowly. The two nephilim had almost reached him when he raised his eyes and looked at Orion. Tomas's gaze burned with blue fire, demonic and unholy. His body turned dark, almost midnight blue.

Orion breathed in and said simply, "No."

Tomas dropped a hand, now growing wicked claws, to stroke the waiting head of the nephilim next to him. The other creature had also come forward and both now stood next to their master, their eyes shining like twin yellow suns. Death's door opened for a being created by the pure terror of dying, a nephilim nearly as powerful as Orion himself.

Three against one, he thought. He knew Thoth would wait for him to fall before destroying them all, but that fact brought him no comfort. His wings sang a metallic note as they bent around him protectively, and his short dagger stayed balanced in his fist. His gaze carefully tracked to his long blade, lying not too far away, but it might as well have been in Edyn. This was going to be a close and brutal fight.

The nephilim that was once Tomas looked at the Aeris lord, his malevolent gaze searching for something. Orion knew comprehension slowly dawned in the creature's mind. These nephilim knew what they were and their purpose, as if some instinct guided them.

Only the dome under which Orion now stood protected the rest of the Aeris realm from the peril they represented, and as the Aeris lord had said before to Thoth, he knew his work.

"You abandoned me," accused Tomas, his recriminating gaze glowing azure.

His attention was caught by movement to his left and right. Orion shrugged, his eyes on the pair that slowly moved to flank him, "You're not Tomas anymore. You're everything he feared. You are despair given life."

The thing that was once Tomas smiled and said, "I'm hungry."

Its body changed, growing taller, becoming stronger. Its features elongated until it looked as feral and dangerous as the others. Then in a guttural voice it said to its minions, "Feast." And in the blink of an eye, all three leapt for Orion.

He moved in a blur, leaning behind his wing and using it like a shield. He rammed the first minion and smashed it to one side. Using that momentum, he rolled under the other's leap, his eyes still on the shade of Tomas. The hulking creature had already pivoted with Orion's roll and would intercept him in a heartbeat.

Then Orion's roll brought him to where he wanted and his hand closed on his long blade, the steel unsullied and gleaming. He rose but one of the lesser shades had already leapt, hitting his wing and knocking him back. His dagger hand came up, stabbing twice, and the thing yelped in pain but did not die. Instead it bit down on his dagger arm like a vise. Only his armor protected him from the thing's teeth and dark touch.

Orion saw dark Tomas just as the creature swung a clawed hand, raking his chest and gouging out three furrows across his breastplate. He kicked out and caught the nephilim in the face, then slashed down with his sword. The blade bit into the neck of the creature on his arm and it exploded into a cloud of black.

Before he could draw a breath a weight crashed into his leg, knocking back down and pinning him. The other minion crawled up Orion's body toward his face.

Orion brought his dagger in a short, brutal arc, stabbing the creature in the ear. The dark being burst into mist and Orion rolled over onto his knees. A brief blur resembling a knee crashed into his visor and slammed him back onto his back.

"Now you would kill me?" dark Tomas cried. He looked around the circle, his eyes coming to rest on Thoth, who watched impassively. "I hunger... why?"

Orion squeezed his eyes to clear his head, then propped himself up until he faced the creature Tomas had created in his death, for in truth this was nothing but an echo of the boy, twisted and corrupt. Orion still felt a need to answer that memory of the Tomas he had watched all these years, and said, "Know that I loved you in life."

The thing that wasn't Tomas turned to face Orion and replied, "I remember me, my life... Jesyn." The creature's glowing eyes looked down at that, as if it truly did remember. For a moment, it looked almost pitiful.

Orion sighed and rose, his long and short blades in hand. He nodded and said, "Your hunger will grow and each Acris you feed upon will fall to your dark touch, creating more. You are a pestilence, a disease that if freed will wipe us from this land."

Tomas crouched, his burning gaze now fixed on the winged lord who meant to end him. His voice came out low and dangerous as he said, "And so you would stand against me, alone?" His form grew more solid, darker, and Orion knew it was time. The transformation was complete. Killing it now within this dome meant it would be destroyed, unable to escape its fate.

He met the creature's burning gaze and nodded. The thing leapt at him, its razor claws outstretched. Orion ducked under his wing as the creature sailed overhead, its claws raking the feather blades out in a shower of white mist and rending that wing to shreds. Orion knew he'd only have one chance and punched upward with his shoulder, slamming into and flipping the nephilim over.

The creature landed on its feet but Orion was already in motion, spinning with his other wing outstretched. It sliced through the chest of the nephilim, even as his dagger followed, punching into its gut.

The nephilim of Tomas fell to its knees in front of Orion, looking up at him. Its form shrank until it looked just like Tomas had in life, except for the eyes. "It's not fair."

Orion stepped forward, his long blade grasped in both hands, point down. "I mourn for thee."

With that he stabbed his blade into the mouth of the creature and through its body, impaling it to the ground. Tomas disintegrated into a fine black mist, leaving the blade standing upright and alone with Orion's dagger clattering next to it. Orion knelt before his blade sobbing. Tomas was dead, and with him, their chance to Ascend together.

The dome fell, and Thoth came to stand next to him. Tej ran over, hugging him as her head pressed against his arm.

"You did what you must," the Keeper said, softly.

Orion didn't look, but instead drew a deep, shuddering breath. Then he let it go with a curse and snapped his visor up. "I always do."

Thoth placed a hand on Orion's shoulder and continued, "There will be others. You may yet Ascend with one that proves worthy."

Orion shrugged off the arm and snarled, "I'm saddened for Tomas, not myself. He would have been a stalwart ally but was hurried to Trial."

He gently disengaged himself from Tej, then stood slowly, retrieving his blades. One wing hung in tatters, and his chest plate and greaves showed the damage from the creatures' claws. They were slowly healing, his armor alive and part of him. Orion knew he would be physically fine, but his heart felt broken. "I am not fair company, Keeper. I feel today is just a harbinger of what is to come."

He didn't wait for an answer, but gestured to Tej, who followed with her head hung low. Behind them trudged Helios, his orange and red armor like a sunburst on a cloudy day, somehow disconcerting in this now mournful place.

The group walked away slowly, with Orion's thoughts on Tomas and what could have been. Possession, what Lilyth and her Furies offered, wasn't an option for him. Ascension was the only path to joining with the people of Edyn, and Orion would uphold that with his last breath. Though Thoth was right and there would be others he could endure the Trials with, the loss of Tomas was almost too much to bear. He could not be near the place where the boy had fallen.

As if echoing his thoughts, a spear of light lit the world behind him and his companions, and he knew the Keeper had also departed.

BRIANNA

The first sip of power can become an unquenchable thirst,
the thirst itself becoming the center of one's thoughts.

- Rai'kesh, The Lens of Leadership

Arek rode the nephilim Cainan as they flew toward
Lilyth's abode. He had thought her castle much
closer, but the immensity of the pyramid upon which her castle
stood played tricks with gauging distance. It was just too
difficult to comprehend something so big, and the result was the
queer feeling of having traveled a great distance only to look up
and see that nothing seemed to have changed.

After a flight lasting the better part of the morning Arek
called a halt, pointing to an overhang that offered some
protection from being directly viewed by any passersby. Below
them lay the ravine they still followed, leading straight to the
city of Olympious like the swipe from a gardener's hoe
furrowing the ground. Cainan tilted his wings and fell,
swooping down to the spot indicated and depositing Arek gently
to the ground.

No sooner had they touched down when the dark shade of

Piter appeared, his arms crossed in front, his hands tucked into each opposite's sleeve. He smiled and bowed, "A nice place to relax."

Arek realized that Piter's appearance no longer triggered the sudden vertigo or pausing of time. Piter seemed somehow more independent here, as if his existence did not rely so heavily on Arek's actions. In fact, the shade seemed more a part of this world than he had back in Edyn.

"That's it? Nothing more helpful?" Arek asked, more than a bit frustrated at their slow progress. "You brought me here. What now?"

"I will try harder to be helpful, Master," Piter replied.

That was strange, to have the shade be so amicable. It made the hairs on Arek's neck stand up. Breathing out, he pulled himself together and motioned to the two and said, "I trust you can both stay out of sight once we arrive? No sense in having other Aeris react as Cainan did."

To this the dark shade did not respond, as if nothing of the old Cainan's emotion and ire survived. Arek wondered about that and whether his consumption of the Aeris lord had created a being less independent than Piter. Clearly, much of whatever made Piter unique had survived his creation. The same could not be said about Cainan, at least not yet. The shade was silent and grim, staring straight ahead unless spoken to directly.

As if contradicting Arek's last thought, the dark Aeris lord turned his glowing blue eyes to the horizon behind them and said, "Someone approaches."

Arek immediately turned to look in the direction Cainan indicated. Seeing nothing, he gestured to them to gather closer, crouching as he quickly thought through options.

"On foot or by air?" He peered past the legs of the dark Aeris lord but could still see nothing.

"They have a prisoner on foot," Cainan responded. The dark shade squinted, holding one hand out as if gauging distance. He crouched next to Arek and pointed.

Arek sighted down Cainan's arm. From under the overhang, they could see down into the ravine and across the green expanse to either side of it. The sun splashed its color generously from behind, lighting Arek's field of view and giving him the ability to pick out details with a clarity so acute it almost hurt his eyes.

It only took him a moment to catch the flash of light, the sparkle of sun striking metal, wavering in the rising heat. He squinted, and could soon make out what seemed to be a party of warriors moving two abreast, their armor catching and reflecting the sunlight in brilliant bursts of silver and gold.

Between the columns came a figure, stumbling with the weariness that bespoke a long journey afoot. Arek quickly adjusted their position to better keep them from sight.

Then something occurred to him. "Why walk?"

Cainan did not respond, but Piter said, "You mean, why not fly?"

Arek did not take his eyes off the two columns when he responded, "No, I mean that Lilyth has the power to gate people. With that, why expose a prisoner or your men to possible capture?"

"A trap for us?" asked Piter, genuine concern in his voice.

"Maybe," Arek said, looking at the columns more closely. There was something strange. The Furies escorting the prisoner were large, as large as Cainan himself. That made them three times taller than the average person from Edyn, yet the prisoner stood just over half the Furies' height. In fact, he or she was quite a bit thicker in limbs and... dwarven!

Arek sat back, shocked. The memory of the fight in the

bowels of Bara'cor came rushing back, and with it an emotion he found hard to control: anger. The dwarven leader, Prime, had been a dangerous enemy and would have killed them all if not for... Arek looked sidelong at Piter.

The shade, for all his rancor, had saved his life then. Arek realized with some chagrin that he'd never thanked him for that act. When Prime threw his poison daggers, Piter's intervention had been the necessary catalyst for the discovery of his own flameskin. Arek looked back at the prisoner, quelling his hate for a moment, letting rational thought work its way in.

Though this person was of the same race as the assassin, he or she was still a prisoner of these Furies, and by extension, of Lilyth. Did he dare interfere with her plans for this person, or as her 'son,' was this his prisoner as well by some twisted logic?

He also realized that any affiliation with Prime was not yet certain. Perhaps this person could be a valuable ally. To find out, they would have to investigate, and the question of why these winged Furies were walking never strayed far from his mind. It seemed on the surface to be a tactically unsound decision, but Arek kept his mind open to other possibilities.

"We should steer clear of these," said Piter. He looked at Arek and continued, "They can end us if they kill you."

Strange, but Piter seemed actually scared, a far cry from his usual acerbic self. Arek considered this, then looked back at his minions and said, "I don't die easily." When he looked at the dozen Furies leading their prisoner he could feel his own hunger rise. Understanding why a dwarf would be prisoner to Lilyth's forces was an important piece of intelligence. He would have answers before facing the demon queen who called herself his mother.

He looked at Piter and Cainan and said, "I intend on taking these Aeris and adding them to our ranks. You hide yourselves.

When I approach, attack from the flanks. Turn them to our cause. I will deal with the prisoner."

Cainan bowed. "As you command, Master."

"Are you sure?" Piter asked, "What use is one dwarf?"

Arek arched an eyebrow and said, "That dwarf is a prisoner of Lilyth. I want to know why."

The shade who had once been his fellow apprentice looked apprehensive, almost sick, as if the idea of attacking these Furies was terrifying. Piter stood there for a moment longer, but when Arek refused to respond, he bowed with obvious reluctance and said, "Yes, Master."

Arek watched the two fade from sight. He then turned his attention to the nearing columns, winding their way along the bottom of the ravine toward Olympious. Now that they were closer more details became clear. That the prisoner was female was easy to see, but other things were harder to understand.

The dwarven prisoner stood in the center of four chains locked to a ring that encircled her neck. Occasionally her form would blur, as if vibrating at a very high speed. Whenever it did, the men's stances tightened in anticipation. Whatever they thought would happen however, never did. The blur made Arek recall when Prime's body sank into stone, and he found himself wondering if the ring was somehow blocking her from doing the same.

A reason for walking now became slightly clearer. If they intended on transporting her with her collar attached, flying would have served as a hangman's noose. Whatever Lilyth's plan was, it seemed to at least to include keeping her alive.

The other Furies had taken station between these four chain bearers, creating two columns of six men in each. They trudged along with a warrior at the front finding a path through the rubble and rock scrap littering the ravine floor. All had wings folded neatly along their backs, and were garbed much like Cainan had been, with mail and blade. None, however, had the magnificent armor and deadly bladed wings of the two Watchers he'd seen at the henge. They had been stunning to behold in action, their prowess reminding him of the effortless puissance of the masters of the Isle.

Arek recalled with perfect clarity how the silver one had tucked under his wing, then spun and brought the razor-sharp tips of his other wing down to spike a nephilim into the ground, before ripping it apart with a casual flick. No move had been wasted, no counter missed. He reminded himself not to underestimate these Watchers should he face them in battle, despite Cainan's derision.

"The Lady's Blades," Cainan's voice floated in from off to his right. Something like an undercurrent of anticipation colored the soft declaration.

Arek guessed and asked, "Your men?"

He could almost imagine Cainan nodding as the voice drifted back with anticipation, "Some... a small company led by Brutus. They will be useful."

Arek thought about what his creations were about to do to these unsuspecting Furies and a small smile lifted the corners of his mouth. He tracked down the ravine to the point where they would come closest to his position, then up the embankment to identify the fastest way down. Though a normal person might balk at the precipitous drop, the descent held no real challenge for someone with his training.

Off to his right he heard Cainan begin to pant like a wolf, and it occurred to him this wasn't anticipation he was hearing in the dark shade's voice, it was hunger.

"If you know him, lend a hand when the time is right." He didn't expect a reply, but instead watched as the party neared the place they would meet. Arek mentally timed the right moment and then jumped from his spot, landing lightly and vaulting immediately to the next stone. His feet barely touched the surface as he flew down the embankment to land in a small cloud of dust directly in front of the lead Fury.

The man towered over him but with a shocked expression on his face. Arek had covered the distance in less than a few heartbeats. To them, it must have seemed he'd appeared out of thin air. The man's hesitation didn't last long. Blades sang from their scabbards as the threat was recognized, but Arek raised his hand.

"I would parley with you," he said, looking at the leader in front. "Perhaps we can avoid bloodshed," he lied.

The Fury didn't answer, instead looking up at the top of the ravine walls, no doubt to try to determine if their position was covered by archers, or worse. Seeing no obvious signs, he turned his eyes back to Arek's own and said, "Parley? How did you come to know our route?" Suspicion bled through every word.

"Why walk at the bottom of a ravine?" replied Arek. The hunger grew within him again, but held himself in check. A moment, maybe two, before it would be time to act.

"We don't answer to you," the man sneered, drawing his arm back.

"Hold, Brutus!"

When the leader of the Furies turned to look, his face turned white with fear. "Captain?"

Cainan stepped forth from the shadows and said, "You'll stay your arm, Commander."

"By the Lady, what has happened to you?" the question came out as a gasp, but quickly the man fell back closer to his companions as the truth was revealed. "You have been turned!"

Cainan said to Arek, "Now, Master."

The explosion of blackfire was Arek's only reply. It erupted out in a cone, taking the four lead Aeris near the front of the column by surprise in a flash of power and heat even as Brutus rolled out of the way. It engulfed them in liquid black flame, beginning their transformation even as they fell clutching at their skin and faces.

Cainan dove into the column nearest to him, cutting into those left, his blade swinging with honed ferocity. Wherever an opening showed itself, he would reach out and touch his opponent, watching as the blackness spread from his touch like an ink stain.

Brutus had risen to his feet after avoiding Arek's initial blast. Now he ran forward and swung, his blade racing for Arek's neck.

Arek watched, but did not raise his arms in self-defense. When the man's blade vaporized in the heat of his flameskin, his only reaction was to tilt his head and smile, as if grading one of his students in a flawed attack.

Then he burst into action, knocking aside the half blade with his forearm and grabbing the Aeris lord's massive wrist. Shock turned to horror as bones snapped and broke in his crushing grip, his flameskin growing brighter at that point of contact, melting through the mailed sleeve. When bare flesh was grasped, it instantly blackened, partially because of the heat but also because of the change Arek's touch inflicted. In an instant the leader fell to his knees.

The blackfire consumed him as it had Cainan, leaving the Fury kneeling in place as the blackness spread throughout his body and transformed him from the inside out. Innumerable particles of black light flowed from the dying Aeris, flooding into Arek as the young adept breathed in his knowledge and power. As the essence of what had been Brutus became one with Arek, he knew Cainan had been right, these beings would be useful indeed. He took a deep breath, his being suffused with joy at the thought that something better than Brutus would now rise in his place.

He looked up in time to see Piter clumsily block a strike and then grab his opponent, the last of two. As the Fury tilted off balance, Piter clawed at his throat without discipline or finesse. It disturbed Arek to see a Brown attack like an animal. The Fury fell gagging under Piter's dark form. Blackness spread under his skin and spread slowly outward until it was a midnight blue.

The sounds of a struggle pulled his attention to another sight, that of Cainan feeding, the blackened bodies of at least four others lying beside him. Each face was frozen in anguish as the nephilim's touch took hold of them, changing them from within.

In moments, it was over. Arek could not believe the ease in which they had taken these winged creatures. It was far easier by his reckoning than the fight at the henge. Unlike elves, these Furies did not seem particularly good at fighting his nephilim, a thought that brought another smile to his face. He liked the sound of that: his nephilim. Still, Piter's flailing attacks made him question how much of his classmate had survived his transformation, and whether or not his consciousness was slowly eroding. Would Cainan and the rest also become nothing but animals in the end?

A sound drew his attention to the prisoner, who pushed herself to her knees, still weighted by chains. Her eyes were wide. She managed to wiggle clear of the bodies undergoing their transformation and knelt in the small clearing at the center.

Arek approached, noting the whorls painting her skin in intricate patterns, unlike anything he'd seen before. They seemed almost alive, shimmering with a dark iridescence. It was not so unlike his own nephilim, the midnight blue-black sigils catching and reflecting the light at odd moments. He pulled in his flameskin, letting it simmer just below the surface, ready in case he needed it.

He gestured to the dwarven woman and asked, "Do you want to live?"

She hesitated, looking around, then nodded vigorously.

"Your name?"

"Brianna."

Arek inspected her chains and collar. Something about it seemed strange. Oh, the chain links were normal enough, but the collar itself was... shifting. His gifted vision could see it phasing in and out, as if it existed in two places at once.

"What does the collar do?" he inquired, kneeling in front of her to finger the chain. He walked his fingers up slowly until he held the link closest to the collar. He grabbed it and pulled her massive frame down so that she was sprawled on all fours, her eyes even with his own.

A sudden breath escaped her lips, an involuntary gasp of fright. She'd seen what he could do. He hoped that would solicit the truth from her, for there was no doubt in him that if she did not prove her worth, she would become part of his growing legion.

"It prevents me from... escaping."

It seemed she wanted to live a bit longer. His fingers flashed once with blackfire and the chain link dissolved, vaporized by the heat. The chain connecting it fell away, leaving her with only three chains securing her in place.

Arek met her eyes, his gaze unflinching, and said, "That is obvious. You should know I've seen your type before. A black-clad assassin who stalked me and my friends. He died—"

"I don't know who they are," she interrupted, swallowing quickly. "I don't know who any of you are."

Arek leaned back, considering. What was his purpose now? He'd come here under Lilyth's invitation as a prince returning to his kingdom, ostensibly to meet his father. Instead Valarius had attempted to kidnap him, and it had been revealed his 'father'
was a Galadine. That fact made him doubt the man could be his pater. But something about meeting his mother did not feel right, either. Something was still missing, still wrong.

He looked back down at the prostrate form of the dwarven woman and asked, "Why would dwarven assassins hunt me?"

She had her hands open, looking up at him, then closed her eyes and dropped her chin to her chest. "I told you, I don't know."

Arek considered that, then blackfire burned bright between his fingers again, melting another one of the four links. The chain fell heavily to the ground as he said, "I reward the truth."

Two chains were left, and the woman raised her head again. Arek could stand and look up at her, but not eye to eye. Even kneeling she stood well above him in height.

"Where are you from?" he asked, noting that she had not attempted to stand despite no one actually holding the two chains that were left.

"Far from here," was her simple reply.

Arek scoffed. "I told you I reward the—"

"I awoke, but my memories are not clear," she interrupted again, one hand raised. "If I knew more, I'd tell you. Nothing makes sense."

Arek paused, his mind working quickly. "The dwarves are from Dawnlight, which disappeared. Did it shift into this realm?"

Brianna looked lost. "Dawnlight? I've never heard of it. But shifting..." Her hand slowly came up to touch the collar and she said, "this prevents me from doing the same."

Never heard of Dawnlight? How could that be? Arek waited for a moment but it was clear she wasn't going to add any more detail. The fortress was part of Edyn's history, a place every child knew. How could a dwarf not know of the mountain from which she came? Despite her lack of a clarifying answer, Arek found his curiosity growing. A brief flare and a third chain fell away. Only one remained.

"Tell me," he said, "if I remove your torc, what will you do?"

The woman's eyes turned down and stared at the ground in front of her. Arek's hunger grew into a longing to consume everything in this world. The large nephilim behind Arek breathed in shallow pants, a sign that he too was getting hungry again. She shook her head slowly, as if understanding her fate should she answer wrong. Then she went to her hands and knees, touching her forehead slowly to his feet.

"I would try and escape," she said in a small voice, "but with this collar on, I will do what you ask of me." As she uttered these words, the tattoos under her skin shifted and changed, their pattern becoming something new. They grew up her arms, winding and twisting, reconfiguring themselves as if her words affected them, and somehow they now reflected that change.

Arek looked at them in surprise, then at Piter and Cainan. "How long do we have before these turn?" he asked, gesturing to the fallen warriors of Brutus's command.

"Not long, Master," Piter said in a voice filled with poison, "but why do we need her? Let us have her."

He thought about that and about those of his legion. They

would always do as he asked, but he needed counsel from someone not compelled to obey. Perhaps this woman would serve? And the mystery of her origin still tugged at him.

Of course he would still meet with Lilyth, but not for the reasons she suspected. It was clear there was a war going on between the demon queen and Valarius. Where he fell in this struggle had yet to be ascertained, but he intended on shaping his own destiny. This woman might yet hold information valuable to him, including what happened to the dwarves after the Demon Wars.

He burned through the last chain with a flick of his fingers, then stepped back as the woman rose. He did not release the collar.

"I'm going to find a place for myself in this world, Brianna," Arek said, "and you're going to help me."

TRUTH

*No tool is more useful to those who would rule
than the silence of the just
and the trust of the innocent.*

- Argus Rillaran, The Power of Deceit

H e's untrustworthy," stated Dazra, flatly.

"You're so sure?" retorted Tarin. "They were being hunted by Sovereign's forces, just as we are. And why do you trust Jesyn so quickly?"

"I took a chance," Dazra said, "and in the Offering I saw no deceit in her."

"And you suppose that he's on a different mission than she is?"

Dazra got up, smacking his thighs. He'd tested the girl and Jesyn had been honest with him. The other one, Dragor, clearly her senior, was guarded. Further complicating things was the fact that during Tarin's diagnosis, the image of his brother, Tamlin, had revealed itself. There was no mistaking the face, nor the obvious truth that his brother was dead.

He hadn't known enough to see if Jesyn also had seen his brother's face, but Tarin had been convinced they both must know. Now they had the unenviable dilemma of deciding to trust neither, one, or both of them.

Unfortunately, he couldn't take the chance and therefore had refused to give Dragor access to Dawnlight. Jesyn thus far had been forthright, but she did not know that he could end her life with a thought, the entat within her body growing to infiltrate every organ and muscle.

Tarin had argued this was the best way to control any potential threat Dragor might represent, but he disagreed. Giving him an entat allowed him access to many of Dawnlight's defenses, their history and lore, and worse, the ability to gift others with the same entatic powers. Though these capabilities were secured, who knew what the adepts were capable of? He'd taken a chance with the girl only because of her actions when they first met. Dragor hadn't earned anything yet, and worsened his stance further still by lying.

Dazra looked back at Tarin and sighed. "What do we do now?"

"Let's separate them," Tarin replied, "and then ask them each to tell their story and compare what they say."

Dazra smiled. "Spoken like a true investigator."

"I'm happy practicing my medicine," Tarin said with a shrug, "but wouldn't mind a break for something easier."

"Easier?" The dwarven leader laughed and said, "Don't let Chermak hear you. The man believes everyone is a criminal waiting for an opportunity."

"Nice to be surrounded by those you have to catch," replied Tarin. "Sort of like being surrounded by everyone who says they're sick. They just don't know it until I examine them. Convenient." She smiled back and then looked over her shoulder.

"Bring the two here," she said to two men waiting by the entrance to their tent. When they'd saluted and left, she turned back to Dazra. "We can't stay much longer. We have to shift before Sovereign locates us."

Dazra moved back over to the chair he'd been sitting in and sat down heavily, "We're no closer to finding our brothers and sisters. Can you take Jesyn and look in on their dwarven prisoner? I'll speak with Dragor."

Tarin nodded and said, "Of course."

A few minutes later the guards reappeared with their two guests in tow. They both entered the tent but the dwarven healer moved forward and tapped Jesyn's arm and smiled.

"Come, I need to show you something."

When the girl hesitated and looked at Dragor for direction, Tarin added, "He'll be fine. Dazra just wants to talk to him."

Dragor nodded, and Jesyn followed Tarin out into the dark night.

Dazra watched as the dark-skinned adept moved deeper into the tent. At his gesture the man took a seat, seemingly content to wait until spoken to. The dwarven leader pursed his lips and chose to address the issue directly.

"Tarin saw my brother's face in your memory. Tell me what happened." He purposely gave as little information as possible, wanting to see how much this man revealed.

If Dragor was taken aback by his directness, he didn't show it. He met Dazra's clear gaze with one of his own.

"I'm not at liberty to discuss our mission. It should be enough that we were being attacked by the same assassins you claim are attacking your people."

Dazra looked at him in silence. Then he said slowly and deliberately, "Why is my brother's face in your memory?"

Dragor shrugged and looked away. The dwarven leader let go of a breath, then stood and walked over to the seated adept. He put his hands on his hips and looked down.

The man was intractable. Dragor's hesitation to speak only made the dwarven leader less certain the man's intentions were harmless.

"You live by my grace, and I've treated you with openness and honor. I expect the same in return. Now, under what circumstance did one of our citizens encounter you?"

Dragor shook his head and said, "Until I ascertain that I'm not in fact a prisoner of the same dwarves that attacked my Isle, you must understand I can't give you more information."

Dazra's felt his face grow hot with anger, but a noise at the entrance distracted him before he said or did anything Tarin might consider foolish. As if summoned by his thoughts, the doctor appeared, with an apprehensive Jesyn in tow. Before they fully entered he motioned for them to remain outside.

Dazra looked back down at Dragor and said, "You'll excuse me for a moment."

He didn't wait for Dragor's acknowledgment, but instead stepped outside to join Tarin. They conferred in low tones, speaking in their dwarven tongue. It was short, ending with Tarin saying, "Ask her."

Dazra risked a quick glance back into the tent, then ushered the two women a bit farther away. He looked down at his arm and tapped a few symbols. In response, a small whorl on Jesyn's wrist lit up.

She looked down at it and asked, "What does this do?"

Dazra said, "It blocks any sort of communication to you. My hope is that you'll tell me the truth, without any coaching from your companion, knowing we've treated you fairly and honestly."

Dazra then said, "My doctor saw the face of my brother in Dragor's memory. Tell me why."

Jesyn looked at Dazra, clearly weighing her options.

Whatever she'd decided came quickly, however. The younger adept cleared her throat and said, "Our Isle was attacked by a team of six assassins. They were quick and merciless, killing one of our teachers and her class of children before heading for the main halls. Our lore father sensed them and cast an illusion letting them think they were succeeding.

"Dragor and another adept, Master Kisan, each went to face them before they could do more harm. Kisan had changed her form to look like one of them, but could not protect anyone without giving away her subterfuge. In the end, Adept Dragor faced them alone. Our lore father's illusion feigned Dragor's death so Kisan could infiltrate them in disguise. He did this though it cost him his own life."

Then the younger adept looked up and met Dazra's eyes again and said, "The man Kisan killed was named Tamlin. We know because she read his memories in order to infiltrate the team. These memories were given to me and Dragor in case we needed them during our search for the assassins' origin."

Dazra watched as the she bit her lip, then she offered, "We didn't know he was your brother, Dazra, and I'm sorry for your loss."

He considered what Jesyn had just said, then asked, "Did Tamlin remember us, did he remember me?"

The young girl swallowed, then said softly, "I don't know. The memories transferred by Master Kisan were incomplete, but nothing I've seen pointed to your brother remembering this place."

"What did he remember then?"

"Bits, pieces," Jesyn replied. "It takes time to assimilate someone's life and Master Kisan was on the run. It's a wonder she got anything."

Tarin moved closer then, her voice soft as she coaxed,

"Let's rejoin Dragor in the tent. You know you have the truth. What must be decided now can be done in the open."

Dazra didn't like the older adept. The man looked like he was always calculating, scheming. He wasn't cooperative, and it felt like he'd brought an ill omen upon the camp. Dragor rubbed him wrong, and Dazra had survived this long by listening to his gut.

A wind whispered through their camp, creating a small susurrus of leaves tumbling by. The dwarven leader breathed it in, letting the cool mountain air clear his mind. The calmness spread, and when he opened his eyes, it was to the smiling face of Tarin, who it seemed knew he'd purged his earlier turmoil from his encounter with Dragor.

"Very well," he assented, and the three made their way back and into the tent containing Jesyn's stubborn companion.

At their arrival Dragor looked alarmed, "I was worried. You went silent."

Jesyn nodded and said, "The entat can block our mindspeak." She looked at Dazra then, worried she'd endangered their trust.

To her surprise, it was Dazra who continued, finishing for her with, "Our entats are designed to secure Dawnlight from harm. Until I am satisfied you pose no threat, we'll continue to take measures to ensure our safety. If our situations were reversed, I doubt your people would do any less."

Surprisingly, Dragor agreed. "I'm trying to be as open as I can, for the same reasons," he said.

"Then complete Jesyn's admission, adept. My brother, Tamlin, was killed by this woman named," he looked at Jesyn, "Kisan. His memories were transferred, then shared with you." Dazra licked his lips and then asked, "What does he remember of us?"

There was silence, then Dragor said, "His memories are disjointed, piecemeal. Kisan managed to get some but there is no order to it."

Dazra stared at the adept for a moment, then nodded and said, "Jesyn said the same. Perhaps—"

Dragor held up a hand and added, "He did remember something called the 'Citadel.' It was a training academy of some sort, though I've never heard of it."

"It is much more than a training academy... it's what we call home, though now it has been taken by Sovereign.

"Anything else you haven't told me, Adept Dragor?" asked Dazra. The fact that the adept had offered the information about the Citadel blunted some of Dazra's frustration, but it had now become a matter of principle that Dragor earn his trust.

As if he understood this, the adept leaned forward and said, "Before Lore Father Themun Dreys died, he said the name *Armun*. Later the new lore father and I found out the name referred to Themun's brother. In looking through our archives it became clear Armun disappeared here, somewhere near Dawnlight, some one hundred and fifty years ago. Our quest is to find him, to see why his name was the last word our lore father uttered."

Dazra could not tell if he said this in order to make amends, or because he sensed how close to being banished he was.

Finally, he looked at Tarin and said in dwarven, *"What do you think?"*

"I believe her," she replied.

He switched back to the common tradespeech and said, "So do I, for now."

Then, he took a breath and then gestured to the room, commanding them to gather around the table and taking his seat at its head. When they'd all settled he said, "I've given Jesyn access to our entats, but I've decided that you will remain unsullied."

Dragor sat up, "We need to stay together to accomplish our mission."

"Perhaps," said Dazra, "but I can't risk the safety of our people. You've not yet earned my trust, Adept. At every turn you chose the path of an adversary, and that cannot be undone."

"I can't help you on my own," Jesyn said to Dazra.

"I'll not gainsay your skill, either of you," Dazra said, "but in this war you do not tip the scales. Furthermore, I have no idea who this 'Armen' is. I've never heard of him. I couldn't help you find him even if I wanted to."

"Ahh, but I can," Dragor said, tapping his head. "The assassin's memories are becoming clearer to me, and I can lead us to where Armun is being held."

"You see this place?" Dazra said with a scoff. "Convenient, now that we do not wish to burden ourselves with your care."

"You misunderstand," said Dragor. "I have seen where these assassins are holding many people. Some may be yours. As more time passes, I can lead us there."

Dazra was quiet, considering this. Then he said, "And having seen this place, you still doubt us? You wonder still if you're prisoner of these assassins?"

The adept looked down, his expression vaguely ashamed. "We got off on the wrong step with each other, and I would offer my apologies."

Dazra got up and walked slowly forward until he stood directly in front of the adept. He looked down at him and said, "I don't trust your heart—" he held out his hand, asking for Dragor's—"but I can't dismiss an opportunity to find our people."

Dazra did not ignite fire, nor did he infuse Dragor with

entats the way he had with Jesyn. Instead, he asked for Jesyn's hand as well and placed the two together. Then he traced a symbol that fell like black ink, a concentric circle that began on Dragor's hand but ended on Jesyn's. When he'd finished he stepped back and said, "I've aligned your perception with ours. So long as you stay near someone with an entat, you may phase with us into our realm. However, should you wander away or I feel you risk the safety of my people, you will be sent back here immediately."

"Here?" asked Dragor, clearly confused.

Tarin stepped forward then and smiled, laying a gentle hand on Dazra's own. She met Dragor's gaze and said, "There are many places in the multiverse that overlap, where the walls between worlds are thin. Dawnlight is one such place. It exists here in Edyn, and also in Arcadia, and perhaps a thousand other worlds. Our Citadel lies within a third place, the Dawnlight *in phase*, a place protected from attack because it exists in between realms. You are standing within the outskirts of it now, but because you cannot phase the city is closed to you."

"So long as you stand near one of us," said Dazra, "you may accompany us."

"And if I disappoint anyone, you send me back here," finished Dragor.

"Verily," said Dazra, "though 'here' may be anywhere I deem you will do the least harm."

"Great," muttered Dragor, "just great."

Truth

COMPLICATIONS

*Those who mourn learn the tree of life
is not the tree of knowledge.*

- Toorval Singh, Memoirs of a Mercenary

Giridian looked down at the body, cold now in death, laid upon the stone slab and surrounded by candles. It was held here as custom demanded, until the funeral rites could be performed. The lore father had begun to hate the beach and the sound of the ocean. His eyes were red from tears shed for Tomas, hurried and rushed to his death. He'd not been ready, something the lore father in hindsight could see clearly now. He'd let Thoth cajole and push him, and the boy had paid the ultimate price.

"He won't be the last if you stop training them," said a voice, the sound echoing hollowly through the Memoriam.

Giridian swallowed, then said, "Get out."

"I won't," replied Thoth. "You act as though only you lost someone. If you could see how it is on the other side—"

"Get out!" shouted Giridian, wheeling on the Keeper. Rage at Tomas's death consumed him, but his own part in it eroded any truly righteous anger. Slowly it diminished and Giridian felt drained... exhausted.

Thoth waited. "I mourn with you," he said at last. "Tomas was a good boy."

Giridian sighed. Finally, he raised his eyes and looked at the Keeper.

"The Phoenix Stone... you were going to determine where in the Shattered Sea I should be looking."

Thoth nodded, gesturing to the exit. They walked together in silence, ascending the stairs from the underground crypt. The opening at the top was delineated by a blinding square of white light. Giridian moved through it, exiting into sunshine.

Thoth was there waiting for him. Giridian didn't bother to look back down the stairs. The fact that the Keeper could instantaneously move from place to place was no longer a surprise. Also of no surprise was the frozen time into which he walked, and he knew this conversation was happening only in his mind.

He sat down on a bench near where the Keeper stood, clasping his hands in front of him.

Thoth gestured and a map of the world shimmered into being. It moved, sunlight sparkling off small waves, forests gently swaying as if pushed by an unseen breeze. Giridian couldn't help but smile, his appreciation for knowledge and lore of any type giving him a welcome distraction from Tomas's fate.

"What do you see when you look here?" asked Thoth, pointing to the Shattered Sea.

Giridian shrugged and said halfheartedly, "Islands in a circle."

Thoth nodded patiently. "Be open to me for this small bit of instruction." He pointed to the circular sea and said, "This is where a very large object impacted your world, many eons ago. It blasted the land here into this shape."

Giridian shrugged absentmindedly. "Falling stars, we see them now and again."

Thoth agreed but corrected, "This object was the Phoenix Stone. Now it lies on one of these isles surrounding the impact point."

"And we must recover it." This last was stated without emotion, the choice obvious to the lore father.

"Yes, lore father. As you've already surmised." Thoth looked uncomfortable, eliciting more scrutiny from Giridian.

Then the Keeper said, "There is a bit of news we withheld from you." Thoth paused, then said, "Your masters faced a red mage called Scythe."

"According to Kisan he leads the barbarian forces against Bara'cor," Giridian said. "He may also be responsible for the destruction of the other fortresses of the Altan Wastes."

"Yes," the Keeper said uncomfortably. "Duncan Illrys is that red mage who Silbane and Kisan encountered. Even now he journeys through Arcadia to rescue his family."

"What?" Giridian exclaimed. "Why wouldn't you disclose this?"

"We thought he died in the explosion that swept away the nomad army. It was not until he was reported in Arcadia that we realized he'd escaped."

The lore father couldn't help but pause at that, assimilating this new information. How could Duncan be alive, and what family did he have? He glared at the Keeper.

Thoth nodded and said, "I understand your confusion, and there is much to tell. Let me start with this: Duncan and Sonya are Arek's true parents."

The lore father couldn't help but start laughing, his head

slowly dropping into his hands. At the quizzical look he got from Thoth, Giridian explained, "You withhold information that might've changed priorities for my masters. You compound that with misinformation about Arek. I sent Kisan to kill Arek because of *your* orders. How likely is it that Duncan will help us once that deed is done?"

"Worry not," said Thoth reassuringly, "I can find them in Arcadia and deliver a message. All hope is not lost."

"You'll understand that my faith in your competence is waning, Keeper. With strategy like this, it's no wonder you've been fighting Sovereign for so long." He stared at Thoth until the older man looked away, his discomfort plain to see. "You can send a message to my masters. Can you do more?"

"More?" inquired the Keeper.

"Can you transport us into Arcadia? Can you return them to me?"

The Keeper shook his head. "You forget that I'm not 'here' in Edyn, Lore Father. I am a construct, an image cast from Arcadia itself. I no more exist here than any other Aeris, not without a body, and Lilyth has absolute control of the Gate."

"But in Arcadia you're real?"

"If by 'real' you mean I can be hurt or killed, yes," the Keeper replied softly. "Though the death of a Keeper is tantamount to the death of knowledge. No Aeris would dare that, so worry not for me."

"I have two masters in Arcadia and two adepts near Dawnlight," Giridian said with frustration in his voice. "My most senior student lies dead. What would you have me do?"

"Have patience, Lore Father. Find the Phoenix Stone. The Conclave will find a way for you to use it to set things right."

"Just in time for me to die upon it," he muttered, but he gave the Keeper a half smile. "Do not worry, I will die a thousand times if it would save this world."

Thoth looked down, not saying anything. His demeanor seemed almost respectful, and when he finally did speak, it was of Arek.

"I can protect the boy within Arcadia, but when he emerges here, he must die."

"And how will we do that and convince Duncan to help us?"

Thoth breathed in and then let it out with an explosive sigh. "I never said this would be easy, Lore Father."

Giridian nodded, his head resting back in his hands. "No, but I never expected it to be quite so hard."

Complications

THE GALADINE WAY

Against an opponent do such overwhelming harm
that his vengeance need never be feared.

- Kensei Tsao, The Lens of Blades

Duncan awoke to an intense pain stabbing his shoulders and wrists, piercing through him to the point where he thought his bones had split. Cracking open one eye, he realized he was hanging from vines entwining what looked to be two wood posts. Something was wrong with his other eye as it stubbornly refused to open, and repeated attempts sent bolts of pain lancing through his head.

He slowly brought his feet under him and stood shakily, his head swimming with vertigo. The vines tightened on his wrists. While there wasn't enough available length for him to sit, he could at least ease his shoulders. He slowly tried to bring his arms down. Judging from the pain that flooded through his chest, he'd been hanging there for some time. He took a shallow breath and his body doubled over from a new type of agony as his lungs expanded from near asphyxiation. He was quite sure had he not awakened, he would have suffocated to death.

He opened his one eye again and saw his arms were still not completely down. He'd hung for so long they felt as if they were at his sides, but in fact stood out in a cone shape that would have been comical if it hadn't hurt so much. He focused, bearing the pain as he slowly finished bringing his hands together in front of him. The movement was excruciating and slow, his labored gasps escaping through pain-clenched teeth.

When he finally could look around, he realized he was standing in an open area. For some reason he'd assumed he was in a cell, but taking stock of his surroundings he was in fact in an audience room made out of a smooth, polished wood. A small upraised bowl in the center, also made of wood, grew seamlessly from the ground. In fact, everything seemed to be made of wood. From behind the bowl came another shock.

Crucified on the wall opposite him was the mummified body of a man. It hung there, its flesh desiccated and ancient. The arms were entwined on a wooden circle, much like the iron one he'd held Rai'stahn to. The dead body stood with arms outstretched like a god giving benediction to the still waters contained in the bowl beneath. Something in Tulien's memory, something he'd absorbed, tickled at Duncan's thoughts, but nothing he could use surfaced.

Then a man stepped into his field of view. Judging from the vast stillness of the place, he could have been there the entire time. He was tall, garbed in gold armor etched with a phoenix. His skin was as white as parchment. Amber eyes stared unblinkingly at him, reminding Duncan somehow of a wolf's. The man's hair fell below his shoulders, also pure white and long, held back by a circlet of gold set with a green gem.

Duncan blinked his eye to clear his vision, knowing that the weight around his neck was the torc of the magehunters, blocking his path to the Way. He tested one of his wrists. In response the vines retightened their hold.

He looked back at the man. The face was bearded, yet Duncan still felt he should know him. Pain and fatigue conspired as allies to slow his thinking and dull his senses. He couldn't connect what he knew was likely obvious. That, or the collar was interfering with his thoughts.

"Release me," Duncan croaked, surprised by the sound of his own voice. Sudden thirst made him realize how long it had been since he'd had any water, and he let out a ragged cough.

The man smiled and said, "Duncan Illrys, I have dreamt of the day I would see you again."

That voice! Duncan knew immediately who this man was and said, "Val..." He raised his head and met the yellow eyes of his captor and finished, "death fits you."

"Not so dead... not quite alive." Valarius paused, moving a bit closer, inspecting his face with an intensity that was both thorough and unsettling.

"The Way changes you here. I take on the aspect of my children, for their faith gives me power."

It was true. As he came closer, Duncan could see that except for his parchment-white skin, Valarius looked just like one of the blue-skinned elves. His gaze shifted and he broke eye contact, unable to experience camaraderie at their reunion. "Fate doesn't have the sense to be rid of you."

"Rid?" The backhand caught Duncan unaware, rocking his head back as Valarius struck him viciously across the jaw. "It is only because of me that Edyn survives!"

He fell, only to be dragged painfully back to his knees by the vines, his shoulders and arms in agony. His head whirled and he hung there, limp. His mouth was too dry to spit so he swallowed the blood, finding a strange satisfaction in the small act of defiance. Slowly, he regained his senses and managed to get to his feet.

He looked at the archmage thought dead so long ago and said, "Yet you're still so humble."

Valarius smiled, a feral, merciless grin. Then he motioned to someone outside of Duncan's field of view. "I'll not have you die so easily."

Duncan's head was jerked back and a spigot put in his mouth. Cool water flowed, at first threatening to drown him, but he gulped or spit as quickly as he could. Then it was yanked away.

He hacked and coughed, trying simultaneously to both clear his lungs and retain whatever precious life-giving water he could. Fresh agony speared his chest and ribs, but the cool water was pure bliss. He could almost feel death retreat as his body absorbed every drop.

"I saved you all. When Lilyth struck, I extended myself and deflected the blow that would have ended your lives. And you repaid me with this." Valarius touched his own face.

"I thought you said your children gave you that."

Another slap rocked him back, but this time he was ready for it. It only made his vision go black for a few moments and purple and yellow stars exploded across his vision. When they'd cleared, he raised himself and opened his one good eye.

"You let the demons in. The king decreed mages be killed because of—"

Valarius raised his hand again, but did not strike. Instead, he said, "Do not speak of my brother! He has been reborn to a greater purpose! But you... still have much to answer for, including what you did to him."

Duncan blinked at the vehemence, and the random thought of how prisoners under his own hand had fared came to mind. Mercifully the torc that blocked his connection to the Way also robbed him of his newfound clarity, and with it the burden of perfect recall. His memory was vague, stifled, a hazy recollection at best of the atrocities he'd committed over the centuries. Yet through it all Duncan knew his reasons had been noble—to find and recover his family.

He looked at the elven highlord that had once been Valarius and said, "You want to be thought a savior? Release me, and you'll start with the one person who might believe you."

"Ahh," Valarius smiled. "I have more than one." He looked to his side and said, "Sonya."

The air shimmered and the shade of Duncan's wife stepped into view. Something in her demeanor made him feel she was not here by choice, but she wore a smile laced with pity, and there was still no love in her eyes when she looked at him. She came up next to Valarius, put her hand upon his robed arm and said, "I told you not to come."

Duncan stared, the sight of her standing at his arm confirming his worst fears. It was a dagger to the gut, deflating any sense of purpose he might have had. His quest now seemed a mockery of everything he'd cherished or held dear. His head sagged and a bolt—a lightning quick surge of rage—turned his skin red and made his vision blur.

When he looked back up, he was greeted with a smile on Valarius's face that drove his hate for the man to new heights, but still he said nothing. He'd not give them the satisfaction, and with this collar on it was unlikely anything he did would be useful. *Better to wait*, a voice said, and a small titter escaped before he could clamp his mouth over it.

Valarius raised an eyebrow at that, but when it was clear he would not speak, the highlord said, "We've known each other now for two hundred years. What commitment could she have to a man who abandoned her here, compared to our lifetime together?"

While the words were logical, they were delivered with a malicious smile, as clearly Val was enjoying this moment. He pulled Sonya in tighter, and she went willingly into his embrace.

He refused to look at Valarius. Instead, Duncan's eyes bored holes into Sonya's until she looked away. She still appeared just as she had when she'd left him, as if time had frozen her in this guise. Perhaps it had. Perhaps his obsession had played its part in casting her in this form, he thought, a gravestone to his own memory, but nothing else. It seemed so when her ghost appeared, and here again in the bedrock of the reality he now faced. Sonya was no longer his. Another part of his mind, the part that was becoming more and more vocal, wondered in a detached way why elves didn't banish shades with their touch. How could Valarius put his filthy hands on her?

"Do you know what we do here?" Valarius asked, his words attempting and failing to pull Duncan's eyes to his own. When there was no response, the highlord continued, "We are the only thing standing against the demons of Arcadia." He said this with a gesture meant to encompass everything. "We are proof against Lilyth and her Furies, who invade Edyn and possess our people."

"Congratulations," Duncan sneered, speaking to Sonya, but it was Valarius who responded.

"Edyn has remained safe for two hundred years, because of me!" He stepped forward and blocked Duncan's view of Sonya, forcing him eye to eye. "I hold them from invasion. My elves keep them contained, sacrificing themselves for you."

He stabbed a finger into Duncan's chest, "I never abandoned the land that abandoned me so readily."

Duncan finally looked at Valarius, instead of looking through him, and said, "Lilyth sent me here to kill you, Val." It was stated simply, but the rage behind it couldn't be hidden no matter how much he tried.

"A lamb sent to kill a wolf." He laughed and said, "She couldn't have picked worse." The highlord turned and said, "Mikal."

A curtain to one side of the hall parted. From behind it stepped the king who had loosed the arrow at Duncan and Sonya. Though he was blue-skinned and winged, the man's face had been burned into Duncan's memory. Here, too, perhaps he'd had some influence, for the people he remembered most were the least changed.

A part of him wondered at why Valarius was so different, but the thought was asked and answered in the same breath. He thought Val dead, and therefore never obsessed over him. The world of Edyn did, most remembering him as the bringer of demons, and the reason their children had been taken. He also understood his fixation for analysis at this moment, a defense to keep him from breaking down. Analysis provided emotional distance and... apathy.

I should be silent, the voice in his head warned with sudden immediacy.

Mikal Galadine came forth and bowed to Valarius, then knelt before Sonya, his eyes downcast and his shoulders slumped as if carrying a great weight. "My queen, forgive us," he said while breathing out softly.

Sonya for her part looked down on the penitent king. "Rise," she said.

That she could show love to the man who had put an arrow through her was almost too much to bear, so Duncan fled back to noting every detail. The man wore silver armor much like Valarius's, with the same phoenix symbol on pauldron and chest. No weapons seemed evident, but he was carrying a bundle in his weapon hand, the hand that drew the bowstring that had changed Duncan's life.

Valarius reached and Mikal handed him the bundle, which moved and squirmed. A gentle hand removed the cloth and inside was a small baby, its pink skin and face marking it as a child of Edyn. For a moment, Duncan forgot that Arek was his son and thought this babe would in fact be revealed as his true offspring. The sickening clench in his stomach abated with Valarius's next words.

"Though we have stopped the full invasions of the past, we cannot end Lilyth's raids. Children are still taken." Valarius looked at Mikal and then handed the child over. "This one was lucky, rescued by my elves." Then he and Mikal went to stand before the crucified form on the ring, with Sonya in tow.

Valarius took the center, in front of the small upraised bowl, and met Duncan's eyes. "Do you know how we fight Lilyth?"

The sick feeling returned, a sudden dread that Valarius would harm the child in some sort of sacrifice. Duncan licked his parched lips and said carefully, "It's an innocent child."

"Said from a man who has butchered almost everyone he's met," replied Valarius, "men, women, and children." Then he smiled and added, "Do not fear for the child. I'm not as cruel as you, and he has a far greater destiny."

Mikal removed the cloth and gave the naked baby to Valarius, then turned and pulled a small piece of desiccated flesh from the crucified form, not more than a speck to Duncan's eye. The king turned and traced a circle on the baby's forehead. He placed the speck on the baby's tongue.

Valarius then dipped the baby in the water of the bowl, submerging and pulling him out quickly. When the baby emerged it was covered in a black liquid tinged red in the dim light. Duncan realized with horror that the babe had been consecrated in blood.

The yellow flash of a binding Oath startled Duncan, though no words had been uttered. It was intense, so much so that for a moment the scene was a sunburst of color and light.

"From my flesh and blood, be reborn as the angel Sorath, who gave himself for his brothers. You will be Fate's Lyre, your music will change the world." Valarius finished, kissing the child's forehead.

The baby Sorath was handed off to Mikal, who cleaned and swaddled him again. The three then made their way around and back to the shackled archmage, who could only watch in silence as the baby's skin began to change.

It darkened, then slowly became a soft blue, glowing with health and vitality, visible even to Duncan's now mundane vision. The bundle seemed to grow a bit, and he was sure if Mikal removed the blanket, he would see fledgling wings.

He looked slowly up from the baby, to his wife, then to Valarius. "What have you done?"

"We need angels to fight demons. Blood and faith lets us create them, but living flesh is still needed." He looked at Mikal and said, "Tell the warforged that Sorath has returned to them, stronger than before."

"You turn children into elves?" Duncan asked, though his outrage seemed to be fading the longer he was blocked from the beneficence of the Way. Why it did not heal him in Edyn was unclear, but here it was a panacea of sorts to his constant mental anguish. Still, it did nothing to banish his hate and rage.

Valarius shook his slowly. "These are far greater than my elves, though they too are forged from my blood. Of the thousands of children stolen by Lilyth, I rescue those few I can and give them a higher purpose. If they carry the bloodline of the first families they become my angels. You bore witness to the birth of one just now. If they carry the noble Galadine blood they receive the greatest gift of all, serving as archangels in our war against the demons. We are Edyn's sacrifice and carry the burden of her safety upon our shoulders."

Duncan just looked at him, blinking. Was he serious? His eyes searched Val's face, but the man's amber gaze was steady. He turned to Mikal, who would not meet his gaze and looked away. Was that shame he saw flit across the king-murderer's face? Duncan felt no pity for him. Finally, his gaze came to rest on Sonya.

To her, he said, "What about our son? Did you let Val do this to him?"

Valarius stepped in between the two and answered, "How do you think Arek came to be?"

Duncan's suspicion turned to dread as he wondered if he even wanted to hear what the highlord was going to say. He could care less about whatever sacrifices the man had made with the children of Edyn, but the idea that he'd tampered with Duncan's son, his property, filled him with a malicious envy and hate. He'd lost everything, to the Galadines, to Edyn, and most of all, to this man.

"What did you do?" he asked carefully, a sudden calm descending over him. He realized his mind was flipping between experiencing his former madness and the serenity Arcadia had bestowed upon him since his arrival. He didn't trust himself to say more, and literally bit his tongue to keep from losing whatever semblance of control he had left. Who knew how long this moment of clarity would last?

"Arek was our greatest creation! He was born of your and Sonya's blood, and consecrated by my blood and Oath. He's as much my son as yours, and will serve his purpose in this war... and so will you."

Duncan surged forward, his control immolated by a white-hot fury at all that had been taken from him. He struggled, brought short by the vines, until he'd spent what little reserves he had left. He sagged back down to hang by his tortured wrists, no longer caring about the pain. All he wanted now was to destroy Valarius and burn everything to the ground.

The highlord came and knelt in front of him, grabbing him by the hair and raising his head until their eyes met. "You will be reborn and take your place beside my brother and the rest who betrayed me. You will serve me as we destroy Lilyth and finally bring peace and order to our world."

The highlord gestured and the wooden poles grew, becoming vaguely humanoid shaped trees. Each had Duncan entwined by an arm and as they straightened, Duncan's feet left the ground.

"Take him back to his cell," Valarius said, "and strip the flesh from his bones, but keep him alive."

The two creatures bowed, then walked off with Duncan suspended between them. He could not see Sonya, and a sudden wash of clarity brought with it agonizing pain.

THE END BEGINS

War is cruelty.
The worse you can make it,
the sooner it will end.

- Galadine House of Arms, *Battle's Focus*

Lilyth walked the garden, enjoying the sun as it flooded the area with its warm orange-yellow light. The health of the land surrounded her, a vitality that permeated every blade of grass and leaf within sight. The thought brought an abrupt wave of sadness, for she knew this world would soon be consumed, ashes laid upon the altar of sacrifice, just to stop Sovereign.

She took a breath, banishing such ill thoughts. Today would be the beginning of the end. If all proceeded the way she'd planned, it meant victory and life for her people. She closed her eyes and steadied herself against self-doubt. Today, she would have to play her hand perfectly.

Booted feet tromping to the internal rhythm of a soldier's march neared. It was a cadence born from a lifetime—and more,

Lilyth thought with a smile—of service. Without turning, she said, "Deft."

The undead magehunter stopped, her silence the equivalent of a salute.

"What do you want?" the demon queen inquired, inspecting a white blossom tinged in purple.

"Baalor has gone silent," was the curt reply.

Lilyth turned to face Alion Deft and said, "Then he's entered Dawnlight. We must stay on schedule or he'll be left—"

Her eyes widened in shock and she looked up at the afternoon sky, searching. The lens had just fixed its own position, which meant it had found its way into Avalyon. *So soon!*

Deft did not address her queen's unfinished reply, but merely asked, "Your orders?"

Lilyth walked past the soldier, her mind whirling. She'd known today would likely be Baalor's entry into Dawnlight but had not dreamt the archmage would gain access to Avalyon so quickly! Tracking the lens hadn't been of any immediate concern until Baalor had finished. More importantly, her next phase of action had to be synchronized carefully because now that her second had entered the dwarven mountain, all communication with him was lost.

She focused her thoughts, seeking the lens through the eddies and currents of the Way. Her gaze was pulled up to the peaceful blue sky. There! Her eyes narrowed at a pinprick of light, sparkling like a diamond to her enhanced vision.

Lilyth chewed her lip, thinking. Dawnlight was impregnable to her forces until Baalor succeeded in his mission, which meant if she committed her forces to assault the heart of the elven city, they would be unable to attack and subjugate the dwarven mountain when it fell out of phase and appeared here. It would leave the dwarven survivors at the mercy of whatever Aeris might happen upon them rather than her own forces. Could she risk attempting Edyn without her builder army?

Still, to breach Avalyon was not a chance one allowed to slip by. Duncan had succeeded, and faster than she'd believed possible. Whether he'd been captured, lived, or died, didn't matter a whit to her, but Valarius could not be allowed any respite. The man was too cunning, too shrewd for his own good. Given the chance, he'd escape and continue to be a nuisance.

No, she thought, *better to be rid of all my pests at once.*

The Eye of the Sun looked at Alion Deft and smiled. "Avalyon is revealed. Prepare the Furies. You will burn Valarius and his cursed elves out of the sky."

"What of Mithras?"

Lilyth said, "We will move our transition to Edyn up. He will take the lead. That leaves Avalyon to you, Queensmark."

Deft's half-eaten face gave a rare smile, bone-white teeth revealing themselves as the rotting flesh pulled back. She looked up in the direction Lilyth had looked, and something about her stance made Lilyth realize the queensmark was about to ask something, something very important to her.

"What of the red mage?" The question was delivered with a hungry anticipation Lilyth seldom heard from the undead warrior. "You promised him to me."

She nodded, waving her hand in dismissal. "He is yours. Kill the rest. Leave nothing in Avalyon alive."

She looked back up at the sparkling star and thought, *I am the Eye of the Sun and goddess of all I see. Let Deft do what she does best. In the end, I will sift through the detritus of Avalyon and save all who believed, for I know my own...*

The End Begins

AFTERWORD

AFTERWORD

READER'S GUIDE

Affinities – Areas of concentration where a given monk has more skill or power. Affinities do not have to be chosen; however, once they are, it is difficult to return to the balance of the center.

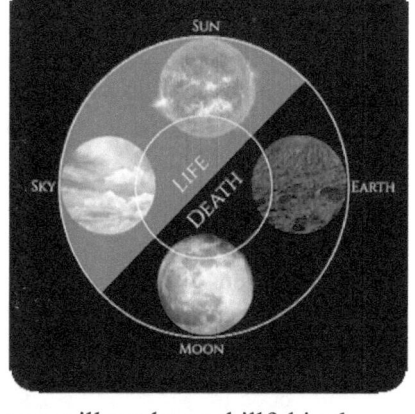

Affinities are arranged diametrically, such that a practitioner with skill in one area will not be as skillful in the affinity directly adjacent to their own and will have almost no skill in the area opposite their own. Note that Life and Death may be combined with ANY of the first four Affinities:

Sun – the use of fire, heat, and light.
Moon – the use of water, ice, and darkness.
Earth – the use of earth, plants, and lore.
Sky – the use of air, weather, and divination.
Life – sensing life, healing, and rejuvenation
Death – the use of time, wounding, and degeneration

Aging – Those on the Isle who practice the Way (see the

Way) age more slowly than normal people. They are typically only a third of their age in appearance. A hundred-year-old adept would appear to be in his or her midthirties. This is a by-product of their training and begins once they attain the rank of adept (see Ranks).

Arek Winterthorn – Apprentice, Affinity – Unknown. Sixteen-year-old apprentice to Master Silbane, known to be able to disrupt magic. Like all sixteen year-olds, hopes he's special, but fears he's not, maybe even disposable. Unfortunately for him, the adepts think the same, making him a prime choice to be sacrificed. Keen if somewhat paranoid outlook, great with blades, knives, and unarmed combat, mostly horrible at picking friends.

Alyx Stemmer – Pragmatic squad leader who acts as aide-de-camp and squire to the Firstmark of Bara'cor. Assigned to safeguard the princess of EvenSea, Yetteje Tir. Probably wishes she'd not been transferred to Bara'cor just before the heat of summer, and oh yeah, a siege. Used to the soldier's luck, wishes the dice would roll differently for her every now and then. Too bad for her, they will.

Ash Rillaran – Armsmark and second-in-command of Bara'cor. Military strategist, master in bladed combat. Attended the War College in Shornhelm, graduated third in class, known for his insight into battle tactics and his skill with swords. Gets entangled with the blade, Tempest. Has had his share of crazy relationships, but Tempest is definitely a new kind of *crazy*.

Aspects – The basic act creating magic with the Way is an act of creation from within. The monk or mage uses the Way from within his body to generate power to perform what he wants. These channels are called 'Aspects,' and govern the Senses, Movement, Attack/Defense, Creation, Transmutation, Channeling, and Domination. If you're going to learn only one, the last one is pretty darn good.

Lord Azrael – Ancient Celestial and warlord of the Aeris. The dragons believe if freed, he will oppose Lilyth and her Aeris army. No one knows for sure, which makes Azrael a prime candidate for something awful to happen when he is freed... and you *know* this is going to happen.

Lord Baalor – General of Lilyth's army and lord of storms. Ancient, powerful, and honorable, Baalor seeks justice for his fallen Aeris brethren and fights without fear. Able to channel the Way in its purest form. Demon of storms and lightning... not so good at small talk.

Bara'cor – Ancient fortress and stronghold, built by the Dwarves. Held by King Bara, then abandoned shortly after the Demon War against Lilyth, for unknown reasons. It now is held by King Bernal Galadine and his forces. The fortress itself is bigger than the current occupants seem to need. That's either good for expansion, or bad if the original tenants decide to return home.

Ben'thor Tir – King of EvenSea, ruler of the eastern stronghold by that name and father to Yetteje Tir. Defender of the East and longtime friend to Bernal Galadine. Married to Bernal's sister. Wonders now if he might have misjudged Bernal Galadine's shrewdness, as he used to think the man wasn't the sharpest blade in the pile, yet somehow *he* got stuck with

Bernal's sister as his wife.

Bernal Galadine – King of Bara'cor, ruler of the western stronghold by that name, father to Niall Galadine and Defender of the West. Barely graduated from the War College in Shornhelm. Would have been expelled, but grandfather Galadine pulled some strings, and also blades. But for what Bernal lacks in diplomacy, he more than makes up with that trait every great war hero has – he just won't quit. Wielder of the mighty runebow, Valor and the ensorcelled blade, Anzani.

Conclave, The – An ancient group dedicated to safeguarding life on Edyn. They are custodians of knowledge and guardians against anything that would endanger the Way. Their representative to Edyn is the Keeper named Thoth, a guy who's tired of withholding information all the time, or having to speak in prophecies and riddles... so he does what no one usually does in these kinds of situations – he blabs it all in a straightforward vomit of truth and clear, simple instructions... and yet everyone still f's it all up.

Cycle, Summer, Turn, Year – All refer to the passage of one year on Edyn. Depending on your age and/or level of debt, that's either a very long time, or not.

Dragor Dahl – Adept, Affinity – Moon. Originally from the southern continent of Koorva, master rank in unarmed combat and illusions. Teacher of Jesyn Shornhelm, whom he found as a baby, abandoned in the Shornhelm Wastes. Prime candidate for local tough gone good, not too happy with the guy-to-girl ratio on the Isle.

Flameskin – A protective halo made of ethereal fire earned when one has gained the rank of Adept. The color of the fire signifies that person's attunement to the Way. The weakest are purple and slowly progress until they shine pure and white. Great at defending one from harm, but also getting you the magehunters' version, your own personal burning at the stake.

Giridian Alacar – Adept, Affinity – Earth. Keeper of the Vault, master of artifacts and other magical items. Sixty years old, teacher to apprentice Tomas, scribe and chronicler of the adepts. Appears to others as a man in his late twenties. Known for his penchant for brewing teas and other mixtures he says are just 'herbs' he grows in his garden. Not the guy you'd ever think would be bad ass, until he is.

Houses – There are four great Houses in Edyn:

House Galadine – Led by the Imperial King Bernal Galadine and Queen Yevaine Galadine (of House Aeonian). House Galadine holds the fortress of Bara'cor. The King and Queen have one son, Niall, who is about to embark on his "Walk of Kings." The King's sister, Clarysa, is married to the King of EvenSea, Ben'thor Tir.

House Cadan – Held by King Rory Cadan and Lady Ilandra (of House Justeces). House Cadan holds the fortress of Shornhelm. They have one son, Durnal, who is still an infant. His sister, Morgan, is married to the King of Dawnlight. They are served by Algren Justeces, Ilandra's brother and Legate for Shornhelm in the capital city of Haven.

House Tir – Held by King Ben'thor Tir and Lady Clarysa Tir (of House Galadine). They hold the fortress of EvenSea. They have one daughter, Yetteje, current ward to House Galadine and staying at Bara'cor as part of her "Walk of Kings" ritual. Ben'thor has a brother, Ellis Tir, who serves as Legate of EvenSea in the capital city of Haven.

House Aeonian – Held by King Temar Aeonian and Lady Morgan Aeonian (of House Cadan). They hold the fortress of Dawnlight. Their daughter, Yevaine, is married to the Imperial

King Galadine. They are served by Merric Spaiten, who serves as Legate for Dawnlight in the capital city of Haven. No hints, but with a name like 'Spaiten'… you know he's not destined to be the good guy. *(Okay, that might be a hint.)*

Minor Houses: House Kalindor, House Justeces, House Spaiten, House Rillaran, House Stemmer, House Naserith, House Petra, House Illrys, House Alacar, and more…

Hemendra – U'Zar, leader of the nomads of the Altan Wastes, military strategist assaulting Bara'cor. Responsible for the destruction of Dawnlight, Shornhelm, and most recently, EvenSea, under the command of Scythe. (See, Scythe.) Hemendra has all the traits you love about barbarians, including being well-read, thoughtful, calm, and respectful of others' personal space.

Jesyn Shornhelm – Initiate, Affinity – Sun. Apprenticed to Dragor, training for her adept's Test, last name taken from the region where she was found. Adept rank in bladed and unarmed combat. Ascended to full adept to meet the growing danger in Dawnlight. Has had her pick of boyfriends on the Isle but as usual, selects the one worst for her long term prospects.

Jebida Naserith – Firstmark, leader of Bara'cor's military forces, longtime friend of Bernal Galadine. Distrustful of magic since the death of his wife and daughter at the hands of creatures that appeared through a rift. Hates magic, but also pretty much hates everything else, so it's difficult to tell when he's upset.

Kaffe – A black drink made from a dark bean soaked in

boiling water. Its effects are a clearing of the mind, sudden energy, and a decrease in appetite. It's said that if someone could just come up with a way to harvest and sell this magic bean, they could make a lot of aurum.

Koken – Similar to Kaffe, except this nut is dried and mixed with honey to hide the bittersweet taste. Normally chewed, the effects are quite a bit stronger than kaffe and therefore used by some for a quick source of energy. However, koken nuts quickly have deleterious effects on the consumer, such as insomnia and babbling. Thought to have no medicinal purpose and no real value, except to smugglers, pirates, and ne'er-do-wells.

Kisan Talaris – Master, Affinity – Moon. Youngest to attain the rank, skilled in illusions and unarmed combat. Willful, strong, impatient, the kind you love to watch kick ass but would never hang out with. Assigned to back up Silbane should the need arise, and possibly the worst choice for that particular assignment. Teacher to Piter, then to Tomas. She recognizes the growing powers of Yetteje Tir. She's also the only master who doesn't care about how powerful she is. If it's enough to kill magehunters and people who don't agree with her, well that's just fine.

Lilyth – Demonlord (often called Demon Queen) and Celestial, Lady of the Aeris. Ancient, better than most in seeing the truth of things. Seeks entry into Edyn's plane of existence, ostensibly for retribution for centuries of enslavement of the Aeris, but in reality her motivations are much more complex. Smart and practical, takes calculated risks, cares for her people in a more honest way than your average demon demagogue. She can make you happy to slit your own wrists, and sad you got her floor messy with your disgusting blood… but she's actually not that bad.

Mikal Galadine – King during the Demon Wars, leader of the forces that forced Lilyth back at the battle of Sovereign's Fall. Victorious, then did an about-face and decreed all magic was outlawed and mages were to be killed on sight. Really bad timing for any mages who happened to have front row seats at the reading of the decree. Brother to General Valarius Galadine (the archmage who ironically did everything opposite of his brother, including starting a war). Mikal is a seriously disturbed man who ultimately becomes more than he wished for in Lilyth's realm.

Mindread – The ability of a practitioner of the Way to assimilate and read the thoughts of another person. Extremely taxing in power, so the information retained is often incomplete or jumbled. However, it can lend situational context when paired with the caster's own perceptions. Generally never used at parties or during a first date by those who don't have this ability.

Mindspeak – The ability for a practitioner of the Way to reach out and speak telepathically with another practitioner. Extremely taxing in its use of energy, but provides a near instantaneous connection through which thoughts and energy can be shared. Conversely, almost always used at parties to get someone to turn around and look for 'voices.'

Niall Galadine – Crown Prince of Bara'cor, seventeen years old. Trained in weapons combat, but you get the idea he skips a lot of classes. Hasn't yet made the transition from combat in tales to combat in real life. About to initiate his rite of passage to manhood, known as the Walk of Kings. A bit entitled, a bit insufferable, tries to be noticed. With the right guidance, he could make an average king. With the wrong guidance, a memorable tyrant.

Piter Winterthorn – Initiate apprenticed to Kisan, training for his adept's Test, last name taken from the region near where he was found, master rank in bladed combat, adept rank in spellcraft. Because he's seen from the eyes of bullies, Piter seems both churlish and annoying. Ostracized by Arek, Piter yearns to be accepted by just about anyone, and boy is he going to get his wish. Unfortunately, his personality *does* make him annoying, so nothing good is going to happen.

Rai'stahn – Ancient dragon, defender of the world, now inhabits a small part of the Isle where the adepts train. Predator, powerful in the Way, able to regenerate, and able to assume many forms. Skilled in combat (immeasurable by common mortal rankings). Does not involve himself in the world's affairs, until the emergence of Arek and the Gate at Bara'cor. Now, some of the actions he took during the Demon Wars are coming back to haunt him, as these kinds of things usually do. Not self-aware enough to realize he's the root cause, but very good at blaming and then killing others for his mistakes.

Rai'kesh – Ancient dragon and king of the dragonkind. Leader of the Conclave and instrumental in giving Valarius Galadine a vision of the true nature of the Way. Some argue this caused Valarius to go down the fateful path he chose, others think it was the next thing that pitched Valarius over the edge.

Ordered Rai'stahn to kill Valarius at the battle of Sovereign's Fall, but only after the archmage won. Most agree this caused Valarius to lose his marbles and harbor a tad of resentment against the Conclave of Edyn.

Ranks – There are four tiers of rank, with many subdivisions. These four tiers are initiate, adept, master, and archmage.

All apprentices, once they pass their Test of Potential and earn their Green rank, are initiates.

Once an initiate passes his Test of Ascension, he or she wears the black uniform and gains the rank of adept.

From there, they test again for the rank of master.

At the beginning of the Mythborn series, there are two masters on the Isle: Silbane, and Kisan.

There are also three adepts: Giridian, Thera, and Dragor.

Tomas, Jesyn, Piter, and Arek are initiates preparing to Test for the rank of adept.

Lore Father Themun Dreys is the only Archmage on the Isle, and as such administers the tests of rank. He also plans all the parties.

Ranks are also used to denote someone's skill along these same four tiers, so a person with a master's rank in bladed combat would generally be better than one with an adept's or initiate's rank. Unless they fought with their left hand, in which case they'd be about the same, or maybe worse, depending on if their left hand was their off hand.

Scythe – Archmage, red-robed wizard who seeks Lilyth's Gate, allied with Hemendra of the Nomads, archmage rank in all things magical, possessor of the Old Lore, and able to wield it as the Old Lords did. Just on this side of crazy, and because of that, more dangerous. Really, really, really focused on getting someone back whom he lost due to a slight error in judgment. Hopes they remember it differently.

Silbane Darius Petracles – Master, Affinity – Sun. Skilled in all forms of combat and combat magic. Eighty years old and teacher of Arek Winterthorn. Appears to others as a man in his late thirties. Pragmatic, self-confident, perhaps enjoys life a little too much. You'd send him into hell to save the world, but he's not the right guy to watch your kids, ever.

Sovereign, the – Ancient guardian and caretaker of Edyn's first people. His plan is simple: kill everyone to make the world a better, safer place. That way someone like him won't show up and kill everyone to make the world a better, safer place. Er… unfortunately, he's as serious as a heart attack and if he succeeds, literally nothing will be the same.

Techniques – A monk may combine various Aspects with their Affinity. These are called *Techniques* and usually require a physical action as well. If one thinks of Affinities as the raw power of the Way and Aspects as the areas in which that power is focused, Techniques are the method by which an Aspect affects or uses an Affinity.

Tempest – Ancient sentient sword, given to Arek for his protection. Said to have the power to heal its wielder from grave injury. Particularly fond of Ash, and Arek. Not a really good example of balanced and rational thinking. Bad at love in a sort of crazy, possessive way. It turns out she's pretty horrible at healing, too.

Themun Dreys – Archmage, Affinity – Sky. Lore Father of the Second Council of adepts, initiates the quest to ascertain the disposition of Lilyth's Gate, master illusionist. Easy to anger, slow to forgive, he's not your typical balanced and rational leader. However, his force of will and tenacity have proven more than useful in keeping his people alive. Although over two hundred years old, appears to others as a man in his sixties. Absolutely didn't want the job, but got stuck with it when his brother skipped out and left him holding the carved runestaff of office.

Thera Dawnlight – Adept, Affinity – Sky. Master's rank in herb lore and medicine, skilled in healing and defensive arts. Closest thing the Isle has to an activist, would definitely chain herself to a tree, a bear, or a dragon to save it, whether they wanted it or not. Orphan and found near Dawnlight, appears to others as a woman in her early forties.

Thoth – Guardian of the Archives, member of the Conclave, a group made up of the Elder Races and dedicated to safeguarding life on Edyn. Tries to state things simply, often making things worse by panicking those around him who can't handle the truth. Then wonders if maybe he ought to go back to speaking in riddles. Just waiting for someone to get it right for once.

Tomas Dawnlight – Apprentice, Affinity – Earth. Apprenticed to Adept Giridian, then to Master Kisan. Preparing for his Test of Ascension. Strong, brave, dumb, but he's dating Jesyn so maybe he's smarter than he looks. Skillful in combining magic with strength, lifting with strength, eating with strength, reading with strength... uh, you get the idea.

Sadly, not great at getting hurt and keepin' on. Unfortunate weakness if you're trying to be an ultimate martial fighter.

Valarius Galadine – General and High Marshal of the King's forces at Sovereign's Fall, Archmage and Lore Father of the First Council of Adepts, known for causing the first cataclysm of the world. Powerful, strong-willed, championed the idea that demons were actually the source of magic and ruin in this world, then promptly went off and summoned the most powerful one. Once he preemptively started a war with the Aeris, he was stripped of his title and rank. Didn't seem to slow him down or even make him pause. Self-reflection is not his strong suit.

The Way – An eldritch force that exists within the very fabric of space, allowing those that can tap into it the ability to manipulate time, space, and matter. There are many manifestations, limited only by the practitioner's imagination and discipline. The Old Lords of the First Council used it to create spells that could alter the nature of the world. The Second Council has honed it into a power that manifests itself in their bodies when they engage in martial combat. The Third Council will likely focus on knitting, cleaning, and other mundane tasks. They think this will keep them unqualified to play any part in saving the world from its next problem... and yet they'll probably *still* be chosen.

Yetteje Tir – Princess of EvenSea, cousin to Niall Galadine, on her pilgrimage to ascend to the royal throne of EvenSea, with her final stop on the Walk of Kings at Bara'cor. She is seventeen and stubborn, hates authority but loves she's one of the 'haves' and not the 'ewww, have-nots.' She's brave and good with a blade, but has no desire to be a hero. It's too bad she's in *this* story, because Yetteje is one of the few who consistently makes sense, you know... like a hero.

Yevaine Galadine – Queen of Bara'cor, wife of Bernal. She is sent from Bara'cor at the siege's start with the young and weak. They are evacuated to Haven, capital city of Edyn, to deliver their refugees and return with reinforcements. You get the sense she's the mom who'd camp in the backyard with you and bring the bow and arrows. Doesn't seem squeamish, knows the business end of a blade. Clearly the one in charge of everything at Bara'cor, as witnessed by what happens when she leaves. Within a day, the fortress is overrun by demons and her son is missing. Updating her is not going to be a high point for King Bernal Galadine.

ABOUT THE AUTHOR

Vijay Lakshman was born in Ottawa, Canada. He spent his early years in Bangkok, Thailand. When he was nine, his father took him to a martial arts exhibition and his life changed forever.

He dedicated four decades to mastering the martial arts, his quest taking him from Thailand, across the U.S. and Europe, to Hong Kong and China. In 1991 he earned his black belt and has accumulated thousands of hours in the ring.

His true passion however, is writing. Mythborn his first epic fantasy series, and pays homage to a lifetime spent mastering the arts of combat and to his passion for writing fantasy and science fiction.

Vijay has created over eighty-five titles in his career as a video game designer and architect of game-based learning software, but spends his free time entertaining his curiosity. This includes researching almost anything on Google, building aquascapes, and flying (and crashing) quadcopters.

His life experiences include graduation from the Harvard Business School's elite General Manager Program, four decades of training in karate, sixteen years of close combat grappling, fifteen years of kendo, six years of long-distance cycling, and taking various things in the house apart.

Putting everything back together is the job of a future, better, version of himself–hopefully one with rechargeable batteries.